Jeff Gulvin was born in 1962. He is half Scottish and half English and has lived in various parts of the UK and for a time in New Zealand. He is the author of one previous novel featuring Aden Vanner, *Sleep No More*. He lives alone in north Norfolk.

Also by Jeff Gulvin

Sleep No More

Sorted

Jeff Gulvin

HEADLINE

First published in Great Britain in 1996
by HEADLINE BOOK PUBLISHING

First published in paperback in 1997
by HEADLINE BOOK PUBLISHING

10 9 8 7 6 5 4 3 2 1

ISBN 0 7472 5385 4

Typeset by
Letterpart Limited, Reigate, Surrey

Printed and bound in Great Britain by
Cox & Wyman Ltd., Reading, Berks.

HEADLINE BOOK PUBLISHING
A division of Hodder Headline PLC
338 Euston Road
London NW1 3BH

In researching this novel the author was accorded access to various units of the Metropolitan Police Force. He would like to thank those concerned for their assistance and confidence.

A special thanks to Paul Cox

For the Nail File Gang

One

The Wasp climbed concrete steps in the darkness.

On the second landing he paused and lit a cigarette, the damp of the night on his face. A boy skipped down the steps and almost bumped into him. The Wasp clutched a handful of collar. He held him, drew him close and inspected him like a hunter his prey. The boy shrank back, face disappearing into the hood of his sweat top. The Wasp pushed him aside.

Ninja sat in the flat, resting an E on his thumbnail. He flipped it into the air and tried to catch it in his mouth. He cursed as it fell out of the line of his vision. In the kitchen the girl ironed his T-shirt. The doorbell screeched in the hall.

'You finished yet?'

The T-shirt spun through the air and landed across his arm. He peeled it over his head, the weight of his hair falling across his back. The girl hung in the doorway, looking at the rain through the open windows. The doorbell screeched again.

'You coming back later?' she said.

Ninja reached for his cigarettes. He met The Wasp on the landing.

Vanner nursed whiskey and chasers in the corner of the pub. Through the window behind him, a fan belt squealed in the rain. Two motorcyclists swapped engine notes and cackled hysterically afterwards. A fat man pushed against his table as he passed, slopping beer onto the mat. Vanner glanced at him, then dipped

1

his finger in the spilt beer and traced a mark on the table.

'Vanner.'

He looked up at McCague.

The phone rang in the hall. From the arm of the chair he lifted the remote control for the TV and turned the sound down. In the hall he picked up the receiver.

'Hello?'

'It's me.'

'I've told you not to call me here.'

'Your mobile's switched off.'

'What d'you want?'

'Are we on?'

'Yes.'

'Good.'

'It's a mistake. There's no need.'

'There's every fuckin' need. You ought to be where I'm standing.'

Silence.

'You listening to me?'

'It's on. All right.'

'I want to hear about it.'

'You will.' He hung up and stood for a moment in the darkness. Then lifting his coat from the peg, he went out into the rain.

McCague pushed himself into the seat next to Vanner. 'Come here a lot do you?'

'That some kind of offer?' Vanner scraped a cigarette from the emptying pack on the table and fumbled with his lighter.

'You look like hammered shit,' McCague told him.

Vanner pulled on the cigarette.

'How long've you been sat there?'

'A while.'

'Go home.'

'Later.'

'You've had enough.'

2

'If you've come here to lecture me – you can fuck off again.'

McCague squinted at him. 'No wonder you drink on your own.'

At the bar a man slid off his stool, glanced at Vanner and made his way to the payphone. Vanner finished his whiskey and set down the empty glass.

'Where've you been?' McCague asked him. 'You don't answer the phone.'

'I've been around.'

'Not so's anyone would notice.'

Vanner shrugged.

'You look awful, Vanner. You living on whiskey and cigarettes?'

'What're you – my nursemaid?'

'Think yourself lucky I'm interested.'

The Wasp drove. Ninja sat next to him, one hand pressed against his belly, his half-length Samurai sword on the floor by his legs. The Wasp glanced at him. 'Bad guts?'

Ninja nodded. The mobile rang on the seat beside him. He lifted it to his ear and listened.

'Let me speak to The Wasp.'

Ninja offered the phone, slack-handed. The Wasp took it from him. 'We're on our way,' he said.

'Good. Eversholt Street. He's drinking in the King's Head.'

'How d'you know?'

'I just know. I'll call you in the morning. Make sure you get it right.' The phone died and The Wasp passed it back to Ninja.

McCague bought more beer and set the glasses down. Vanner was sitting straightbacked, staring at the table top. McCague looked at his cigarettes.

'Help yourself.'

McCague shook his head. 'I've only just packed it in again.'

Vanner drew a cigarette from the pack.

'How long're you going to keep this up?' McCague asked him.

'Keep what up?'

'This. You're pissed and it's barely ten o'clock.'

3

'Pissed? I'm not even merry.'

'You only lost one rank, Vanner. DI. There's still a job if you want it.'

'I don't want it.'

'They could've ditched you you know. There's those that pressed for it. Especially after you walked out on the hearing.'

Vanner shook his head. 'Sarah Kennett was barely cold and they're sitting on me like vultures.'

'That's why you're still technically a copper. They took it into consideration.'

'And I'm supposed to be grateful?'

McCague sighed. 'So you're not coming back then?'

'I never go back.'

'Right.'

Vanner looked at him. 'What d'you expect, McCague? You really think I'm going to just walk on back with my hands up and my prick stuck in my mouth.'

McCague scraped at a palm with his thumbnail. 'It's only one rank, Vanner. But they won't wait forever.'

Vanner was quiet for a moment. 'Where's the DI's job anyway?'

'2 Area Drug Squad.'

'Who moved on?'

'Westbrook. DCI with 13.'

Vanner looked at the barmaid, chatting to a couple of punters. 'She's Australian,' he said.

'Aren't they all.' McCague glanced at him. 'You going to let this bug you forever?'

'Let what bug me?'

'Oh, come on. You know what I mean.'

Sarah Kennett. A face in his mind, flesh on his flesh and darkness over a cliff. He closed his eyes and swallowed the dregs of his glass. McCague looked at his watch. 'You want another or have you had enough?'

Vanner gave him the glass.

* * *

He stood watching from the inside of the window. No music tonight. Just the darkness and rain falling against streetlamps. From the other room, he could smell alcohol. Anton Cready. He wished he could have watched, but Cready was very particular. He looked at his watch. Ten-thirty. He moved to the desk where the computer screen was dark. Idly, he dragged his fingers over the keys and then took out his handkerchief and wiped them. Hands in his pockets now, he moved back to the window. He looked at the row of unopened watches on the shelf and smiled to himself.

Vanner watched McCague push his bulk through the crowd and hand the glasses to the barmaid. He looked beyond him, gaze blurring into the bottles that lined the back of the bar. Christmas Eve on the Norfolk coast. The wind howling over the cliff and the shadow of a woman and then nothing. If he closed his eyes he could relive the darkness now. He did not close his eyes. He watched McCague come back with the drinks.

McCague sat down next to him. 'The DI's job's yours if you want it. The word is in, but the board won't wait forever.' He looked at him. 'Back on the street, Vanner. Where you belong.'

Vanner thought about it then, through the haze of drink that swathed his brain in a bandage of numbness, which he had to fight now to penetrate. He felt vaguely queasy and crushed his cigarette in the ashtray. People thronged about their table. He could no longer hear rain on the window. McCague looked at his watch. 'I'd better go,' he said.

The Wasp drove past Camden Palace and onto Eversholt Street. Ninja watched the road ahead of them, blinking with his one good eye. Behind them a siren blared and a fire engine hurtled towards Kentish Town. The Wasp grinned in the mirror. 'Mickey Blond-hair,' he said, 'set fire to his mum again.'

McCague got up to leave. Vanner sat where he was. McCague looked down at him, hands in the pockets of his coat. 'You sticking around then?'

5

Vanner grunted.

'Don't get shitfaced. And think about it, Vanner. You need the job. What else are you good for?'

When he was gone the silence descended from within. Vanner looked at his empty glass. Three people forced themselves onto the bench that McCague had just vacated. He glanced at them. The men, cropped hair, T-shirts and tattoos. The girl smoking hand-rolled cigarettes. One of the men stared at him. He stared back. The man leered at him.

'Want a picture?'

Vanner stood up. 'Choosy what I put on my walls.'

Outside the rain fell in sheets. It cooled him, only his head sang with beer and with whiskey and too long in the confines of the pub. For a moment he leaned on the wall.

Across the street, Ninja sat straighter. The Wasp started the engine.

Vanner walked in the rain, coat over his arm, jacket plastered against his flesh. A car drove slowly past him and turned off behind the Parcel Force building. Vanner put on his coat and got wetter. He shrugged his shoulders and crossed the road. At the corner, he paused where the Parcel Force depot butted the station. Buildings blistered the skyline beyond it: the three towers topped in yellow and red and blue when the light of day fell across them. He needed to pee. He stepped round the corner and moved into the shadows.

He felt rather than saw them, a presence in the lee of the wall. He zipped up his fly and for a moment he stood where he was, trying to penetrate the gloom with eyes wearied by drink. A figure stepped towards him. He was holding something long and heavy. Vanner's head cleared. He could not see the face, dark or hooded or something. He stood a moment with his arms hanging at his sides, and then from behind him, the sound of metal pulled against metal.

All at once he was sprawling, hands out into puddles. A foot against his spine. He rolled to his right and a crack rang out on the pavement. He kept rolling and was stopped by a second kick, that knocked the breath from his body. He tried to get up. If he got up he could fight. But as he raised himself something heavy and wooden came down between his shoulder blades.

Scrabbling now, crablike; two dark figures circling him. He rolled away from them, smashed against a dustbin on wheels and half-squatted. The one with the bat moved towards him. The other held something too, but it was shorter and thinner and curved. Breathing hard now, Vanner launched himself at the bat, catching the assailant and bowling him over backwards. He lost his footing, the drink and the rain on the concrete. Where was the other one – the kicker? He could not sense the kicker.

And then he was in his face. Vanner half-standing, the smell of damp cloth in his nostrils. Hooded. The eyes: something odd with the eyes. He felt something blunt in his gut and doubled once more. He could barely see them. They moved around him so quickly. Darkness on their side.

Escape. He could not fight them. He searched the gloom, back the way he had come. Path blocked by the bat. The blade arcing towards him, up and down and scything the air by his face. He dodged right but it cut him, nicking his shoulder and slapping off his upper arm. Again he was against the dustbin. Wet metal on his back. The blade came once more. This time he moved left and the bat clapped against his forearm. Pain shot to his shoulder and he forced down a cry. He kicked out, high and to his left and caught something. A grunt. Staggering feet. A gap. Vanner dived for the gap, right arm dangling, bone chafing the flesh. He tripped and threw out both hands in front of him. As he fell so the blade came down and scored the length of his back.

Hands and knees now, hugging his right arm to him. Blood, like salt in his mouth. A glimpse of his reflection where street light blackened the puddle. He could hear the sound of their breathing. Then headlights, sudden and brilliant in his eyes and feet retreating away from him.

Two

Jane's face floating above him; dark hair, stripped away from white cheeks and the blood red of her mouth. He reached into darkness and she faded. Opening his eyes, he felt the ache of his body.

The nurse had her fingers about his left wrist and was looking at the upturned face of the watch, pinned against her breast. Vanner could smell her. He closed his eyes and he breathed.

'Back with us?'

He opened his eyes again. Young face, smiling at him. He looked beyond her to the window and the sky, bright now with stars.

Some time later he opened his eyes again and the lights were sharp against them. An old man lay asleep in the next bed to him, face all sagging and grey; toothless mouth hanging open. Hospital. Rain and night and a bat and a blade. He touched chapped and swollen lips with a dry tongue. He was thirsty, desperately thirsty.

The pub: faces all mixing and blurring and weaving in and out of his head. How many beers? How many whiskeys? He remembered McCague. A DI's job in the Drug Squad. Australian barmaid all lipstick and chest and those two at the table. He frowned, seeing the old man's face in the bed next to him and not seeing it. He tried to roll over but pain shot through his back. His arm throbbed, encased in an inflated bag. The nurse glanced at him. 'We'll do that soon,' she said. 'Be more comfortable for you.'

Vanner watched her and said nothing. Three other beds beside

9

his and the old man, a sixth but that one was empty. Beyond the lights, night blanked the city.

He woke and it was morning. Two men in suits sat beside the bed. He looked for the nurse but he could not see her.

'Feeling better, Guv?'

Vanner glanced at the speaker: youth still in his face. 'Look like a copper, do I?'

'They didn't take your wallet.'

He pushed himself into more of a sitting position, ignoring the tearing sensation in his back. His tongue filled his mouth. He looked at the jug of water by the bedside. 'That fresh?'

The constable shrugged.

'Get me some. Will you?'

The constable poured some water into a plastic beaker and passed it to him. 'You want any help?'

'No.' Vanner drank, spilling it from the sides of his mouth. It was warm and it tasted of plastic. But it was wet and it soothed the heat in his tongue.

'Took a bit of slap, Guv.'

'You don't say.'

'What'd they look like?'

'Don't know. They had hoods on.' Vanner looked from one of them to the other. 'Where you from?'

'Fennell Street.'

'Who's your Guv'nor?'

'McKinley.'

'Don't know him.' He moved his arm and pain bit from his shoulder.

'You didn't see their faces then?'

He tried to think back. It was more of a blur than it had been. 'IC1,' he said. 'One of them at least.'

'You could tell?'

'His eyes.' He bunched up his face. 'Something odd about his eyes.'

'You saw them?'

'Yes.'

'Up close?'

'For a moment I did.'

'But IC1?'

Vanner nodded. 'He was, almost certainly.'

'Well, that's a start at least.'

Vanner looked at him then. 'What's your name?'

'Jenkins.'

'It wasn't a mugging, Jenkins.'

'Do what, Guv?' Jenkins sat forward.

Vanner motioned with his good hand. 'You said yourself, they didn't take my wallet.'

'They were disturbed, Guv'nor. Car came round the corner. Picked you up in the headlights.'

Vanner shook his head. 'They had no intention of taking my wallet. Or if they had it was an afterthought.'

The two constables exchanged glances. Jenkins stood up. 'We'll leave you in peace, Guv. Talk to you again a bit later.'

McCague came in that afternoon. He pulled the curtains round the bed and sat down. Vanner looked at the curtains. He was sitting up now, his back against three pillows. 'What d'you do that for?'

McCague looked round. 'Don't know really. More private I suppose.'

'Open them,' Vanner said. 'Claustrophobic enough as it is.'

McCague opened them again and sat down. Vanner looked at him. 'No grapes then?'

'You've had enough already.'

Vanner grinned. 'Grapes and malt and hops.'

'Exactly.' McCague moved his bulk in the chair. 'Who d'you pick a fight with?'

'If I knew that I wouldn't be in here.'

'Walking home?'

Vanner nodded. 'Couple of blokes fancied it in the pub after you left. Skinheads. Tattoos and that.'

'Give you trouble?'

11

'Nothing I couldn't handle.'

'You think it might've been them?'

'Maybe.'

'Told Fennell Street? It's their job.'

Vanner laughed. 'What, those two who were in this morning?'

McCague looked at him. 'You were a DC once.'

Vanner held his eye then and McCague's gaze did not waver. 'You were well out of it last night.'

Vanner twisted his mouth. 'Tell me about it. Sober – I'd have been able to see them.'

'No idea who they were?'

Vanner shook his head. 'One of them had a knife.'

McCague raised his eyebrows. 'You're telling me he did. There's thirty-seven stitches in your back and your shoulder's split to the bone.'

Vanner glanced at his broken forearm. 'Other one had a bat.'

'You didn't get a look at them?'

'Too dark. They had hoods on.'

'Black or white?'

'The hoods?'

'The bodies, you prat.'

'One was white I think. Funny eyes.'

'What d'you mean?'

Vanner made a face. 'Can't tell you. Something odd that's all. I only saw for a second.'

'You told that to Fennell Street. About the eyes, I mean.'

Vanner nodded. McCague got up then. 'I'll come and see you again,' he said. 'By the way, I phoned your old man. He's coming down tomorrow.'

Later that evening the nurse came back. She came over to his bed and rearranged his pillows, the weight of her breasts on his arm. 'Have you eaten anything?'

Vanner shook his head. 'Don't fancy it.'

'Maybe tomorrow then.'

'Maybe.'

She stood straight, hands on her hips, arms bare to the elbow,

12

the skin fine and soft and warm. 'You shouldn't drink so much. Last night we had trouble finding blood in your alcohol.'

He smiled at her. 'What's your name?'

'Valesca.'

'Beautiful name.'

'Thank you.'

He looked at her. 'I'll try to remember. About the drink I mean.'

'Do that.' She smiled then. 'Too much drink spoils your looks.'

'So that's what's been wrong all these years.'

He watched her check the other patients and then he lay back with his eyes closed. Her's had been the face he had seen when he woke up. But before that, drifting in and out of sleep or coma or just unconsciousness, it had been Jane. When he closed his eyes now he could see her as if it was yesterday. Weakness, he told himself. It was weakness. The past closed in when he was weak. He felt it now, deep in his gut, a sensation he had not been aware of in a long time. He felt alone. People around him, but as alone as he had ever been. Alone was okay, alone was normal. But this alone – this was almost lonely.

He could not sleep. Maybe it was the drugs or the pain in his back or maybe it was the ghosts of his past as yet unaccounted for, that drifted in and out of his head. Last night, the night before, whenever. Sitting in that pub until he could barely sit at all. And then the chilled March rain on his face and the desperate need to take a leak. Two hoods in the darkness and his wallet still in his pocket.

The following afternoon his father came to see him. Vanner was half-dozing, the clatter of cups shook him from the pillow. He looked up at his father, tall and white-haired and dressed all in black.

'You look like a priest,' Vanner said.

'I am a priest.'

His father sat down and looked at him. He placed a bag of fruit on the side table. An orange rolled from the bag and dropped onto the floor. He bent to pick it up and when he straightened their

13

eyes met. He sat back in the chair. 'You okay?'

'Not bad.'

'Much pain?'

'Had worse.'

'Bad enough though eh?'

Vanner nodded.

Silence between them; a strained dullness as if both of them had things to say but neither could remember how.

'How's Anne?' Vanner asked him.

'Worried about you.'

Vanner smiled. 'There's nothing here that won't mend.'

'Two of them?'

'Bat and a blade between them.'

'You were lucky.'

'I was pissed, Dad.'

'Then you were very lucky.' His father looked about the room and then back at him.

'Mugging?'

'What?'

'Just a mugging was it?'

Vanner pulled his mouth down at the corners. 'I've still got my wallet.'

'What then?'

'I don't know.'

Again silence between them. His father said: 'When do they let you out of here?'

'They haven't told me. Soon, I hope. Can't take much more of this lying around.'

'What're you going to do? You can't exactly fend for yourself.'

'I'll be all right.'

'Anne doesn't think so.' His father looked at him. 'I don't think so. Come up to Norfolk. Better to recuperate up there than down here on your own.'

Vanner looked at him for a long moment, then finally he nodded.

* * *

14

His father drove. Vanner in the passenger seat, sun against the windscreen. Silence, save the drone of the old engine, as they moved along the country roads with the tang of the sea drifting through the crack in the window. His father looked sideways at him. 'You okay?'

Vanner nodded.

'Small car. No good for your back.'

'I'm okay, Dad.'

So many memories. These roads, so often travelled, younger days when his mind was stretched and hopeful. He tried to sit back in the seat but the bandages that swathed his middle restricted his movement, tightening the breath within him. His father seemed to sense his discomfort.

'When do the stitches come out?'

'They haven't said. I'm supposed to check in with a GP up here.'

'You can use McMahon. He's a good man.'

They drove on. Vanner watched the gnarled and beaten skin of his father's fist as he clutched the gearstick. The trees were full of leaf, the fields ripening with the freshness of the wind and the fall of the sun across them. Everywhere he looked the countryside bloomed with life and yet all he saw was wilderness. His shoulder ached, his arm itching interminably under the confines of the plaster cast.

'Anne'll have food ready.' His father made the comment as if to break the weariness that stretched, chiselled but unworked between them. Vanner said nothing, thought nothing, looked out on abundance and saw nothing.

'Will you take the job?'

'Job?'

'DI's job in the Drug Squad. McCague told me about it when he phoned. Good man, McCague. On your side, right through that other business.'

'I don't know,' Vanner said.

His father looked at him then, as fathers do, with confusion and

15

uncertainty, as if to say something, but yet nothing to say. Vanner stared through the windscreen. Father's thoughts. Son's thoughts. Family. Why did he have so much difficulty with family? There had been no family to speak of: only his father and churches and the army. Uniformed men and drinking and laughing and fighting.

They came closer to the coast and Vanner rolled down his window to smell the familiarity of the sea. Gulls cried: he could see them in the distance against the flattened line of the horizon. The city left behind, the emptiness of the life that was his there. Now the sea seemed to beckon him, a distant reminder of some other kind of life that he had known, long ago. The scent of her: she had never been here; but now, as he drew closer, he could smell her.

His father got his bag from the boot and Vanner adjusted the sling on his shoulder. Anne came down the steps, her feet crunching on the gravel drive of the rectory. The sun had dipped behind the house and the weight of it all seemed to descend upon him.

'Aden.' She reached up and kissed him, cupping his cheek with her hand.

'Hello, Anne.' He avoided her eye, looking beyond her into the house: the width of the hall; the wood panels of the floor, reminding him of the empty house he had bought and left behind. Gently, his father kissed Anne. Vanner watched him, glimpsing the unspoken warmth that passed between them. Anne smiled at him and nodded towards the open doorway.

'Go on. I've made up a room for you.'

Lips curling back over a red and dripping tongue. Red eye. White face. Half the devil looked back at him. He hummed as gently he wound the mangle, one strip through and then tearing slowly at the perforated edges that Cready had ruled when the paper was still soaking. One clean sheet of acid squares. Hundreds of laughing faces.

He wore a cycle mask over his face, the type used by those brave enough to risk the stench of the city. Eyes wide, blinking against the strength of the alcohol that sloshed now in the trays. His head thumped but that might have been with the music that drummed in his ears. He cut fifty sheets then went through to the main floor and closed the door behind him. Stripping the mask from his face, he drank from the bottle of water.

Earlier today, as he had paid more cash into the box, he had questioned whether this was in fact the right way. For the moment at least, logic told him that any other way was too dangerous, and as yet wholly unnecessary. No point in taking risks for risk's sake. The first rule of any business. The existing policy had been a calculated strategy: to do other would be to launch into the unknown. That was before Saturday though. With Saturday so many things had changed. He stood now with the heat of crystal soaked in alcohol buzzing in his head, and contemplated the difference. His hand had been forced: that was how it had felt and that was no good to him. He would have to consider alternatives.

Vanner stood naked before the full-length mirror that misted as the bath filled. Half-turned, he could see over his shoulder and take a first real look at the spider's legs of stitching that criss-crossed his spine. How many did McCague say – thirty-seven? His shoulder too was stitched and the plaster weighed on his arm. He stared at the grey of his face in the mirror. They told him he had lost quite a lot of blood. Maybe that accounted for the pallor. The mirror clouded and he lowered himself into the water and felt the stinging sensation all across his back. Sweat gathered in sticky globules that rolled from his brow to his lips. Through the uncurtained window he could see the height of the church spire, climbing against the moon. He closed his eyes. Anne still looked like Jane. It occurred to him then in a warped kind of way, that maybe it was why he had married Jane in the first place.

They ate dinner in the kitchen, though still he could find no appetite. His father made small talk and Anne smiled at him. He felt uncomfortable. He always did. They knew it. Afterwards in the lounge he drank his father's Scotch. His father sipped coffee.

17

Anne came through after a while and they sat together in the silence. At ten o'clock feigning fatigue, Vanner went up to bed.

He lay in the darkness but could not sleep. The curtains remained undrawn. He had hauled the sash window fully open so the breeze that had risen with the evening could break the silence of his room. He could hear them speaking in small voices as they went to bed, and then the house stilled into a dullness that echoed in his head. The weight of his arm was difficult. He had not bothered to re-strap his back so at least tonight his breathing was easier. He wondered if he would bleed on the sheet.

Superintendent Morrison walked the length of the corridor and knocked on McCague's door. He straightened the knot of his tie and tugged at the sleeves of his jacket. He heard a gruff command to enter and he opened the door. McCague looked over the desk at him.

'Sit down, Andrew.'

Morrison sat. McCague closed the file he was working on and sat back. He looked over fisted hands at him.

'Settling in?'

'I think so.'

'Different to CIB.'

Morrison allowed himself a smile. 'Back in this field. It's what I always wanted.'

McCague looked at him. 'But not like this.'

'Sir?'

'Come on, Andrew. I'm your Guv'nor. You can be candid with me. You fucked up over Vanner and this is a sideways shift. You know it and I know it. Why ponce about?'

Morrison looked steadily at him. If he wanted to be jaundiced he would say that McCague was enjoying this.

'I got it wrong over the Watchman Killings, Sir. I'll admit that. But my motives were sound.'

'You investigated Vanner for assaulting Gareth Daniels in an interview room. That got him suspended. Then you decided he was a murderer. You never had a shred of evidence. You took

18

inference and supposition as fact. That's why Garrod shifted you.'

'Vanner had a past, Sir.'

'So what. We all have a past. You let personal feelings cloud your judgement.'

Morrison looked at the floor.

'Vanner may be an awkward, selfish bastard, and he shouldn't have smacked Daniels. But he's no killer.'

McCague pushed himself away from the desk. 'Like I said. The past.' He sighed. 'We're not here to talk about the past. You know he's been demoted.'

'I heard.'

'And you also know he was mugged.'

Morrison nodded.

McCague paused then. 'I've offered him the DI's job with the Drug Squad.'

Morrison was suddenly cold. 'You mean the North West job?'

McCague nodded.

'I don't want him.'

'I didn't think you would.'

'You asked me to be candid.'

'That's why we're having this meeting.'

'He wasn't responsible for the Watchman murders, but he was involved with Sarah Kennett. She killed five people and then killed herself.' Morrison shook his head. 'Don't you think that makes him just a little bit unstable?'

'You forget,' McCague said. 'Vanner was a soldier. He's seen death in Ulster and he's seen it in the Falklands. He'll get over it. That's why he's in Norfolk. If he's hung up on anybody it's his ex-wife – not Sarah Kennett.'

For a few moments neither of them spoke, then Morrison said: 'Has he accepted the job?'

'Not yet.'

'He won't.'

'No?'

Morrison shook his head. 'Vanner would never go back. Not the kind of man to accept demotion.'

'He will.' McCague sat back again. 'He might not have done. But now he will.'

'You mean because of what happened to him?'

'That's exactly what I mean. Vanner'll want to find out who hit him.'

'He was mugged. Hundreds of people get mugged.'

'That's not how he sees it.'

'Then with respect, Sir, that makes him even more of a liability.'

'Possibly.'

'And you're happy about that?'

'I'll live with it. It'll give him an edge. Vanner's good with an edge.'

Morrison crossed his leg on his knee. 'With respect, Sir. I don't agree with you. Vanner in the Drug Squad with a grudge is not going to help us at all.'

'They're rudderless down there, Andrew. Have been since the reshuffle. They've been without a DI for two months.'

'What about Ellis? He's acting DI.'

'Ellis is a good skipper. But Vanner's a good DI.'

'Sounds like the decision is made, Sir.'

'It is. I just wanted to let you know.'

Vanner sat in the spring sunshine in a deckchair. His father was digging out flower beds, in his wellington boots. Anne brought Vanner a cup of coffee and sat down on the bench beside him. 'How are you today?'

'Getting there.' He glanced across at his father. 'How's he?'

'He's okay. He misses you though, Aden. I know he'd like to see more of you.'

Vanner looked back at her, clearly, unflinching and yes she reminded him of Jane. Hair pulled back, the height and beauty of her face still evident despite her fifty-odd years.

'You find it difficult being around me don't you, Aden.' She said it flatly, no hint of emotion or testiness in her voice. He opened his mouth to deny it, but then he closed it again. She smiled from deep in her eyes. 'Why?'

He could not answer her. He looked beyond her to his father, who leaned on his fork and studied the ground at his feet.

'You make him happy,' Vanner said.

'Do I?'

'You know you do.'

'We have a nice life now he's retired. He still locums of course. But it's quiet up here and we get along. He misses you though. He's seventy-two now.'

'You mean his time is running out?'

'Not just his, Aden. Yours.'

Vanner looked towards his father again. 'He's not ill or anything is he?'

'No. He's as fit as ever. But you're his only son.' She shook her head. 'You know you're both so alike.'

Vanner smiled then. 'You think so?'

'Don't you?'

They were quiet for a moment and then she said: 'I remind you of Jane, don't I?' Pain in his chest. He sat forward and placed his cup back on the saucer.

'Have you never tried to see her?'

'She's married, Anne. What would be the point?'

'D'you know where she lives?'

'No.'

'It's been such a long time.'

'Yes. You're right. It has.'

Day died over the city and two boys played eight-ball pool in the Neasden Road Bail Hostel. A third boy rolled a cigarette in a corner. Every now and then he would glance out of the window.

'You should've seen the cunt.' The red-haired boy bent low over the table, the glint of adrenalin still in his eyes. 'Nearly shit himself when I wave this fuck-off blade in his face.'

'How much d'you get?' the other boy asked him.

'Hundred.'

'Shit. A ton? In one hit?'

'Yep. What about you?'

'Twenty-five. All fuckin' day. Two buses and a tube train for that. Cost me more in fares.' He lowered his voice as the warden walked past the open door. 'Some old bag on the top deck. Last one of the day. Twenty-five quid and a bar of fuckin' chocolate.'

In the corner a bleeper sounded and the lad with the cigarette glanced down at the face of his watch. A number flashed on the panel. He looked up at the others. 'Give me your dosh then. They'll be here in a minute.' He stood up and moved to the door. There was no sign of the warden. He hitched at baggy jeans with his elbows and looked back across the room. 'Come on, Sammy. I'll nip out while Michaels isn't looking.'

The red-haired kid fished eighty pounds from his pocket and passed it over. The other one looked up at him. 'Thought you said a hundred.'

'I did.'

'So where's the rest?'

'Pocket money. He can afford it.'

The other lad looked at him, shook his head and then shrugged. 'Your funeral,' he said.

Pocketing the money, he moved back to the window and saw a grey BMW pull up in the car park. 'They're here,' he said. 'Sammy. You make sure the old git's not about. I'll take this across.'

The red-haired boy went out to the kitchen.

The boy with the money ran to the car park and crouched down on the passenger side of the BMW. The window was wound down. Ninja leered at him from out of his good eye. The boy shrank back a little. He always did this close. The left eye was a mass of whitened pupil with scars crisscrossing the lids. His right earlobe was missing. The Wasp leaned across, holding a small, padded envelope in his hand. 'What you got?'

'Hundred and five.'

'Not bad.'

'Bloody good.' Again the boy looked at Ninja, arm hanging out of the window, a cigarette burning between black-nailed fingers.

The Wasp took the cash and passed over the envelope.

'Respect.' The boy stood up, hesitated and glanced back at the hostel. 'Hey, Wasp,' he said. 'Sammy's holding out on you.'

The Wasp drove towards Cricklewood. Ninja counted the money. 'That's seven hundred,' he said. 'Only Archway to go.'

The Wasp nodded. 'Pretty good for the day.' He glanced at Ninja. 'Sammy fuckin' Johnson. You'd think he'd know better by now.'

The bleeper sounded on Wasp's wrist. He pulled over beside a phone box. Leaving the engine running and Ninja sat in the car, he dialled the number on the watch face.

'Wasp?'

'Yeah.'

'What's happening?'

'We've just done Neasden. Only Archway to go.'

'How much?'

'Seven hundred and a few.'

'Not bad.'

'One thing.'

'What?'

'Kid in Neasden. You know – Sammy Johnson. He's holding out on us.'

The voice in his ear went cold. 'Maybe you'll sort that for me.'

Vanner stayed a week with Anne and his father and then the confines of their house became too much and he knew he had to move on. He met his father in the drive, sorting some rubbish from his car. He looked up as Vanner walked over. 'What is it?'

'I can't stay here.'

His father rested his hand on the roof of the car. 'You're not fit enough to look after yourself.'

'I'll be all right.'

They looked at one another. 'You can't go back to London.'

Vanner shook his head.

'Where then?'

'I thought I'd go to the cottage.'

Slowly his father lowered the boot lid and crunched across the gravel towards him.

'You sure that's wise, Son?'

'I need the peace, Dad. I need to be alone.'

They stood together on the step and watched him loading his bag into the boot of the car. Anne looked across the roof at him as if she understood. Vanner smiled at her. His father drove him to the village and dropped him outside the shop. He switched off the engine. 'Power's on and everything, Son. There's plenty of wood for a fire. We spend a few weekends there, Anne and I.'

Vanner nodded.

'You got your phone?'

'Yes.'

His father pushed out his cheek with his tongue. 'I'll probably pop across – see if you're all right.'

'Sure.'

Vanner got his bag from the boot. His father started the engine and nodded to him through the open passenger window.

'Thank Anne for me. Will you, Dad?'

'Of course. Take care, Son.'

Grass bent to the wind across the headland. Waves kicked into bone-coloured horses that sculled the lip of the beach. A few people walked dogs. Vanner stood with his bag between his feet and looked out to sea. His gaze was dragged momentarily across the line of the shore to the lighthouse and beyond, where the land was split by sugarbeet fields and his father's chalet stood on its own. Sarah Kennett had died there: thrown herself off the cliff rather than face trial for the Watchman murders and spend the rest of her days in Broadmoor. They had been lovers for a while, but she had never replaced Jane. He bent his eyes to the sun and stared out to sea once again.

He sat in the chair with his jacket still buttoned as the darkness drifted against the window that faced the sea. Beside him, unopened, lay his bag and the small parcel of food he had bought from the shop. In his unplastered hand he held a whiskey glass. On the floor at his feet, the bottle stood with the top off. He stared into his reflection as it grew in the darkness of the window. He glanced at the fire, empty save the murmur of ash. When he came for Sarah there had been candles. No candles now. No dripping wax. The floor had been covered with photos. As he sat there he saw them again.

Later, in the bathroom he dried himself carefully and inspected his wounds. His shoulder was healing. With each day that passed there was more movement. His back would be bitten by scars forever. Beneath the plaster cast his arm itched. He got dressed again and went back to the fire he had lit in the lounge. Salt-crusted wood hissed and smoked in the grate. He poured a large measure of whiskey and lit himself a cigarette. Then he took his mobile phone from his jacket.

'Jabba?'

'Mr Vanner. How's the back?'

'You heard then?'

'Word gets about. I thought you had gone away for good.'

'No,' Vanner said. 'Just for a while.' He paused then: 'Jabba?'

'Yes?'

'I want to find out who hit me.'

He sat down beside the fire and put out his cigarette. Jabba had been his best informant for years. They went way back to when he was just a PC. The word would go out and the word would come back. With Jabba it always did. He finished the whiskey, thought about another then put the lid back on the bottle. He picked up the mobile again and dialled McCague's office. He got no reply so he tried him at home. This time McCague answered.

'It's me. Vanner.'

'How are you?'

'Getting there.'

'How's your father?'

'He's all right. Listen. The DI's job in the Drug Squad.'

25

'What about it?'

'I want it.'

'I thought you might.'

'You know why then?'

'I figured.'

'Is there any word from Fennell Street?'

'Not a whisper.'

'They interviewed the two from the pub?'

'It wasn't them. Whole bunch of witnesses. Stayed in the bar till closing time.'

Vanner nodded to himself. 'Anyway,' he said. 'I'll be back as soon as I'm fixed.'

'One thing I didn't tell you, Vanner.'

'What's that?'

'Your Divisional Super. It's Morrison.'

Three

Vanner sat at his desk with July heat beating at the window. Two sheets of blue absorbent paper lay before him and six hundred faces stared up at him. Half the face was human, white, blue-eyed; the other half was red, the grinning face of the devil. Somewhere he had seen it before, but he could not remember where. Ryan looked over his shoulder.

'Denny,' he said.

Vanner looked up at him. Longish brown hair, sharp blue eyes.

'Nothing till three months ago and suddenly they're everywhere.'

'Who's Denny?'

Ryan shrugged. 'Fuck knows. That's what the kids call them.'

'Where does it come from?'

'Don't know.'

'E's as well as these?'

'Yeah.'

'And it was this type that killed the lad at the rave?'

Ryan nodded.

Vanner stood up. 'I think we should talk to your dealer.'

They left the Drug Squad office on Campbell Row and drove through Wembley, traffic choking the High Road. 'There's a few cartoons that we know already, Guv,' Ryan said. 'Fiver a square. Small-time most of it. But the market's growing again. E costs you fifteen, twenty quid a tab'. Acid isn't Ecstasy. But it's cheaper.'

Vanner thought about the squares pinned on the office wall.

'Hearts, strawberries, the test-tube twins,' Ryan went on. 'Ren

27

& Stimpy's quite new. But we know it's been around in the States. We've found it in Australia as well. Denny, we've never seen before now. We've checked across the water, but they haven't seen it. Nothing as far as we know in Holland. So the source of the artwork is here.'

Vanner looked at him. 'Which makes your dealer a catch.'

Ryan nodded. 'Half a sheet on him. Undercover buy. He got wise and legged it.'

'So you pulled him.'

'We got lucky. Good snout. Geezer I nicked dealing heroin wraps from his foreskin.'

Vanner looked sideways at him.

'Straight up, Guv'nor. I knew he was dealing. But when we strip-searched him we couldn't find anything. He was getting dressed when I noticed the shape of his helmet. Little bumps, making the skin very white – you know.' Ryan grinned then. 'Five wraps up his foreskin. Tiny little bubbles of clingfilm. He'd sit in his car with his flies undone, sell what he had then fuck off home for some more. Nearly got away with it too.'

Vanner laughed. 'Intimate search was it? I trust you got the Super's permission.'

'Didn't need to, Guv. I just told him – either you take them out or we hold you down and we do it.'

They moved on again and Vanner settled back in his seat. A sari-clad Indian woman stepped off the kerb and Ryan jerked the wheel to avoid her. Vanner watched the traffic in front of them. Three weeks in and the summer half over. His shoulder hurt him a little still, whenever he moved it too sharply, or first thing in the morning. His back was fine, but badly scarred. His right forearm was mended.

Sid Ryan was a face from the past. They had both been PC's in Tottenham, nearly ten years before. They had worked together for a year and then he had moved on. Ryan's was the first name McCague had mentioned to him: a DS now, who had been with the squad for three years. He was the most experienced of the twenty-strong team that Vanner had inherited from Westbrook.

'So you settling in then, Guv?' Ryan said as they turned off the High Road and cut down towards the Stadium. Vanner nodded and glanced at him. 'What was the word when you found out it was me you were getting?'

Ryan squinted at him. 'Well, if you must know we thought it was funny.'

'Funny?'

'Yeah. You know. What with Morrison being Division Super.'

Vanner snorted. 'Bit of friction in the barracks.'

'Keeps things interesting doesn't it.'

They sat in the interview room at Neasden Police Station, with the young, black dealer sitting across the table from them. Ryan rolled a liquorice-papered cigarette and passed it across. 'There you go, Ringo. Better with a spliff in. But it'll do.'

Ringo did not smile. He was very black, short-cropped hair grazing the height of his skull. He wore baggy jeans and basket-ball boots.

'Where d'you get the squares, Ringo?' Ryan said.

'I'm not talking to you, man.'

Vanner leaned his elbows on the table and looked him in the eyes. 'Bit young to play the hard man aren't you.'

'I want a lawyer.'

'Do you?'

'Yeah. I do. I ain't talking till he comes.'

'Done this before have you?'

'Before?' Ryan blew smoke at the ceiling. 'This Borstal. That Borstal. Half your life in a bail hostel. Isn't that right, Ringo?'

Ringo looked dull-eyed at him.

Ryan pushed the plastic bag across the table. 'Half a sheet of squares, Ringo. Not to mention the E's. Must make you the main man on your block.'

Ringo looked at the floor. Ryan leaned towards him. 'You know one of these days you'll do yourself a favour and talk to us. Lot of stuff in the papers about E's.'

'No one forces it down their throats.'

Vanner looked at him then. 'And that makes it all right does it?'

29

Ringo blew smoke in his face.

'You want to watch yourself, Ringo,' Ryan said. 'We let it out you're an E dealer – people might think that boy in Archway died because of you.'

Vanner tapped the squares. 'This is new. This Denny. Very new. Suddenly it's everywhere. That puts you in the frame.'

'I just deal.'

'Who supplies you?'

'I don't know.'

Vanner cocked an eyebrow at him. 'You're looking at a lot of bird, Ringo. Pretty boy like you should enjoy that.'

'I want to see a lawyer.'

They drove back to Campbell Row. Vanner lit two cigarettes and passed one across. 'He doesn't want to go down, Guv.' Ryan said. 'We tread carefully we might get somewhere.'

Vanner nodded. 'Who's the brief?'

'Just the duty.'

'No bail?'

'Not right now anyway.'

Morrison was in Vanner's office when they got back. He was looking at the acid squares on the desk. He looked up as Vanner came in. 'What're these?'

'New artwork. Slippery picked up a dealer.'

'Small-time?'

'Half a sheet. Sort of bloke we want to talk to.'

'Many of them about?'

Vanner nodded. 'Our patch mostly. Ecstasy too.'

'Have you flagged it with the AIU?'

Vanner just looked at him.

Morrison stepped past him and closed the office door. Vanner looked out of the window. Thus far he had managed to avoid Morrison. But something was on his mind. He had seen it the moment McCague met with both of them in Hendon. He turned to face him and Morrison looked up. His face was closed: pale skin, green eyes, the red rash of his hair. 'Settling in, Vanner?'

'Yes.'

'The squad?'

'Good team.'

'Been together a while. McCague thought they were leaderless.'

'They were.' Vanner leaned on the radiator.

'What else are you working on?'

'This and that.'

Morrison's eyes dulled. 'I need to know, Vanner. It's my job.'

'You will know, Sir. When there're things to tell you. Right now you know as much as I do.'

Morrison moved away from the door. The room was too small for both of them, a desk, a filing cabinet, two telephones. He half-paced and stepped back again. Vanner stood where he was. 'You went to Daniels' trial?'

'Had to give evidence.'

'Went down like a lamb didn't he.'

'Mr Apologetic.'

'Maybe he meant it.'

'Maybe.'

'They're not all bad, Vanner.'

'Aren't they?'

Morrison folded his arms and leaned against the door. He pulled at his lip with his teeth. 'Rumour, Vanner.'

'What's that?'

'About you. Only been back a few weeks and already a rumour. The word is – you only came back to find out who hit you.'

'Is that right?'

'It's what I'm hearing.'

'You shouldn't listen to rumours, Sir. You, of all people, know that.'

Morrison flared his nostrils. 'You were mugged, Vanner. That's all. It's a Fennell Street deal. I want it kept that way.'

'Not been anywhere near them, Sir.'

'So far.'

'They've not exactly come up with anything have they.'

'No room for private crusades, Vanner.'

'Or vendettas.'

Morrison looked at him. 'Just watch yourself. You're on proba-tion remember. You might have the Chief Super on your side. But there are others.'

Vanner did not say anything.

Morrison opened the door. 'Friendly word, that's all. You know how I play it. By the book, Vanner. Down the line. If you look good – who knows? – you might get your pips back.'

Jimmy Crack stood at the urinal in Gallyon's Nightclub. Next to him the bouncer zipped up. There was no one else in the room.

'Who's the blonde sort with Bobby?' Jimmy said.

The bouncer washed his hands. 'Lisa Morgan. Tom. Very high-class.'

'Some looker.'

'Five hundred a trick.'

Jimmy shook off the drops and zipped up. The bouncer was drying his hands. 'That doesn't include the suite. Got one most nights at the Clarion. You know – off Trafalgar Square. Seven-fifty a throw. So the punter's into her for twelve-fifty a night.'

'I should hope he is at that price.'

The door opened and two men walked in. The bouncer gave them the eye, as bouncers always do, and then he walked outside. Jimmy dried his hands.

Back at the bar, Anne Barrington passed him a drink. 'Not bad overtime this. Maybe I'll get lucky and pull.'

Jimmy glanced up at the balcony where Gallyon leaned on the rail, surveying the hubbub of his empire. 'The looker's a Tom,' he said. 'Regional plant just told me. Five hundred a time.'

'Nice if you can get it.'

'It very probably is.' Jimmy looked across the dance floor and saw the blonde-haired prostitute dancing by herself. Men approached her now and again but she ignored them and they walked away.

A man in a white grandad shirt under a black box jacket walked across the dance floor. Slim, not very tall, but an attitude about him that made people move aside. Jimmy watched as he went up the stairs. Halfway up he glanced across the floor, caught the Tom's eye and nodded to her. She lifted her hand in reply. At the head of the stairs the man shook hands with Bobby Gallyon. Jimmy Crack watched as they sat down at Bobby's table.

Michael Terry drank a Bloody Mary and watched Lisa on the dance floor. Even from here she aroused him. Gallyon was talking to one of his doormen, at the head of the stairs. Terry stood up, drink in hand, and leaned over the rail. On the dance floor below him a man approached Lisa and he smiled to himself as she rebuffed him. A moment later she looked up, caught his eye and Terry tapped the face of his watch. She nodded, once, then went back to her dance.

Gallyon came back, signalled to the barman and sat down.

'Busy night?' Terry said.

'Not bad.'

The barman set more drinks before them. When he had gone Terry said: 'I'm going to Amsterdam this week.'

'So soon?'

'Why not?'

'Selling well then.'

'You know it's selling well.'

Gallyon nodded. 'When does the next load arrive?'

'In my yard on Wednesday.'

'And the price?'

'Price is good.' Terry looked over the dance floor once more.

'You like Lisa. Don't you,' Gallyon said.

Terry looked back at him. 'She keeps me amused. Must be good for business.'

'A fixture.' Gallyon nodded. 'Tell you what,' he said. 'Tonight I'll do you a favour.'

Terry lay back on the bed and watched as Lisa peeled herself out of the dress. Arched back, hair falling across her shoulders. She

33

stood there in suspenders and high heels, giggled at him then sat down in the chair. She jiggled the string of pearls that fell between her breasts, then crossed her ankle on her knee. Terry sat up. 'Come here,' he said.

She just looked at him, the pearls between her teeth now.

'Come on.'

'Why?'

'I've got something for you.'

She stood up, hands on her hips, naked save the black of her stockings. Terry made a grab for her and she danced back, shaking her head. She moved to the bathroom door.

She knelt in the shower and gave him a blow job, water falling over them. Terry stood rigid, hands knotted in the mass of her hair, he kept her eyes upturned to his. Still wet, he walked her over to the bed and made her lie face-down. He moved his weight on top of her, probing between her legs with stiff fingers. He spoke with his mouth close to her ear.

'You like it up the backside don't you.'

'No.'

He pushed himself against her. 'I said, you like it up the backside don't you.'

'It's extra.'

He pushed her face into the pillow. 'Darling. I can afford it.'

Later, body still moist, he lay on his side on the bed. Naked, Lisa sat on the floor, looking at the small white tablet in her hand. 'Funny face,' she said. 'What a funny face.'

'Funny ha ha or just funny?'

She shrugged her shoulders, popped it into her mouth and swallowed some champagne. Terry touched her hair, then he curled his fingers into it and pulled her up from the floor. She cried out. He smiled, twisted her head round and pushed her face into his groin.

The Wasp watched Sammy Johnson leaning against the car-park wall with his mates. His hair flopped over his eyes as he laughed.

Ninja watched him too and ran his thumb along the edge of his sword. The Wasp glanced at him. 'We ain't going to cut him, man.'

'What then?'

'Break the fucker's arms.'

They saw Sammy take a packet of cigarettes out of his jacket pocket, flip open his Zippo and cup his hands to the wind. The Wasp curled his lip. 'Look at the wanker. Thinks he's fuckin' big-time.'

Ninja shifted in his seat. 'Let's just smack him and go.'

Vanner unlocked his front door and stepped into the cold, silent hall. A pile of letters looked up at him. He stepped over them and went downstairs to the kitchen. There was no furniture. He had none. The house was a purchase that had come upon him all at once when he had returned to his flat at Christmas. He had realised he did not own anything and for some reason it mattered. He had walked up the road one day, on the way back from a meet with Jabba, saw the board, looked in the windows and bought it. There was a Greek Taverna on the corner and a pub directly opposite. Camden Town. Why not?

In the kitchen he bent to the fridge. A single pot of yoghurt on an otherwise empty shelf. Standing up again, he closed the door and then plugged in the kettle. He unplugged it again and went back upstairs. The lounge was empty, his feet echoing on the stripped wood of the floor. All the floors were stripped. Maybe that was why he had bought it. Upstairs, he tossed his jacket on the bed. Apart from a hanging clothes rail, bought from a closing-down shop sale, the bed was his only furniture. He took a shower, got dressed again and crossed the street to the Taverna.

Costas was there as usual, whistling as he poured cold beer into a frosted glass. Outside, the orange of street lights reflected off the roofs of the cars. Vanner ate Moussaka and Greek cheese, and drank two more bottles of beer. He could see his new, empty house from here. When he was finished eating he smoked a cigarette and watched the comings and goings from the pub.

35

Good to have Slippery as his DS. He could mind for him. No doubt he would need to. The rest seemed able enough. Drug Squad, good men on the street. McCleod would be on his side, as would China. Kevin Davies too. Ryan had said as much. Ellis was the one maybe. He would need to watch Ellis. The other DS, with his Inspector's Board coming up. No doubt he had had his eye on this job.

Morrison. He smiled to himself. Nice to see the little bastard floundering. Tables turned by McCague. He could have laughed aloud at the irony. Garrod had lost him pretty quickly after the CIB debacle. Sideways shunt and everybody knew it. Unblemished career, suddenly with a great big stain on it.

Michael Terry was speeding. Not in his car, in his head; mind racing as he counted the notes on the table. Two nights on the trot. Five hundred a time. Jesus Christ. Was it worth it? He looked down at the naked shape of Lisa, lying on her side with half an arm tucked under the pillow. Her hair fell back from her face. Silly fucking witch. Funny how she disgusted him afterwards.

He took the lift downstairs and studied himself in the mirror. Looking good, he told himself. Looking very good. He waited in the lobby while the doorman found a taxi. He sat in the back as the cabbie cut down through the West End and headed towards the river. Vodka and wine mingled in his head and he could smell Lisa Morgan on his clothes. A police car was parked along the Haymarket. Two uniforms were talking to a couple of likely looking lads in green, nylon bomber jackets.

In his flat he poured another vodka and stirred in tomato juice. He drank it, standing against the height of the window which filled the wall, overlooking the river. He could see Gabriel's Wharf and the back of the Sea Containers building and beyond it the glass of the water. He loved to stand here on nights like this, with his sacks emptied and his head buzzing. He liked to watch the lights on the water, listen to the traffic rumble over Blackfriars Bridge. He could see St Paul's and the city beyond it. Five years ago he had nothing.

* * *

Vanner scraped his face, then finished with a splash of cold water. Outside a car's horn hooted. Drying his hands, he went to the window. Ryan had his car parked in the middle of the road and was rolling a cigarette on the roof.

They sat in the charge room at Neasden. Ryan looked over at him. 'No furniture in your place then?'

'Haven't got round to it yet.'

The Custody Sergeant brought Ringo out. He looked bleary-eyed and lonely. Vanner glanced at Ryan. 'His brief seen him yet?'

Ryan nodded. He stood up as Ringo got to them. 'Another night on the tiles? Told you before about that.'

They sat in the interview room. Vanner looked Ringo in the eye. 'D'you want your solicitor here?'

Ringo shook his head. Ryan rolled a cigarette and he looked hopefully at it. Ryan stuck it between his own lips, lit it and drew the smoke in hard. He talked as he exhaled. 'Not much sleep last night then. Sarge out there tells me you had a right bunch of hooligans in. Sang all night did they?'

Ringo said nothing.

Vanner leaned forward. 'Get used to it. Prisons are very noisy.'

Ringo wet his lips with his tongue. 'I don't want to go away,' he said.

Vanner looked at Ryan and then back at Ringo again. 'Little bit late for that isn't it?'

Ryan passed Ringo the cigarette and he sucked greedily on it. Vanner kept on staring at him and the hunted look grew in his eyes. Ryan sat back in the chair and tapped his lighter on the table top. 'Maybe there's something we can do, Guv'nor?' he said.

Vanner shook his head.

'You don't think so?'

'No.'

Ringo glanced at Vanner. 'I could help you.'

'How?'

Ringo shrugged. 'I could tell you things.'

'What sort of things?'

'Man, I ain't just gonna cough.'

Vanner stood up and looked at Ryan. 'No,' he said. 'I don't think so.' He walked out of the room.

Ryan was rolling a second cigarette. He twisted up one end, placed it in the corner of his mouth and it flapped up and down as he spoke. 'Listen, Ringo,' he said. 'You play ball and I might just be able to do something.'

'What?'

'Square this with Mr Serious back there.'

'Get me off?'

'Not off. Get you bail. Get you to help us maybe.' He lit his cigarette. 'Tell me what you know and we'll see.'

They sat down in the canteen and Ryan poured out the tea.

'So?' Vanner said.

'He's been dealing for three months.'

'What does he know?'

'Not very much.' Ryan spooned sugar. 'He sells to other dealers. Very small-time. A few squares here. A few E's there. Spreads it out a bit. Nobody we want to talk to. It's a good scam, Guv. He doesn't know who supplies him.'

'What d'you mean?'

'He's got a post office box.'

'And?'

'Fifty quid a year. One application form, but two cards for signing. He sends off for the box, giving proof of his address. Lives up at Bream Park. You know – the arsehole of the world, where you only leave your car if you're looking for an insurance job.'

Vanner sipped at his tea.

'Anyway. The deal is he applies for two cards. Post Office'll issue them so long as the box owner takes responsibility.'

'And he's the box owner?'

'Yes. Card comes with a box number and a postcode. All he

does is sign for the stuff he picks up. The source posts him acid and Ecstasy with the Denny logo. It comes in padded computer-disc envelopes. Doesn't really weigh much. Could be anything inside. Anyway, all pretty boy has to do is waltz in with his card, sign the bit of paper and pick up the gear. When he gets outside he posts another envelope back with the cash in. Some time later number two cardholder arrives and picks up the dosh.' He sat back. 'Very bloody simple.'

'You come across it before?'

'As a method of supply?' Ryan shook his head.

Vanner rubbed his jaw. 'Who's the second cardholder?'

'He doesn't know.'

'How does he know when to collect the gear?'

Ryan tapped his wrist. 'His watch, Guv. Built in pager. A phone number flashes up on the face. Ringo makes a call, presumably to a phone box. He reckons the numbers are different most of the time. Anyway, that's how he gets his instructions. You see the watches advertised on the walls of the tube stations. Hundred and twenty a time.'

'So who recruited him?'

'Some kid in a bail hostel over in Chalk Farm. He was tucked up in there after being charged with assault.'

'Can he give us the name?'

'Says he can't remember. Kid's gone now anyway. He got off his case and Ringo hasn't seen him since.'

Vanner sat back as Ryan's breakfast arrived. 'So he's supplied with a box, a watch, and fifty quid for the rental. He gets two cards for the box and he never sees anyone.' He took out his cigarettes. 'What did he do with the second card?'

'Got picked up from him. Number to call on the watch. Told to stand outside Wembley Central and wait. Cyclist picked it up. You know one of the fancy type messengers, all racing bike and lycra and radio.'

'What did he look like?'

'Couldn't tell. Helmet and smog mask. Two seconds to take the card and ride on.'

'And that's it?'

'Says it's all there is.'

'You believe him?'

'He isn't looking to go down, Guv.'

Vanner sat forward again. 'So we set him up? Get him to lie down for this one. Give him a couple of weeks on remand and then don't oppose the bail.'

Ryan nodded.

'Will he go for that?'

'I reckon.'

'And you'll handle him?'

'Yes.'

'Okay. Let's do it.'

Vanner sat in his office with the door open. His mobile lay on the desk before him. He heard Ryan start singing 'Jimmy Crack Corn' from the outer office and he shook his head. Another face from the past. Jimmy 'Crack' McKay. One of the original members of the now disbanded Crack Squad that had been set up when everyone thought the US Crack epidemic would follow suit over here. But it didn't and the squad was disbanded. Jimmy remained, however, as the Crack Liaison Officer, working for the Area Intelligence Unit. He was a big man, black hair. Vanner had fought him in the Lafone Boxing Championships in 1988.

The mobile phone rang on his desk and he picked it up.

'Mr Vanner. This is Jabba.'

Vanner pushed the door to with his toe. 'Jabba,' he said. 'What news?'

'Not so much. The world is very quiet.'

'Meaning we're not paying you enough?'

'No no. Would I say that, Mr Vanner? No, I mean what I say. The world is very quiet.'

Vanner sat down. 'It's nothing that Fennell Street are looking at?'

'Not so's I've heard. Who hates you, Mr Vanner?'

'You want a list?'

Jabba chuckled. 'That's the place to start.'

'It's a long list,' Vanner said.

'Whose name's at the top?'

Vanner lifted his foot to the edge of the desk and pondered. 'Six years ago I was in D11. Forerunner to the Gunships we have now.'

'I remember.'

'Franklin Tate,' Vanner said.

'He's dead.'

'I know. I shot him. Armed robbery. Brought him down in a warehouse in Hammersmith. He tried to take me out with a sawn-off.' Franklin Tate. Gut shot. Always the worst kind. Blood seeping like water and all that time to think about dying before finally you lose consciousness. Tate had lost it in the ambulance. He was dead on arrival at hospital.

'He has two brothers,' Jabba said.

'Alexander and Christian. They both went down for the blag.'

'So, it's not them?'

'They're inside.'

'Christian Tate is out.'

Vanner sat very still. 'You sure?'

'Very. A cousin of mine has seen him. Lives in Croydon with his mother.'

'They were a Streatham family.'

'Not any more.'

Vanner thought about it. Christian Tate, the brother of a man he had killed. Two hoods in the darkness, a baseball bat and a knife. 'When did he get out?'

'February.'

'Why didn't I know?'

'You tell me, Inspector.'

Vanner sat forward again, shaking his head. 'Do some digging, Jabba. Let me know what you find.'

Four

John Phillips had his back to the class as he looked out of the fourth-floor window to the sunfilled concourse below. Three men stood talking, jeans and boots and motorbike jackets in spite of the heat. He felt the hairs rise on his neck.

'Sir?' He heard the voice from behind him, but did not reply. He was watching the three men. Did they know which was his class? Could they see him? Did they know he was looking at them?

'Sir?'

'What is it?' He whirled around and saw one of the students holding up two wires.

'Black negative?'

'What?'

'Is black negative?'

For a moment Phillips stared at him. John was about his age. 'Yes. Of course it's negative.'

The boy lifted his chin. 'Sorry,' he said. 'Only checking.'

Phillips turned back to the window. The concourse area was empty.

At three o'clock he stacked his books into his bag and sat down behind his desk. Long day. He rubbed his face with his palms. Always was on a Tuesday. Solid teaching. He should never have agreed to the timetable, but at least the term would soon be over. His nerves were tattered. It was beginning to get too much. He knew it was past time he went to the police. But what could they

43

do? What could he prove? They would lie low maybe, if he was lucky. But they would be back. Their kind always came back. Slowly he got to his feet, closed the catch on his case and wandered down the stairs.

The heat blistered the tarmac, setting it mushy under his shoes. He walked towards his car, one hand fumbling for the keys in his pocket.

'Hello, Mr Phillips.'

He stopped, chill all at once on the neck. He stood a moment then turned around. The tallest of them leered at him; long hair, half a beard. Phillips looked him in the eye. The small one, with the blackened teeth, stepped between them. 'Where's John, Mr Phillips?'

Phillips looked down at him. He was aware of the tension in his muscles. 'I don't know.' He tried to step round him but the other two took his arms and forced him against the wall.

'We think you do.' Bad-teeth breathed in his face. 'He comes home to do his washing.'

'If he does – it's not when I'm there.'

'You're a liar.'

Phillips bristled then. God how he'd like to smack the little bastard. In the old days he would have done.

'We want him,' Bad-teeth said. 'You should teach him to pay his debts.'

Phillips made a move towards him and he stepped back. The other two gripped his forearms and pushed him back to the wall. He looked beyond them for help. But all he could see was a lad. Mark Terry, it looked like. One of John's old friends from school. For a moment Phillips stared at him.

'Maybe we'll take a look at that little girlie of yours,' Bad-teeth went on. 'Must be old enough to bleed by now.'

Phillips' face twisted. 'You even . . .'

Bad-teeth jabbed him in the chest with stiff fingers. 'We want our money. You think about that.' They took his case, scattered his papers all over the car park and then left him alone.

Phillips slowly collected the papers. He could feel tears behind his eyes. Fifty years old and he could feel tears. A shadow crossed his and he looked up. Mark Terry stood there with his bag over his shoulder, heavy-lensed glasses half-covered by his unbrushed hair. The sun was still high overhead and he had his coat fastened to the neck. 'You all right, Mr Phillips?'

'Fine.' He said it gruffly. 'I'm just fine.' Snapping the fastener on his case, he marched over to his car. The boy followed him. Phillips paused and his shoulders sagged. 'It's okay, Mark. Really, I'm fine.'

Mark looked towards the gates. 'What did they want?'

'Oh, nothing.'

'I heard them talk about John. Are they looking for him?'

Phillips looked round then. 'Yes, Mark. They are.'

'Why? What's he done?'

'I don't know. I haven't seen him for ages.'

'You don't know where he is?'

Phillips ran a hand through his hair. 'I have to go, Mark.'

'If you see John . . . Say hello for me will you. I'd like to see him again.'

Phillips nodded.

'Is he in trouble?'

Phillips felt the threat of tears once more. 'Promise me something, Mark,' he said.

'What?'

'You'll have nothing to do with drugs.'

Ryan registered Ringo May as an informant with the Yard. He gave Vanner the details. Ryan would handle him on his own. Vanner would manage the relationship. The two of them sat in Vanner's office in Campbell Row.

'Sorted?' Vanner asked him.

Ryan nodded.

'What's his pseudonym?'

'Milo.'

Vanner arched his eyebrows.

'It's a chocolate drink. Comes in green boxes from Safeway.'

45

'Why Milo?'

'Fuck knows. Maybe his mother fed him it.'

Vanner shook his head. 'They'll know he was pulled,' he said. 'Let's hope they still go for it.'

'It'll be all right. He's been away a fortnight. Long enough to allay any suspicions. He'll tell them we nicked him for possession – that's if they ask. The way this is set up he can't do them much harm anyway. We just have to wait for a delivery then set up a plot on the box.'

Late afternoon, he sat in the park with his jacket undone, watching a man and a woman dragging a spaniel along the path. Black and white thing, scruffy, dragging its ears on the ground. They walked arm in arm, their heads very close. They did not seem to notice the dog. Thirsty, he thought. That dog looks thirsty.

He sat back, looking at the crystal blue of the sky. The sweat formed on his brow and dampened his shirt at the armpits. A child toddled in front of him, on reins held by its mother, a sinking 99 ice cream dripping all over its hand. He smiled at the mother. She ignored him and concentrated on guiding her child.

Standing up, he glanced at his watch and wandered over to the phone box. It rang as he got to it. 'What took you so long, Wasp?'

'I was busy.'

'Well don't be. I don't call for the good of my health.'

'Hey. Fuck off, man. I was with a woman.'

'It's the middle of the afternoon.'

'I like it in the afternoon.'

He took a breath and leaned into the booth. 'Was she any good?'

'I don't know. I got interrupted.'

'Listen,' he said. 'One of the gang is down.'

'Who?'

'Ringo May. Wembley.'

'So what? He knows less than I do. Stuff gets dropped. He drops off the cash. If he don't Ninja and me kick his head in.' He paused, seemed to think. 'Anyway, how come you know?'

'Because it's my job to know, Shithead.'

For a few moments there was silence then he said: 'He's been out of the game for two weeks. He's just now been released.'

'How come you know that?'

'Because I watched him come out of Neasden Police Station.'

'You saw him?'

'That's what I said.'

The Wasp was quiet. 'Man, you get about don't you. You want another dealer?'

'No. Not yet. I want to watch for a while. Get in touch and find out what went down.'

'Okay.'

'And Wasp.'

'What?'

'There's something else you should know.'

'What's that?'

'There's a new man on the Drug Squad.'

'So.'

'His name's Vanner. Small world isn't it.'

John Phillips sat with his wife in the living room. She chewed at her nails, her face still very red. 'They came right into the college?'

'Yesterday afternoon.'

'Why didn't you tell me?'

He looked beyond her, through the window to the street and the mass of parked cars that seemed to crowd and box him in. He stood up, looked again, then sat down and twisted in the seat. 'I didn't want to worry you.'

'Worry me?' She stared at him. 'You think I'm not worried already?'

'Exactly,' he said quietly. 'I didn't want to worry you any more.'

She paced the room, hugging herself. She moved in front of him, walking to the window and back again.

'Nobody's out there,' he said.

'Not now maybe. But they will be. Tonight. Tomorrow night. The next day.'

'Do you want me to call the police?'

'And tell them what?'

Exactly, he thought. And tell them what? That three men had scattered his papers in a college car park, that they had threatened him. Only Mark Terry had witnessed it and he was not going to bring him into this. And then his impotence hit him, and for an instant he could look back over fifty long years and wonder how he ended up sitting here. A whole lifetime had passed. His lifetime. A career. Two careers. First the Army and now lecturing. A wife, two children, an ageing, infirm mother and an inert fear in his gut that ate at him day by day. He looked again at his wife, sitting now, perched on the arm of the settee. Wearily he stood up. 'I'll make some tea.'

She followed him into the kitchen. He boiled the kettle, settling the bags into the brown, earthenware teapot and reaching for the cups and the sugar. She got milk from the fridge and fetched a spoon from the drawer. 'It's Anna I worry about. I wish you hadn't told me about Anna.'

He looked round then, as the kettle began to hum behind him. 'Don't worry about Anna. I'll watch out for Anna.'

'Oh, yes. And how will you do that? Every minute of the day – how can you?'

Again the feeling of helplessness. He turned his back to her, squaring his shoulders. He felt her touch then, between his shoulder blades and for a second the tension went out of him. He turned, took her in his arms and held her very close to him.

'It's okay,' he said. 'Honestly. It'll all be okay.'

'If only we knew where he was. I hate not knowing where he is.'

He was not listening to her. His mind was wandering, back to younger days when he wore a uniform and could face situations like this. Things had been different then. In those days there was only him and his mates, one looking out for the other; half a dozen blokes to watch your back while you and half a dozen others watched theirs. So much easier then: the rules were there and the adrenalin alone was enough.

'John?'

He looked down at her. 'Sorry. What?'

'Oh, nothing.' She pulled away from him and emptied the contents of the kettle into the teapot. 'I was saying I wished we knew where he was.' She placed the cosy over the pot and rattled the cups in the saucers. 'I just don't understand it, John. Why us? Why him? Why any of it?'

He could hear the sobs rising in her voice and he half reached out to comfort her. But then he realised there was no comfort and slowly he drew back his hand. She splashed pale tea into cups. 'He was always such a good boy. How did it end up like this?'

John Phillips Junior squatted in the disused warehouse and felt the breath of wind off the sea. Through the cracks in the door he could see the lights of the dock and the weight of the container ship that sprawled the length of the quayside. It was cooler now it was dark and he could think a little more clearly. He sat on an upturned wooden crate and his coat lay on the floor beside him. Half-hidden amongst the folds was a length of rubber hose and a fully-charged syringe.

Behind him he had lain the ancient overalls he had stolen from the wash bins that tonight would be his bed. He looked once more at his gear: shoot this lot up and he was down to nothing again. He would have to steal a car and get it back to London. His gaze carried once more to the dockside. Yarmouth in the season, plenty of nice motors around just waiting for tricky fingers like his. He thought about that and it pleased him. One thing he did well. There was nothing he could not get into.

He got up and moved to the door. He could hear water slapping the side of the dock. He glanced up and down the quayside: open here, no fences or security men or dogs. He went back to where he had lain his coat and sat down. Rolling up his sleeve, he checked the inside of his left arm and made a face. Pulling the sleeve down again, he pushed up the other. Not quite as bad but almost. He flicked at the vein with his fingernail. Nothing. No life. No pigging blood in him. Shot to fuck, John, he told himself. You're all shot to fuck.

Still, he took up the rubber hose and twisted it into a tourniquet above his elbow. He bent the arm, so the pressure built and slowly his hand went numb. Again he swatted the skin, trying to lift a vein. He slapped it, flicked it, harder and harder until a vein finally lifted. He tightened the hose with his teeth and picked up the brimming syringe. He could hardly see. He did not want any air in it. Now that would be a waste.

And lying back with the needle lost to the floor and the fuzzing in his head and his arm limp beside him and the warehouse high overhead as slowly the darkness descended.

Mickey Blondhair left Archway Tube with his mate. They swaggered into the sunlight and stood for a moment on the street. Mickey wore a long-sleeved sweat top which gathered almost to his knees. His hair was cropped to the neck, yet long and dangling in front. Beside him his mate stood in his T-shirt, his hands stuffed into baggy jeans. The laces of his boots dragged on the pavement.

Mickey moved along the street, swinging his shoulders and eyeballing the shoppers who passed him.

'Cashpoint?' his mate said.

Mickey nodded. He could feel the edge of the blade against his backside as he walked. Two banks on the street. But he knew there was a third, round the corner on the edge of the industrial estate. It was where all the Paki shopkeepers paid in their daily takings. A panda car drove slowly past with two white-shirted coppers in the front seats. They glanced at him and he glanced back. They turned left at the lights.

They stood beside the benches. Behind them the cashpoint. Mickey rested one foot on the bench and watched as a young mother pushed her twins up to it in a double buggy. She got a few quid, stuffed it hurriedly into her purse and moved on. Mickey's mate looked at him. Mickey looked away.

A few minutes later a car drew up. Big car. German. Mickey looked more closely. A tall, thin man got out, wearing a two-piece suit and a tie tight at the neck. He left the car door open, and walked up to the cashpoint. Mickey looked to his mate and nodded. He felt the adrenalin rise, the slow rushing of blood that gathered pace in his head until it thumped against his temples. The man was keying in his number. He stood back for a moment. Mickey moved off the bench.

At the wall the man waited for his money. His card returned to him and he pocketed it. Then the jaws of the machine opened and ten crisp twenties rolled out to him. And then he was down, his legs gone from under him. He still held the cash, but the next moment it was snatched from his hand. He half-cried out, half-looked round and glimpsed two figures running away from him. A coloured woman came round the corner. They almost knocked her over. He tried to get up, but his legs would not work. Sweat, heavy on his brow. He propped himself on an elbow. Blood spewed from his knees.

'Help me.' Small voice, very unlike his own. 'Please. Somebody help me.'

He stood on the corner, watching as the cab waited for the lights to go green. Vanner on the Drug Squad and Ringo May wanting back in the game. He tapped his polished shoe against the kerb and put out his hand as the cab approached. The cab pulled over and he climbed into the back. 'Covent Garden,' he said to the driver.

The street heaved with people. Piccadilly at night. He walked round the cab and paid the driver. He did not wait for his change. Crossing the road, he paused under the Sanyo sign and looked back at the statue of Eros. Finding a phone box he dialled.

'Wasp, it's me. I told you Ringo May was back on the street.'

'I ain't working tonight, man. I'm going out.'

'Contact Ringo. Tell him he's still in the game.'

'Not tonight, man. I'm out tonight.'

51

'Tonight, Wasp. One phone call. It'll only take you a minute. I'll talk to you tomorrow.' He hung up. The whine in the Wasp's voice. He would make the call. He always did. Ringo May could deal. He would deliver in a couple of days and then maybe they would see.

The power. He sauntered up the road and dwelt for a moment on the power. Hard to keep the smile from his lips. People hugged the street, great weighty bunches of them: English and Chinese and German and French and black and white and yellow. London. Turning up Windmill Street, he came to the intersection with Brewer. Soho at night: fat old men huddling round the windows of video shops and music thumping from peep-shows.

He stood across the road from the gay bar on Old Compton Street and watched the shaven-headed men in the window. They looked back at him. Pretty, no doubt, they thought. The black girl beyond the counter of the strip joint opposite, called out to him. 'Want to see a live show, Sir?'

He turned to her, chocolate-coloured breasts thrusting at the neck of her top. 'Later, maybe.' He crossed the street once again.

Covent Garden. He wanted to see wankers in suits popping Denny E's in a wine bar. The buzz almost gave him a hard on. Blake's Bar on Long Acre. That's where Maguire had his pitch. 3527 – Maguire. A number on a computer screen. A name on a post office box and money in brown padded envelopes.

Blake's was thick with drinkers. He had to carve a path to the bar and when he got there he could hardly turn round. He bought a beer and carried it to an alcove where a group of people rested glasses on a chest-high table. He could smell the perfume, the aftershave as part of the atmosphere. Silk shirts, baggy turned-up trousers. Resting his back against the wall, he sipped beer from the neck of the bottle and watched them. He stayed an hour. No sign of Maguire. Too early in the week for him. One time on a Friday he had been in here and Maguire had offered him his own stuff without knowing it. The kick, like a drug in itself pumping around in his veins. Still he looked about him. What he wanted was some jerk in a £500 suit, popping a Denny Ecstasy tablet. But tonight he was disappointed. He stayed another half-hour, then he shrugged his shoulders and left.

Ryan climbed between the sheets and smelled the warmth of his wife. Naked, back to him, he rested his palm in the cup of her side. She stirred, dragging one leg up the bed, foot against his shin. He brushed her neck with his lips. The mobile rang by the bed. He cursed and picked it up.

'Mr Ryan. It's Milo.'

Ryan sighed. 'What d'you want, Milo?'

'They buzzed me. Bleeped me on my watch.'

'Who?'

'Them.'

'Who's them?'

'I don't know. The ones who contact me.'

'What did they say?'

'They've told me I can deal. They'll deliver in two or three days.'

Ryan sat up straighter. 'Good boy. Give me the number they asked you to call.' Milo told him and he wrote it down. 'When the gear comes in you call me. You understand?'

'Yes.'

'You can't deal, Milo. You deal and we nick you again. That's how it goes.'

'I understand.'

'Good. Bell me and we'll sort it from there.' Ryan switched off the phone. His wife's breathing was even beside him. He looked at her and sighed. 'I suppose a fuck's out of the question?'

Five

Vanner sat with Ryan in his office. 'We can't justify a body behind the counter, Sid. We'll just have to trust that the teller's on the case.'

Ryan looked doubtful. 'This is the same post office that can't tell us how many boxes have two cards. Right?'

'They don't have a separate register.' Vanner made a face. 'Why should they? You told me yourself you'd never come across it before.'

'We could ask them to count them.'

'What, all the boxes in London? There must be thousands.' Vanner stood up. 'Right now we have one box. We'll watch it.'

For three days they watched. Ryan outside with China, sitting in a car down a side road near Wembley Central Post Office. Others took turns inside. Anne and McCleod and Ellis. At the end of the third day Ellis challenged Vanner. 'I know this is half a sheet, Guv. But can we justify the manpower?'

Vanner looked at him. 'The artwork is new, Paul. Like you said – half a sheet. That means he's close. The distribution is flat.' He glanced at Ryan. 'Am I right?'

Ryan lit a Camel and nodded.

Vanner looked back at Ellis.

'Okay.' Ellis held up his hands. 'But how long're we going to keep it up.'

'As long as it takes. There's fifteen hundred quid in that box. Nobody's just going to leave it.'

He stood in the bus shelter and studied the blue Vauxhall Astra parked in the side road. Two men in it. Putting the headphones in his ears, he wandered into the post office and bought a book of stamps. He glanced about the hall. A woman in the far corner, half-reading a V10 form. He made his way up to the counter where the post office boxes were kept and saw a buck-toothed man checking forms.

He went home and put on a suit. At lunchtime he went back and posted a letter. The man behind the counter had been replaced by a girl. In the hall the same woman was there. He smiled to himself and left.

Later, darkness had fallen outside, he sat before the computer and scrolled. Jackson. Damien Jackson. He phoned him from the box at the top of the road. He dialled the number of his watch and then walked to the box at the tube station. He got there as the phone started ringing.

'You call me?' A hushed voice in his ear.

'Sorry it's too late.'

'No problem. What is it?'

'Tomorrow. You're scheduled to make the Wembley pickup.'

'Yeah.'

'Old Bill's watching the box.'

Silence on the end of the phone. 'I'll give it a miss then.'

'No you won't. My money's there.'

'Look, I ain't about to get nicked.'

'You'll be fine. Go at lunchtime. Between twelve and one. The regular guy isn't there then. Just some little pretty with a space between her ears.'

'I don't know.'

'Ride a pushbike. Steal one if you have to. Wear the gear, helmet and mask. No one will see you.'

Again hesitation.

'Trust me. They won't pick you up. There's an Astra parked down a side road. It might be a different car but it'll be there. Check it out before you go in. There'll be two coppers in it. You know what they look like – stick out a mile. When you come out you'll lose them in the traffic.'

'I don't know.'

'You can do it. They won't pull you outside. They'll want to see where you go. Lose the bike. Lose the gear and walk away. Piece of piss.'

Again a strained silence.

'There's money in it for you. Bonus.' His voice chilled then. 'It's that or you're out of the game.'

The following afternoon at five o'clock they were gathered back at Campbell Row. Ellis looked sourly at Vanner and Vanner held his eye. 'At least we know he showed.'

'Right. But we don't know who he is.'

He had collected at lunchtime. The girl was on the counter. Two other people to serve. Boyfriend trouble the night before. She was in tears when Vanner had questioned her about it. He had come in and gone again without them even knowing until the main clerk got back from lunch. Ryan moved off the desk. 'So it's a mistake. It happens. She'll get her arse kicked. At least she remembers him.'

'Hardly a description,' Ellis said. 'Cyclist with smog mask and helmet.'

Ryan glanced at Vanner. 'That fits the one Milo gave us. Whichever way you look at it we're getting somewhere.'

Vanner stepped into the middle of the room. 'At least we know they don't suspect anything. We know when gear is delivered. Next time we'll try and get someone behind the counter.'

Jimmy Crack drank coffee at Euston Station with the Regional plant from the nightclub.

'Who's the snappy dresser with Bobby?'

'Businessman. Name's Michael Terry.'

'We know him?'

'Some. Fraud Squad nicked him five years ago. Property dividend scam.'

'What does he do now?'

'Imports plant at Dartford.'

'So what's the connection with Gallyon?'

'Don't know. I think he's just there for the Tom.'

'Lisa?'

The bouncer nodded. 'Seems to like them expensive.'

Jimmy sat back. 'You know I don't think Gallyon's into crack.'

'He's into coke. Why not the lowlife?'

Jimmy stirred his coffee. 'Too much trouble.'

'We know he's got outlets with spades.'

Jimmy shook his head. 'Doesn't feel right. I've got other things to do. Maybe you could tell your Guv'nor.'

Two weeks after they had lost the plot at the post office Vanner sat in his office, leafing through a sheaf of reports from the B team. Ryan poked his head round the door. 'Got a call from Milo, Guv.'

'About time. They delivering again?'

'Next week.'

'Good. Maybe we'll get it right this time.'

Ryan scratched his head. 'Milo reckons there's a consignment of Denny E's being traded at a minicab office on Kilburn High Road.'

Vanner looked at him. 'How does he know that?'

'Whisper from the contact.'

'Why would he tell Milo?'

'He's talkative, Guv. Milo reckons he's let things slip before.'

'How many E's?'

'Couple of thousand.'

Vanner raised an eyebrow. 'New player?'

'Maybe he does more than just boxes.'

'When's it coming in?'

'Tomorrow night.'

'Do we know this minicab outfit?'

Ryan nodded. 'I had a chat with Jimmy. The place is a crack house. Kilburn want it closed down.'

Vanner looked at him. 'What're E's doing at a crack house? Crack's predominantly black.'

'Yeah.'

'And E's are raves and suits and white kids.' Vanner pushed his foot against the desk. 'Doesn't that strike you as odd?'

Ryan grinned. 'It's all gear, Guv'nor. Markets cross all the time. Jimmy reckons this place is a bit of a centre. Sort of midnight supermarket for lowlife.' He paused. 'We can't let it go.'

Vanner sat forward. 'Let me have a word with Jimmy.'

He sat in his swivel chair and rocked himself from side to side. Oasis played through his headphones. Before him the screen flickered as it went through its pre-boot checks. He bobbed his head to the music. In his hand he held Sammy Johnson's pager watch, thoughtful of the Wasp to get it back when they broke his arms.

The power. Better than the drugs themselves. Silly boy Sammy, swapping the bail hostel for hospital. It would be a lesson for others. The word would spread: Neasden, Archway, Chalk Farm and the rest. Ninja's reputation went before him. Nobody else would cross him.

The screen popped up the menu and he keyed in his password, then waited until the codes played through and the log lifted before his eyes. He scrolled with rubber fingers until he came to Sammy's details and he hesitated as he counted the numbers. Pity he got so greedy. Sammy had been productive. But supply was supply and the demands of the market were great. What he didn't take others would and he could not have people holding out on him. They got him cash. He supplied them with their kicks. That was the deal. Nobody held out on him. He looked at Sammy's name and then pressed the *Delete* button on the keyboard.

In the training room at Kilburn Police Station Ryan was joking with the boys from the TSG. Jimmy Crack stood with Vanner. 'What time's your snout reckon then, Guv?'

'Pickup's supposed to be at ten. He's going to phone.'

'And the spotters are over the pub?'

Vanner nodded.

'We'll wait for the sniffer, then Slippery and me can brief them.'

They went over to the canteen where the two handlers were sitting with their dog leads tied across their shoulders like bandoliers.

'So what're you working on with the Regional?' Vanner asked him.

'Bobby Gallyon.'

Vanner lifted his eyebrows. 'Big-time.'

'Old family, Guv.'

'Tell me about it.'

'Regi's had a U.C. in there for three months. Doorman. Took them forever to get him in.'

'Miracle they did. That family's been tight as a drum for years. What's the deal – Gallyon importing coke?'

'So we think. Colombia. His couriers take a few hits now and then. Couple the other day with solution in rum bottles. But we never get near *him*.'

'So what's your angle?'

'Regi think Gallyon might be trying to spread crack to the white community. Sort of thing the Americans warned us about when the squad was set up.'

'So you're watching him.'

'I go in as a punter now and then, see if I can spot any faces. I think they've got it wrong though. I've told them but you know how it is.'

Vanner nodded. 'You know much about this place tonight?'

'Three guys. They deal crack, relatively small-time. But they do a bit of other stuff. There've been trades there before. Bit of smack. Bit of speed. But mostly it's crack.'

'You want it closed down?'

'Local boys do, Guv. Hell of a lot of Toms hang about outside. It's getting bigger by the day. We won't win. But it's nice to slap them down now and then.'

'This Denny deal fits then?'

'Why not? Everyone's looking for expansion.'

Vanner nodded. 'Cabs. Post office boxes. It's all movement I guess.'

Back in the training room the Drug Squad were gathered. Vanner looked at his watch. Seven forty-five. Ryan was eating a curry from a foil container. Ellis sat in the corner on his own. China looked up from where he was sitting with a polystyrene cup of coffee between his hands. 'Definitely no firearms then, Guv?'

'Not so's we know.'

'No Gunships tonight then.'

Davies blew cigarette smoke. 'Just as bloody well. Last spin we did like this we had SO19 halfway round the block when the call came to stand down.'

Vanner lit a cigarette and sat down next to Ryan. Ryan spooned the last of his curry into his mouth and glanced up at the TV screen, which played on the wall above their heads. 'So what's Grant up to then?'

'What?' Vanner looked at him.

'Grant Mitchell. *Eastenders*.' Ryan nodded to the TV. 'Oh, never mind.' He took a cigarette from Vanner's pack and lit it from the one he was smoking.

'What's the word from Milo?' Vanner asked him.

'Reckons about ten-thirty, Guv.'

He stood up and went over to where Jimmy Crack was talking into his mobile. They stood together for a moment and then began the briefing. They did it between them. Nothing was on paper. Jimmy drew a rough map of the target area on the SASCO board. He indicated the forward position to be taken up by the unmarked van. It was agreed that two members of the Territorial Support Group would be in the first van. The rest would come behind in the other. The two in front would handle the battering ram. There was a main door which opened into a foyer where the glass counter was housed. Beyond that a second door which was locked.

Vanner sat at the far end of the table. 'Back entrance, Jim?'

Jimmy nodded. 'High fence to get over first. But there is one.'

'We'll need a couple round the back then.' Vanner glanced about the table. 'Ellis, you and Davies take the back.'

One of the dog handlers shifted his position by Vanner. 'You'll have to watch the dogs then,' he said. 'We'll be out the back. If they come out that way don't chase them. Dog'll go for the runner.'

Vanner stood up. 'You got the warrant, Sid?' Ryan nodded and tapped his pocket. 'I need an exhibits officer,' Vanner went on. 'China. The 101?'

China nodded and Vanner looked at his watch. 'We've got a while to wait. No doubt the TSG will get a cardschool going. I'm going to do a drive-by if anyone wants a looksee.'

He drove with Ryan. Three cars were parked outside the minicab office. Two Fords and a Nissan. 'How many in there?' Vanner asked.

'Three main drivers. Target 1 is called Nathan. Jimmy says he's the pickup boy. Sometime about ten-thirty he'll go and pick up the gear. His is the Nissan.'

'The others?'

'Old fella and another young one. Little guy with dreads.'

'Any other drivers?'

'Maybe.' Ryan nodded to the pavement outside the office, which was thick now with girls. 'Toms are out, Guv. At least we know there's crack. Blow job to pay for the gear.'

'Milo?'

'In the pub. The OP's above. He talks to them on the payphone.'

Vanner nodded and drove on.

He locked the room and went outside into the night, being careful to lock and padlock the outside door to the warehouse. Briefly, he looked up at the windows and then walked up to the main road. Buildings sprawled and scratched at the sky all about him. From the estate he could hear someone yelling.

At the top of the road he turned left and walked down towards the tube station. When he hit the High Road he stuck out his hand for a cab.

'Where to, mate?' The cabbie twisted in his seat.
'Kilburn.'
'Whereabouts?'
'I'll tell you when we get there.'

The cab slowed at the junction of Cricklewood Lane and Chiselle
Road. He asked the driver to head down Kilburn High Road and
drop him off by the park. He tipped him and then set off walking,
back up the road once again. He sang softly to himself, hands in
the pockets of his suit. He loved the metallic sound his quarter
tips made on the pavement. He crossed the intersection and kept
on walking, up towards the minicab office with the pub and the
church across the road. A huge Day-Glo sign lifted above the
street from the church. JESUS SAVES, it read. Ringo May came
out of the pub.

Vanner sat in the front of the van, Jimmy Crack driving, Ryan
squashed between them, a baseball bat on his knees.
'That regulation issue is it?' Vanner said.
'Lives in the boot of my car, Guv'nor.'
In the back the rest of the team were bunched together with the
two uniformed TSG men. One of them held the battering ram.
The van idled. Ryan glanced through the windscreen to the height
of the tenements all round them. McCleod called from the back:
'How much longer we going to sit here, Guv'nor? Some old sod's
going to ring up the target and tell him there's a van full of Old
Bill plotted up round the corner.'
'We're waiting for the call, Sam.'
Jimmy leaned back in his seat. 'Sammy's right, Guv. We can't
sit here forever.'
Ryan looked at his watch. The mobile rang in his lap. He
picked it up, listened, then nodded once to Jimmy.

He watched from the darkened doorway of a shop. A white
unmarked van hurtled round the corner so fast it was all but on
two wheels. It jerked to a halt outside the minicab office. Side

door open and men crashed to the street. Two of them ran for the back. A second van pulled up, marked this time. A whole stream of uniforms tumbled out. Dogs barked, voices shouting, the sudden splinter of wood. He stood a moment longer then he slipped quietly from the door and walked back down the street.

Vanner kicked his way through the hole in the panelled door. It had opened outwards instead of inwards. They had had to go through the middle. Precious seconds lost. He saw a woman and a tall, thin black man.

'Stand still,' he said.

Ellis' head appeared through the window at the back of the corridor. Stairs leading down before it. Vanner moved towards them, Ryan alongside, baseball bat in his hand. They ran down the stairs and kicked open a second door. Four men played dominoes.

Vanner stepped into the room. Naked women paraded on the TV screen above his head. Ryan followed him and McCleod. Two ragged couches and an armchair. A bar area at the back of the room and beyond it the open door of a toilet. They could hear the sound of it flushing. Vanner's eyes were drawn to a handwritten scrap of paper, pasted over the bar. '*Drug Free Zone*' it read.

Ninja and The Wasp moved along the landings of the Kirstall Estate in Kentish Town, listening to the silence and the racket that lifted in turn from the flats. Two o'clock in the morning. Ninja carried his half-length sword, pushed up the sleeve of his jacket. They climbed stair after stair until they came to the top floor of the building. Then through a final door and metal steps to the boiler room. Light crept round the lip of the door where it did not fasten correctly. From within, they could hear the murmur of conversation. Ninja slid the sword the length of his arm and slipped it from the scabbard. The Wasp grinned at him in the darkness. He stood on one side of the door and quietly took hold of the edge. Ninja pushed the weight of his hair from his face and blinked with his one good eye. The Wasp ripped the door open.

Ninja sprang in, sword waving, a snarl creasing his lips. Bedlam. Boys and girls crying out, rushing for the walls and the door. He could smell the pungent aroma of dope. Very casually The Wasp stepped in behind him. Denny squares cut into singles lay on the floor at his feet. He caught sight of the faces and belly laughed. Mickey Blondhair got up from where he crouched behind some piping, hair hanging over his face, gold stud in his nose. 'You fuckin' wanker, Wasp.'

Ninja put his sword away and lifted a joint from the kid nearest him. The Wasp closed the door and sat down on a box. Mickey Blondhair squatted across from him. A pager watch hung from his wrist. 'What d'you want – anyway?'

The Boiler Room Gang. The Wasp scanned the faces. Mickey Blondhair was the eldest at thirteen. 'The money of course. How much've you got?'

Mickey got up and stuffed his hands in his pockets. 'Fuckin' shitloads, Wasp.'

The bleeper sounded on Wasp's wrist. He cursed and looked down at the face. 'Anybody got a phone?'

Mickey Blondhair produced a Nokia. 'You'll have to pay for the call.'

He sat before the computer screen and yawned. Weary now, long day and much longer night. No headphones. No music, just the silence and the electronic figures before his eyes. He tapped the desk and waited. The mobile lay next to him with the digits illuminated. Dangerous to receive a call on a mobile. But tonight . . . He waited. The phone finally rang. 'Yes?'

'It's me.'

'What're you doing?'

'Collecting funds.'

He narrowed his eyes. 'Where?'

'Boiler room.'

'How much?'

'Dunno yet.' The Wasp spoke away from the phone. 'Hey, Blondie. How much?'

'Three-fifty. Split this cunt's knees at the cashpoint. Got two hundred myself.'

He heard. 'Good,' he said. 'Very very good.'

'What d'you want, man?'

'Ringo May.'

'What about him?'

'I want you to kill him.'

Six

Ryan stood with Vanner and Jimmy Crack beside the TSG van. He rolled a loose cigarette and passed it to Vanner. 'One lousy rock of crack,' he muttered. 'In the bin of all places.'

'No bodies,' Vanner said. 'It happens.' He cupped his hands to the match. China came out of the minicab office with the 101 form flapping in the breeze. 'You all done?' Vanner asked him.

'All but, Guv.'

Jimmy held up the rock, yellowed and shaped like a tooth and heat-sealed in clingfilm. He looked at Vanner. 'I'll give it to the DI at Kilburn, Guv. Stick it in the 66. Gives us a reason to crash the door at least.'

Vanner looked back at Ryan. 'Where's Milo?'

'Gone.'

Jimmy made a face. 'You think he's lifting our leg?'

'He showed didn't he.'

Jimmy looked back at the cab office where Nathan, the dealer, was watching him. 'Love to nick that bastard. So bloody cool.'

Vanner touched his shoulder. 'Next time,' he said.

John Phillips Junior walked along Great Yarmouth front with the wind buffeting him from the sea. The 'Pleasure Beach' thumped with disco music behind him. Children crying. Girls screaming on the waltzers. Skeletal rides, stark against the skyline. It was hot but he walked with his coat hugged about him and the blood very thin in his veins.

Two cars were parked side by side in a road that led towards the town centre. He paused and looked them over. M reg. Volvo and a Mercedes 190. That was worth having a go at. He might get a few grand for it in the arches. Two women walked towards him though, pushing young children in buggies. Across the road in the park, an old man threw bread for grey pigeons. Dismissing the Merc, he walked on.

He was hungry. He could not remember eating. His face felt drawn and pinched and he was aware of the puffiness in his eyes. His hair straggled about his face. He could smell himself and he longed for the feel of a bed. All he needed was the right car and a few minutes alone with it. Then it could be London, a wedge and a bath in his mother's house.

He moved towards the city centre and spotted the bleak mass of the multi-storey car park. Across the road, the shopping arcade hummed with people. He was not keen on car parks. They were okay if you got away quickly. But if an alarm went off or the lock out was a pain in the arse, they could be tricky. It just depended on how good the attendants were. Some of them – most of them in fact – could not give a toss: but there were always the odd one or two.

He stood at the end of the road, the sun on his back but cold inside himself. The wind licked his hair, sticky, like the fingers of a child. As if in some unspoken warning, a police car crossed at the lights in front of him. He stood on the pavement with his arms folded and watched as they swung left on the one-way system. He paused a moment longer, looked back toward the sea. Then he looked ahead again and crossed the road to the car park.

Vanner met McCague in Hendon. They bumped into each other as Vanner climbed the stairs towards Morrison's office.

'How are you?' McCague asked him.

'Not bad. Spin last night in Kilburn. Didn't get in till three.'

'Result?'

'No.'

'It happens. Much tackle with you?'

'TSG. Dogs. No Gunships.'

'I heard about the last one. Stand Down at the eleventh hour.'

'That's snouts for you.'

McCague looked at him then. 'How's the back?'

'Looks like a wild woman's knitting.'

'Nothing from Fennell Street?'

Vanner shook his head.

'Still think it was more than a mugging?'

Vanner shrugged his shoulders.

McCague took him to one side of the stairs as two WPC's moved past them. Vanner watched them. 'Best looking plonks always were at Division.'

'Why d'you think I work here? Listen, Vanner. Morrison's been bending my ear. You're supposed to keep in touch with him.'

'I'm on my way to see him now.' Vanner folded his arms. 'He's always busy. He's got surveillance plotting the entire manor on Eagle Eye.'

'It's political.'

'It's a waste of fucking time.'

McCague tapped him on the shoulder with his index finger. 'He's your Guv'nor, Vanner. Report to him.'

In the corridor outside Morrison's office he met Frank Weir. Thin face, sparse hair, grazing his head like a burn on a hill. He chewed gum habitually. AMIP. Scouser. Vanner had always hated him. One of Morrison's cronies and a hard man with it. They looked at one another, Weir tugging the cuffs of his suit. 'Vanner,' he said. 'You look worse than one of your dealers.'

'And you look like a tart's handbag.' Vanner went into Morrison's office without knocking.

Ryan was waiting for him back at Campbell Row. He was drinking coffee in the kitchen and chatting to a sergeant from the Firearms Enquiry Team. Vanner walked past them and into his office without speaking, Morrison's dressing down ringing in his ears. *Three P's, Vanner. Remember the three P's? Property. Prisoners. Prostitutes. Right now you're way down on property. Keep me informed. That's the way we do things.*

69

Ryan came into the office behind him. Vanner was sitting at the desk, a mound of papers in front of him.

'Old man giving you stick, Guv?'

Vanner glanced up at him. 'I need you to mind my back, Sid. Ellis is Morrison's snout.'

Ryan grinned. 'Old numb nuts. Acting DI, Guv'nor. Not a happy soldier when you blew in.'

'Sid, I need a minder.'

Ryan sat down on the edge of the desk. 'I've spoken to Milo.'

'And?'

'Doesn't know what went wrong. E's could have been there, though I doubt it. Reckons the info was Kosher.'

Vanner sighed. 'Well, bugger all we can do about it now. What else have we got?'

'Nothing. There's been no drops at the post office.'

Vanner looked up at him then. 'Maybe we should keep an eye on Milo.'

'I've told him to bell me daily.'

'Good.'

'Another thing, Guv. I meant to tell you before.'

'What's that?'

'The night Milo called me at home. When they bleeped him with the drop. The phone number he had to ring was a call box in Kentish Town.'

'So?'

'So nothing maybe. But he said they'd used it before.'

Ninja sat in the passenger seat and took a lighted cigarette from The Wasp. 'You never told me he lived here.' He rubbed fingers over his belly and stared through the windscreen into the darkness of the Bream Park Estate. A warren of broken-down flats. Burn marks on the exterior walls of the car park, where innumerable cars had been set light to. The Wasp looked at him. 'It's no worse than ours.' He nodded to Ninja's midriff. 'What's up with you anyway?'

'Guts are bad.'

'Again? You should see a doc. I told you that. You'll drop dead on me one day.'

Ninja twisted his head all the way round so he could see him. 'I ain't going to no doctor.'

The phone rang on the dashboard. The Wasp pressed SND and put it to his ear.

'We're here.'

'Did you get the gloves?'

The Wasp glanced at the surgical gloves on the back seat. 'Yeah.'

'Good. No mistakes. Just do it and get out. We'll talk again tomorrow.'

The Wasp put down the phone.

Ninja looked out of the window again. 'I'd never've come if I knew he lived here.'

'We'll be all right.'

'You will. You're black.'

The Wasp grinned then. 'Come on, man. You're Ninja. The fuckin' Gypsy. Everyone knows who you are.' He reached over and stroked Ninja's long, matted dreadlocks.

'You're almost a brother ain't you.'

'Fuck brothers.' Ninja opened the door. 'If we're going to do it – let's do it.'

The Wasp led the way up the first flight of stairs from the pavement. Ninja walked behind him, sword hidden in his jacket. On the first landing they surprised two young kids, smoking dope. They ran off as soon as they saw them. The flats were off the corridor, which was carpeted after a fashion and windowed off from outside. It gave the impression of being in a void.

'Which one is his?' Ninja asked, as he surveyed the array of doors.

'It ain't on this floor.'

'Where is it then?'

The Wasp pointed into the heart of the building.

'I just knew it fuckin' would be.'

Ninja walked with his sword out, scabbard in one hand, open

71

blade in the other. The Wasp grinned at him. 'Man, nobody's going to have a go at you.'

'How the hell do you know?'

'Just look at you. One eye. No fuckin' ears.'

'I got ears.'

'Well one and a half. Jesus, man. Put the fucker away. We're not supposed to draw attention to ourselves.'

Reluctantly, Ninja sheathed the sword again and slipped it back in his jacket. He scowled at the emptiness of the corridors. He could smell piss and paint and cigarette smoke.

They walked up two more flights of stairs and then the length of another corridor. Ninja said: 'How come you know the way?'

'Been here before.' The Wasp looked back at him. 'Black, ain't I.'

'What we gonna do?'

'Knock on his door.'

'How'd we know he's in?'

'We don't.'

Ninja shook his head. 'Ain't gonna answer no door. Is he? Three o'clock in the morning.'

They climbed a final flight of steps and came out on another hallway. 'The end one,' Wasp said. '252.'

Ninja looked out of the window. At the far end of the concourse a small fire was burning in a dustbin. He could make out shadows gathered about it. He glanced at the graffiti covering the walls. 'Makes ours look pretty.'

'Hey,' Wasp said.

'What?'

'You ever killed anyone before?'

Ninja thought for a moment. 'Don't think so. You?'

The Wasp shook his head and Ninja half-smiled. 'Don't worry, Wasp. I'll do it.'

They finally got to the flat and The Wasp looked back the way they had come. The corridor was empty. They stood in front of the door and Ninja slid his sword down his sleeve until the hilt was gathered in his hand. The Wasp knocked on the door.

'What if he ain't on his own? What if he's got pussy with him?'
The Wasp shrugged. 'Then we'll kill her an' all.'

He knocked again, louder this time and they waited. Ninja moved lightly from one foot to the other. He glanced behind him again and caught his reflection in the dark of the glass.

Then they heard a voice on the other side of the door. 'Who is it?'

'Me. Donny.' The Wasp winked at Ninja.

'Donny. Right.' The door was unlocked and Ringo stood there in his underpants. Ninja stepped into the hall.

Ringo lay face-down with one arm tucked underneath him, lost now in the blood that drained from his stomach. Ninja sat in an armchair with the blood moving towards his feet. He looked down at Ringo's face, eyes open, staring at a patch on the wall. The Wasp leaned in the kitchen doorway, drinking a bottle of beer he had found in the fridge.

Ninja pointed with the bloodied blade of his sword. 'Very dead ain't he.'

The Wasp nodded as he drank. 'You want any of this?'

'Naw. Gimme a smoke though.'

The Wasp tossed him a packet. The blood moved closer to Ninja's shoes and he lifted his feet over the arm of the chair. 'Lotta blood.'

'Yeah.' The Wasp bent and dipped the finger of his gloved hand in it. 'Thick ain't it.'

'Buckets of the stuff. I never would've figured it.'

'You cut the bastard open, Ninja. What did you expect?' The Wasp looked about the sparseness of the flat. 'Nothing worth nicking. We ought to go.'

Ninja stood up and farted. 'Christ,' he said. 'I got to take a shit.'

'Now?'

'Yes, now. Fuckin' guts are killing me.'

Vanner stood with Ryan at Campbell Row. 'Heard it from a mate over in Tufnell Park,' Ryan said. 'PC on the Crime Group.

Thought you might want to know, Guv. Geezer in Archway had his knees slashed at a cashpoint.'

'Slashed?'

'Yeah. Bloody great knife or something. He was stood there collecting his readies. Next thing he knows he's on the deck with blood pissing out of his legs. Two of them. Took two hundred quid off him.'

Vanner looked beyond him. Christian Tate in his mind. 'Random mugging was it?'

'That's how they're treating it. Kind of thing that'll send Morrison ape-shit. The geezer's in hospital. Tendons are shot to pieces. He's up to his neck in plaster.'

Vanner stood at the door of the ward and glanced at the beds. Not so long since he had occupied one just like it. The man he wanted was nearest the window. He was sitting on the bed with his back in pillows and his legs stretched out in front of him. They were bandaged from the thigh to the ankle. Vanner walked over to him with his hands in his pockets. The man lay back with his eyes closed. Vanner glanced at his notes.

'Mr Boyd?'

The man opened his eyes.

'Detective Inspector Vanner.' He sat down on the seat by the bed.

Boyd looked like a ghost. He was about forty, thinning brown hair and blue eyes. Vanner looked down at his legs. 'How're you feeling?'

Boyd managed a smile. His bloodless lips tracing the faintest of lines in his bloodless face. 'How do I look?'

'Nothing like a stupid question eh?'

Boyd looked at Vanner's legs crossed now over his knee. 'I've already told everything I know to the other officers.'

Vanner nodded. 'Did you get a good look at them?'

'Not really. They came from behind me. I saw them running away.'

'Did you see the knife?'

Boyd swallowed and the lump rose and fell in his throat. He looked down at his legs. 'I didn't see anything. It all happened so fast.' His eyes glassed then. 'D'you know how long it's going to be before I walk again?'

Vanner did not say anything.

'Months. I might not be able to properly. They've cut all the tendons around the knee cap. I'll need months of physiotherapy.'

Vanner sat forward. 'All the more reason to find out who did it.'

Boyd's face softened and he closed his eyes once more. 'I've told your colleagues all I know,' he said. 'There was a witness apparently.'

'Witness?'

He opened his eyes again. 'A woman saw them running off.'

Vanner thanked him and left.

In the car there was a message on the mobile from Ryan. Vanner phoned him.

'What's up?'

'I haven't heard from Milo.'

'Since when?'

'Day before yesterday.'

'That's a problem?'

Ryan was quiet for a moment. 'Usually calls in the morning.'

'Phone him then.'

'I did. No answer.'

Vanner shrugged. 'Too early to start the checks. Go round if you want to.'

'Me on Bream Park? Got to be Old Bill haven't I.'

'Leave it a while,' Vanner said. 'He'll phone you.'

He sat with Mrs Emery in the café where she worked. He had got her name from Ryan's contact in Tufnell Park. He passed the sugar for her coffee.

'Kids,' she said. 'They were just kids.'

'You sure?'

'Of course I'm sure.'

'How old?'

75

She moved her shoulders. 'I don't know. So hard to tell these days. Earrings. Nose rings. What will they pierce next?'

'One of them had an earring?'

'I've told all this to your friends.'

'I want you to tell it to me. Did one of them have an earring?'

'No. He had his nose pierced through.'

'Was he white or black?'

'White. Blond-haired. The other was white too. But I didn't get a good look at him.'

'He ran by you – the one with the blond hair?'

'Nearly knocked me over.'

Vanner sat back. 'So you'd recognise him again?'

She looked at him then. 'Oh, I'd know him all right.'

He sat at his desk. It was done. A lesson learned just like Sammy. No room for loose cannons, no freelancers trying to go their own way. If they were loyal then he was loyal. They should know that. It was why The Wasp stayed in line. He watched the computer screen and eased the volume a little higher on the Walkman. He scrolled through the list of names and stopped at the letter M. M for May. Ringo May of Wembley. 2517-May. Deleted.

Seven

Ryan sat in West End Central Police Station and looked at the three Ecstasy tablets. They were laid before him on the desk, wrapped in a plastic bag. Carter, one of his counterparts from Central, emptied them out and moved the end of a pen amongst them.

'Not seen these before,' he said.

'No?'

Carter shook his head. 'We see doves all the time, or just plain ones. This is a new one on me.' He looked up. 'Good stuff?'

'The best. We've had Lambeth check them out.'

'Heard you'd picked up a few.'

'Acid mostly,' Ryan said. 'This is newer. The label's only been around for a few months.'

'Fresh artwork then.'

'Yeah.'

'You close to anybody?'

'Not so far. Picked up a dealer in Wembley. First lead we got. Half a sheet of acid. We got him to lay down and shoved him back on the street.'

'Anything come of it yet?'

Ryan frowned. 'Had word there was a stash in a crack house in Kilburn. Gave it a spin the other night but got nothing.'

'Wind up?'

'Possibly. Could have been the wrong night, wrong gaff, whatever. You know how reliable the average snout is. This one needs his hand holding big-time.'

Carter looked again at the tablet. 'Denny?' he said.

Ryan nodded. 'Whatever that means?' He took out his tobacco. 'Where d'you find them?'

'Blake's wine bar in Covent Garden. Fella trying to sweeten his girlfriend.'

Ryan grinned. 'She'd fuck all night on these.' He lit his cigarette. 'Who's dealing?'

'Not sure. There is a face. Irish fella from Barnet. Maguire. We've seen him about. Tends to stick to the upmarket joints. When I ran a check on this the AIU came up with your flag.' Carter sat back. 'I've got an address for Maguire if you want it.'

John Phillips sat in the front room, watching television. Upstairs he could hear his wife running a bath. He was half-watching *Newsnight*, but his mind was wandering elsewhere, waiting for the cricket highlights afterwards.

The window smashed by his head. Curtains suddenly billowing. Phillips was on the floor, hands over his head, waiting for the rumble of explosion and the rushing of air from the room. It never came. Seconds ticked by and he remembered he was in London and there was peace so far in Belfast. Getting to his feet, he saw half a brick lying amid chips of glass on the carpet. He pulled back the curtains. The window was all but gone. He peered into the street. Nothing. Only parked cars and streetlamps and other, quiet, houses. The door opened behind him and his wife stood there in her dressing gown. She stared at him and he saw the grey in her face. Bending, he picked up the half-brick. 'Phone the police,' she said.

When the two constables had gone, Phillips went to the shed at the bottom of the garden and took a folded removal carton from where it was stacked against the wall. With hammer and nails he boarded up the window, while his wife and daughter sat huddled on the sofa.

'I want to move,' his wife said.

Phillips sighed and laid down the hammer. 'I'll make some tea.'

'I don't want tea. I want to move.'

She followed him into the kitchen. 'Don't you understand what this is doing to me?'

He turned to her, face all red and crumpled where she had been crying so much. He reached for her but she pushed his hands away and her face buckled again.

'I can't take any more of this, John.' She shook her head. 'Why can't they leave us alone?'

'John owes them money, love. They mean to get it from us.'

'Then give it to them for Christ's sake.'

'We don't have it,' he said quietly. Anna watched from the doorway. 'Besides, they would only come back for more. John will always owe money.'

'That's it. That's it. Just give up. God, that's typical of you. Wash your hands of him.'

'I'm not washing my hands of him.' He tried to keep the edge from his voice. 'But he's a heroin addict, Mary. He will always owe money.'

'He needs help.' Tears fell from her eyes.

'Yes. And if we knew where he was we'd give it to him.'

Later, just before he finally locked all the doors, he went back out to his shed. On the wall, his long-handled axe hung between two hooks. He lifted it down and ran the end of his thumb over the blade. It was sharp. He always kept it sharp, though they never burned any wood.

His wife was already in bed. Anna was in bed, though he could see the glow of her lamp beneath the foot of the door. He went into his bedroom in darkness. Mary was lying on her side, facing away from him. He undressed slowly and, as he got into bed, he slipped the axe underneath.

Michael Terry watched Lisa in the shower. She always showered with the curtain pulled back, water splashing over the floor. She liked him watching. He could tell by the way she soaped herself that she liked him watching. He scratched his lip. The smell of her on his fingers. A woman flying on E's. He exhaled very slowly.

Rolling onto his stomach he looked at the small round tablet with the grinning half-devil looking up at him. Then he placed it back on the table and stood up. Stripping off his bathrobe, he climbed into the shower.

He rolled off her and lay sweating in the half-light. He stared at the ceiling, feeling the buzzing of champagne in his head. She lay still beside him, her side rising and falling. Vaguely he reached for her breast, cupped the nipple and squeezed it between his fingers.

He got up and left her. On the table beside the bed, four Denny Ecstasy tablets lay on top of the plastic bag. He looked down at them and grinned. Let her have them, plenty more where they came from.

Vanner stalked into his office and closed the door. A pile of papers rose up to greet him and he had half a mind to sweep them into the bin. There was a knock on the door behind him.

'What?'

Ellis stuck his head round. 'Phone call for you, Guv'nor. Ten minutes ago. Inspectorate want to make a visit. They want a presentation on what we do.'

Vanner looked up at him. 'We chase fucking drug dealers. What do they think we do?'

Ellis held up his hands. 'Just passing the message.'

Vanner went through to the kitchen. Jimmy Crack stood there in sweatshirt and jeans, black hair sticking up from his skull. He spooned coffee into mugs. 'You want one, Guv?'

Vanner nodded. 'Where's Slippery?'

'Don't know.'

Vanner looked at his watch. 'He's late. Why is he always late?'

'He's late because unlike some, he was still in West End Central at one o'clock this morning instead of home shagging his wife.'

Vanner looked round at Ryan, who stared out of slanted and bleary eyes at him. 'Good morning, Guv'nor.' He looked at Jimmy Crack. 'Mine has two sugars all right?'

Vanner followed him into the office. Ryan dropped a plastic bag on the table and lit a cigarette. He rubbed his eyes with the heel of his palm.

'West End Central?' Vanner said.

Ryan nodded. He gestured to the bag on the desk. 'Skipper down there picked them up. Spotted my flag. AIU gave me a bell.'

Vanner looked at the face on the tablets. He knew he had seen it before. Somewhere in the past. 'Where'd he get them?'

'Covent Garden. Blake's wine bar. Geezer looking for a high-tension knee trembler from his bird.'

Vanner lifted one eyebrow.

'You ever shagged a bird on this stuff?' Ryan shook his head. 'Thinking of taking one home for the wife.'

Vanner grinned at him. 'So what've we got?'

'Irish dealer. Maguire.'

'We know him?'

'Central do. He hangs out in the West End. Hails from Barnet though. Our turf.'

'Do we have an address?'

'We do.'

'I wonder if he's got a post office box.'

Night smudged the window, heavy cloud tonight. Before switching on the lamp he had been sitting in the darkness. He always thought best in darkness. He could sit for hours, with just the hum of the music in his skull and the strategies gradually building. He had built an empire on thought. Watches and boxes and padded envelopes and acid from America and Ecstasy from Amsterdam. Mr Plod. Mr VAT man. What the hell did they know? They were so short-staffed it was a joke. The rules of the game were not even fair.

But now Vanner on the Drug Squad. Somehow that changed things, if only a fraction. A little irony which disturbed him. But so far what had they got? Ringo May's box. Ringo May was dead. There was nothing yet to worry about.

He hunched over the keyboard, wound the volume up in his ear and tapped in his password. The screens rolled and three options lifted before him. He pressed the letter O for Operatives and waited. A list of names and addresses filled the screen. So many now. Such a small investment. £120 for a watch, sixty post office boxes at £50 a time, and an empire built on losers. He rolled through the names and stopped at the letter P.

The Wasp flicked ash in the darkness. Next to him the silent warmth of a woman. He rolled onto his side away from her, drew on the cigarette and flicked more ash. She stirred beside him, body still hot with his sweat. He looked at her. Did she know she slept with a killer? Of course she didn't. She, like all of them, knew nothing. He sucked hard on the cigarette. He was not the real killer though. He just stood and watched, as Ninja, crooked smile on his crooked, mashed-up face, buried that blade into Ringo. Man, but how blood gushes when you prick someone. Short sweeping blow with all the force of the gypsy's arm. And Ringo May, his insides falling out of him, on his knees on the carpet.

He got up from the mattress. All this work and still only a mattress. He found his phone, crushed out the cigarette and dialled. Funny how he needed to talk tonight. Three days but now he needed to talk.

Ninja lay in the darkness, all the windows were open and the night blowing into the room. He lay on his back, naked; no blanket covering him. Next to him the girl slept, shrouded in the duvet. The phone rang beside him. He pressed the button and listened.

'Hey, babe.' The Wasp. Who else would call him at this time. 'Whatcha doing?'

'Just lying here.'

'Fuckin' cold tonight.'

'Is it?'

'Yeah. You sleeping?'

'No. Just lying.'

'You got pussy with you?'

'Julie.'

'Good?'

'She'll do.'

'Whatcha thinking about?'

'Nothing.'

The Wasp said: 'So much blood in that dude.'

'Lotta blood.'

'Fuckin' everywhere.'

'Yeah.'

'Think there'll be anyone else?'

'To kill?'

'Yeah.'

'Maybe. You keep thinking about it uh?'

'Don't you?'

'Naw.'

'Can't get it out of my head.'

'You got a woman with you?'

'Course.'

'Black or white?'

'White, man. You know I like it white.'

'Pretty?'

'Great tits.'

'She asleep?'

'Put to sleep, my man. Put to sleep. Three times tonight. Can't seem to get enough.'

'You or her?'

'Me. Just can't seem to get enough.'

'Go to sleep, Wasp. Give your dick a rest.' Ninja switched off the phone.

Vanner sat with Ryan, watching the address for Maguire. So far they had seen nothing. The surveillance team were occupied with AMIP, so they had set up the plot themselves.

Ryan chewed on a roll. 'Easiest ones to nick are the ones who do their own stuff,' he said. 'They get careless. Habit gets to them and they fuck up.' He looked sideways at Vanner. 'I told you this before?'

Vanner shook his head. 'I think he's too clever for that.'

'You think so? Maybe he thinks he is. I reckon he thinks he is. Got himself a smart little setup going. That might be his downfall.'

'How many dealers d'you reckon?'

'God knows.'

'All of them with boxes. All of them with watches.'

'If it ain't broke don't fix it.'

'Maguire's box is in his own name.'

'So is Ringo's.' Ryan finished his roll. 'Buck stops with them, Guv. That's the game.' He looked forward again. 'Here we go.'

Across the road a slim, brown-haired man stepped out of the front door of the flats and walked towards a black GTI Golf. Vanner screwed up his eyes. There was something familiar about him. Ryan started the engine. Vanner lifted the radio. 'Control from 2–1. Target on the move.'

'Received, 2–1.' The voice crackled back at him.

'IC1,' Vanner said. 'Blue shirt, chinos, brown shoes. Driving a black VW Golf.' He read out the number as Ryan pulled out from the kerb.

They followed him to Blake's Bar. Friday night, early, the streets thick with August drinkers. They stood at the bar drinking beer from the bottle. Ryan leaned with his back against the wood. 'Loads of Totty, Guv'nor. I might get a move to Central.'

They watched two women in short skirts, seated at a table by the window, a cold bottle of chablis between them. They were laughing, heads close, sharing Friday night jokes. Maguire sat on a stool a few feet from them and chatted to the barmaid. Vanner watched him: good-looking, about thirty, blue Irish eyes, a heavy gold band on his right wrist. On his left, a watch with a pager.

He smoked soft-pack Marlboros and sipped Becks from the bottle. Every now and then he would glance about the room, catch an eye, then look back to his beer. Nobody approached him. Vanner looked for likelies.

After about half an hour, Maguire slid off his stool and cut a path for the toilets. Ryan watched now. Vanner watched. Two men left their girlfriends and backslapped their way after him. Vanner pushed himself away from the bar. 'Taking a leak,' he said.

Maguire stood at the urinal. The other two alongside him. Nobody spoke. Vanner moved beyond them into the cubicle. He heard one move off the stand and then the sound of water running. He flushed the chain and walked out. Maguire was gone. The other two were laughing.

Ryan said. 'Anything?'

Vanner took the fresh bottle of beer from him. 'I think so.'

'You didn't see?'

'Couldn't. Only three pans. I had to go in the box.'

Ryan looked at the two men now back at their table. 'They look happy enough.'

'Watch them,' Vanner said.

Ryan watched but saw nothing. Maguire lifted his cigarettes from the bar and went back to the street.

In the corner he watched Vanner. He had not been this close before and the thrill of it fluttered in his chest. He sat on his own, drinking beer, hair slicked back from his face. He had spotted Maguire, seen him go to the toilets, seen those two jerks follow and then Vanner after that. Vanner was cannier than he looked. Where had they got Maguire? Vanner and Ryan left. They finished their drinks, said goodnight to the barmaid and walked after Maguire. In the corner he shook his head and smiled.

Maguire made his rounds. As he moved from bar to bar he was picked up and watched. Vanner and Ryan waited in the car. At midnight he got back in his Golf. They followed him north and west, up to Euston Road and round Regent's Park. He stopped outside Bobby Gallyon's nightclub. They watched him go inside. Vanner drummed his fingers on the steering wheel.

'Regional plot, Guv.'

Vanner nodded. 'I'm going in anyway.'

Ryan looked at him. 'On your jack?'

'Why not?'

'Who clubs it on their own on a Friday?'

Vanner thought for a moment. 'Who've we got on the plot?'

'Jackie.'

'Jackie?'

'Jackie, Guv. You know – B team, Jackie.'

Vanner picked up the phone. 'Jackie? This is your Guv'nor. What're you wearing tonight?'

It was much cooler now, the stars climbing over the city. Vanner left Ryan with the car and met Jackie outside Gallyon's. She wore leggings and a baggy T-shirt. The doormen eyed them. Vanner returned the look and they went inside.

Terry climbed the stairs to the upstairs bar, a stack of cash in his pocket. He looked for Lisa but could not see her. Getting a taste for that girl. Maybe it was what she did with a champagne bottle after they had finished drinking it that appealed to him. The barman mixed him a Bloody Mary. Gallyon stood by the rail and nodded to him. Terry brought his drink over and looked down on the dance floor. He saw Maguire sitting alone at a table.

'You're becoming a bit of a regular,' Gallyon said.

Terry sipped vodka. 'Might as well mix business with pleasure.'

The music jarred. Vanner bought Jackie a drink and they stood together at the bar. Maguire sat at the table right under the stairs, talking to a couple of men. Vanner scanned the room and felt the gaze of one of the bouncers: squat man, short-cropped hair. He stared at Vanner. Vanner leaned into Jackie's neck. 'Regional plant,' he whispered. 'Don't look. Over by the door. Cropped hair. Knows we're job and not happy about it.'

Maguire was on his own again. Vanner looked upstairs and saw Bobby Gallyon looking down at the dance floor. A slim, good-looking man stood next to him, drinking what looked like tomato juice. Black box jacket. White collarless shirt.

Maguire moved from his table and leaned on the bottom of the banisters with his beer bottle resting against his lip. He was watching a woman dancing on her own, red-blonde hair, wearing a white silk shirt over black, skintight leggings. Upstairs Gallyon and the dark-haired man were seated at a table, their heads close. Vanner hugged Jackie.

'Something going on up there.'

She followed his gaze. 'Do we know him?'

Vanner shrugged.

The downstairs bar got crowded as the last drinks of the evening were being ordered. Vanner got up from the table where he and Jackie were sitting. 'Get you a drink,' he said. 'Upstairs.'

Gallyon was still sitting with the dark-haired man. Vanner moved past them to the bar. He ordered the drinks and watched. The good-looking girl from downstairs was seated on a stool next to him. Every so often the dark-haired man with Gallyon would glance across at her. Vanner paid for the drinks and slipped his wallet back into his pocket.

'Got a light?' She looked into his face and smiled, holding a white filtered cigarette between scarlet painted fingers. Vanner flicked his lighter. She steadied his hand with hers, looked again in his eyes. 'Thank you.'

'Pleasure.' He picked up the drinks and turned. The dark-haired man was watching him.

Gallyon tapped Michael Terry's arm. 'Don't get jealous. She's a working girl.'

'I want her.'

'Not tonight.'

Terry stared at him.

'She's busy tonight.' Gallyon nodded over his shoulder and Terry looked round. An Arab in a Jermyn Street suit had sidled onto the stool next to Lisa. She had her hand on his thigh. Terry finished his drink and got up. 'I'll see you, Bobby,' he said.

Vanner watched him go, down the stairs, face dark. He glanced at Maguire as he passed him and stalked across the dance floor.

Vanner looked back to the balcony. The girl with the Arab raised her glass.

Lisa took the pile of notes from the table, flattened them and folded them into her bag. The Arab lay on the bed, nothing on but his socks, a drink-sodden smile separating his beard. Lisa zipped up her bag and started to unbutton her shirt.

Downstairs in the foyer two Vice Squad officers from West End Central were talking to the night manager. 'Room 202,' Jenny Bennett tapped her warrant card on the reception counter. The Manager looked at her.

'It's occupied.'

'I know it's occupied. It always is.' She smiled at him. 'Lisa Morgan. Prostitute.'

'I don't know what you're talking about.'

Collins, her male counterpart, took the warrant from his jacket pocket. 'Yes you do. Every night you let her in, different room, different punter. She gives you a nice little kickback. You see we've been watching you.'

Colour slipped from the Manager's face.

'Now,' Collins said. 'We can do this very quietly, or if you like – we can make a fuss.'

Fifty padded envelopes lay on the table against the far wall. The door to the back room was ajar and the faint smell of alcohol clouded his head. Weeks now and still it lingered. He sat at the table and put Denny's face onto E's with the pharmaceutical stamp.

He looked at his watch. Three o'clock already. He should never have begun this. But he needed to think, and while he thought he might as well work. The thrill and yet the disturbance from earlier plagued him and he knew sleep would not come. A pity, there was so much to do in the morning. When he was finished with the stamp, he folded bubble wrap round the batches of tablets and slid them into the envelopes. Then he wrote the box numbers and postcodes on each one and marked them off on the computer.

Maguire was in his head. That smug Irish fuck. My God but he loved himself. There he was large as life, dealing in the toilets with Vanner from the Drug Squad watching him. How had they got Maguire? He must have got careless, nothing like success to breed complacency. What separated the great from merely the good.

Vanner was becoming something of a thorn in his side though. First Ringo and now Maguire. No doubt they would employ the same tactic, watch the box for a pickup. They must know about the two cards, Ringo and his flappy mouth, permanently closed now at least. He sat there and thought it through. If he were Vanner he would look for the second cardholder. One dealer was nothing. They could pick them off one by one but it did not get them any further. No, it was the collector they wanted. A risk with Damien Jackson over Ringo's box, but he had had to know. The fifteen hundred was irrelevant but the information was not. He had got away with it once, but would he do so again? He knew he needed to be vigilant. If he had not been out tonight, he would not have seen Vanner. The knowledge gave him an edge. But he would have to consider Maguire.

Saturday morning, and Vanner stood before Morrison's desk in Hendon. Morrison had papers stacked neatly in front of him. The desk was neat, the twin pen and pencil set mounted in silver. High-backed chair. The files all tucked carefully in order on the shelving behind it. Even the window was clean. Vanner thought of his own office and sat down.

'You went to see Alan Boyd.'

'Alan who?'

'You know who I mean.'

Vanner looked at him.

'Had his knees slashed at a cashpoint.'

Vanner folded his arms. Morrison's gaze was keen, green eyes slanted, chin stuck out as if he was enjoying himself. 'You also went to see the witness. What d'you think you were doing?'

Vanner looked at him now. 'There were similarities between that attack and mine.'

'Vanner, these were kids. The witness will have told you as much. It was a mugging. Random. Like yours.'

'Random.'

'Yes.'

'Just another street crime.'

Morrison threw out a hand. 'You know it was. Listen . . .' He pointed at him then. 'Mugging is nothing to do with you. Boyd is nothing to do with you. Tufnell Park are dealing with it. They don't want DI's from the Drug Squad poking their noses in. Do I make myself clear?'

Vanner stood up. 'Is that everything, Sir?'

Morrison sat back. 'I've told you already, Vanner. I don't need a loose cannon in my division. You do any more of this and I'll shift you.'

Ryan met him at Campbell Row, a sloppy grin on his face. 'Good night with Jackie, Guv?'

'Not in the mood, Sid.'

Ryan followed him into his office.

'Anything from the post office box?'

'Nothing.' Ryan folded his arms. 'We do have a development though. Central again. Vice this time. We're due down there now. I'll tell you about it on the way.'

They drove down to West End Central. 'High-class Tom,' Ryan said. 'Real looker apparently. Ought to be a diversion at least.'

Vanner glanced at him.

'Clarion Hotel. Off Trafalgar Square. Every bloody night.' He shook his head. 'D'you know how much a suite there costs? Five hundred a night. That and the trick. She's got some serious punters.'

They were met by Collins and Bennett. Collins sat down with Ryan. 'Tasty as they come, mate,' he was saying. 'Tasty as they come.'

Jenny Bennett glanced at them. 'She isn't that bloody tasty. I did the strip-search remember.'

Collins looked to the ceiling.

'Denny Ecstasy?' Vanner said.

Bennett nodded. 'Three tablets. White with a face marked on them. I'll get them from properties,' she said. 'She's in Interview Room 2 when you want her.'

She left them then and Collins looked at Vanner. 'She's pissed off, Guv. We've been after this one for weeks. Scam running at the hotel. Night Manager taking back-handers. Owners have been trying to stamp it out, so we've had a body in there watching.'

'Who is she – the Tom?'

'Lisa Morgan. Works for Bobby Gallyon.'

Vanner stared at him. 'What does she look like?'

'Slim. Reddy-blonde hair. Drop-dead gorgeous.'

Vanner glanced at Ryan. 'Let's go and say hello.'

She sat with her hands clasped on her knee. Slim, willowy, a mass of red-blonde hair. Vanner stood behind the chair opposite her and she met his eyes, face intent but expressionless. Ryan pulled back a chair. Bennett stood by the door with her hands behind her back.

'I'm DS Ryan,' Ryan said, 'and this is DI Vanner. North West London Drug Squad.' Lisa was not looking at him. She continued to stare at Vanner, her face tilted, haughty almost. Vanner looked back at her, the height of her cheekbones, the fine line of her nose, the fullness of a mouth without lipstick.

Ryan said: 'This is an informal interview, Lisa. But if you want you can have a solicitor present.'

'I don't need a solicitor.'

Vanner took out cigarettes. He offered the pack to her and she shook her head. Not once had she looked at Ryan. Bennett placed the plastic bag, sealed at the neck with a twistlock, on the table between them. Vanner picked up the bag and fingered it carefully. Three Ecstasy tablets. 'Where did you get these?' he said.

She did not say anything.

'I'll ask you again. Where did you get them?'

Still she did not say anything.

Ryan yawned. 'Not much of a conversation.'

She looked at him for the first time. Then she looked back at Vanner. 'Could I have some coffee please?'

Vanner glanced at Ryan and he stood up. Lisa spoke without looking at him. 'Black,' she said. 'No sugar.'

When he had gone Lisa picked up Vanner's open packet of cigarettes and lit one. She fanned out the match and dropped it in the ashtray.

'You know,' Vanner said, 'you could help yourself if you want to.'

She leaned her elbow on the table, her chin in the palm of her hand. 'Oh. And how could I do that?'

'Well . . .' Vanner started.

'Arrest is an occupational hazard in my profession, Vanner.' She looked him hard in the eye. She knew her business. It was as if she wanted him to know that she knew it.

He sat back in the chair. She did not take her eyes off him. So sure of herself, not in any cocky or arrogant way, just a total awareness of her situation and exactly what she could do about it. Bennett looked over her shoulder at Vanner, hawkish. Vanner glanced up at her. 'Could you leave us alone for a moment?'

She frowned. 'You know I'm not supposed to, Sir.'

Lisa swivelled in her chair. 'It's all right,' she said. 'I don't mind.'

Bennett pursed her lips, opened the door and Ryan came in with the coffee. He placed the plastic cups on the table. Bennett held the door open. When they were alone Lisa looked at Vanner. 'I saw you in the club last night,' she said.

'Did you?'

'Never forget a face.'

Vanner half-smiled.

'She's very pissed off isn't she.'

'Bennett?'

She nodded and indicated the E's on the table. 'Those make me more valuable to you than to her don't they.' She clicked her tongue. 'Shame. She's been watching me for weeks.'

'In the club?

'The hotel.'

Vanner sipped coffee. 'Why carry on – if you knew she was onto you?'

'Business, Vanner. My profession. I'm very, very expensive. I have schedules. My punters aren't just bods off the street. When I say they can see me – they expect to see me.'

Vanner leaned an arm over the chair. 'All very professional.'

'How else can you run a business?'

He poked a finger at the E's on the table. 'You take a lot of these?'

She smiled at him. 'I'm always in control.'

'You like control.'

'Don't you?'

He looked evenly at her. 'Bobby get them for you?'

She folded her arms.

'The Arab you were nicked with then?'

'Don't be silly. Arabs don't do E's. They do champagne and good malt whisky.'

'Who then?'

She put out her cigarette and lit another. Vanner leaned towards her once more. 'You don't have to say anything. It's up to you. But they've got a good case against you. It could be very serious.'

She looked keenly at him then. 'That would depend on the judge.'

He stared at her for a moment. 'Like to wear their wigs do they?'

'Some of them do. Yes.'

For a moment he was lost. She held his eye. He looked right back at her, but could think of nothing to say.

'I know the ropes, Vanner. Occupational hazard. It won't change anything.'

'What about Bobby?'

'What about him?'

'Piss him off won't it. Man like Bobby Gallyon.'

'He's just a nightclub owner.'

He laughed then and shook his head. 'Tell you what, Lisa. You're good. I'll give you that.'

She flicked ash in the tray. 'I'm a lot better than good.'

For a moment they stared at one another; Vanner sat deeper in the chair. She leaned on her palm again and her eyes were big and blue and intent upon his. He felt gooseflesh rise on his cheeks. She picked up her coffee, still looking at him, and sipped it. She made a face. 'He put sugar in it.'

'That's his sense of humour.'

He passed her his own coffee. 'So how long've you been on the game, Lisa?'

'The game? I'm not on the game.'

'Tom. Hooker. Prostitute.'

She wagged her head at him. 'Disgust you does it?'

He looked at her for a long moment and then he sat back again. 'You like drug dealers, Lisa?'

'Not especially. They make a living.'

'Just a business then. Like yours.'

'Nobody forces anyone to do anything, Vanner. It's all a matter of choice.'

'So it doesn't matter that people get hurt, that families get broken up, that kids puke to death in a warehouse.'

She laughed now. 'Sentimental bullshit. It's a business like everything else. Supply and demand. Where've you been the last fifteen years?'

Vanner looked at her now. 'Last night,' he said quietly. 'That guy with Bobby Gallyon.'

For the fraction of a second her eyes flickered.

'What's his name?'

'I don't know.'

'You're a liar.'

'Tough guy now are you?'

Again he held her eye, his face very cold. 'Punter of yours is he? I saw how he looked at you, getting all nervous over there at the table while I was lighting your cigarette. Who is he, Lisa? Mate of Bobby Gallyon's. Do a few deals do they? What is it – he gets you at a discount?'

'I don't give discounts.'

He tapped the plastic bag. 'He gave these to you. Didn't he.'

She sucked smoke and blew it in his face. 'I've got nothing more to say.'

Vanner waved the smoke away and stood up. 'They've got the hotel manager for his night owl bit. You should've been more discreet, Lisa.' He picked up the bag of tablets.

'And then of course there's possession. If you fancy a chat we could think about the possession.' He peeled a card from his wallet. 'That way you might not go down.'

She parted her lips a fraction. 'Oh, I always go down, Vanner.'

Mickey Blondhair sat in the boiler room and blew smoke rings. Ninja sat opposite him, cross-legged, looking at the short, curved sword resting against Mickey's thigh.

'Cut your toenails with it do you?'

'You ain't the only fuckin' knife man.'

Ninja looked round at The Wasp. The Wasp grinned. Ninja's own sword poked from under his jacket.

'Competition for the Gypsy.'

'Bollocks,' Ninja said.

Mickey flattened his cigarette. 'You a real Gypsy?'

Ninja levelled his eye at him.

'Caravans and that?'

Ninja stood up. 'No air in here,' he said.

Mickey watched him go and then looked back at The Wasp. 'Don't like rooms do he?'

'Don't like anything much.'

'Is he a Gyppo?'

'Yeah.' The Wasp lit the joint he was rolling, sucked at it and passed it across. 'What did you want to talk about?'

'I don't want to thieve no more.'

The Wasp peered from under his dreadlocks at him. 'What you saying, man? You want out? There is no out. You know Sammy Johnson?'

'Neasden Bail Hostel.'

'That's right. Well he wanted out. We broke his fuckin' arms.'

Mickey smoked the joint and looked back at him. 'I didn't say out, Wasp. I just said I don't want to thieve no more.'

The Wasp looked at the sword. 'What the fuck d'you buy that for then?'

'I liked the look of it. Okay?'

They were quiet for a moment. Mickey relit the joint and passed it back.

'So what *do* you want to do?'

'Deal.'

The Wasp laughed.

'Don't laugh at me.'

'Where the fuck would you deal?'

'School, you arsehole. At school.'

Eight

Vanner went home after he left West End Central. When he got there he phoned Jimmy Crack. 'Sorry to bother you at the weekend, Jim.'

'No problem, Guv'nor. What's up?'

Vanner looked out of the window. 'Gallyon's nightclub. You told me you look out for faces?'

'That's right.'

'D'you ever notice a bloke sitting upstairs with Gallyon?'

'He sees a lot of people, Guv'nor.'

'About my age. Black hair. Well dressed.'

'Oh, him. Name's Michael Terry. Imports plants over at Dartford.'

'Big mates with Gallyon?'

'Don't know. 6 nicked him five years ago though. Fiddling shareholders or something.'

'Regional boys got a flag on him?'

'No. They think he's there for the Tom.'

'Thanks, Jim.' Vanner put down the phone.

Michael Terry picked his son up from Kirstall Estate. 'Sorry I'm so late,' he said. 'I got held up this morning.'

Mark shrugged his shoulders.

The Wasp watched them from his window. Terry glanced up at him, then opened the door of his Mercedes and got in. He sat for a moment and looked at his son, hunched uncomfortably in the seat alongside him. His hair fell over his eyes. Pity about the glasses, made him look so awkward. That came from Jennifer's side of the family. Her old man – blind as a bloody bat. Maybe he should buy him some contacts.

They drove south, a flat silence between them. 'You're not working today then?'

Mark shook his head. 'They're redecorating the shop.'

'They can afford to be closed? How much do they pay you?'

Mark did not laugh. His father eased the wheel through his hands and sighed. 'D'you fancy coming over to Dartford with me? I've got a load in I want to look at.'

They drove through the city and headed out towards the East End. 'You know you can bring a mate over one Saturday if you like,' Terry said. 'You're always on your own, Mark. I never see you with anyone.'

Mark shrugged his shoulders.

'All you do is sit at the bloody computer. Haven't you got any mates? What about John? You ever hear from him these days?'

Mark shook his head. 'Haven't seen him in ages.'

'Used to be good mates didn't you? We had a laugh when he slept over.'

Mark looked round at him. 'He's doing drugs, Dad. I think he's in some kind of trouble. I saw three blokes having a go at his father – right inside the college.'

His father frowned. 'I didn't know his old man worked at your college.'

Mark nodded. 'Teaches electronics.'

Terry stopped the car outside the yard, under the shadow of the Queen Elizabeth Bridge. He got out and looked at the sky, where dark clouds were gathering at last.

'Nice if it rained,' he said. 'Haven't seen any all summer. Still, summer'll soon be over and then we'll all complain.' He unlocked the chains on the twelve-foot iron gates, and pushed them open. He looked back at Mark. 'You want to drive the car in?'

Mark looked at the steering wheel.

'Go on. You can do it.'

Mark shook his head.

Terry rested a fist on the roof. 'It's easy. Automatic. You just put it in *Drive* and press the pedal.'

'No. It's all right. You do it.'

Terry shook his head and climbed back in the car. He drove inside and parked by the two-storeyed portakabin. 'I'll teach you to drive if you want me to.'

'I've got my bike, Dad.'

'I know you've got your bike.' His father hissed air through his teeth. 'But you're old enough to drive. I could teach you. Not in this. We'll get a smaller car. One with normal gears.'

Mark lifted his shoulders. 'Maybe,' he said.

They got out of the car and Mark looked across the yard at the two Caterpillar dump trucks, their cabs still blackened by fire. 'Are those the new ones?'

'Yes.'

'They just came in?'

His father nodded. 'Shipped over from Amsterdam.'

'You go there a lot. Don't you.'

'My business, Mark. You know the auction's in Amsterdam.' Terry took out a cigarette.

'I'll take you again if you want.'

'I've got to go to college, Dad.'

Terry looked at the sky. 'Whatever.' He climbed the steps and unlocked the upper cabin door. Mark wandered towards the trucks. 'Don't mess about with them, Mark. You'll only get yourself filthy.'

Vanner drove through the West End. He cut his way through cabs and buses and took all the short cuts to Westminster. He crossed the bridge and followed the South Embankment to Lambeth Road and headed for the belly of the city. It was beginning to get dark. Not long now and the nights would start to draw in. Further south the traffic eased and he listened to the radio. Lisa Morgan filled his mind and he felt himself begin to stir. He wondered if she would phone him.

He thought about how she cupped his hand with hers when he

lit her cigarette in the club. He thought about the scent of her skin
as he stood next to her, body still hot from her dancing. He
thought about how she had looked at him, head to head, unflinching in the interview room. Then he thought about Morrison,
watching his every move.

He took the A23 and came down Streatham High Road. Here
the memories of Tate were vivid. Hard, South London family. Not
in the old days' class, but classy enough, he supposed. One dead
and two away. Only one of the two was out now. Jabba had been
on the phone. Apparently Tate had been shooting his mouth off.
Vanner fingered his shoulder and drove.

He came down Purley Way and stopped at the lights, then he
made a left turn and drove past the Waddon Arms. Harrison's Rise
was a few streets away and he looked for somewhere to park.
Switching off the engine, he sat in the steadily dwindling twilight
and watched. There were a few people about. On his right an
off-licence. On the corner a chippy with people queuing out of the
door. He assumed the chips were good. Tate's street was the first
turning right. Vanner got out of the car and slipped on his jacket.
The nights were definitely cooler now. No stars above the street
lights. If they were lucky it might even rain. A woman pushed
past him with a toddler straggling behind her. He watched her
turn right and after a few moments he followed.

From the corner the road lifted steeply. He could make out a
couple of small business premises on his right and across the
street the houses climbed sharply. Number 1 was the first house
on the left. Light stole from behind the curtains of the front room.
The phone rang on his belt.

'Guv'nor. It's me.'

'Hello, Sid.'

'That Tom give you a bell?'

'Not yet.'

'Too early I guess. You think she will though?'

'I don't know.'

'I reckon she fancies you, Guv.'

'Ha bloody ha.'

Ryan chuckled. 'Looker though eh. I don't care what the plonk said. That's what you call a strip-search.'

'What else is new, Sid?'

'Just thought I'd let you know – I'm going over to Bream Park.'

Vanner looked at the sky. 'That a good idea?'

'Milo, Guv. Bastard still hasn't called me.'

'It's early days, Sid. Breaking all the rules.'

'I'll pretend I'm a dealer. Always worked before. Besides, I've got a bad feeling. I need to know what's happening.'

Vanner was quiet for a moment. 'You going on your own?'

'I can handle it. Unless you want to come.'

Vanner looked again at Tate's house. 'No can do.'

'On a promise are you?'

'Something like that.'

'I hope she's good, Guv'nor.'

Across the street a man came out of Number 1. Vanner stepped back around the corner. 'She'll do, Sid. She'll do.' He switched off his phone and slipped it into his pocket.

Tate walked ahead of him. He watched him cross the dual carriageway and head towards the church. At the corner Vanner paused. Tate crossed the road and went into the Black Bell pub.

Ryan drove to Bream Park. He stopped in the car park and locked the door very carefully. A group of kids stood in the doorway to C block. Ryan turned up his collar.

Vanner watched Tate playing pool with a black man with dreadlocks. Vanner stared at him. Hoods coming off, hair flying in the rain. He remembered it now. The last thing he had seen. The bar was crowded with Saturday night drinkers. The benches outside were full. He could see the pool table however: Christian Tate bent over it, sizing up a yellow striped ball for the bottom corner pocket. His partner chalked the end of his cue. Vanner ordered a pint.

Tate potted the ball and played on. His mate sat down on a stool. Vanner watched Tate, the way he moved, the way he bent over the table. He was tall enough. One of them had been white. But then again the eyes. What had it been about the eyes? Tate missed the black, leaned for a moment against the table and then stood up. He looked straight at Vanner. Vanner looked straight at him. Tate moved to the stool while his partner set about the spotted balls on the table. Vanner raised his glass to his lips. He drained it, looked again and Tate was back at the table. Vanner placed his glass on the bar and waited for the landlord to finish serving the man next to him. He looked back at the table. The game was over and the black man was stuffing money into the slots. Tate chalked his cue and watched him.

Vanner's pulse lifted. Many a pub in the past, many a dark and lonely night. London, Edinburgh and before all of that – Belfast. He took out his cigarettes and lit one. Still Tate watched him. The black man framed the balls with the triangle and set himself to break.

Ryan stood outside Ringo May's door and knocked. The landing was empty. From downstairs he could hear the sound of an engine revving. He knocked again. No answer. 'Come on, Milo. You fuck.' He knocked again, then he crouched down on the floor and lifted the flap on the letterbox. The smell hit him. He stiffened, sniffed again and then he stood up. All at once he was cold. All at once the sounds from the estate banged in his head. He moved back from the door and thought for a moment. Then he lifted his foot to the wood.

Slowly Vanner drank his second pint and slowly Tate and his mate played out their second game. The black guy was watching Vanner now, a moment ago their heads had been together. So now there were two of them. Vanner felt the adrenalin begin to flow. The scars on his back seemed to throb, but it might have been in his head. He put out his cigarette, shook out another and lit it. Tate sat on the stool and watched him.

Ryan caught the full force of the stench the moment the door gave. The hall was in darkness. He fumbled along the wall for a light. He found a switch and the bulb glimmered dully. The door to the sitting room was open. Milo lay on the floor in dried and crusted blood, one arm thrust beneath him, his eyes open and staring.

Ryan took out a handkerchief and held it to his nose. He moved closer and looked down at the almost naked body. The flesh was open and chafed on his belly, the skin punctured and lifted. Ryan stared, blinking against the reek that lifted from the body. Broken and blistered flesh, the weight of his entrails buckling him to the floor. He looked about the room: a beer bottle lying on its side on the table. Another smell mixing with the bloated and gaseous flesh. On the floor by the chair, a pile of dried-up excrement.

Outside on the landing he phoned Vanner. He was transferred to the answer machine. 'Fuck you, Guv'nor,' he muttered. 'Never there when I want you.'

Vanner had moved to a table. Tate was sitting at the bar now, a group of lads around him. Every now and then one or other of them would glance over Tate's shoulder at Vanner. Big man: the original hard man of old. Then Tate turned and looked at him. Vanner raised his glass. Tate slid off his stool and pushed his way through the drinkers towards him. Vanner sat straight-backed, glass held loosely, and watched him every step of the way. Tate stopped at his table and rested both fists on it. They looked one another in the eye.

'What d'you want?'

'You've got a big mouth. I'm just seeing if that's all you've got.'

'You want to watch what you say. You want to watch where you drink.'

Vanner stared at him. 'Somebody had a go at me. I thought it might be you. But now I'm here – I don't think you've got the bottle.' He looked beyond him then to the gathering at the bar and creased his mouth into a shallow smile. 'Frankie. Now he had the bottle. But Frankie's dead isn't he.'

Tate stared coldly at him. 'I could call this harassment.'

'Could you?'

'Yeah. I could. You know I report to Croydon Nick twice a month. Got myself a tame probation officer. I might just tell him about you.'

'Why don't you do that. From what I hear you like to talk.'

'You shouldn't listen to gossip.'

'Maybe not but I do.' Vanner emptied his glass and stood up. He looked again to the bar.

'Glory days,' he said. 'All you've got left isn't it.'

He drove home and thought about Tate standing across from him. Too small. Nothing wrong with his eyes. When he got to his house he replayed the messages on his answerphone. He listened to the crackle and then Ryan's voice from his mobile. 'Guv'nor. Phone me. Somebody killed Milo.'

He parked his car next to Ryan's on the Bream Park Estate. An ambulance squatted with its lights flashing and half a dozen uniforms moved about in the doorways. He saw Morrison's Granada between two patrol cars. He showed his warrant to the uniforms and climbed the stairs. He followed the corridors into the bowels of the building and came out on Milo's landing. Ryan leaned against the window, smoking a cigarette. He looked up but he did not smile. 'In the flat, Guv'nor. I could smell him through the letterbox. Must have been dead for days.'

Vanner glanced towards the open doorway. 'SOCO?'

'SOCO. AMIP. The whole bloody shooting match.'

'AMIP?' Vanner looked back at him.

'Major incident isn't it. Weir came down with the old man.'

'Why didn't you call me on the mobile?'

Ryan looked at him. 'I did, Guv'nor. Switched off wasn't it.'

Vanner felt in his pocket. He had switched the phone off before he went into the pub. He had forgotten to turn it back on. Ryan sucked on his cigarette. 'Sorry to spoil your evening.'

Vanner stepped across the threshold. Morrison stood in the doorway to the sitting room. The ambulancemen were lifting the brittle form of Milo onto a stretcher. The stink hit Vanner. Morrison looked round at him. 'You took your time.'

Vanner ignored him. He moved to the doorway and a white suited SOCO stepped aside. The floor was caked in dried blood and intestine. Vanner looked at the excrement near the chair.

'Always do it on the floor.' Morrison shook his head.

'Their statement.' Vanner looked at Milo. 'How long dead?'

'A few days at least.' Weir's voice from behind him. Vanner turned. Weir stood in the kitchen doorway, chewing gum.

Vanner turned back to the sitting room. The carpet, thin and ill-fitting, was bunched where the body had been. One of the chairs had been moved back. A brown, empty beer bottle lay on its side on the table. A forensic man was dusting it. Vanner scanned the room: nothing in it save the table, two ruined chairs and a broken-down TV set. Weir was talking to one of the SOCO men. He pointed to the excrement.

'That do us any good?'

The SOCO man made a face. 'DNA?'

Weir nodded.

'There's DNA in it, yeah. But not his. Or if it is his – it would take a year and a day to find it. The DNA would be that of what he's eaten.'

Vanner listened to him. Then he bent lower and looked at the faeces. Taking a pen from his pocket, he scraped the nib through the pile. He felt Weir's gaze on his back.

Vanner stood up and looked at the red-brown mess on the nib. He moved to the white-suited SOCO. 'Get a bag,' he said. 'Some of this is blood.'

Weir stood by the chair. 'Your snout was he, Vanner?'

Vanner turned. 'Ryan handled him.'

'Just Ryan? No co-handler?'

'I managed it.'

Weir smiled. 'Did you?'

Vanner ignored him. He looked at Morrison. 'Incident room?'

'Of course.'

'It's a Drug Squad murder.'

Morrison picked teeth with his finger. 'So it would seem,' he said.

Vanner felt a chill brush the back of his neck. He knew Weir was watching him.

'Castle Hills the nearest nick with a Holmes Suite.'

'Already on the move.'

'IO?' Again he felt Weir on his back.

'We'll talk about it in the morning. Be in my office at nine.'

Michael Terry dropped his son off at the edge of the Kirstall Estate. 'Sorry it's been so short, Mark. I know you normally stay but there's things I have to do tonight.'

Mark nodded and opened the door. His father laid a hand on his arm. 'You don't mind?'

'I don't mind.'

'Want me to walk you up?'

'I'm seventeen, Dad.' He got out of the car and his father drummed the steering wheel.

'See you in a couple of weeks then. I'll be in the States for a few days. But I'm home for the weekend if you need me.'

Mark nodded and closed the door.

He walked up the flight of steps to his landing. The Wasp leaned in the stairwell with a girl on his arm. He smiled at Mark, showing the white of his teeth. 'Hey, college boy.'

Mark started to move past him, but The Wasp blocked his path. 'Daddy's car? Very nice.'

Mark looked at the floor. The Wasp poked him in the ribs with long fingers. 'Buy you an ice cream did he?'

Mark stepped by then and The Wasp laughed in his ear.

Vanner sat in his car on Bream Park, Frank Weir's face in his mind. Morrison and Weir went way back. He knew Morrison was about to give the murder to AMIP and make Weir the Investigating Officer. Nine o'clock in Hendon. If he was to avoid that then he needed an edge, something more than he had. And what did he have? One dead informant, Maguire, the dealer from Barnet and

Lisa Morgan the prostitute. He thought back to the interview room, her eyes on his, the certainty in her voice, and her hand cupped about his as he lit her cigarette in the nightclub. He thought of the man with Bobby Gallyon, Michael Terry, the look on his face when their eyes met. Lisa's reaction this morning when he had asked her about him.

Taking his notebook from his case he looked up her number and dialled. No answer. He sat and he thought for a moment. He glanced at his watch. He needed the edge before the meeting with Morrison. He started the car and drove to Gallyon's nightclub.

He sat in darkness, at his desk in the warehouse with only the light of the computer in front of him. He had spoken to The Wasp, who jokingly informed him of Mickey Blondhair's desire to switch from the street to dealing. He thought hard about it now, rolling the cursor down the line of figures that represented Mickey's contribution to the team. For a thirteen-year-old he was good. He virtually ran the Boiler Room Gang. He was the one with the watch. Such ingenuity, versatility. Not just the cashpoint stuff or the women on buses, but the burglaries. That had been his own idea. His team had gone as far north as Hampstead. They made the bail hostel gangs look like amateurs.

He sat back, rocking on two legs of the chair and switched on his headphones. Who would run the Boiler Room? That would be a question for Wasp. Not a bad idea perhaps to move Mickey on, especially after the last incident at the cashpoint. A good haul, but messy and apparently a witness. School, though. So far he had avoided schools. Although it filtered down. His dealers were half-sheet men. They had their own networks beneath them. He did not know who bought and then sold on. He did not care. He had his market and beyond that, well, other people had theirs.

That was the way of things. Business rolling on. The pyramid working its way downwards. He had avoided the dirty stuff, smack and crack and so on. Acid was good because a crystal went a long way and the squares were easily posted. He could vary the jiffy bags with normal envelopes, a variety of shapes and colours so as to avoid suspicion in the boxes. E's were more difficult but the profit outweighed the risk. And of course if they were caught, the box was registered to the dealer. Just one more name to replace.

But other conundrums. Vanner knew about Maguire. He would have to think about that. And Mickey Blondhair, with his imitation of Ninja. Maybe he was best moved on. He could consider it promotion. The Wasp could supply him. Switching off the machine, he went downstairs in darkness and out onto the street.

Vanner sat behind the wheel of the car, across the street from the club. He watched the two bouncers at the door and then Lisa came out with a wrap around her shoulders. Terry held her arm and one of the doormen flagged down a cab. Vanner started his engine. He drove, one hand on the wheel, the other resting in his lap. The cab cut through the traffic ahead of him. They drove east. He followed them through the City and down towards the river. They crossed on Blackfriars Bridge and for some reason Vanner thought of Roberto Calvi, God's banker, hanging from the end of a rope. On the south side of the river the cab pulled over beside the Express Newspapers building and Lisa and Terry got out. Vanner stopped the car and watched them cross to a block of apartments.

He had no way of knowing which apartment they had gone into but something about Terry's attire told him the view would be over the river. Getting out of his car, he walked to Gabriel's Wharf and looked down into the oil blackness of the water. Somewhere in the middle of the river a refuse barge chugged west under the bridge. The breeze lifted and Vanner buttoned his jacket to the collar. He lit a cigarette and flicked away the match. It died before it hit the water. He smoked in silence, watching the traffic on the far embankment. The dome of St Paul's dominated the City. Leaning lower on the rail, he looked down between his feet. Then he turned and glanced at the building. He could see windows; huge, opaque: some of them were lighted, some of them were not. He could make out no figures against them.

He thought about Michael Terry, inside somewhere with Lisa

Morgan. For a moment he wondered what he was doing to her and he shook the thoughts away. Who was Michael Terry? Gallyon imported coke from Colombia. The RCS were watching him. Jimmy Crack was watching him. Something told Vanner that this Michael Terry had given the E's to Lisa. Maguire had been in the club however. Maybe she scored off him. But would Maguire, a small-time Irish dealer, supply E's in Gallyon's club? Maybe Gallyon supplied. Maybe Terry got them from him. But everything SO11 had on Gallyon told them that he only dealt with cocaine. E's were a whole different ball game. And acid, most of the Denny label was acid, a different market again. He looked back at the river and knew he was clutching at straws. But tomorrow he needed an edge and he had to know if there was one.

Back in the car he dozed. At nearly five in the morning he was awakened by the dieseled rattle of a cab. He sat up, rubbed his eyes and squinted at the apartment building. He saw Lisa come out of the revolving door. The cabbie was out of his seat. On the fourth-floor balcony, a man stood in his dressing gown.

Vanner followed the cab back across the river then west on the Embankment. They skirted Pimlico and West Kensington and the cab finally pulled up outside a squared block of flats in Chelsea. He saw no money change hands. Lisa stepped onto the pavement and moved past a red, chequered barrier towards the apartments. Vanner got out of his car. He followed her into a silent, square concourse in the middle of the block. The flats rose on four walls around them. Lisa was at the door to the right. Vanner stepped out of the shadows.

Her apartment was on the third floor, softly furnished in white peach. Vanner stood in the middle of the lounge with his hands in his pockets. Lisa tossed her keys onto a small table and yawned. 'You look like a policeman,' she said.

He did not smile.

'You sat out there all night?'

He nodded.

'Don't you have a home to go to? No wife? I normally see coppers with wives.'

He squatted on the edge of the settee. Lisa sat down in the chair opposite, kicked off her shoes and eased her feet beneath her. 'Drink, Vanner?'

'Got any Irish whiskey?'

'Darling, I've got everything.' She indicated the cabinet set into the wall and Vanner fetched a bottle of Jameson. He poured two glasses and handed one to her.

'So talk, Vanner. If *that's* what you came for . . .'

He sat down again and looked at her. Her skin flushed red at her throat, the heat of the room perhaps. He could make out the height of her breasts beneath the material of her shirt. He looked briefly at the floor. 'I need to know who gave you the E's, Lisa.'

She shook her head at him. 'And there's me thinking you wanted conversation.'

He looked at her, hair on fire, a light in the depth of her eyes. She yawned then and lifted her hand to her mouth.

'Been a long night?' he said.

She widened her eyes at him. 'Very long, Vanner. Good and long and slow.'

For a while they sat in silence. 'Have you always been into drugs?' she asked him.

'Not always.'

'What then?'

'Robbery. Murder. Armed Response.'

'Guns. You know you look like a gun man.'

'Do I? And what does a gun man look like exactly?'

'Like you, Vanner.' She lit a cigarette and tossed him the packet.

'I need to know, Lisa.'

'So you say.'

'It's that guy you were with tonight isn't it. Michael Terry.'

She got up from the chair and sipped her drink, one hand on her hip. 'What're you looking for, Vanner? An informant? Snout. Isn't that what you call them? You pay them don't you?'

'If you like.'

110

She laughed then. 'You couldn't afford me. Either way you couldn't afford me.'

He rolled the glass between his palms. 'Lisa, tonight we discovered a dealer lying in his flat with his guts ripped open.'

'Dead was he?'

He stared at her. 'He was no more than a kid.'

'So.'

'He was killed by whoever supplies those tablets we found on you.'

Her face sobered then. 'All the more reason to tell you nothing.'

He looked beyond her. Hendon awaited him with Weir and Morrison together, in less than four hours. 'Did he pop much tonight – your man?'

'Only me, darling.'

Vanner felt inexplicably wounded. She shook her head. 'Just a job, Vanner. Hand job. Blow job. Any old job you want to pay for.'

Vanner stared at her. 'Oh yeah. How much?'

'What?'

'You heard me. I said: how much?' He stood up and they faced one another. Lisa looked at the floor. 'Sorry, love. I'm not working tonight.'

'No? Tired are you?'

She looked him in the eye. 'Absolutely fucked.'

Vanner stood where he was for a moment. He could smell her. For a second he imagined Terry with her. He pushed his hands into his pockets and moved to the door.

'You know an Irishman called Maguire? Comes to the club. Was in the other night.'

'Lots of people come to the club.'

'Does he know the punter you were with?'

'How would I know, Vanner? I don't know him.'

'Brown-haired guy. Earring, wears a gold band on his wrist.'

'No bells ringing.'

He opened the door. 'Terry always goes upstairs does he? Always chats with Bobby?'

'You tell me, darling.'

111

'He doesn't dance.'

'I've never seen him.'

'He doesn't dance with you?'

'He's a punter, Vanner. I don't dance with punters. I fuck them.'

He looked at her standing there, head to one side, feet slightly apart. 'Thanks for the drink, Lisa.'

'Vanner.'

He turned back from the door.

'Don't follow me any more.'

He rested his shoulder against the door frame. 'I'm not following you, Lisa. All I want to know is whether Terry gave you the E's. You tell me and I'll leave you alone. If you don't I might *just* follow you.'

She held his eye. Then she looked at the floor and pushed out her lips. 'You're a bastard aren't you, Vanner.'

'The very worst kind.'

She stared at him for a moment. 'Okay,' she said, 'he gave me the E's.'

Nine

Vanner climbed the stairs to Morrison's office at three minutes after nine. McCague was there. Vanner allowed himself a smile. Morrison covering his back. Weir poured coffee.

'Come in, Vanner,' Morrison said.

Vanner glanced at Weir and nodded to McCague. He sat down in the vacant chair.

'Coffee?' Morrison offered.

Vanner shook his head. Weir sat down next to him, crossed his ankle on his knee and stirred black coffee.

Morrison steepled his fingers. 'I had a phone call at home this morning, Vanner,' he said. 'Superintendent Burke of the Regional. He wanted to know why 2 Area Drug Squad are messing up his plot.'

Weir sipped his coffee. McCague sat with his hands clasped.

'Friday night,' Vanner said. 'We tailed a suspect to Gallyon's nightclub. Maguire. Dealer from Barnet. Central know him from the bars in Covent Garden. He's supplying Denny Ecstasy.'

'Have we pulled him?' Morrison said. 'I don't remember reading about him.'

Vanner sat forward. 'No, Sir. We haven't pulled him. I'm not pulling anyone else at the moment. We know him. He doesn't know us.' He glanced at Weir. 'Milo told us about post office boxes with two cards. We know Maguire has a box in Barnet. We also know there's a second card.'

'But we don't know who has it?'

Vanner shook his head. 'The applicant for the box is the dealer.

113

He applies for it in his own name. Fifty pounds up front for a year. If a second card is requested, it's given out on the basis that the applicant is responsible. All that cardholder has to do is sign it and they make sure the signature matches when he collects. It's really very simple.'

McCague said: 'So that's how they make the pickups. Drugs are mailed in and collected. Then the cash is mailed in by the dealer and the second cardholder collects.'

'That's it.'

Morrison looked at McCague. 'Not a system we've come across before, Sir.'

'Ingenious.'

'It works,' Vanner stated. 'The source is never traced. We make a bust, all we get is the dealer.'

Morrison sat forward. 'Now we need an incident room.'

'We do. Milo changes everything.'

Morrison glanced at McCague. 'Really is an AMIP deal.'

Vanner shook his head. 'I don't think so, Sir.'

Weir glanced round at him. 'Murder, Vanner. Drug Squad don't investigate murder.'

Vanner looked back at him. 'I think we do in this case. Milo was killed because they found out he was a snout. We know this source is new, at least in this form. He might have been on the periphery of things for a while but the Denny cartoon is a new one.'

'Where does it come from?' McCague asked.

'The cartoon?' Vanner shrugged. 'We've never seen it before. It's not been used in the States. Most of what we see over here they've had over there at some time.'

'Still murder,' Weir said. 'My team should be involved.'

'I agree.' Vanner looked at him again. 'I want them involved. The Drug Squad has other inquiries to work on.' He looked at Morrison and then at McCague. 'The Investigating Officer has to be Drug Squad though. It's Ryan's informant, killed after being set up over the crack house in Kilburn. Ryan knows the case and I know the case.'

'But, Vanner,' Weir said. 'If you're working on the murder, who runs the squad?'

'Skipper. Paul Ellis can do it. He was doing it before I came and he's got his Inspector's Board coming up. I can liaise with him if I need to. But he's been there for two years. I've only done two months.' He looked straight at Morrison. 'And it's not as if I've no experience of a murder investigation. Is it, Sir?'

Morrison sat back in his chair then and touched his collar. Morning sun drifted through the window. 'I'm not sure,' he said.

McCague looked at him. 'Why not? Makes sense from where I'm sitting.'

Weir glanced at Morrison. Morrison thought for a moment and then looked back at Vanner. 'What've you got, exactly? I mean apart from two small-time dealers.'

'The dealers aren't small-time. Milo had half a sheet. But apart from that, I've got a Tom being supplied by a punter from Gallyon's nightclub. Not just a punter – a face who spends most of his time there talking to Gallyon. We know Gallyon imports coke. That's why Regi are staking him out. They think he's looking at crack. That's why the crack man from the AIU's been involved.'

'Maybe it's a Regi deal full stop then,' Weir said.

Vanner looked sideways at him. 'When's anyone handed anything to the Regional that they don't have to?'

Morrison pushed out his lips. 'Who's the punter? Do we know him?'

'Name's Michael Terry. I saw the Tom last night. She confirmed it was Terry who supplied her.'

'In the club again?' Weir lifted one eyebrow.

'Don't be stupid. We know he likes her with no knickers on. He was pissed off on Friday because she had another punter, so I waited for them outside the club then I tailed them to his place. He lives in a block of flats on the south side of the river. She left at five. I followed her home. She gave me the word at five-thirty this morning.'

He looked at Morrison. 'Terry was a property man in the late eighties. We nicked him for defrauding shareholders in 1990. I've spoken to Holborn. He only got a slap but it's form.'

McCague caught up with him outside. 'You know how close you were to Weir being the Investigating Officer?'

'Tell me about it.' Vanner walked down the stairs. 'Why d'you think I tailed some Tom halfway round London last night?'

McCague took his arm. 'You did well in there. Without that name, Morrison had a case for Weir.'

'You're on my side then, Sir.'

'No sides, Vanner. Just logic. What you said makes sense. Weir's team are Weir's team mind you, so you might have to deal with the politics.'

'Been doing it all my life.'

Michael Terry made a phone call. He stood before his open balcony, with a breeze coming off the river to flick at the skirts of his dressing gown.

'James. Sorry to ring you on a Sunday, but I wanted to let you know the two Cats came in.'

'Were they what you wanted?'

'Spot on.'

'Just make sure it's reflected in my fee.'

'Don't I always. Listen, there's a big deal coming up. So I need some more in a hurry.'

'I'll see what I can do. But I can't promise anything.'

'Well, keep them coming and I'll close my account with the auction.' Terry laughed and put down the phone.

Vanner drove into the Bream Park Estate, fatigue plucking his eyes. Ryan's car was there and two marked pandas. He crossed the car park and found Ryan at the head of the stairs. He looked bleary-eyed, unwashed hair hanging about his ears. He was holding a plastic binliner.

'You okay?'

Ryan made a face. 'Hate losing a snout.'

Vanner opened his cigarettes and Ryan took one from him. 'Smoking too much,' he muttered. 'Wife's giving me gyp.'

'SOCO turn up anything?'

Ryan looked up at him. 'Good job you peeked at the shit, Guv'nor. To coin a phrase they'd have dumped it.'

'Blood,' Vanner said.

'Not much. But enough.'

'A start then.'

Ryan nodded.

'Anything else?'

Ryan opened the neck of the binliner. Vanner looked inside and saw a single surgical glove.

'Always the way, Guv. Think they're clear because they wear them and then they go and dump them. Found this in the bin at the bottom of the stairs. There's blood on it. Wiped, but not properly. If we're very lucky we'll get a print from inside.'

Vanner felt himself relaxing. He sat down the steps, arms over his knees. 'Had to fight off Weir,' he said. 'Morrison wanted AMIP to do it all.'

'So you're the IO?'

Vanner nodded. 'We'll split the team, Sid. You and me and one or two of the others. The rest of it will be AMIP.'

They watched as the pathologist stripped off his gloves. Milo lay on the table in front of them, eyes closed now, body unbuckled.

'So what killed him?' Vanner said.

'Sword, I would say.'

'Sword?' Thin and curved and arcing through darkness towards him.

'Not full-length, but a long blade anyway.'

'Could it have been a knife?'

'I don't think so. The cuts are extremely deep and they're tattered at the edges. Have a look, you'll see.'

'I looked already.'

'The angle isn't right for a knife,' the pathologist went on. 'The killer would have to be standing much closer to him and if he did that then the shape of the lacerations, their depth, would be different. No, I'd say it was a sword of some sort.'

'Curved sword?' Vanner said. 'Like a . . . I don't know – Samurai maybe?'

The pathologist looked over his glasses at him. 'I would say it was certainly curved.'

Later that afternoon, Vanner was talking to Sergeant Platt at the incident room. He was a local man from Castle Hill, the office manager for the inquiry. Morrison came down the stairs. The girls from the Holmes Suite were gathered. Vanner had his team. Ryan, Anne Barrington, China, the bodybuilder and the ginger-headed McCleod from the Drug Squad. Five AMIP detectives, bossed by a skipper called Wainwright. Vanner and Platt followed Morrison into the office at the back of the room.

Morrison looked at his watch. 'Right, let's get started,' he said. 'I've got a meeting with the Child Protection Unit at three-thirty.' He looked at Vanner. 'What d'you want in the docket?'

Vanner gave the action sheets to Ryan. 'Where's Jimmy Crack?' he said.

'On his way, Guv.'

Vanner looked at the AMIP team. The skipper he knew, Weir's man. That meant Weir would know every step they were taking. Probably Morrison's idea. Just in case he stepped off the line. Nice to know he had such confidence backing him up. Jimmy Crack came down the stairs and unclipped the mobile phone from his belt. Vanner went over to him. 'Everything sweet with the big boys?'

Jimmy grinned. 'Oh wonderful, Guv. The Super's pissed off. Reckons the whole thing's connected. Should be a Regional job.'

He took his seat and Vanner moved to the front. Gradually the hubbub of conversation died down. 'Okay,' he said. 'For those of you in AMIP who don't know, I'm DI Vanner. The Drug Squad team are Slippery, Sam, China and Anne. Introduce yourselves.

'The victim was Milo,' he went on. 'Pseudonym. He was Slippery's snout. Ringo May. Eighteen.' He watched their faces.

'So far we have a glove with blood on it. It went to the lab this morning. We hope to match the blood to the body and get a print from the inside of the glove. The murder was on Bream Park as you know, which means witnesses will be few and far between. That being said, the AMIP team'll do the rounds. You've all got your action sheets.' He paused again. 'The Doc thinks Milo was killed by a sword. Long blade, thin and curved. His belly was ripped open. Death from organ damage and blood loss.' He paused. 'So who do we know with a sword?'

He scanned their faces. 'We also have excrement left on the floor. You've all seen it before. Adrenalin pumping. Nice to know he was human at least. He looked again at their faces. 'We've found traces of blood in it. Piles, maybe. Whatever. Anyway it's in Lambeth for DNA. It'll take a while, but we might get lucky. The name on the street is Denny,' he went on. 'Apart from Milo we have one other dealer. Irishman called Maguire.' He broke off for a moment. 'You've seen the Denny cartoon. We've got it on acid squares and E's. We don't know what it means or where it comes from. It's new though, which makes the dealers close to the source. In other words – a pretty flat organisation. In my opinion that counts Bobby Gallyon out as the source.' He glanced at Jimmy Crack. 'There is a connection however. We've got a face who's close to Bobby, and we know he supplied E's to a Tom called Lisa Morgan. For those of you who don't know the Gallyon family, they import coke. The RCS have been looking to nick them for years. The word is Gallyon's trying to introduce crack to the white community, to spread their operation to the lower end of the market. They're not known for E's or acid.' He paused again. 'We might get some political flak over Gallyon. Regional's pissed off because we've been stomping all over their plot.' He nodded to Jimmy Crack. '007 here's going to liaise, make sure feathers don't get too ruffled.'

He went on to tell them the rest of the story. 'AMIP take the estate,' he finished. 'Anne and Sammy – Maguire. We've asked the Post Office for a list of the boxes where they've issued two cards but they can't give us one. The two cards are only listed on the relevant file. We've got surveillance today and tomorrow. After that it's up to us.' He stopped talking again. 'As I said, it might be a long haul. The suspects are tenuous to say the least. But that's just how it is. You know the form. Platty's Office Manager. Use the 50/20's for intelligence info and get it fed into Holmes.'

Ryan and China followed him into the office. 'You two,' Vanner said. 'I want chapter and verse on Michael Terry. I want to know who he is, what he does and how he does it.' He closed the door behind them.

John Phillips junior chewed the end of a hotdog roll and wiped mustard from his lip. The food lay heavy in his gut but he knew he had to get something inside him. He stood by the wrinkled metal of the 'Wild Mouse' with his feet deep in the sand. Children squealed above him. He felt weak, sick all at once in his stomach. He sat down on the wall and dipped his head between his hands. He could not believe he was back here so soon. The last one had been easy but the bastards in the arches were getting wise to him. Three hundred quid. Barely enough for a score. Now he was broke again and worse than that, the last of his gear was gone. He could not stay in London. The mob from the Bull's Head were going to break his legs.

So he was back in this grockle filled, godforsaken place where nobody knew him and people were careless with their cars. He shivered again, despite the height of the sun. He thought about the car park. He hated fucking car parks, but the last one had been a cinch. He had to do it: his hair was filthy, his clothes filthy and this time he needed a big one. If he could just get a decent set of wheels, they'd have to pay him a wedge and then he'd be flying again. He looked out to sea, his stomach settling once more. Just this one and then maybe he'd quit.

Getting up, he felt in his pockets. The last of his change had gone with the hotdog. He shivered again. Extending his hands in front of him, he looked at how they were shaking. He hugged them under his armpits.

He wandered the sideroads along the seafront, trying to figure out whether or not to wait until later. Tonight was no good, the car park would be closed. It would have to be in daylight. And if it was in daylight, it might as well be now. He shook his head as he wandered nearer the centre. Never do the same place twice. At least not the same car park. So he wandered the streets and looked for other options.

An hour later he stood across the road from the car park, leaning with his back against the blacked-out window of the sex shop. The steps leading up were directly across the road and the weight of the levels ran out to span the dual carriageway. He pushed himself from the window and his heart began to thump. He crossed the road to the steps, and he went through the door, a policeman came out of the music shop.

He climbed to the third level. Last time had been the top, but that was open and he did not want to risk it again. He stood in the stairwell as shoppers passed him and he scanned the ranks of parked cars. Nothing stuck out immediately. He felt in his pocket for his keys, closing his fingers over the metal. It concentrated his mind, made him focus beyond the ache in his guts and the ripple of blood in his veins.

He moved among the cars massed side by side, hunks of quiet metal, dulled in the poor light that drifted through the open sides of the car park. Astra. Cavalier. Nothing to entice him. He made his way deeper into the lanes then something caught his eye. Soft-top BMW. 325 in red.

Behind him, the policeman stepped out of the stairwell.

John crouched by the side of the car. He touched the rim of the hood. He had a knife in his pocket but that would make his two grand fifteen hundred and he needed every penny. He worked away at the window.

Inside. The alarm going off and he was at the dashboard. Sudden footsteps behind him. He looked into the face of the policeman.

'Lost your key did you?'

* * *

121

Vanner pushed an empty trolley around the supermarket. Friday night men trailed after their wives with their children trailing after them, while tins and milk and bread and beer were stacked into the metal cask of their trolleys. He browsed among vegetables, picking up some pre-wrapped broccoli and putting it back again. He caught a glimpse of his reflection in the mirrored walls which dipped over the display cases. He could smell Lisa Morgan and it bothered him. A young couple moved behind him, laughing, pushing the trolley between them, loose arms about one another as if the supermarket was some kind of delicious aphrodisiac that surpassed all else on a Friday. Outside it was dark already, days growing ever shorter. He stared at the vegetables. A harassed-looking woman with greasy hair chastised her three children. He watched her. She stared for a moment before moving on. Leaving his empty trolley where it was, he walked back out to the car park.

The traffic was in his face. He listened to the news but all he could hear was the bickering of politicians and he switched the radio off. Tonight Jane was in his mind and he was sick of her. Nearly eleven years and still she could haunt him. Maybe if he had seen her again, replacing the last image he had of her, alone in their house on the base, when she sat there with tears in her eyes and a packed suitcase in the hall. Hair pulled back; gathered at the back of her neck so her face was full and high and perfect. Apart for the glistening of tears, that was exactly how she had looked the night she had seduced him in front of her father's fire.

Now she was married again, to Andrew Riley of all people, the best man at their wedding. Betrayal, bitter still on his tongue.

After Jane had gone he had remained there long enough to climb the stairs, look one last time at the rumpled mess that had been their bed and the remnants of the belongings she had left behind. A few of her clothes, oddments, some of the things he had bought her. He had gone downstairs then, closed the front door and got on a plane to Belfast. He had never been back. As far as he knew she had never been back. When the house was cleared he was sent a bundle of her belongings which he burnt, unopened, in a dustbin while the rest of the barracks was sleeping. That had been it. From then until now, nothing. Eleven years and he was left with an unfinished memory.

Ninja and The Wasp waited in the car park behind the Neasden Bail Hostel. Goldie played on the stereo. Across the road three lads were collecting money. The tallest one, dark hair, was squinting out of the window. He looked at the watch on his wrist. 'Come on. Come on,' he said. 'They won't sit there all night.' In the corner Sammy Johnson sat on his own, staring at the floor. Both his arms were in plaster. For a moment the dark-haired one glanced across at him, then looked back at the others. 'Will you shift your arses.' He moved to the door, the money in his hand. 'Where's Michaels?'

'Upstairs.' The smallest boy, with the lisp, said.

The dark-haired one nodded. 'Go up and make sure he stays there.'

Outside, The Wasp drummed his hands on the wheel. The dark-haired boy sprinted across the car park and dropped between the cars. Ninja leered at him. The dark-haired boy passed the money through the window.

'How much?' Wasp said.

'Seventy-five.'

'That's not very much.'

'It's all there is. There's only three of us now and Smithy's a waste of space.'

Ninja still stared at him.

The boy looked at The Wasp again. 'It's straight, Wasp. There is no more.'

The Wasp revved the engine. 'Do better. This don't even pay for the watch.'

Across the road the warden watched from an upstairs window. The car lurched out of the space and muscled its way into traffic. Michaels came out onto the landing and saw Tony Smith, the lisper, looking at him.

'Yes?'

'Er, washing-up, liquid, Sir. Where is it?'

'Under the sink where it always is.'

Downstairs, the other two were watching TV. Johnson sat on his own. Michaels looked at them, so casual in the chairs. 'You two,' he said. 'Go and help Tony with the dishes.' When they had gone, Michaels sat down in a chair. He looked at Johnson.

'Worried about court on Monday, Sammy?'

Johnson half-moved his head.

'Think you'll go down?'

'Dunno.'

'They'll wait till your arms are healed. Might even adjourn the case.'

Johnson did not say anything.

'You still don't want to tell me what happened?'

Johnson looked at the floor.

'Sammy?'

'I told you. I fell down the stairs.'

Ten

At the window, he watched the night sky arcing above street lights that set the stars in a haze. From here he could see the mass of the estate: the clouded, troubled buildings abutting the railway line. He was thinking about Maguire, so smug and cocky and sure of himself. But what did he know really? Vanner watching Maguire. It should not bother him: sooner or later a dealer grew careless and was watched. Maguire had grown careless, carried away with the money in his pocket and the reflection in the mirror. Dealers came and dealers went, like Ringo May, the corporate traitor, or even Sammy 'Greedy' Johnson for that matter. But with Vanner it was different. After what happened in March Vanner had a grudge of his own and that made him dangerous. Maybe he should delete Maguire. Not delete exactly, in the manner of Ringo May. Just take him out of the game. No more supply. Cut off the merchandise at a stroke. He could do that. His was the power. Sort of controlling the money supply.

Wasn't that how Friedman had put it? Take control of supply and let the market fend for itself. But what was the money supply? What was money except a row of digits on a screen or the weight of a plastic card in your wallet. Press a few buttons and you had as much money as you wanted. Friedman was only half right.

He could delete Maguire. He did not want to but he could. The first rule, survival. Expend the expendable. The likes of Maguire did not come easy however. Other money was tighter now. The hostels were doing less business. Only seventy-five from Neasden. Ringo May out of the game and Wembley vacant, ripe for another mover and shaker to take hold. The Boiler Room Gang minus Mickey Blondhair was, as yet, an unknown quantity. A pity too about Johnson. For all his other faults, Johnson had been a performer. But he could afford no mistakes. He could not risk Damien again. His instincts told him he was being attacked: not open and frontal, but the niggling shadow of a sniper.

He considered his options, sitting again at the desk with the headphones plugged in and music alive in his ears. Maybe the suits could go elsewhere and maybe he could find other markets. But he liked the thought of them popping his Ecstasy tablets. The pickups were a problem though. They were watching the box. He had seen them, the fools in their white Escort van with the clothing racks piled in the back. Maybe Vanner would grow bored of such vigilance and take out Maguire himself. Save him the bother of a decision. At least Ringo would be a deterrent. But the Maguires of this world were not that easy to come by. All very well for The Wasp to spread the word through the estates and pick up the odd street thief, or a dealer worthy of a box, but Maguire was a coup in himself.

He thought back to the old days when there had been the three of them, the brains and the brawn and the daring to recruit from the street. Now there was only him. One of them prattish enough to lose it one night and now paying for the consequences, albeit comfortably, with plenty of cash banked for his 'retirement'. Like so many others he had squandered opportunity. How many times had he seen that? A slip here, a slip there and then back to old ways and another missed opportunity. But one man's misfortune was another man's profit. For every winner there were half a dozen losers. Only the strong could survive. At least his silence was guaranteed.

But the third, he was a big-time loser. He should have spotted it years back and checked him once and for all. Loose cannon now, disappearing and reappearing and only the code to protect him.

He stood in the phone box and dialled. When the phone was answered he said: 'Vanner is watching you.' He could hear the

Irishman breathing on the other end of the line, faint and light but evident. He delighted in the power. Knowledge was power. Information was power. Real power.

'Who's Vanner?'

He laughed then. 'Drug Squad. Didn't you see him? He watched you dealing in Blake's bar.'

Maguire sucked breath. 'You were there?'

'Evidently.'

'I never saw you.'

'Fool,' he said. The fear was suddenly tangible, a charge coming down the line. 'He knows you have a box in Barnet.'

'Nothing's been delivered.'

'He knows all the same.'

'Doesn't that worry you?'

'Why should it worry me? Nothing's been delivered because I haven't delivered anything. Maybe it should worry you.'

'What d'you want me to do?'

'Do? Nothing. Leave it alone. You've got a watch. I'll contact you again when you're clear.'

'How long'll that be?'

'However long it takes.'

'But, shit. I've commitments. What'll I do for money?'

'Get a job.' He put down the phone.

John Phillips sat in his front room and waited for his wife to come home. He glanced at the window, recently fixed, and wondered how long it would be before it would need fixing again. The police had done nothing. But what could they do? He knew who they were of course, knew where they drank, but could prove nothing against them. His work was suffering. Some of the students were talking. He had heard them, in the refectory when they did not know he was there. If they were talking then some of the staff would be too. The worst of it was walking around with a fear in his gut that seemed to carve out the very middle of him. A fear for his son. A fear for the rest of his family. Anna was only fourteen and already she was terrified to go out on her own. But at least now John was safe. Not out of harm's way, but safe all the same.

The front door opened and his wife came in. She was unwinding the scarf from her head as he stepped into the hall. 'Mary,' he said, and she turned.

'What is it?'

'I know where John is.'

She almost visibly wilted, half-closing her eyes. 'Where?'

'A police station in Great Yarmouth. He was caught stealing a car.'

Vanner sat in his office. Outside the girls worked on the computers. He glanced through witness statements from Bream Park. Witness statements, no one had seen anything. Not a whisper. Not one word. He sat back, hands on his head and looked through the window at Wainwright. They had gleaned a print from the inside of the surgical glove, but had nothing in the records to match it.

Ryan and China came down the stairs and Ryan lifted a briefcase onto his desk. Vanner went through to the incident room. 'What've you got, Sid?'

'Enough.'

Vanner looked at the clock on the wall. 'Tell me about it over a pint.' He looked at Wainwright. 'You want a drink, Fred?'

Wainwright shook his head. 'I'll man the phones, Guv.'

They went to the Irish pub on the High Road. Vanner helped himself to Ryan's cigarettes.

'Terry runs a pretty mean business, Guv,' Ryan said. 'Got a yard in Dartford. Down by the new bridge.'

'I know about the yard. What does he do exactly?'

'Imports damaged plant, fixes it and sells it on again. Big stuff. Good money in it. Caterpillar mostly. Diggers, dump trucks, that kind of thing.'

Vanner lifted one eyebrow. 'There's money in that?'

'Lots of it, Guv'nor. Tell him, China.'

China rested massive arms on the table. 'The secondhand plant market is huge,' he said. 'Like Slippery says: diggers, lorries, excavators. Some of those big Cats are worth half a million apiece.'

'Where does he get them?'

'All over the world. Seems a lot of stuff gets damaged. It's sold off by insurance companies and generally ends up at auction.'

'Where?'

China smiled then. 'There's one big Auction house, Guv'nor. Merricks. They have one in the States, one here and a really big one in Amsterdam.'

Vanner looked at Ryan.

'Yes, Guv'nor. Spends a lot of time there too. He's been three times in the last two months.'

'Where else does he go?'

'The States.'

'Customs know about him?'

'Only as a plant dealer.' Ryan leaned his elbows on the table and took a long draught of his beer. 'He brings the kit in from Holland and then has spares shipped in from the States. Crates of engine parts. The bulk he uses – it saves him a fortune. They cost a packet if you go through the dealers.'

Vanner tore the edges off a beer mat. 'Holland and America.' He looked again at China. 'What does he do with the stuff when it's fixed?'

'Sells it on. Some in this country. Some of it goes to Israel. Some to South Africa. It all seems to come through Dartford though. He's got two rigid-body Cats in his yard now. That's a quarter of a million on the market. He seems to sell a lot to South America.'

'Where in South America?'

'Colombia mostly.'

Vanner sat back. 'Gallyon.'

Ryan lifted his hands. 'Deals big-time with Colombia according to Jimmy Crack and the Regional. But he imports, Guv. Not exports.'

Vanner looked at his empty glass and China went to the bar. Vanner leaned forward. 'You've been busy, Sid.'

'There's more. We've been digging into his past.'

'And?'

'Seems he was a serious City boy in the eighties. We reckon he's about thirty-eight. Started out as a stockbroker. From Romford originally. Sort of bloke Norman Tebbitt would've been proud of. You know – *Got on his bike*. Anyway, big-time braces boy. Made a few quid and then got into property. Some of the big development deals that were done in the late eighties.'

China set fresh drinks on the table.

'He went bust,' Vanner said.

Ryan shook his head. 'Not bust. Never bankrupt. Done for fraud. Not very serious when you consider some of them. It broke him though, lost a bloody great house in Hampstead and all the rest of his assets.' He sat forward. 'Had a wife and kid apparently. Upped and dumped them when things went wrong.' He paused for a moment and said: 'He's a good-looking bastard right?'

'Yeah. So?'

'So, when it all went wrong he cleared off with this sort from a record company. Samantha Clay. President of one of the UK subsidiaries of a Yank parent company. Anyway he dumped said wife and kid, shagged this Clay bird a few times and Bingo, he's playing again.'

'What happened to her?'

'Don't know, Guv. But she's not on his arm any more.'

Back in the incident room Anne was sitting with McCleod. Pierce was there, a DC from AMIP, who had been back out to the Estate. He stood up as Vanner came in. Vanner nodded to him and looked back at Ryan. 'Get onto the record companies, Slippery. I want to find this Clay woman.' He looked back at Pierce. 'What've you got?'

'I think I've got a car, Guv'nor.'

Pierce told him he had taken a statement from an old man who had seen two men driving away from the estate at four o'clock on the morning of the murder. He could not sleep and had been making a cup of tea in his kitchen. He had no number but the car had been grey or silver and he thought it was a BMW. He had seen the two men however, although not clearly. One was black and the other white. Both had very long hair.

Vanner leaned a fist on the table. 'Nice one, Pierce,' he said. 'How'd you get him to talk?'

Pierce shrugged. 'Just knocked on his door, Guv.'

Vanner lifted one eyebrow. 'That's a first for Bream Park. Someone prepared to say something.'

'Old school,' Pierce said. 'From Jamaica in the fifties. Pentecostal church and all that. You know the type.'

'Isn't he worried that someone might have a go?'

'Trusts in the Lord.' Pierce made a face. 'Says he's never seen the car before. Bit of a watcher. Sees most things he reckons.'

Vanner sat on the edge of the desk. 'Somebody coming in from outside? Must be bloody sure of themselves.'

'I've got him coming down in the morning. We're going to look at some pictures. Don't know how reliable he's going to be mind. He's knocking on a bit.'

'Show him all the pictures you want.'

Anne stuck her head around Vanner's door. 'We've lost surveillance again, Guv. Can't do anything till Friday.'

Vanner shook his head wearily.

'I don't think it matters really. Plot's waste of space. Maguire hasn't been near the box. I've talked to the teller. Nothing's been delivered or collected for at least a couple of weeks.'

Vanner drew up his brows. It was two weeks since this investigation began, two weeks since he had spoken to Lisa Morgan. He stared at the wall and wondered. Ryan tapped on the door. 'Samantha Clay, Guv. The lady boss of the record company. She isn't a boss any more.'

'Got an address?'

'Maida Vale.'

Vanner nodded. 'We'll talk to her tomorrow.'

John Phillips' mother looked across the interview room at her son. His face was pale, thin in the cheek with dark hollows crawling beneath his eyes. He needed feeding. She fought all at once with her tears. 'Why, John?' she said.

He chewed hard at his nails, looked at the floor then at his father. 'You getting hassle from them, Dad?'

His father opened his mouth to speak and his wife's glance burned his cheek. 'You just worry about yourself, lad. I can take care of the rest.'

'How much do you owe, John?' his mother asked him.

'Five grand.'

She sat back and looked at him.

'They bothering you for it?'

She took his hands and squeezed. 'Don't worry about us, son. We're just glad you're safe.'

'How's Anna?' John said. 'They threatened to do things to Anna.'

'Anna's fine,' his father said. 'She's with your Nan.'

'Nan. Jesus. I haven't seen her in ages.'

'She's fine too.'

'Must be her birthday soon.'

'Next week.'

John nodded, thumb once more at his lip. 'Get her a card or something from me will you. Tell her I'm sorry.' He looked back at his mother and his seventeen-year-old face suddenly showed all of its youth. 'I am sorry, Mum.'

The constable stirred at the door. Phillips looked up at him. 'Just a few more minutes please.'

The constable nodded and moved back again. Phillips said: 'What happens to you now?'

'Magistrate's court in the morning.'

'Will you get bail?'

John sighed. 'I doubt it. I was already on bail remember.'

His father sat back. He could feel the frustration welling up inside him. There was nothing he could do. This was his son and there was nothing at all he could do.

'They reckon I'll get remanded someplace.'

'Where?'

'Norwich Prison probably.'

His mother passed a hand across her face and now she did sob. John leaned forward but she held up a palm. 'I'm all right,' she said.

His father looked him in the eye. 'You can handle it, son.'

John suddenly grinned. 'If you can't do the time don't do the crime.' His mother took his hands in hers again. 'We'll visit you.'

He nodded. 'Are you going back now – to London, I mean?'

His father shook his head. 'We'll book into a guesthouse. Be there to support you tomorrow.'

Terry undressed Lisa. Normally he liked to watch her undress herself, but he wanted control tonight. He stood in front of her and unbuttoned her shirt, slowly, one-handed, the other tightened in a fist at his side. He pulled her shirt clear of one shoulder, revealing her breast, the nipple puckering beneath the movement of his fingers. He squeezed hard and smiled. When she was naked he stepped back and looked at her, his nostrils flaring slightly.

She stood there, legs arched and firm in black high-heeled shoes, the muscles standing out against the scattered gooseflesh of her thighs. Terry felt himself stiffen. The curve of her hips, the flat of her belly, nipples hard now, erect under his gaze. She moved towards him then let her hand fall across his groin. The muscles tensed in his own legs. Lisa unbuckled his trousers then she took him in her mouth.

Later, she moved about his bedroom, naked save her shoes. She hugged herself though it was warm. Paintings hung from the walls, huge original canvases from Japan and Mexico and Spain. Terry lay back on the bed. He sipped champagne and watched her. 'You like my house?'

'Expensive.' She trailed her fingers over the dark wood of the Peruvian box at the end of the bed. 'You must make a lot of money.'

He felt himself stirring again. 'I do.'

'You do business with Bobby?'

'You ask a lot of questions.'

She looked at him. 'Would you rather I just lie back and think of England?'

'I'd rather you shut up. I'd rather you came over here.'

He strapped her ankles to his bed with two neckties, forcing her face down against the sheet. Then he took his belt and with a sneer creasing his mouth he buckled her round the neck. For a moment she gagged. He eased the pressure and then he tightened again.

'I can't breathe.'

'Shut up.'

'Michael. I can't breathe.'

'Shut the fuck up.'

With the free end of his belt he fastened her wrists behind her back, hauling tight so her shoulder blades punched against the skin. Her head was forced right up, like a horse in a bearing rein. She tried to cry out but her voice was lost in her throat. Terry stood up, kicked away his clothes and masturbated over her face.

She sat on the edge of the bed, her back to him and massaged her forearms where his belt had bitten her. She touched her neck where it was raw and felt the indentation of the buckle. He lay on his belly, trailing patterns in the carpet with his fingers.

'You hurt me.'

'You can handle it.'

'You never hurt me before.'

'I know you better now.'

'Hurting me is extra.'

He pushed himself up on his elbow and swigged from the glass of champagne. Then he took his wallet from where it lay on top of his discarded trousers and peeled off a ream of notes. He tossed them at her and they fluttered against her breasts. 'Get dressed,' he said. 'And get out.'

Frank Weir had a drink with Morrison. Double Bacardi with ice and no coke. Morrison sipped at a pint of bitter. Weir took the gum from his mouth and pasted it under the table. 'Vanner's got a snout called

Jabba,' he said. 'Indian fella. Apparently Christian Tate's been shooting his mouth off about Vanner in a Croydon pub.'

Morrison looked at him. 'You're well-informed.'

'I get about.'

'Who's Christian Tate?'

'Brother of the bloke Vanner killed in that warehouse.'

'Ah,' Morrison remembered the properties log in Hammersmith from a year ago.

'I reckon Vanner might be thinking that Tate's behind the mugging.' Weir looked at Morrison. 'That's the only reason he came back.'

'I know.'

Weir shook his head. 'Not much of a reason for being a copper is it.'

'So far he's walked the line. And you know McCague's behind him.'

'Yeah. McCague.' Weir sipped his drink, swirled the ice around and sipped again. 'I was on the Squad with McCague.'

'You rate him?'

'Top man.'

'He's always backed Vanner.'

'Vanner's a maverick. They have their supporters. Man like McCague – solid, reliable. Someone like Vanner lets him breathe now and again.'

'You don't like him?'

'Vanner?' Weir lifted an eyebrow. 'Squaddie wasn't he. Too gung-ho for me. You see it with the boys on 19. Guv'nors are all right, but some of the young ones . . .' He twisted his lip. 'Vanner's one of them after all.'

Morrison bought more drinks. He looked at his watch. He never usually drank at lunchtime. He was supposed to be home early today too. He had promised Jean he would look after the boys. But Weir drank at lunchtimes. He always walked out sober. But he liked to drink at lunchtimes.

'What about the Tom?' Weir looked sideways at him. 'He got her registered?'

'No.'

'But he's talking to her?'

'I don't know. He doesn't tell me very much.'

'My boys working out okay on the Milo deal?'

Morrison looked sideways at him. 'You mean you don't know?'

Weir grinned then. 'What about the Gallyon connection? From what I hear Burke is one unhappy man.'

Morrison moved in his seat. 'There's always politics with the Regional. Unfortunately I find myself allied to Vanner on this one, Frank. I need a result here. Career is on hold till I get one.'

Samantha Clay looked all of her forty-eight years. She had short-cut hair dyed to auburn and crow's feet bunched at her eyes. She sat on a leather couch with her feet drawn up and sipped tea from a china cup. Vanner sat opposite her. Ryan in the seat alongside. Vanner stirred his tea. 'Thank you for seeing us,' he said.

'My pleasure, Inspector. I don't think I've ever been visited by the police before.'

'First time for everything,' Ryan said.

She looked at him and smiled, then she picked up Vanner's card where it lay on the coffee table. 'Drug Squad?' She lifted her eyebrows. 'I gave all that up years ago.'

'You're the one,' Ryan said.

Vanner put his cup and saucer on the table and looked at her. 'You know a Michael Terry, Ms Clay?'

Her face clouded and she sat up straighter. 'I did.'

Vanner cocked his head to one side. 'Forgive me,' he said. 'Your tone. Not a happy memory?'

She looked at him then, and gathered her blouse where it was loose at her neck. 'Why're you asking about him?'

'You see him now?'

She shook her head. 'No,' she said. 'I don't.'

'But you did.'

'Once upon a time. Why d'you want to know?'

Vanner glanced at Ryan. 'Just routine. A few questions that's all.'

She looked again at his card. 'What's he done exactly?'

Ryan moved in his seat. 'We don't know that he's done anything.'

'No? Then why're you here?'

'His name's cropped up in an inquiry.'

She looked at him and smiled. 'And that's all you're going to tell me.'

'When did you last see him?' Vanner asked her.

'Years ago.'

'Not recently then?'

She shook her head. 'What's all this about, Inspector? You think he's dealing in drugs?'

Vanner looked away from her. 'We don't know,' he said. 'We're trying to get some background on him. You know – talking to people he knew.' He opened his hands.

'How well did you know him?'

'He used to be my stockbroker.'

'Advised you on investments?'

She looked back at him. 'I used to make money, Inspector.'

'Not any more?'

'Something else I gave up.'

Vanner sipped tea. 'You had a purely professional relationship?'

'I don't think that's any of your business.'

Vanner smiled. 'What did he do for you, exactly – the investments, I mean?'

She tipped back her head, hand touching her neck. 'He was a good broker. Used to work with another man, James somebody. He left the company though. Went off on some other venture. Reinsurance or something.' She shook her head. 'It was a long time ago.'

'How long ago?' Ryan asked her.

'When I first met him? Eight years.'

'He left the City didn't he,' Vanner said. 'Why did he do that? I thought brokers could print money in the eighties.'

'They could. He was always very ambitious though. I think he wanted a higher profile than just a dealing house. He went into property.'

'Along with the rest of the world,' Ryan said. 'Tell me about it. Negative equity and all.'

Vanner said: 'He was into property in a big way?'

'He was for a while. All went horribly wrong though. Some of those deals in the docklands. Plc's were tumbling.'

'We arrested him,' Vanner said. 'Fraud Squad.'

'He claimed it wasn't his fault.'

'Defrauding shareholders?'

'His back was to the wall. He was just looking to survive.'

'At someone else's expense.'

She looked at him. 'That's the nature of business, Inspector. Every winner has a loser. Sometimes the rules got forgotten.'

'Maggie's farm.' Ryan shook his head. 'Mind if I smoke, Ms Clay?'

She indicated the ashtray.

Vanner crossed his ankle on his knee. 'So Terry had a property company?'

'He had a dozen companies, Inspector. I think he liked the feeling of power it gave him.'

Ryan squinted at her then. 'You don't like him do you?'

'Not very much. No.'

Ryan glanced at Vanner. 'We don't like him either. Or at least we don't think we do. Trouble is we don't really know him. What we need is someone who can tell us about him, I mean what he's like as a bloke.'

She picked up Vanner's card once more. '*Is* he dealing drugs?'

'We don't know. But we'd really like to find out.'

For a few moments nobody spoke, then Vanner said: 'Were you involved with him?'

She looked at the floor. 'For a while I was, yes.'

He nodded. 'We don't want to pry into your private life, Ms Clay. But if there's anything you can tell us . . .'

She did not say anything.

'He went bust didn't he.'

'Not exactly. He was never declared bankrupt or anything.'

'He lost all his money though.'

'He lost everything. House in Hampstead. Cars. A boat. You name it.'

'And then he came to you?'

Again she looked away from him. 'He left his wife and child. I always regretted that.'

'You had a relationship then,' Ryan said it gently.

She tugged her lip with her teeth. 'For a while we did, yes.'

'What's he like?' Vanner asked her. 'What's he like as a person?'

She looked him in the eye. 'He's a class-A bastard. The very worst kind. He's a user. Manipulator. Liar.'

'He lied to you?'

'Of course he lied to me. Soft words in my ear. The kind of thing a silly, forty-year-old woman falls for.' She sat back again. 'He smoothed his way into my life, my house, my bed. Left a wife and child to fend for themselves. Then – when he got what he wanted – he was gone. Nothing. Zilch. Kaput. Just upped and walked away.' She laughed. 'Oh, I should've seen the signs. He walked away from his family with not so much as a backward glance.' She looked down at the floor.

Vanner watched her. 'How did he get started again?'

'I funded him. I mean totally. I was so stupid. I handed him money on a plate. He set himself up and off he went. He has a yard in Dartford with no mortgage. Well if there is one it's small. I think he borrowed against the cash I gave him at first, but he seems to have moved on since then.'

Vanner looked at Ryan.

'He got back in touch with his friend. The one I told you about. Apparently between them they came up with some scheme. Importing stuff I think. I don't know much about the business. But he seems to have done pretty well.'

'You ever see him now?' Vanner said.

'No. I haven't laid eyes on him since he walked out of my house in 1991. We were together for only a year.'

'The friend's firm,' Vanner said. 'Does it have a name?'

'I've got a card somewhere. I'll get it for you before you go.' She looked at Vanner then.

'What's he done, Inspector?'

Vanner looked back at her. 'We really don't know yet.'

'His wife and kid,' Ryan said. 'You say he just dumped them?'

'Yes. That's the bit I regret the most. But then again – if it hadn't been me it would've been somebody else.'

'D'you know where they are now?'

She looked at him then. 'Kentish Town. Some ghastly council monstrosity. One of those fifties estates. Warrens of flat running everywhere.'

Back in the incident room, Vanner looked at the business card Samantha Clay had given him. *Glendale & Watts Reinsurance House*. The name 'James Bentt' was inscribed underneath. He handed the card to Ryan. 'See what you can find out,' he said.

'The estate, Guv,' Ryan said. 'Where Terry's wife and kid live. She told us it's in Kentish Town.'

Vanner nodded. 'Milo made a call to a box in Kentish Town.'

'He did, yeah. Just after we set him up.'

Vanner went through to his office and sat down. He thought about Samantha Clay and he thought about Michael Terry. A few minutes later Ryan pushed open the door, the business card in his hand.

'James Bentt's on his honeymoon, Guv. A month in the Caribbean.'

Vanner shook his head. 'All right for some.'

'There's other directors though. You want to speak to them?'

'Who are they?'

Ryan looked at the note in his hand. 'Bloke called Phelps, another called Simon Smith and a guy called Andrew Riley. You want me to talk to them or d'you want to wait for Bentt?'

Vanner was looking beyond him. He held out his hand for the card. 'I'll do it,' he said.

Eleven

Vanner sat on the floor in the hallway of his house with the telephone between his knees and James Bentt's business card in his hand. Outside the workmen were packing up for the day. He phoned Lisa Morgan. He stared at Bentt's office number but he phoned Lisa Morgan. 'It's me, Lisa. Vanner.'

For a moment she was silent and then she said: 'What do you want?'

He stared at Bentt's card. 'I wanted to talk to you.'

'What about?'

'Michael Terry.'

She was silent, then: 'You asked me for his name and I gave it to you.'

'I know. But I need to talk to you again.'

'Talk to somebody else.' The phone clicked dead in his ear.

He waited a few minutes and then he called her back. 'If you want to book some time – why don't you just ask?'

'Not that kind of time.'

'That's the only time I do. If it's conversation you want get a wife.'

'I had a wife.'

'She left you? You surprise me.'

He was silent, then: 'Are you working tonight?'

'What's it got to do with you?'

He paused. 'I want to see you, Lisa.'

'I've got nothing more to say, Vanner. We had a deal. I kept my part. Now leave me alone.'

* * *

He parked his car in the permit zone and locked it. Cold tonight, stars lifting above street lights, seizing the sweat of a city. His footsteps sounded hollow as he made his way beyond the barrier. Behind him, he could see the lights of the upstairs gym and the bodies pumping iron inside. In the concourse he pressed her bell.

'Yes?'

'Vanner.'

'Go away.'

'I want to see you.'

'I said, go away.'

He pressed the bell again, waited a few moments longer and then the door clicked in front of him.

She had left her front door ajar. He let himself in and closed it. Music drifted as part of the atmosphere. Even from the hall he could smell her. She sat in a chair, dressed in a lightweight bathrobe. Her hair was piled on her head and a silk scarf wound about her throat. She stared at him. He stood there, awkward under her gaze.

'What d'you want Vanner? You said you would leave me alone.'

'I know. I'm sorry.' He sat down opposite her.

'No you're not. Don't say you're sorry when you're not. You're not the kind of man to be sorry.'

He sat back and unbuttoned his jacket. It was very warm in the room. The atmosphere with a slightly rarefied quality to it, damp almost, the remnants of a bath perhaps. She picked up a brandy glass and sipped from it. He studied her; face closed, eyes full of darkness.

'I want you to tell me about Terry,' he said.

'There's nothing more to say. You asked if he gave me the tablets. I told you he did.'

He looked at her then: face still, eyes intent upon his. He looked away again.

'If you want to fuck me just say so. I'm sure we can work something out.'

'I don't want to fuck you.'

'Just as long as you're sure.'

He looked at her again. She had half-lifted one knee, drawing her foot up the settee towards her, the robe fell away from her thigh.

He poured himself a drink and stood by the empty fireplace. He watched her holding her glass, slim painted fingers, long and fine and delicate. He took out his cigarettes and shook the pack at her. She nodded. He lit two and handed her one. She took it without speaking. As she did so, the sleeve of her robe slipped up her arm and he saw purple marks, stretching down to her wrist.

He sat down and indicated her arm with his glass. 'Terry do that did he?'

She looked away from him.

'Last night was it? Likes it rough now does he?'

'What he likes is none of your business.'

'No? I think it might be.' He stared at her for a moment. 'Did he talk to you?'

She looked him in the eye. 'He fucks me. He pays for it. He's not there for conversation.'

'So he says nothing.'

'I just told you.'

They were quiet for a moment, Vanner watching the naked skin of her thigh. She smiled at him then, cocked her head slightly and touched her lips with her tongue. He looked away from her. 'Has he offered you any more E's?'

She shook her head.

'Acid?'

'I don't do acid.'

'He's never offered it though.'

'No.'

'I got the possession charge dropped, Lisa.'

'Don't say you want me to thank you.'

He finished his drink. 'Does he ever tell you about his business?'

'He says he imports things and sells them. He goes abroad quite a bit.'

'Does he bring you presents?'

'No. But sometimes he phones me and I bring him off down the line. Is that what you wanted to know?'

He got up then and moved across to her. She watched him. He dropped to one knee, looked in her eyes and then reached for her hand. He took it gently, holding her gaze. She did not say anything, did not resist. He eased back the sleeve and looked at the bruising. Slowly she withdrew her hand.

He stood up. '*Did* Terry do that to you?'

She flicked ash in the direction of the bowl on the table.

'Lisa?'

She looked up now and a light was back in her eyes. 'What do you care, Vanner? I'm a hooker, a Tom. I can look after myself.'

Vanner lifted his cigarette to his lips. 'Ecstasy and power games.' He shook his head. 'Nasty bastard.'

'You'd know eh?'

He could feel a tightness in his chest. They sat for a moment in silence. Lisa finished her drink and offered him the glass. 'Get me another one. Will you?' Vanner got up, poured a large measure and gave the glass back to her. As he did so their fingers touched. She held the glass to her chest, not looking at him. He remained where he was for a moment, then slowly, almost forcing himself, he moved away from her.

'How old are you, Lisa?' Why it mattered he did not know, but in that moment it did. She looked up at him. 'Twenty-six.'

Jane had left him when she was twenty-six. That made Jane thirty-seven now.

'Why?' she said.

'No reason.'

'Worried about me, Inspector?'

He did not say anything.

'I don't think so – do you? You've got a bulge in your pants.'

Vanner stared at her then, eyes cold, mouth set in a line. She moved her foot back and forward along the settee, the robe riding higher on her thighs. He glimpsed the darkness of pubic hair.

'Why d'you do it?' he said.

144

'Do what?'

'Screw people for money.'

'Because I'm very good at it.'

He swirled the whiskey in the bottom of his glass. '*Did* Terry talk last night?'

'That's not what you want to know.' She sat up now and faced him, breasts pushing at the material of her robe.

He looked again at her forearms. 'What'd he do – tie you up?'

'Maybe.'

'Do you like him?'

'He's a punter. Why should I like him?'

Vanner finished his drink and lit another cigarette. 'Bobby Gallyon know he likes it rough?'

'Why would he care?'

'Damaged goods, Lisa.'

She drew on her cigarette and blew the smoke at him. 'I'll heal, Vanner.'

'What's the deal between them?'

'I haven't got a clue.'

'Bobby bringing in the E's?'

'You tell me.'

'Bobby's into coke, Lisa. Not E's. Terry bringing in E's?'

She stared coldly at him then. 'You talking to me or just thinking aloud?'

She stood up and her robe hung open. Vanner felt a swelling in his throat, mouth suddenly drying. He drank whiskey but that only dried it some more. She unwrapped the scarf from her neck and showed him the marks from Terry's buckle.

'He tied me to the bed, Vanner. That's what you want to know isn't it? Silk ties round my ankles.' She pointed. 'Here and here.' She moved towards him, the robe suddenly wide. 'He tied his belt round my neck.' Her face was cold now, eyes dark. She was standing right in front of him. He could see her, smell her; moist, warm woman. She traced the line of his nose with one finger and dragged the nail across his lip. 'He likes to hurt me Vanner.'

He sat where he was, hunched to the edge of the settee. She

moved her face close to his ear. 'You didn't come to talk about Terry giving me drugs. You already know about that. You came to find out what he does to me.'

Still he sat there, both hands gripping his glass, the scent of her all over him. He did not say anything, eyes averted, the echo of her words in his head.

'You'd like to do it to me wouldn't you, Vanner. Dominate me. Tie me up. Hurt me. You're here because you're almost jealous of him.'

He stood up then. Her words against his back, her breath on his neck. She moved around him, gown open, moisture lining her skin. 'Want to hurt me, Vanner? Like to hurt women do you? That why your wife left you?'

He turned then and stared into her eyes. He took a pace towards her.

'That's it, Vanner. Now we're getting to it.'

He stopped, fist clenched at his side.

'Come on. Why not. Maybe I'll make it a freebie.'

He felt sweat creep on his brow. Lisa moved closer to him. She brushed her fingers over his crotch. 'You want to fuck me don't you. Fuck me really hard. You think that's what women like.'

He wanted to move, go, say something. But he just stood there.

'This isn't about drugs, Vanner. This isn't about Terry. It's about you.'

And then he was pushing her back, forcing her down on the couch, fingers tearing at her robe. He brushed himself against her . . . neck, breasts; the nipples taut between his teeth. He kissed her hard on the mouth, deeper and deeper, one hand at his belt, the other between her legs. Then he was inside her, penetrating, forcing the faintest of gasps from her lips. She held him by his hair and looked him in the eyes while he fucked her.

He caught sight of his reflection in her bedroom mirror as he dressed. She lay on the bed, skin flushed red, and watched him.

'Why *did* she leave you – your wife?'

He stared at her in the mirror. 'That's nothing to do with you.'

'You did hurt her then.'

'No.'

'What then?'

'I was a soldier. She didn't like it when I killed people.'

'And now you hate women.'

'I don't hate women.'

'Yes you do, Vanner.'

He bent and lifted his shirt from the chair.

'How d'you get those scars on your back?'

'Somebody didn't like me.'

'Must be catching.'

He looked over his shoulder at her. 'How much do you want?'

'You can put it on account. I'm sure you'll be back.'

Mickey Blondhair dealt Denny acid squares in the bicycle sheds at school. Black kids, white kids, Asian kids. So much cheaper than an E at five quid a square. So much easier than thieving. Different buzz all right, but a hell of a lot easier. He stood among the triple-locked mountain bikes and took a fiver a time for the squares. Party tonight. Only dinnertime and already he had fifty quid in his pocket. A couple of Bangladeshi lads smoked cigarettes at the far end of the shed and watched the school buildings for him. They were older than he was – Ranjit was almost sixteen and here he was, indirectly working for him. Ranjit looked round suddenly and signalled to him by flapping his arm up and down.

Mickey stuffed the padded envelope down his pants. He stood on tiptoes and looked over the lip of the wall where the corrugated iron roof did not quite meet it. Walker, the PE teacher, was making his way across the playground towards them. It was almost time for the bell to go. Picking up his bag, Mickey made his way to the far end of the shed and slipped out of the gate. He shouldered the bag and walked the short distance to the other gate, then he went back into school as if he had just come back from dinner. He grinned to himself. Him dealing Dennies. So much easier than whacking people at cashpoints. In the pocket of his jacket, he fingered the tiny set of collapsible Tanita scales that he did not need but liked to have on him anyway. That's what dealers carried.

Vanner looked at Pierce. 'Nothing?'

'Not so far, Guv. We've been around the square but he doesn't recognise any of them.'

Vanner sat back and nodded. 'Okay,' he said. 'Keep trying. Any of the others come up with anything?'

'Bream Park's a wall, Guv. Apart from the old man it always was.'

When he had gone, Vanner placed both hands behind his head and looked at Ryan.

'Weir knows about Tate, Guv.' Ryan looked at him as he rolled a cigarette. 'That means the old man'll know.'

Vanner stared at him. 'I didn't even know you knew.'

'Word gets around.' Ryan pinched the threads of his cigarette. 'You reckon it was Tate who hit you?'

'He had enough reason to. Biggest grudge in my cupboard.'

Ryan nodded. 'Guess you've been churning things over in there eh?'

'Bound to aren't I.'

'You still think it was more than a mugging then?'

'Wouldn't you? They left my pockets alone.'

Ryan shrugged. 'Disturbed though weren't they.'

'They were, but only by a car.' Vanner shook his head. 'Beating was planned, Sid. Systematic. You get to know the difference.'

Ryan lit his cigarette and blew smoke at the ceiling. 'You want to pay the ex-Mrs Terry a visit?'

Vanner nodded and got up.

Ryan drove, Vanner next to him, bunched up in the seat. They headed east towards Kentish Town. 'Guv'nor, far be it for a lowly DS to give advice – but you want to watch it with Tate. If he squeals harassment – Morrison'll have a new IO for this deal before you can spit.' Ryan looked sideways at him as he said it. Vanner stared at the traffic through the windscreen. 'It isn't Tate,' he said quietly.

'You know?'

'I can feel it.' He shifted his position. 'Went down there the night Milo was killed.'

'I thought you were with a bird.'

'Chance'd be a fine thing. I sat in the Black Bell pub in Croydon and watched him with his cronies. He's milking the old days, Sid. You know: South London hard man whose brother was shot by a copper. Bunch of kids around him.'

Ryan nodded. 'Maybe you ought to let it alone then, Guv.' He shifted gear. 'Maybe you *were* just picked on. It happens. Hell, who needs a motive in this day and age. Lot of shit goes down where you got smacked. You've got Somerstown and all those Bangladeshi boys. White kids in Euston, just across the road. You take a chance wherever you go. Lad got stabbed for just being there. They never nicked anything from *him* either.'

Vanner glanced at him. 'You think that's how it was?'

Ryan shrugged. 'Well it wouldn't be the first time. Would it?'

Vanner looked forward again. Maybe Ryan was right. Maybe they all were. With all the random, motiveless violence in this city they were much more likely to be right than he was. He did not want to admit it though. It had been his reason for coming back. But then was that really the case? Or was it the only way he could justify the ignominy of taking a step backwards. Maybe his father was right. Maybe McCague was too. No other place to go, and this way, at least, he felt as though he could deal with it.

They drove along Leith Road and Vanner glimpsed a scrawl of white paint on a wall. *868,000 empties in the UK. Homes for all.* The building behind it was derelict. Ryan parked the car outside a row of shops, across the road from the Kirstall Council Estate. This whole area was a warren of flats, some high-rise, some only five floors but spilling out to the street in either direction. The estate was bordered by a small side road of terraced houses which cut an L-shape into the bowels of the station. Beyond the houses an old factory had been split into industrial lofts where young girls churned out cheap Indian saris for some obscene rate per hour.

The ex-Mrs Terry lived in Montgomery House. It was the first block that bordered the road. Vanner and Ryan stood by the car and Ryan gestured to the telephone box. They walked up to it and Ryan checked the number. He came out and nodded to Vanner.

'Let's get a cup of tea,' Vanner said.

They bought two tall mugs of tea from an Indian woman in the café directly across from the estate. Three Irishwomen, with half a dozen teeth and two shopping trolleys between them, smoked cigarettes until the air was thick with it. They coughed and cackled like witches, grey hair faded to blonde by cheap dye and nicotine. Vanner sat with his back to them and stared across at the buildings. The tables were chipped and old and as cheap as the tea before them. On one wall a picture, a small symmetrical water-colour. He stared at it: empty beach, calm blue sea and a paradise isle in the distance.

Ryan sipped his tea and spooned in more sugar. 'You reckon she'll tell him, Guv?'

Vanner shrugged. 'Depends on how much she hates him. We don't even know if she sees him.'

'We don't exactly have much do we. Pierce's witness is a waste of space.'

Vanner looked at him. 'At least we've got him. That's a first for Bream Park.'

'What have we got though really? Couple of geezers getting into a jam jar at four in the morning. So what. No one sleeps on that estate.'

'One black and one white. Long hair.'

'A million geezers, Guv'nor.'

'You always this cheerful, Sid? Or is it only when you're with me?'

They climbed stone steps to the fifth floor of the first block. From somewhere in the belly of the building House music blared. Vanner could hear the sound of a baby crying. The stairs stank of beer and no sunlight, the walls sprayed over with paint. From the balcony of the fifth floor they could see the windows of the loft units, the whirr of sewing machines lifting from within. Number 40 was the second-last door on the landing. Vanner checked the slip of paper in his pocket and pressed the bell.

The door was opened, but only as far as the chain would allow. 'Yes?' A woman's voice. Vanner could barely make her out in the darkness 'Jennifer Carr?'

'I don't need a loan.'

'I'm not selling one. Police, Ms Carr.'

The door was opened fully and the woman looked up at him. Dark hair, tousled about her face, the cords of a dressing gown drawn tightly about her.

'What is it – not Mark? Nothing's happened?'

Vanner shook his head. 'Nothing's happened, Ms Carr. We'd just like a few words with you. That's all.'

She ushered them through to the lounge. It was neat if sparsely furnished. A photograph of a dark-haired boy dominated the mantelpiece. He was not smiling.

'I work nights.' She yawned, easing the hair from her face.

'We got you up?' Ryan said. 'Sorry.'

She flapped a hand at him, yawning still. 'Don't worry about it. Mark'll be home for his lunch soon anyway.'

'Your son?' Vanner nodded to the picture.

'Yes.' She hugged herself. 'Can I get you tea or anything?'

Vanner shook his head.

She went through to put some clothes on. Vanner scanned the lounge. It was tidy enough but he could see traces of damp crawling under the window frame. Ryan was looking at the photograph. Vanner glanced at the furnishings. Two armchairs, an old settee. TV and video. Ryan looked over at him. '*Where* did they live before?'

'Hampstead.'

She came back through, wearing jeans and a light pullover. 'If it's not about Mark then what is it about?'

Vanner showed her his warrant card. 'I'm DI Vanner, Ms Carr. North West London Drug Squad.'

She eyed him then, taking half a step back. 'Mark's not into

151

drugs. He's a very bright boy. He goes to college. He wouldn't be into drugs.'

'We're not here to ask you about your son,' Vanner said. 'We want to know about your husband.'

'I don't have one.' She sat down and indicated for them to do the same. Ryan squatted on the edge of a chair. Vanner stood with his back to the window.

'You were Mrs Terry though. Mrs Michael Terry?'

She nodded. 'For my sins.'

'His name's cropped up in an inquiry. It's just routine,' Vanner said. 'A few questions.'

'What's he done?' Eagerness chafing her tongue.

Vanner looked at her. 'Like I said – it's just routine.'

'He's a bastard. Biggest shit I ever clapped eyes on. He's a bully and a liar and a cheat.'

She dropped her gaze. 'Sorry.'

Ryan looked at her. 'He left you?'

She nodded. 'Went bust. Lost everything. Home, cars, the lot. He left *us*, yes. Me and my twelve-year-old son. We went from a five-bedroomed house in Hampstead to this. He cleared off with some tart from a record company who was old enough to be his mother. Now he lives in a penthouse in Blackfriars, just so he can keep an eye on the City. What else d'you want to know?'

Vanner looked at Ryan. 'Where d'you work, Ms Carr?'

'I clean offices in the West End. Six nights a week. It just about keeps us going. What with that and the family credit.'

'He doesn't give you money?'

'He gives Mark money. Now. CSA finally got to him.' She stared at the window. 'For three years he didn't even set eyes on him. Then one day he swans in here with an armful of presents as if nothing has happened. He always did think he could buy his way into everything.'

'How does Mark get on with him?'

'I think he hated him at first. But every boy needs his father.'

She stood up then and went to the mantelpiece where she picked up the photograph. 'He's the only decent thing that

Michael Terry's been involved in. He's a good boy. Bright. You know he's way ahead of his class.'

'What does he study?'

'Business and politics and maths. He's going to get A's at A-level. Then he's going to university. His father's no more than a barrow boy.'

She replaced the photograph. 'You haven't arrested him again then?'

Vanner squinted at her. 'Again?'

'You must know about it. He was done for fraud five years ago. More misery.'

'Misery?'

'Stealing people's lives, Inspector. That's what he does. He's a callous, greedy bastard. What he wants he gets, no matter who gets stamped on.' Her face was pale and bitter, the line of her lips barely a mark in her face. She looked at the picture of her son again and then back at Vanner. 'I'm sorry.' She held up a hand. 'It's just . . .' She shook her head, then sat down on the settee. 'He stripped me of everything I had and left me and Mark to rot here in this hell-hole. There's three locks on my door and every night I have to go out to clean while Mark stays on his own.'

Vanner was looking out the window. He could see the café from here and their car. Two youths came out of the paper shop. One of them was white and the other black. Both of them had dreadlocks.

The front door opened and Jennifer got up from her chair. 'Mark? In here, darling.'

A slim, black-haired youth, wearing jeans and an anorak came into the room. He glanced at Vanner through eyes accentuated by thick-lensed glasses. He looked quickly at his mother.

'These men are policemen, Mark. They're just asking me some questions.'

Mark looked down at the floor.

'It's okay, Mark,' Vanner said. 'Your mum's not in any trouble.'

His mother patted his arm. 'I'll get you some lunch.' She went through to the kitchen.

Ryan looked at Mark. 'Go to college do you?'

He nodded.

'Where's that then?'

'Tech.'

'Your mum says you're doing well.'

He shrugged.

Vanner went through to the kitchen. 'Seems like a nice lad,' he said. 'Different to most of the kids round here.'

'You can say that again.'

'Not many friends?'

'I never see any. Keeps himself to himself. He had one or two at school, but they moved away. He stays in and plays with his computer most of the time. His father hates the fact that I work at night. He keeps asking Mark to go and live with him.'

'He wouldn't do that though would he?'

'I don't know. He never says very much. I never know what he's thinking.'

'He doesn't see anyone from round here?'

'Not as far as I know.'

Vanner moved to the window. 'Two lads,' he said. 'Dreadlocks.'

She made a face. 'Those two.'

'You know them?'

'Not really. They give Mark a hard time though.'

'Know their names?'

She shook her head.

Vanner leaned on the worktop. 'How often does he see his father?'

'Every other weekend. He didn't want to see him at all to begin with. But that was a couple of years ago. He picks him up on Saturday morning and brings him back on Sunday.'

'So they spend the weekend together?'

'Sort of. Mark works in a shop on Saturdays. System X on Oxford Street. You know the space war things. Combination of computer games and models. He paints the characters from the computer games and they have battles and things on a table. His father drops him off there so they only really spend Sundays together.' She looked up at him then. 'If he's into drugs I don't want Mark anywhere near him.'

They walked back to the car. 'One bitter woman,' Ryan said.
   'Two.'
   'Yeah, right.'
   'She's terrified he's going to take the boy away from her.'
   'Seems like a nice enough kid. Though he looks like a bit of an egghead.'
   'I bet he takes some stick in there. Must be tempting to get out.'
Vanner was staring at Montgomery House. On the second balcony the black youth with dreadlocks was watching him.

David Michaels stripped cushions from the chairs in the bail hostel. The vacuum cleaner, pipe extended, hummed on the floor alongside him. They always stuffed papers and things down the side of the chair, couldn't be bothered to go as far as the bin. He picked up the pipe and sucked. Dust and bits of paper and then something larger and blue, blocking the end of the nozzle. He switched off the machine and withdrew the offending article. He looked closer. A grinning red face looked back at him.

Vanner and Ryan went down the stairs to the incident room. McCleod was there, poring over something on his desk. A man Vanner did not recognise was with him. Morrison came out of Vanner's office and beckoned him over. 'Regional want to know what else we've got on Terry.'

Vanner pursed his lips. 'Why? We're not treading on their toes.'
   'They think we are. I've had Burke on the phone this morning.'
   'Terry's our flag,' Vanner said. 'Gallyon's theirs. I'm not interested in Gallyon.'

Morrison looked at him. 'Not at the moment maybe. But Terry's got an association with him.'

'I think Gallyon launders his cash,' Vanner said. 'But, I'm not about to tell that to the Regional.'

Morrison scratched his chin and looked at Vanner out of pale green eyes. 'Maybe Terry is nothing to do with this Denny cartoon.'

'He has business in Amsterdam. He gave Denny E's to Lisa Morgan.'

'So maybe he got them from Gallyon. We know Gallyon's into coke. Maybe this is a sideline.'

Vanner shook his head. 'Denny's a new cartoon. Why would Gallyon bring in a new cartoon? He's never been into acid.'

'New market. Why not?'

Again Vanner shook his head. 'Gallyon has a network. He doesn't use post office boxes. Why go to the trouble of setting up a new distribution when he already has one?' He sat down on the edge of the desk. 'I don't think it matters now anyway. I only ever went to the club to follow Maguire. We'll leave it alone, Sir. But the Denny cartoon is our flag and it needs to stay that way.'

Morrison sighed heavily. 'Any more from the Tom?'

Vanner looked past him. 'I've spoken to her. Terry hasn't given her any more gear, but she told me he likes his women rough.'

Morrison lifted one eyebrow. 'Have you been seeing her?'

Vanner squinted at him.

'She's not registered.'

'She's not a snout, Sir.'

Morrison folded his arms. Vanner looked to where Ryan was standing with McCleod. 'Who's the visitor?'

'Warden from the bail hostel on Neasden Road.'

Vanner frowned at him.

'He gave us a call after lunch. Found a complete Denny square down the side of a chair.'

Vanner sat across from Michaels and looked at the full square in front of him. A crisscross of perforations, splitting the face in four pieces. 'You found this down the arm of a chair?'

Michaels nodded. 'This morning as I was cleaning. They're dirty little sods, Inspector. Always using it as a bin.'

Ryan squinted at the square. 'Expensive bin,' he said.

Vanner looked back at Michaels. 'What's this about Friday nights?'

Michaels told him how he had witnessed, three times now, the comings and goings on a Friday. The car pulling up in the car park behind the hostel. One of the lads sprinting across and coming back a few minutes later.

'What kind of car?' Vanner asked him.

'BMW. Old one. Grey or silver maybe.'

Vanner glanced at Ryan. 'I don't suppose you got the number?'

Michaels shook his head. 'I tried. The last time. But they were gone before I could get it.'

Vanner steepled his fingers. He looked at Morrison, then at Ryan and finally back at Michaels. 'The lads you've got in there at the moment – what's the form?'

'Two for burglary. One of them for car theft. A couple for mugging . . .'

Vanner looked sharply at him.

'You know, whacking old ladies for handbags.'

'What about the one who crosses the road?'

'Mugging.'

'He's the only one who goes over.'

Michaels shook his head. 'There was another. Sammy Johnson. He's away now. Hospital wing at Brixton.'

'Hospital?'

'Yes. Before he went down, somehow he broke both his arms.'

Vanner got up from the chair and moved to the window. Outside, China and Anne came down the stairs. Vanner turned to Michaels again. 'This lad for mugging?'

'Peter Richardson.'

Vanner nodded. 'Does he wear a watch?'

Vanner addressed the briefing. Friday morning. Everyone was gathered. He waited for them to settle down. 'Okay,' he said. 'I think we might be getting somewhere.' Morrison stood at the back of the room: their eyes met and then Vanner continued. 'Slippery and me paid a visit to Michael Terry's ex-wife yesterday and found the second bitter woman of this little investigation. She lives on the Kirstall Estate in Kentish Town with her son Mark.

Bright lad. Seventeen. Goes to college. Sticks out like a sore thumb and gets the piss taken something rotten.

'We know from Milo that he was phoned from the box at the top of the road there, which places a caller in Kentish Town. We don't know who the caller was, but we do know the phone box has been used on more than one occasion.' He paused for a moment. 'So far we've got nothing more on Terry. But I've found out from Lisa Morgan that he likes it a little rough now and then. We know he's a nasty bastard all round. But that doesn't make him our man.' He broke off again. 'Maguire, the only other dealer we've got, is out of the game. That means that Denny knows we know about Maguire. Denny knew we knew about Milo and now Milo is dead. I guess that means the Irishman will be sweating. If he's sweating he might be useful. I want him picked up and interviewed. We can't nick him, but if he's unemployed he might want to talk to us.'

'If he's sweating too much he won't.' Ryan sat with his arms folded.

Vanner looked at the flip chart behind him. 'We still don't know how many boxes there are with second cards so we need another dealer. The witness from Bream Park gave us two men getting into a BMW at four in the morning. One of them was white. One was black. Both of them had long hair. That's all we know from him. So far he's looked at all the faces we have but he hasn't spotted anyone. The car is something though.

'Yesterday, we had a call from a bail hostel in Neasden. The warden found a complete acid square down the arm of a chair. He told us that on three separate occasions a grey or silver BMW has been parked out the back on a Friday. Each time someone from the hostel has nipped out, bent down at the passenger window and then nipped back in again. There's been two different kids going to the car. The first one has just gone down for assault, only before he took the drop somebody broke his arms for him. The second one is on a mugging charge. Nothing special in that, half the bloody kids in those places nick handbags during the day.' He glanced at Morrison as he said it. 'The difference here, though . . .

is that the kid in Neasden wears a pager watch.'

He stopped talking and looked at them. 'Two things about the Kirstall Estate. Firstly, Michael Terry's son lives there. Terry picks him up every other Saturday. Secondly, there's two lads living on that estate with dreadlocks. One's IC1 and the other IC3.' He sat on the edge of the desk. 'A few threads. A few bits to think about. We'll set up an OP on the hostel tonight. And I want Maguire picked up and interviewed.'

Michael Terry parked his car in Leith Place outside the industrial lofts. He glanced at the estate and locked the car carefully. Then he ducked between the blocks and went into Montgomery House. His ex-wife answered the door, looked at him coldly and walked back to the kitchen. Terry looked at his watch.

'Mark ready yet?'

'Not yet. You'll have to wait.'

Again he looked at his watch. 'He's going to be late. He ought to get up earlier.'

He waited for him, standing in the doorway of the kitchen, looking at Jennifer as she scrubbed pans and wondering what he ever saw in her. Through in his bedroom, Mark was still getting dressed. Jennifer rinsed the last of the grease from the pan and leaned it on the draining board.

'How's he getting on at school?' Terry asked her.

'It's not school. It's college.'

'School. College. Whatever.'

'There's a difference.' She looked stiffly at him. 'He left school when he was sixteen.'

Terry moved to the doorway. 'Look, if he's too much for you he can move in with me.'

'Who said he was too much for me?' She flicked hair from her eyes. 'Anyway. He doesn't want to live with you.'

'Have you asked him?'

'I don't need to.'

'I have.'

'You bastard,' she said.

She leaned a fist on the draining board. 'If you try and take him away from me . . .'

'It's up to him, isn't it.' He looked at her then, lank hair, pale face. His lip puckered as if he had a bad taste in his mouth. 'Not much of a role model are you.' He called over his shoulder. 'Come on, Mark. You're late.' He looked back at Jennifer. 'He's seventeen. It's time he was out and about.'

'What, so he can end up like you?'

He leaned against the door frame, hands behind his back. 'I want to take him on holiday.'

'When?'

'Soon.'

'He has college work.'

'A couple of weeks won't hurt. I'm going to the States. Do him good to come with me.'

'He's got to go to college.'

Mark sat in the Mercedes. His father glanced at him. 'You don't have to live there you know.'

Mark did not reply.

'I've told you. You could come and live with me. That place is full of yobbos.'

Still Mark did not reply.

'Mark?'

Mark stared through the windscreen. He flicked at the seat belt across his shoulder. 'I've got college, Dad. It would take hours to get there.'

'You could go to another college.'

'I like it where I am.'

They drove down Tottenham Court Road and Terry said: 'I don't like your mother working nights. I don't like you being alone.'

'I'm all right.'

'What, on your own every night? I don't think so. It's not as if you ever see anyone. If you lived with me you could go out. We could go out. I could show you things, introduce you to people.' He looked sideways at him. 'Time you started thinking about more than just college books. You're nearly eighteen. By the time I was your age I was making a buck.'

He revved the engine and overtook a learner driver. 'You've inherited my brains, Mark. College is one thing, but there's a whole world out there. Opportunities.' He snaked his tongue over his lips. 'You need a head for business in this world. You won't learn that from a book.'

The traffic buckled into a line before them. Terry tapped on the wheel again. 'You're going to be late. You should get up earlier.'

'Doesn't matter. I'm only painting today.'

'Still doing that? You must be pretty good by now. You liked those cartoons I used to draw when you were a kid. Didn't you.'

'They were okay.'

Terry said: 'Listen, I'm going to the States next month. Why don't you come with me?'

Mark made a face. 'What about college?'

'Won't hurt will it? Couple of weeks together. Won't be as long as the last trip, but then again I won't be as busy. You wouldn't have to fend for yourself so much.'

They were almost to the shop. His father said: 'I might pop back later. Watch one of the games. You never know, I might try my hand at some painting.'

'Did Mum tell you about the police coming round?'

Terry looked startled. 'No. When was that?'

'Thursday lunchtime.'

'What did they want?'

'Don't know. Mum just said – a few questions.'

'What sort of questions? About her?'

Mark shook his head.

'You're not in any trouble are you?'

'I think they were asking about you.'

Terry's fingers tightened about the steering wheel. He looked forward again and braked hard to avoid the taxi in front of them. 'What did they want with me?'

'Routine, Mum said.' Mark looked at him then. 'They were from the Drug Squad, I think.'

* * *

Vanner spoke to Ryan, sitting on his bed with the towel about his waist and his hair still wet from the shower. On the pillow next to him was James Bentt's business card, as yet unused, as yet undeclared to Morrison.

'Total waste of time, Guv'nor,' Ryan said. 'Sat on the plot half the night. Not so much as a whisper.'

'What time d'you get home?'

'About two. Took it upon myself to stand down.'

'No problem. There's always next Friday.'

'Oh, I just love being a spotter on a Friday.'

'Relax. I'll form a rota.'

Vanner hung up and picked up the card. James Bentt of Glendale & Watts and another Director called Riley. Andrew Riley, the best man at his wedding. The man who stole his wife.

Michael Terry watched the kids playing war games in System X. Computer screens on the walls above shelves stacked with models. A large painted table in the middle of the floor. Armies massed against each other. Two lads plotted tactics on the screens and two more implemented them at the table. In the corner, at a smaller table, Mark painted tiny white figures with a fine stemmed brush. Terry was lost in thought. The Drug Squad in Jennifer's house asking about *him*. How did they know? He felt the package of E's in his pocket. And then all at once it dawned on him.

When the shop was closed they drove back to his flat overlooking the river. 'Enjoyed myself today,' Terry said. 'I haven't painted like that in years.' He grinned at the tiny, colourful figure of the dwarf, squatting malevolently on the dashboard. 'Maybe they'll give me a job.'

They drove across the bridge. Terry said: 'Tell me about college then. What're you studying, Mark?'

'German voting system.'

'Additional members. You know we devised that for them after the Second World War. Designed to stop another Hitler rising.'

Mark looked at him. 'They've done okay haven't they. The Germans.'

His father grinned and patted the wheel. 'Make good cars, son. Make good cars. What about business – economics?'

'We're comparing Keynes and Friedman.'

'Are you? Money supply and all that. Full employment.' Terry shook his head. 'Whoever heard of full employment? Nice idea, Mr Keynes. But then that was the thirties.' He smiled cynically. 'All very nice in theory. But the market rules, son. The market will always rule. Supply and demand. The Chicago school of economics. Maggie was right.'

Mark looked at him. 'You still think so? Even after what happened to you?'

Terry made a face. 'One market fell and I was in too deep. All my eggs in one basket. I didn't diversify.' He looked sideways at him. 'Experience, Mark. You can't learn it from books.'

'What about now?'

'Different markets. Different games but the same rules. Up and at 'em again.'

They ate dinner at the long, wooden table in front of the window, darkness closing outside. Terry looked at his son. 'Listen, I'm going to take a shower and then I have to go out.'

Mark looked at his plate.

'There's something I should've done yesterday. I have to do it tonight.' He smiled at him. 'Don't worry though. It won't be until later.'

Mark toyed with his food.

'You'll be okay,' Terry went on. 'Work your playstation. Or watch the TV. There's always a movie on Sky.'

Terry climbed out of the shower, dried himself and went through to the kitchen. Mark was playing his Megadrive.

'You seen the bottle of water? It was on the side.'

'Finished, Dad. I binned it.'

'Oh.' Terry scratched his head. 'I'll get another.'

He phoned for a taxi. Mark watched him from the window, the

lights of London breaking the stillness on the far side of the river. His father got in the cab and he watched it cross the bridge. He mooched about the flat, TV off, thinking about his father, thinking about his mother, when they had been together all those years ago. Sometimes it felt like yesterday. Home alone again now though, with either one of them it was always home alone. But at least with his mother it was because she had to.

Terry sat in the back of the taxi and thought about the Drug Squad asking questions. Then he thought about Lisa, how he had tied her by the neck and the wrists. Maybe he should have tied tighter.

The Wasp drank beer from the neck of the bottle, gripping it under one curled finger and tipping it down his throat. On the TV the film played out to its inevitable conclusion, the kind of conclusion he had seen a million times before. He swore at the box and switched it off. In the next room, the girl dressed and undressed and dressed again as only girls can do. His mobile rang. He looked at it, sank more beer and placed the bottle on the floor. She appeared in the doorway. Bra and knickers. He could see the protrusion of nipple through the cotton. 'You going to answer that?'

The Wasp glowered at her and lifted the phone to his ear. 'Yeah?'

'Wasp.'

'What d'you want?'

'Where are you?'

'In my flat.'

'On your own?'

'No.'

'Ninja?'

'No.'

'Aha. Girlies again.'

His voice was chill on the ear. The Wasp scratched the rising skin on his arm. 'What d'you want?' he could hear him breathing.

Sometimes he could hear music. But tonight only the stilted silence of the Cellnet.

'Coppers on the estate.'

'I saw them.'

'Asking questions, Wasp. Asking a lot of questions.'

The Wasp sat more upright. 'You think they're getting close?' For a moment he could see the body of Ringo May, dying in his own blood. He looked at the bottle of beer.

'Vanner thinks he's getting close, Wasp. I've watched him. Gets about a lot.'

'But he ain't close enough. Right?'

'Right.'

'What then – you want us to hit him again?'

'Don't be stupid. I want you to lie low.'

'What d'you mean – lie low?'

'Just that, shithead. Keep away from everything for a while. I want you for another job later on.'

'What kind of job?'

'You'll know when I tell you. Big bonus though, Wasp.'

'When?'

'I don't know yet. But in the meantime I want you out of sight. That goes for Ninja too.'

'But what about the pickups – the hostels and the boiler room and that?'

'Leave them to me.'

The Wasp felt a little cold. 'You trying to phase me out of the game, man?'

'Listen, Wasp. I'm doing you a favour. Vanner is nobody's fool. Just lie low. Chill out. Enjoy some of the dosh you've been making. Nobody's phasing anyone out. But stay away from it all for the moment. We need to regroup a little.'

'And next Friday?'

'Like I told you. I'll sort it.'

Terry climbed out of the taxi and paid the driver. The two doormen nodded as he passed them. He hung his coat in the lobby and moved

165

into the bar area. Gallyon was not about. His table by the balcony, empty. Terry cursed quietly to himself and scanned the floor for Lisa. He could not see her anywhere. Climbing the stairs to the upstairs bar, he bought himself a drink and then occupied Gallyon's spot by the rail. Quiet tonight. He glanced at his watch. Still early. He sipped vodka and watched the murmur of dancers on the floor, music low as yet, the thump thump in his ear.

She came in, Lisa, looking for all the world as if she owned the place. Terry watched her move across the floor, watched the expressions of the punters and his mouth set in a line. He would never have thought it of her. But then the other night she had been yappy, and the night with the Arab. Smug as fuck, trying to make him jealous. Jealous. For Christ's sake, he was paying her. Denny E's. He cursed himself for a fool.

He waited for Gallyon. Much as he would have liked to take her to one side himself, she was Gallyon's property. And Gallyon was a big man. Nice to rub it with him though, shoulder to shoulder, around a table full of drinks with money going down between them. He looked again at Lisa, leaning now by the downstairs bar. Still she had not seen him. Pity about her, the sex had been ballistic.

She looked up, caught his eye and smiled. He liked it when she smiled. Oh, he knew he was paying for it, but he still liked it when she smiled. The sensation it gave him, even now with the anger rising like sap in his veins. The tightness across his chest and the little charge in his loins. He held her gaze. Still she smiled. He did not smile back.

Gallyon came in at ten minutes to midnight. Lisa was dancing. Terry remained where he was. As Gallyon got to the head of the stairs, Terry signalled the barman.

'Michael.' Gallyon touched his arm, adjusted the knot of his bow tie and sat down.

'Didn't expect you tonight.'

'Didn't expect it myself.'

Gallyon squinted at him. 'Trouble?'

'A little maybe.' Terry looked over at Lisa.

Twelve

Vanner stared across the table at Maguire. Mouse-coloured hair, clear blue eyes looking back at him. They sat in the interview room at Castle Hill.

'I want a solicitor,' Maguire said.

Vanner cocked his head to one side. 'Why? Nobody's arrested you.'

Maguire looked at him. Vanner took out cigarettes and offered him one. He took it cautiously. Ryan flipped open his lighter and Maguire cupped his hand to the flame.

Vanner sat back in the chair. 'You've got a post office box at Barnet Central.'

'Have I?'

'You know you have.' Vanner picked up a photocopy of an application form made by Maguire seven months earlier. He pushed it across the table. '*We* know you have.' Maguire skimmed his eyes over it, drew on the cigarette and flicked ask. Vanner folded his arms. 'You paid for a full year. How come you've stopped using it?'

'I don't need it any more.'

'What did you use it for?' Ryan asked him.

'Business.'

'What sort of business?'

Maguire sat more easily in the chair, the confidence returning to his eyes. 'Mail order.'

'What sort of mail order?'

'This and that.'

'Why did you have two cards?'

Maguire flinched then and recovered himself. He leaned over the table, scraping the end of his cigarette round the rim of the ashtray. 'I needed them.'

'Why?' Vanner said.

'The business. I had a partner.'

'Who?'

'Doesn't matter. He's gone now anyway. Moved on. Like you said, we don't use the box any more.'

Vanner glanced at Ryan and then he hunched forward so his head was close to Maguire's. 'You're a liar.'

He sat back again, crossed his legs and kicked his foot lightly against the table. 'You deal drugs, Maguire. The box was your pickup point. You posted back the cash. The second card was so someone could collect it.'

'News to me.'

'Bullshit.' Vanner held his gaze, dominating him. 'You dealt E's with the Denny insignia on them. Sometimes you dealt acid. Mostly E's though. The punters in Covent Garden prefer E's. Cheaper than coke but not so cheap as acid.'

'I don't know what you're talking about.'

Vanner laughed at him then. 'I saw you. Blake's Bar on Long Acre.'

'Never been there.'

'You want to see the records?' Vanner glanced at Ryan. 'Tell him.'

'You've got a Golf GTI,' Ryan said. 'Black one. H reg. Nice wheels. Alloy right?'

Maguire stubbed out his cigarette.

'We followed you,' Vanner went on. 'Friday night, last month. Good nights for you are they – Fridays?'

'Okay. So I go to Blake's bar once in a while. I like a drink. There's no law against that.'

Vanner smiled from one corner of his mouth. 'I followed you into the gents. Two suits. Remember? I saw you deal, Maguire.'

'So, why didn't you arrest me?'

Ryan leaned forward then, resting both elbows on the table. 'Because it's not you we want.'

Vanner moved in his seat. 'The second cardholder.'

'I don't know what you're talking about.'

Vanner stood up then and leaned with his back to the wall. He stared coldly at Maguire.

'What's it like to be out of the game?'

Maguire looked back at him. 'I've got nothing more to say to you.'

'You know, if you're out of the game you must be strapped. Cash, I mean. Lot of money in E's.' He glanced at the watch on Maguire's left wrist. 'Called you on that did he?'

Maguire shook his head slowly. 'I don't have a clue what you're on about.'

'He doesn't call any more. Does he,' Vanner went on. 'That must really piss you off after seven months of profit.'

'I told you. I'm not answering any more questions.'

Vanner said: 'Tell me about Michael Terry.'

Maguire looked blank. 'Can I go now? If I'm not under arrest then I must be free to go.' He stood up. 'I think I'll go now.'

'Sit down.' Vanner moved towards him and rested his hands on the table. Maguire hovered, then slowly he sat down again.

'Gallyon's nightclub.'

Maguire frowned.

'We saw you there too. Michael Terry was there, upstairs with Bobby Gallyon. Big man Bobby. Old family. Five serious nightclubs. Not the sort of bloke to mess with. Did you deal in Gallyon's nightclub?'

Maguire stood up. 'I really am leaving now.'

'You should talk to us, Maguire,' Vanner looked keenly at him. 'Do yourself a favour.'

Maguire shook his head. 'Not the kind of favour I need.'

Morrison was behind Vanner's desk in the incident room when he went back downstairs. Jimmy Crack was talking to him. Jimmy got up from the chair, but Vanner palmed him down again.

'Maguire?' Morrison said.

Vanner shook his head. 'He knows what happened to Milo. He isn't going to talk to us.'

'And he's the only other dealer we know about?'

Vanner nodded. 'So far.' He sat down heavily and looked at Jimmy. 'More hassle from Regi?'

Jimmy glanced at him, then briefly at Morrison. 'Burke's okay, Guv,' he said. 'No damage.'

'Good.'

Jimmy looked again at Morrison.

Vanner lifted an eyebrow. 'What is it?'

'The Tom, Guv. Lisa.'

'What about her?'

'She's disappeared.'

Vanner sat forward, furrows cutting his brow. 'What do you mean – disappeared?'

'There's a new piece of furniture there now. Black girl called Isabel. The doorman told me that Lisa was in on Saturday and not there on Sunday. On Sunday this new bird is there. Sunday's a good night for Lisa.'

'I don't understand.'

Jimmy sighed. 'On Saturday night Michael Terry comes in. Apparently he wasn't expected. Anyway he and Gallyon have a little chinwag and then Terry leaves. He doesn't speak to Lisa. He doesn't go anywhere near her. Later on Gallyon calls her upstairs. They go out the back together and she hasn't been seen since.'

Vanner parked his car outside Lisa's building and walked into the concourse. He was aware of the sound of his feet on the flagstones. At the exterior door he pressed her bell and waited. She did not answer. He stood there and waited and waited. Still she did not answer. Then a man came down the stairs and opened the door. Vanner held it for him. The man squinted. Vanner ignored him and took the steps two at a time.

Her front door was closed. He knocked, lightly at first; but when the door was not answered he knocked louder. 'Lisa?' He listened, ear close to the wood. 'Lisa?'

She did not answer him. He knocked again, much louder this time. 'Lisa?'

A door along the corridor opened and a woman looked out. 'Can I help you?'

Vanner moved towards her and she shrank back. He fished his warrant card out of his pocket. 'Police,' he said. 'Number 14. D'you know if she's in there?'

'Well, she was earlier. Poor girl. Bandage on her face.'

Vanner went very still. 'Thank you,' he said and turned back to the door.

He waited until the woman had gone back into her apartment and then he knocked again. 'Come on, Lisa. It's me, Vanner. Open the door.'

Still no answer.

'Lisa.'

'Go away, Vanner.' Her voice from the other side of the wood. Vanner leaned with his fingers pressed against it.

'Come on, Lisa. Let me in.'

'Just go away.'

He stood back, folded his arms, unfolded them and stepped forward again. 'Come on Lisa. I need to talk to you.'

'I've had enough talk, Vanner.'

'A minute. Just give me a minute.'

The door clicked and then it was opened the length of the chain. Lisa's face was framed against the light from inside. Vanner thinned his eyes. Her right cheek was covered by a heavy gauze bandage, taped down with plaster.

'Lisa . . .' he started.

She looked at him, then slowly she peeled back the bandage. Her cheek was swollen and blue and lined with ugly, black stitching. For a long moment they stared at one another.

She sat down in the lounge. Vanner stood before her. The curtains were closed. 'Can I get you a drink or something?'

She shook her head.

'Who did it, Lisa?'

'I fell.'

'Oh, come on.'

'Don't pretend you care, Vanner.' She lifted her gaze to accuse him.

He closed his eyes for a moment. 'Michael Terry.'

'No, Vanner. *You.* You wouldn't leave me alone.'

Again he looked away from her. 'I was just doing my job.'

'Yeah. And so was I.'

He stood up, sat down again, made an open-handed gesture. 'Terry saw Gallyon. Gallyon took you outside. Testify, Lisa. Give me a statement and we'll pick up Bobby Gallyon.'

'Grow up, Vanner.'

She got up then and poured herself a drink. She stood with one hand cupping her waist, resting her elbow as she sipped from the glass. Vanner lit a cigarette and watched her.

'I can help you.'

'Like you did before?' She hissed air through her teeth. 'Coppers. Jesus. You're a sad bunch.' She looked at him then. 'You're no better than he is. You want to fuck me again? Come on, Vanner. Let's fuck. That's what you and me do.'

He sat in darkness on the floor of his unfurnished lounge in his unfurnished house in Camden Town. Smoke eddied from the cigarette between his fingers. The emptiness of the room closed about him. A half-filled whiskey glass squatted between the bridge of his legs. He stared at the wall. Jane was in his mind, Jane and Lisa Morgan with her face ruined for all time. Her words rang in his head.

He crushed out the cigarette, burning the ends of his fingers. He lit another, smoked it in the silence, drank his whiskey and poured another. For a moment he closed his eyes and the scars seemed to lift on his back, as if in some wasted display of sympathy. Jane and now Lisa. The same all over again. From his back pocket he took out his wallet and from his wallet he took James Bentt's business card.

* * *

John Phillips stood at the window of the staff room and sipped coffee. Clouds littered the sky, grey and black, hiding the sun as if to echo his mood. Behind him, the hubbub of the other lecturers drifted in monotone. He stared out of the window, the weakness of the afternoon preceding the weight of the night. John was on his mind. Last Thursday, the grey of Norwich Prison, looking down on the city from a hilltop. He looked awful, withdrawn, face pinched and bitter: his eyes bunched in darkened hollows of fear. Cold turkey and prison. God alone knew what he would do in there, anything and everything, with anyone and everyone, just to get his hands on some dope.

He worried about Mary, but on the face of it she seemed quite strong. The strength, perhaps, of motherhood. John safe, at least in her mind. Yet it was not over. The money was still unpaid. This morning he had found his tyres slashed with a knife. What would tomorrow bring? More windows broken, more lives threatened, another petrol-soaked rag through the letterbox. The last one – thank God he had been alone in the house. He was thinking of moving Anna and his wife to his mother's house.

Turning from the window, he caught a glimpse of Alex Hammond, watching him from his easy chair. A brief smile passed between them. Good man, Hammond: perceptive. Taught politics to the A-level students. Funny how they got on, him working-class Tory fodder and Hammond a middle-class socialist. Hammond joked about the deferential vote. Yet they were the same age and maybe, in their own way, they were as weary of their worlds as each other.

Hammond got up from his chair. Phillips turned back to the window and felt him move alongside.

'Going to rain.'

Phillips nodded. 'Looks like it.'

Hammond laid a hand on his shoulder. 'You know what, John: every break, every lunchtime, you stand here and stare at this window. Now either there's something in the glass that only you can see or other things are bugging you.'

Phillips looked round at him. 'You're right,' he said, 'there's something in the glass.'

They sat over two pints of bitter and Hammond wiped froth from his lips. 'Go to the police. Make a statement. You can testify against them.'

'I've been to the police. There's nothing they can do. I can't prove anything. The only other person who's seen anything is Mark Terry. And I'm not bringing him into this. Christ, he's only a kid.' He shook his head. 'I don't know where I went wrong. I always tried to do the best for them. Anna's okay, so far at least. But John . . . Those shits are killing my family, Alex. I mean for Christ's sake – I served with the Paras in Ulster. I was a soldier. Now I'm fifty years old and there's bugger all I can do.'

'And John's in prison?'

'Remand. Norwich. At least it's a long way from London.'

'Heroin you say.'

Phillips nodded.

'Is he a registered addict?'

Phillips shrugged. 'I don't know. What difference does it make?'

Hammond lifted his eyebrows. 'Could make a lot. If he's only on remand and he registers, then you might have a case to get him out of Norwich and into the care of a rehab institute.'

Phillips stared at him, not daring to acknowledge the bubble of hope in his chest. 'You can do that?'

'It's not unheard of. Why don't you try and find out?'

Phillips sat back in his chair and crossed his arms on his chest. 'I've got to do something, Alex. I sleep with an axe under my bed.'

Vanner stood in the incident room. 'Lisa Morgan, the Tom from Gallyon's nightclub has a dozen stitches in her cheek.'

McCleod raised his eyebrows. 'She won't be turning any more five-hundred-quid tricks then.'

For a moment Vanner stared at him. 'Terry'll know we paid a visit to his ex-wife,' he said. 'And he's seen me in the club.' He looked at Terry's photograph on the wall behind them. Then he sat on the edge of the desk and pushed a hand through his hair. 'He goes to Amsterdam an awful lot. Less to the States, but then one good crystal can make three hundred thousand squares. That's how much on the street, Sid?'

'Million and a half, Guv'nor.'

'Right.' Vanner looked at them again. 'Somebody get onto the DLO. It's time we had customs involved. I also want the Dutch and US police notified. I want him tailed the next time he gets off a plane.'

'What about the boxes, Guv?' Pierce asked him.

'Still blank. What we need is the pickup man. It might be more than one, but we know he's handling cash, so I doubt it. It'll be somebody close to the source. The only box we've got is Maguire's and his mouth is zipped tight.' He thought for a moment. 'Somehow Terry's using Gallyon. My guess is to launder the cash.'

He moved round behind the desk. 'We've still got the Friday-night OP at the Bail Hostel. We don't know what's going on, but some inmates are there for mugging. We're always being told that street crime is random. Trouble with that is – there's a kid in Neasden with a pager watch.' He looked at McCleod. 'Sammy, I want you to check with all the other hostels in the area. Find out from the wardens if any of the inmates have pager watches.'

Anne looked up at him. 'You think he's funded this from the street, Guv?'

'I don't know.' Vanner looked at Morrison. 'But Eagle Eye is big news at the moment. I'd hate to think it was organised.'

Morrison caught his arm as he went back into his office. 'How's the Tom?'

'How do you think she is?'

'Don't blame yourself.'

Vanner stared at him. 'You care?'

Morrison shut the door. 'Care has nothing to do with it. You came onto this squad with a grudge, Vanner.'

Vanner sat on his desk.

'Do I need to spell it out? We both know we have a target but very little else. What we don't need is our judgement being clouded by grudges. You should've registered or kept away from her. You did neither. Now forget about it and get on with your job.'

When Morrison was gone he picked up the telephone and dialled. 'Jabba?'

'Mr Vanner.'

'Listen, Jabba. I need a favour.'

'You know it wasn't Tate who hit you.'

'Yes. I know that. He's just got a big mouth. Right?'

'Unfortunately so. I'm sorry about that, Mr Vanner.'

'You only told me what you heard. I need something else though.'

'If I can help.'

'If we win there's a bonus. Four figures at least.'

'I'm listening.'

'You ever hear of Denny?'

'Ecstasy and acid. Good stuff apparently. New face on the block.'

'I need a dealer, Jabba. I've had two. One's dead and the other one's rabbit. I need one who doesn't know I have him. D'you think you can find me a name?'

'Time, Mr Vanner. And money.'

'You can have the money. I can't give you the time.'

Thirteen

Vanner stood in the doorway of the Banca Di Roma on Gresham Street in the City. Across the road was a pair of double doors, one of which stood open. He could see a marbled hallway beyond. It was lunchtime and the narrow street was choked with people; business-suited men and perfectly manicured women. A few of them glanced briefly at him as they passed. He looked again at the open double door. Thrimble and Grace, a gentleman's tailor, crowded it on one side and The Last Wine Bar on the other.

He crossed the road and paused, looking beyond the inner glass door to the foyer. The lift jutted out, blocking half his view. An antique table was placed neatly against the other wall, a mirror rising above it. He read the list of company names that occupied the board to the right of the lift. Glendale & Watts were on the second floor.

The stairs were narrow, curving tightly in a spiral with barely enough room for one person to walk. On the second floor he came out onto a landing, much the same as the ground floor with the lift butting up to the wall. The door to the office faced him, the name of the company, plaque-like, in the middle of it.

For a moment he remained where he was. Andrew Riley. A personal, undeclared interest and Weir waiting in the background. He shook his head at himself, thought about Lisa Morgan and narrowed his eyes. Then the years rolled back, eleven of them and a lifetime of friendship before that. How many times had he dreamt of stumbling across Riley? Nothing premeditated – that would bear out all that they said about him – but just happening upon him. He used to think about it in the night, when the ache in his gut chewed at him as he led his men through Divis.

Inside, the receptionist did not smile. A turquoise suit fastened to the neck: she clutched a retractable pencil between crimson cambered nails and looked him up and down.

'Andrew Riley,' he said.

'And you are?'

'Detective Inspector Vanner.' He pulled out his warrant card and dropped it on the desk.

'North West London Drug Squad.'

She sat up straighter. 'He's not in right now.'

'Where is he?'

'At lunch.'

'Where?'

'He's with clients.'

'Where?'

She hesitated, glanced at the desktop, then looked up at him again. 'I'm not sure. Next door, I think.'

Vanner took his ID back from her and slipped it into his pocket. He looked beyond her then, to the nameplates on the doors. 'What about Mr Bentt?'

'He's on his honeymoon.'

'Simon Smith?'

'Away on business. Mr Phelps is at lunch with Mr Riley.'

'How long will they be?'

'Shouldn't be very long. They've been gone over an hour.'

He nodded. 'I'll wait then.'

He sat in the high-backed chair across from her and lifted his ankle over his knee. He kept his hands in his pockets and watched her. He knew he made her nervous. She kept shifting in her seat, scribbling now and then on her pad. The phone rang and she lifted the receiver almost gratefully. When she put it down she offered him coffee. He refused.

He sat for half an hour before he heard voices from downstairs and then the lift began to rise. His pulse quickened fractionally. The lift stopped. The doors slid open and four men came out into the foyer. The receptionist rose from her desk.

'Andrew. There's someone to see . . .' Her voice dribbled away as Riley looked round at Vanner. His face lost its colour.

Vanner got to his feet. They were the same height only Riley was heavier, his belly flopping over the belt of his trousers.

'Aden.' Riley forced a smile.

'Andrew.'

Riley turned to his colleague. 'John, take our guests into the boardroom will you. I'll be along in a moment.'

Riley's office was spacious and lined in oak. Twin leather chairs faced his leather topped desk and a fuller, deeper chair beyond it. Riley moved to the chair so that the desk was between them. He touched the knot of his tie then offered Vanner his hand. 'Been a long time,' he said.

Vanner kept his hands in his pockets.

Riley sat first. Vanner lowered himself into the chair opposite and looked at him.

'What can I do for you, Aden?' Riley's voice was brusque now, businesslike. 'Is this a social call? Only I'm rather busy with clients . . .'

Vanner took his card from his pocket and moved it over the desk with one finger. Riley picked it up and his eyebrows arched. 'Drug Squad? I don't understand.'

Vanner leaned forward. 'Tell me about the secondhand plant business, Andrew.'

Riley sat back, visibly pushing his chair away from the desk as if he needed the extra room to breathe.

'Caterpillar dump trucks,' Vanner said. 'Komatsu. Ford New-Holland. Tell me about fire-damaged plant.'

Riley played with his cuffs. 'James Bentt deals with that. I never get involved.'

'James Bentt isn't here.'

Riley made an open-handed gesture. 'Well, what did you want to know?'

'Where does it come from?

'Damaged plant? From all over the world.'

179

'What happens to it?'

'As far as I know it goes to auction.'

'Merricks.'

'Generally. Yes.'

'Amsterdam? The States?'

'There's a smaller one here. But those are the main ones, yes.'

'But you know about it before it gets to auction.'

'We deal with insurance companies throughout the world, Aden. Sometimes we deal with their loss adjusters.'

'And what do you do with the information?'

'It's not illegal.'

'Did I say that it was?'

Riley drummed his fingers on the table. 'James has a few clients in that business. He advises them of job lots. It gives them an edge in the marketplace.'

'And they pay you a fee?'

'That's our business. We lay off risk for a fee.'

'Money in it.' Vanner looked round the room.

'We get by.'

Vanner looked back at him then. 'Tell me about your clients.'

'I can't, Aden. That's confidential. Client confidence is everything.'

'Tell me about one client.'

Riley looked at him.

'I bet that's not difficult. You can't have too many clients in that business. If you did they wouldn't have an edge.'

'You're talking about Michael Terry.'

'We arrested him for fraud in 1990. James Bentt worked with him in the City.'

'He did, but that was a long time ago.'

Vanner stared at him then. 'How's Jane?'

Riley coughed and sat forward. 'Look, Aden . . .'

'What does Terry do?'

'I don't know him, Aden. As far as I know he buys plant.'

'You tell him about deals going down. Fire damage. Water damage. Sabotage.'

'There's an element of that. Some of the more aggressive environmental groups.'

'You mean people who prefer trees to roads.'

'There's a lot of them about.'

'So it's a good business then.'

'I think so.'

'Terry makes a lot of money?'

'I don't know. Why don't you ask him?'

Riley sat back again and looked at his watch. 'Look. I'm sorry, Aden. I have a meeting to chair. Those two gentlemen you saw. They've come all the way from Japan. I can't let them wait any longer.'

Vanner sat back. 'Terry buys damaged plant, ships it to Dartford, repairs it and ships it on again. Where does he sell it?'

'I really wouldn't know.'

'What're the good markets?'

'You'd have to ask James. But as far as I know – South Africa. Israel. The Middle East, although there's DTI restrictions in some countries.'

'What about South America?'

'It's a market.'

'Terry supplies there?'

'I don't know. You'd have to ask him. All we do is advise him of potential purchases.'

'Bobby Gallyon?'

'Don't know him.'

'Does James Bentt know him? Michael Terry does.'

'Aden, all James does is advise Terry on deals. What he does thereafter is nothing to do with this company. What we do is not illegal.'

'You don't mind dealing with a man convicted of fraud though.'

Riley sat back once more. 'Anyone can make a mistake, Aden. You should know that.'

Vanner thinned his eyes. 'How *is* Jane?'

'She's fine.' Riley opened his hands. 'Aden, I'm sorry. I . . .'

Vanner stood up. 'I'll want to talk to Bentt when he gets back.'

'Why?'

'Because I haven't got the answers yet.'

'Look, if Terry's into drugs – I can assure you we know nothing about it.'

'Did I say he was into drugs?'

Riley held up his hands.

Vanner moved to the door. He heard Riley get up behind him. 'Aden.' He turned. Riley had a tense expression on his face, the muscles suddenly heightened.

'You know it's funny,' he said. 'Jane and me . . . you being a soldier and everything . . .'

'What about it?'

'Well, I always thought . . .'

'Thought what?'

'That maybe you'd come after me.'

Vanner looked at the floor for a moment, then back in his eyes. 'Maybe I will,' he said.

John Phillips took the phone call in the staff room. Lunchtime was about over, only he and a handful of other lecturers were there. It was Mary, his wife. He could hear the tears in her voice.

'What is it, love?' he asked gently.

'It's Anna.'

'What about her?'

'They had a go at her, John. Outside the school.'

'Where is she?'

'She's here. One of the teachers drove her home.'

'Is she all right?'

'She's very very upset. We're both very upset.'

He found them in the kitchen when he got home. The front door was double locked and the curtains drawn across the living-room window. They were sitting at the table with the blind pulled down over the back door. Anna looked up as he came in and she started to cry once again. He took her in his arms. 'It's all right, love. I'm here now.'

When she stopped trembling he helped her back to her seat. His wife stood up wearily and leaned against the sink. Phillips sat down in the chair she had vacated, still holding both his daughter's hands in his own. 'You okay now?'

She sobbed once and nodded.

'Can you tell me what happened?'

'I went to the shop for some crisps,' she said.

'On your own?'

She nodded. 'They were waiting for me.'

'Who were?'

'The one with the bad teeth. And the other two with motorbike jackets.'

Phillips compressed his jaws. 'What did they do?' he asked quietly.

'They started swearing at me. Horrible, disgusting words. They said all the things they'd like to do to a little schoolgirl. One of them kept trying to lift up my skirt.'

Phillips glanced over his shoulder at his wife. Her face crumpled in red. He looked back at his daughter, trying to keep the stammer from his voice. 'Did they hurt you?'

'One of them kept flicking my hair. He showed me a knife. He told me he was going to cut off all my fingers. He said they were going to follow me every day until you gave them their money.'

Her father took her hands in his again and then released them as if suddenly his impotence made him unworthy. He stood up, moved around the kitchen, trying to keep a lid on the anger that built and built inside him. His daughter looked at him. 'Dad. They said they know where Nan lives. They said they were going to pay her a visit.'

Upstairs, he lifted the long-handled axe from where it lay under the bed. As he stood up, he caught sight of his reflection in the uncurtained window. He stood straighter: his hair was thin, but his belly was flat and he could still feel the strength in his arms. He heard the sound of his wife and daughter downstairs. They were cooking. His mother he had brought over earlier. Siege mentality. He knew he had to put a stop to it. He weighed the axe in his hand. The head was very sharp. The women busied themselves downstairs. Anna was easier now. She had washed her face and brushed her hair, and her Nan had held her on her knee like she used to.

Phillips opened the wardrobe door and switched on the light. Just something he had rigged up to make life a little easier. He was always doing odd jobs like that: this little comfort, that little comfort. Maybe it was a sign of his age. He smiled to himself and realised how much calmer he felt now he had come to a decision. From the shelf above the rail he took down an old, green bundle and unfurled it. His number was still sewn above the breast pocket and the stripes angled into the sleeve. Lifting it to his face, he closed his eyes and smelled the past etched into it. He wished now he had kept his beret. But when he had left the Army Mary had wanted the past to be just that. Time to look ahead, she had told him. So many old soldiers carry their past around them like an albatross. He did not know about that, but men, like women, sometimes needed the comfort of the past.

Stripping off his sweater, he put on the combat jacket. It reached almost to his thighs. Over it he buttoned his overcoat and slipped the axe under his arm. It was cold and strangely brutal against his side. He switched off the light and went back downstairs.

They were all still in the kitchen. He stuck his nose round the door. 'I'm going out for a while,' he said.

'John.' His wife called out to him. 'Don't be long. Dinner will be in an hour.'

It was colder tonight, the final echo of summer drawing away from the city. In a couple of months it would be Christmas. Getting into his car, he took off his overcoat and laid the axe across the back seat. He caught a glimpse of his face in the rearview mirror. His eyes looked old and weary, but they no longer looked so hunted.

The engine fired with the first twist of the key. He engaged the gears and drove off down the road. Tired old car, tired and worn like its owner. But tonight, with the past revisited, he knew it would not let him down. At the far end of the close, he headed around the park and pulled onto the main road.

They drank in the Bull's Head on Tottenham Lane. He knew that from John. Maybe after tonight he would be able to get him out of prison and into a rehabilitation clinic. That had been his hope. He had not said as much to Mary yet, but that had been his hope.

He drove slowly along Tottenham Lane, the traffic clogging about him. Lights in his eyes, headlights and streetlamps and the chill that fell with the night. The Bull's Head sign flapped in the wind that came from the north. He looked behind him to the back seat where the axe glinted in the street light. He passed the pub, saw their battered Ford Escort, with a black motorcycle standing alongside it. There was nowhere to park. He would have to walk with the axe under his jacket.

And now he could feel the adrenalin begin to pump. His backside was loose and he farted as he pulled the car into a parking space in front of a line of shops. Teenagers milled about the kebab house. He could smell the meat that was roasting.

Carefully, he locked the driver's door, the axehead crooked under his armpit like a crutch. He flattened his arm against it to keep it in place. His jacket was just long enough to obscure the handle completely. He stood straighter and adjusted it under his bicep. The cold nibbled at him but still his hands were clammy. Fifty yards to the pub. Early yet, there would not be too many drinkers.

He stood outside, glancing once at their car, bumped up on the kerb. The outer pub door was open. Beyond it the glass panel of the swing door. Slowly, he unzipped his jacket and let the axe slide down his flank. He caught it beneath the head, hefted it and slid his fingers over the shaft. With his free hand he pushed open the door.

He had been right, few drinkers. Just an old man in one corner and the landlord polishing glasses. They were gathered at his end of the bar, two bikers and the little one with the blackened teeth. Cigarette smoke clouded between them. They seemed to be intent on some kind of card game. Phillips started towards them and hefted the axe to his shoulder. The landlord looked up and his mouth dropped open. Phillips was almost to them, fingers tight about the shaft now. The tallest biker looked up, flipping his long hair from his eyes.

Phillips crossed the last two paces between them, both his hands on the axe now. He swung it high and hard and then down and with a cry like a beast, buried it deep in the bar. Glasses smashed. Beer flew. Bad-teeth reeled where he sat. Phillips grabbed him by his collar and lifted him right off the stool. Every muscle alive now, as if all the years had gone and he was young and fit and strong. He held him so high, his legs dangled above the floor. 'See that?' He hissed at the axe, embedded into the bar. 'If you ever come near me or my family again – I'll come back and cut off your head.'

Fourteen

Ninja and The Wasp drove towards the Neasden Bail Hostel. The Wasp stared moodily at the road. Ninja turned to look at him. 'We're doing the right thing yeah?'

'We're killers. We can do what the fuck we like.'

'But Denny, man.'

'What about him? No shithead's going to phase me out of the game.'

Ninja twisted his mouth at the corners. 'We don't know that he is. I mean, do we? Maybe he is looking out for us. Drug Squad on the estate, yeah? Maybe we should just lie low.'

The Wasp looked at him. 'You reckon?'

'Shit, I don't know. We don't know what's happening do we.'

'Fuck it,' Wasp said. 'It's Friday. We make the pick up, Ninja. That way we got his money. If he is giving us shit then we got something to bargain with.'

Ryan scratched his unshaven chin and sipped coffee. He looked at Vanner, then glanced out of the window of the flat once more. Across the car park, the bail hostel was quiet. He could see lights in the downstairs windows, but there was no movement. He looked at his watch and yawned. 'What happened to the bleedin' rota then, Guv'nor?'

Vanner chewed on a sandwich. 'I'm here aren't I.'

Ryan blew on his coffee. 'You find out anything from the broker?'

Vanner swallowed his bread. 'Nothing we didn't know already.

He gives Terry an edge. Sometimes he gets in before the kit goes to auction.'

'Stuff still gets turned around in Holland though eh?'

Vanner nodded.

'Maybe we ought to bust the yard, Guv. Take some of those trucks apart.'

'We'd never get a warrant.' Vanner shook his head. 'Let Customs watch him, Slippery. See what he does when he's across the water.'

Ryan lit a Camel. 'You want one of these?'

'Taste like horse shit.'

Ryan shrugged and stuffed the packet back in his pocket. 'Where's he making the squares?' he said.

Vanner made a face. 'We don't know that *he* is do we?'

'Somebody is.' Ryan sucked on his cigarette. 'Cready was over at the beginning of the summer.'

'Who?'

'Anton Cready. Before you joined us, Guv.'

'Who's Anton Cready?'

'Acid man from the States. About fifty. Willie Nelson looka-like. Throwback to the Woodstock days.' He flicked the end of the cigarette. 'Customs clocked him flying in. Stayed about three weeks and went home again.'

'Was he watched?'

'As much as he could be. But he's a smart cookie. Gave us the slip for a few days.'

'So you're thinking maybe Terry and Cready got together?'

'Why not? Terry's in the States a lot. Cready runs a bunch of psychedelic sixties shops. He's done it before. Set up a supply line of crystal. Fly in once in a while to brew up a batch.'

'Terry couldn't do it himself?'

Ryan made a face. 'I guess he could. But it's bloody delicate. I've been on the Squad three years and I couldn't do it. You've got to get the solutions just right. The timing and everything. Terry could get all the gear sorted, the trays and the mangle and that. But it takes an expert to mix it.'

'So where is it made then?' Vanner said, half to himself. 'Dartford?'

'Hell of a pong, Guv'nor. Alcohol's as strong as it gets. Hangs about for ages after. Certainly get the attention of anyone working there.'

The Wasp turned the BMW onto Neasden Road. He could see the lights of the hostel up ahead.

'What if somebody else is making the pickup?' Ninja said.

'Then we'll find out who he is and skin him.'

They pulled round the corner beyond the hostel and turned into the car park. The Wasp craned his head over his seat. Then he looked at Ninja. 'They won't see the car. Bleep them.' Ninja took the mobile phone from the dashboard.

Ryan was on his feet at the window. 'Guv'nor.'

Vanner got up quickly and came over. Ryan pointed. 'Grey BMW.' He lifted the binoculars to his eyes and spelled out the registration number. Vanner wrote it down. He glanced across the parked cars, as the back door to the hostel opened and a youth ran down the steps. He spoke into the radio. 'You there, China?'

'Already spotted, Guv'nor. We're getting the pictures now.'

Ninja looked out of the window as the black-haired boy came alongside. He dropped to one knee and peered at them. 'What's happening?'

'What d'you mean – what's happening?' The Wasp leered at him. 'The money.'

The boy shook his head. 'Not tonight, Wasp. We had word. Cancelled. We've been told to lay low for a while.'

'Fuckin' hell.' The Wasp thumped the steering wheel. Then he looked ahead and saw two men watching him from a parked car. 'Oh, Jesus.' He pulled out onto the road.

Ninja stared out of his good eye at him. 'I told you we shouldn't have gone. You should've listened to your man, Wasp. He gets about.'

'Shut up.'

Ninja folded his arms. 'Sometimes you're a real wanker. You know that.'

The Wasp drove on in silence, back towards the estate. 'They'll have the number,' Ninja said.

'So what? Won't tell them anything. We were talking to a mate. Nothing wrong with that. Besides, I've never been nicked.'

'I fuckin' have.'

'It'll be cool. What've they got? Nothing.'

'Ringo.'

'We wore rubber gloves. Relax, Ninja.'

Ninja shook his head. 'Relax. Fuck. Fuck relax, Wasp. Fuck it.'

He stood alone in the darkness. The silence of a cool head after the conversation with the hostel. He looked up at the stars through the window, prickling the spread of the night. Slowly he shook his head. The stupid ignorant fools.

He moved over to the desk and sipped from the bottle of water. He rubbed his eye with one hand and sat down in the chair. The payment books were alongside him and the Western Union slips. He looked at them, looked back at the screen. Ninja and The Wasp, like all violent men they had their sell-by date. He sat up straighter. Not yet, though: one more job before he would discard them for being the fools that they were. But that job was still unquantifiable. He would need to humour them yet.

Monday morning and McCleod was with Vanner. He told him that there were seven more hostels in the area. At least one inmate in each had a pager watch. Vanner considered the information. Morrison's Eagle Eye theory blown all to pieces.

Ryan came in with the pictures.

'Any good?' Vanner said.

'Bloody good, Guv.' Ryan was not smiling though. Vanner frowned at him. He shifted the papers from the desk and Ryan began to spread out the photographs. They were well taken. Blown up close-ups of the two youths in the car. One of them was black, one of them white. Both of them had dreadlocks.

Anne Barrington looked up from the phone call she was making. 'Car's registered to one Carlton Bishop, Guv. IC3. More commonly known as The Wasp.'

Vanner peered at the face in the photograph. 'We know him?'

'Sort of. Got in trouble at school. Expulsion etc. We've cautioned him once. But we've never actually nicked him.'

Vanner looked up at her. 'So we haven't got a print then.'

He looked closely at the picture of the white man. There was something odd about his features. Ryan was sitting with his back to the glass partition. 'Only got one eye, Guv'nor,' he said. 'That's what you don't notice at first.' Slowly Vanner lifted his head and for a moment they looked at one another.

'I know him,' Ryan said, cupping his cigarette between his fingers. 'I nicked him when he was eleven. Well he claimed he was nine but I reckoned about eleven. He was dealing smack. Eight years ago.'

Vanner sat down opposite him.

'We banged him up, locked him in a cell while we tried to find his mother. He went loco. Absolutely mental. Never seen a kid kick and scream and bite so much in all my life. Claustrophobic, big-time. Took three hairy-arsed coppers to stick him in the cell. Little bastard wrecked it. He had a gold sleeper in his ear. He was so fucking wired he tore it out. Ripped off his earlobe in the process.' He got up and drew on his cigarette. 'Look at his ear. You'll see a bit is missing.'

'What about his eye?'

'Always had that. He's a Gyppo. That's why we couldn't tell how old he was. No birth certificate. You're all right if he's Catholic. You might get a baptismal certificate. Not in his case though. Lost his eye in a fight, so his mother said. About six he had been. Some kid poked him with a stick. He's got scars above and below it. Makes him very distinctive doesn't it.' He stopped talking, pulled on his cigarette and tapped it out in the metal of the bin. 'His mother was dealing the smack. Using him as her front man. We couldn't prove he was older than ten so we had to let him go. I always thought what a mean bastard he would be – if he ever grew up.'

'What's his name?' Vanner said.

Ryan looked at him. 'Ninja. The Gypsy.'

Vanner sat back, lifted his fists to his chin and looked again at the pictures. 'Get Pierce,' he said to nobody in particular. 'Get his witness back in. I want him to look at these.' Ryan went out to find Pierce. Vanner looked at Anne. 'Do we know where they live?'

'Don't know about the Gypsy, Guv. But The Wasp lives on the Kirstall.'

Vanner bought coffee from the machine. Jimmy Crack came in with another man from the AIU. 'Bull's Head,' Jimmy was saying. 'Went right in and left the axe in the bar.' Vanner sipped frothy, cheap coffee. 'Guv,' Jimmy said.

'Jimmy. What's happening?'

'Nothing much. Saturday night was quiet.'

'Terry?'

'He showed. Pissed off with the new Tom on his arm.'

Vanner thought of Lisa Morgan. 'What's this about the Bull's Head?'

'Oh, that's something different, Guv. I was up at St Anne's on Saturday. Blokes there had nicked this ex-squaddie for burying an axe in the bar. Landlord's doing him for criminal damage.'

'Bull's Head's a smack house isn't it?'

'It is. Small-time though. Local boys watch it from time to time. Not a major priority.'

'Anyone we know – the soldier?'

'Phillips, I think his name was. Apparently some pushers have been terrorising his family, only he couldn't prove it. Obviously lost it, Guv.'

Vanner frowned. 'What outfit was he with?'

'Your lot I think. 9 Para' or something.' Jimmy put change in the machine. 'One thing though – might be interesting.'

'What's that?'

'He's a lecturer now. Teaches electronics in Kentish Town.'

Vanner went back downstairs. Ryan was sitting on the corner of his desk. 'Guv'nor, Morrison's just been on the phone. He didn't sound very happy.'

'When does he ever sound happy?'

'No. I mean seriously pissed off.'

'What's he got to be pissed off about? We're getting somewhere aren't we.'

Ryan looked at him. 'Glendale & Watts, Guv. He asked me if I was aware that you knew Andrew Riley.'

Vanner closed the door and sat down. He took out his cigarettes and toyed with the box in his hand. He could feel Ryan looking at him.

'He's one of the directors isn't he. Do you know him, Guv?'

Vanner did not reply.

'You didn't declare it then?'

Vanner shook his head. Ryan lifted one eyebrow and took the packet of cigarettes from his hand.

'I haven't seen him in eleven years, Sid.'

'So, how do you know him?'

'He's the man who stole my wife.'

He parked his car near Alexandra Park and looked for the house. Phillips was a lecturer at the college where Mark Terry attended. Maybe he knew Mark's father. On top of that Vanner wanted time to think before he faced Morrison over Riley.

He found number 57 and rang the doorbell. It was opened a crack, just the length of the chain and a tall, grey-haired man squinted at him.

'Yes?'

'John Phillips?'

'Who wants to know?'

'Detective Inspector Vanner, Mr Phillips. Once upon a time it was Captain Vanner.'

Phillips poured coffee and Vanner lit a cigarette. 'So you were with 3 Para, Sir?'

Vanner nodded. 'A long time ago.'

'I could've done with you. Really I could've – over the last few months.'

'Your son?'

Phillips nodded. 'Heroin addict. He's only seventeen.'

'You want to tell me what happened?'

Phillips recounted it all to him, and apart from the few words he had had with Alex Hammond, he realised that this was the first time he had fully articulated the whole story to anyone. When he had finished Vanner sat back in the seat. 'So finally you'd had enough?'

'My daughter, Sir. It was when they messed with my daughter.'

Vanner put out his cigarette. 'And now they're doing you for criminal damage?'

'Ironic isn't it. I'd do it again though, Sir.'

Vanner thought for a moment. 'Your lad's on remand in Norwich?'

'Yes. He was caught nicking cars in Great Yarmouth. Don't ask me what he was doing there. The holiday season or something. Trying to keep out of London.'

Vanner was still. 'My father lives in Norwich,' he said. 'I spent some of my childhood there.'

'There's a fella I work with, Sir,' Phillips told him, 'thought I might be able to get John out of prison and into the care of a doctor or something. Apparently it happens sometimes, if the offender's a registered addict.'

Vanner nodded slowly. 'It does happen now and again, yes. My father,' he said. 'He was a priest. He might know some people.'

Hope flared amid the liquid of Phillips' eyes. He looked at Vanner. 'You think he might, Sir?'

'I can ask him. No promises, mind. It'll depend on the magistrates.'

They sat for a while longer and then Vanner said: 'You teach now, right?'

'At the Tech. Kentish Town.'

'You know a student called Mark Terry? Bright Lad. Politics and Business Studies.'

Phillips nodded. 'I know him well. He and my boy John were mates. They were in the same year at school.'

Vanner looked at him. 'What's he like – Mark?'

'I don't teach him. But from what I remember he was always a nice kid. Bit quiet. Keeps himself to himself. Doesn't seem to have many friends. I guess he's a bit introverted because of what happened to him.'

'What was that?'

'His old man cleared off five years ago. Dumped him and his mother. They live on a council estate. The Kirstall. Right hovel it is. He used to live in Hampstead.'

'You know his father?'

'Not personally. I've seen him about the college from time to time. Why?'

'No reason.' Vanner stood up. 'I'll make a call for you, John. See what I can do.'

They shook hands. 'If there's anything I can do in return, Sir . . .'

Vanner nodded. 'I know.'

Morrison sat on the radiator. Vanner stood on the other side of the desk, listening to the rain rattle the window. 'You should have declared your interest, Vanner.'

'Our interest was James Bentt.'

'Yes, but yours was Andrew Riley.'

Vanner looked at him. 'Another director. Bentt was on holiday. I didn't know it was the same man.'

Morrison cocked his head at him. 'Come on.'

'There must be a hundred Andrew Rileys in London.'

'You knew he was in reinsurance. You must've known it was him.'

Vanner looked at him then. 'How do you know I knew that? Oh, sorry. I forgot. My past is a pet subject of yours.'

Morrison shook his head. 'Don't, Vanner. You don't have the legs.'

Vanner looked at the floor. Morrison was right of course. A

personal interest could get him sidelined. Not declaring it probably would. He could almost hear Weir, champing at the bit.

'You should've told me,' Morrison said.

'I was going to.'

'When?'

'When I was sure.'

Morrison pushed himself off the radiator and looked through the office window. Ryan was on the phone at his desk.

'Tell me about Friday night.'

'We've got two faces in a BMW. They live on the Kirstall Estate, or at least one of them does. McCleod's checked all the other hostels on the manor. Seven have kids with pager watches.'

Morrison looked back at him. 'Why weren't you here this morning?'

'I was checking out something Jimmy Crack told me. Man called John Phillips.'

'Oh, yes. I heard about that. Left his calling card at the Bull's Head in Tottenham.' Morrison studied his face. 'Crony of yours was he?'

'We've both been in the Army, if that's what you mean.' Vanner sat down. 'He's been terrorised by heroin dealers from that pub. His fourteen-year-old daughter was abused by them. You've got kids, Sir. How would you feel about that?'

Morrison blanched slightly. 'I wouldn't take the law into my own hands.' He touched the knot of his tie. 'Anyway that isn't important. What's he got to do with us?'

'He teaches at the Technical college where Target 1's son goes. He knows him well. He and his own son were friends.'

'So?'

'So, we have another perspective on Terry. I thought it worth pursuing.'

Morrison leaned his backside against the desk. 'This thing with the broking house,' he said more quietly: 'in your opinion – will we need to talk to them again?'

Vanner looked at him then. He had been waiting for the word to come. *Sorry, Vanner. Off the case. Enter Frank Weir.* Then he realised that now was not the time to shift him. They were beginning to get somewhere. The incident room had gelled to the point where the team were pulling for one another. Any *them and us* friction was long past. Morrison was too good a policeman to disrupt things unless he really had to.

'If we do – I'll send someone else.'

'Do that, Vanner.'

Ryan opened the door and they both looked round at him. 'What is it?' Morrison asked. Ryan grinned then. 'Result, Guv'nor. That was the Lab on the blower. The shit we found in Milo's flat. There *was* blood in it. Lab reckons whoever left it has a duodenal ulcer. He's bleeding. If it gets any worse he'll start puking it up.' He looked from one of them to the other. 'It fits the Gypsy. The street for most of his life. He eats crap food and does a bit of gear.' He paused. 'The blood gives us DNA.'

Vanner stood on the pavement and looked at his watch. Ten forty-five. The pub doors were shut but unlocked. He went inside and closed both doors behind him. One man, cleaning the surface of the bar. He stopped polishing and stared at Vanner.

'We don't open till eleven.'

Vanner moved towards him. He could see the split in the bar where Phillips' axe must have rested.

'I said, we're not open yet.'

Vanner moved up to him. He was squat, all but bald, a few traces of wispy black hair clinging in desperation about his ears. 'You the landlord?'

'Who wants to know?'

Vanner showed him his warrant card.

The man squinted at the card and then he seemed to relax. 'Come about the bastard who messed up my bar have you?'

'In a manner of speaking,' Vanner stared at him. 'I'm Drug Squad.'

The landlord's eyes flickered.

Vanner looked beyond the line of hand pumps. 'You've got a hole in your bar.'

'You don't say.'

'I take it you're insured.'

'Yes. But . . .'

'You know, if I were you I'd make a claim and put it down to experience. Be a talking point for years. Good crack for your punters.' He paused then. 'You see we know who your punters are. And you know what – we don't like them very much. Come to think of it – we don't like you very much.'

The landlord shook his head. 'You can't do this.'

'Can't do what exactly?'

'Threaten me.'

'Is that what you think I'm doing?' Vanner lifted one eyebrow. 'You'd know if I was threatening you. You see, I'd say something like: if you go on with your complaint then maybe I'll take an unhealthy interest in your pub. I'll have the TSG and sniffer dogs and great big coppers all over the manor. I might even close you down.' He paused and upturned a palm. 'You see I'm bound to find something.' He leaned then on the bar. 'Understand the difference? All we're doing is having a chat.'

The landlord chewed his lip. Vanner pushed himself away from the bar. 'Oh, one other thing,' he said. 'I reckon you can tell the three shitheads they ought to cut their losses. If they haven't got the message already then maybe it's time that they did.'

The man seemed about to say something. He looked at the hole in the bar and then his body sagged.

'I enjoyed our little talk.' Vanner opened the doors and set them back on their hooks. 'You have a good day now.'

That evening he phoned his father. He had not spoken to him since August.

'How are you, son?' his father asked him.

'Busy, Dad. Incident room stuff.'

'Ah. I understand.' A fractured pause between them. 'What can I do for you?'

'I need a favour.'

'Ask.'

'Bloke I know down here – his son's on remand in Norwich Prison. Name's John Phillips. He's a heroin addict. I want to try and get him out, maybe into a clinic somewhere. If he's registered it happens sometimes.'

'What did you want me to do?'

'You've got some contacts haven't you. Maybe you could have a chat. Go and see the boy maybe, see if there's anything you can do.'

'Yes, I could do that.'

'I'd appreciate it, Dad.'

His father was quiet for a moment. 'You should come and see us more often, Aden. Anne misses you.' Which meant he missed him. At that moment Vanner missed him too. There was so much to be said between them.

'I will come, Dad.'

'What about Christmas this year?'

Christmas. That lost time between December and January when the world stopped for some and ran away with itself for others. 'Haven't even thought about it.'

'Will you be working?'

'I don't know. I guess it depends on the inquiry.'

'Difficult one is it?'

'Liable to drag on.'

'I see.'

Vanner bit his lip. 'I'll do my best, Dad. It'd be nice to get away for Christmas.'

'See what you can do then.'

'Yes.'

'I'll work on this other business and give you a ring in a few days.'

'Thanks.' Vanner put down the phone.

The cyclist pulled onto the pavement and rested his bike against the wall. He pushed his helmet back and wiped the grime from his face, then readjusted the smog mask. Careful to lock his bike, he pressed the buzzer on the doorpost. Up one flight of stairs with the empty bag lying across his shoulder, he came to the small reception area. An Asian girl sat reading a magazine.

'You're new,' the cyclist said through his mask.

She nodded.

'Sven-Lido.'

She got up and went through to the back room. He waited, lightly tapping his half-gloved fingers on the desktop. She came back with a sheaf of padded envelopes bound in two elastic bands. She handed them to him. He thanked her and stuffed the envelopes into his bag. Then he went outside to his bike.

Andrew Riley poured himself a large measure of Bells and watched as evening drifted over the city. James and the others had gone home. A good day today, the Japanese deal finally closed which would make the last quarter look very good indeed. So good he'd have to talk to the accountants.

Vanner was in his mind. He sipped the whisky. Eleven years of silence and then suddenly there he was, large as life and sitting in his office. To walk in like that and see him after all these years, enough to give an older man a heart attack. That night he had gone home and looked at Jane: the beauty in her face, the depth of her eyes and the fire that still burned in them. He had not told her about Vanner.

He remembered when he had been best man at their wedding, he had known it would not last. What she saw in Vanner had been transient. Explosive, yes. A challenge, certainly. But explosions fade. Challenges are taken up and conquered. Vanner was the stuff of the immediate, not of the duration. He had known it then and he had bided his time. Oh, he knew he had wanted Jane the first time that he saw her. And his betrayal had begun at hers and Vanner's wedding. The life they had now, the home, the friends: he had imagined such a life with her all those years ago when first she had married Vanner. But he did not plot it so much as wait for the inevitable.

It had not been difficult. Vanner in Belfast all the time, with his men – his foolishly precious men. Jane on an Army base, in married quarters, for God's sake. Whatever was Vanner thinking of. An open invitation for a girl like that. He had been around. That much was deliberate. But, he told himself, it was as much for her as for him. And then when the time came, after Vanner got back from the South Atlantic, a visibly changed man, it was only a matter of when.

But the man unnerved him. Once he had called him friend and no matter how he tried to justify it, the taint of betrayal lacquered his shoulders. That was how Vanner had seen it. How else would he? It was true what he had said the other day: he had waited, wondered, lain awake at night and thought about getting into his car or getting out of it or going to the office and finding him there. But Vanner had melted away. Stayed in Ulster. Fought terrorists or whatever it was he did there. That was until last year when suddenly he was thrust at them out of the front of a newspaper, when those hit and run drivers were being executed.

But this. He looked again at Vanner's card, deliberately left for him perhaps as some permanent reminder of his responsibility for the past. Drugs and Michael Terry. Bobby Gallyon, he knew of now. James had told him about the man after he got back from his honeymoon. According to James, Terry knew Gallyon of old. He had acted for the family over their share dealings when he and James worked for the same stock-broker. James had been uneasy even then, everyone knew the rumour as far as the Gallyons were concerned. But Terry liked to sail close to the wind. The thrill of it all was what drove him. James had no idea Gallyon was involved with Terry now. Or at least, he said he hadn't.

Riley had been unsure about getting involved when James approached the board with Terry's plan for the trucks. Vanner was right about the ethics of his past. Terry had approached James when he resurfaced a couple of years after the fraud inquiry. But as James had said: the past was the past and the fees were potentially huge. Terry had shown him fresh, unencumbered stake money and a decent freehold in Dartford.

He himself had been aware of the market of course, but only vaguely. The firm dealt with the big insurers worldwide. Loss adjusters were part of it. Risk and reward: the old underwriting adage. But Terry had been right: buying early, before the auctions, gave someone an edge. And there was a hell of a fee in it. But this Gallyon getting involved. Thank God he had never met the man.

It occurred to him then that, according to James, Terry spent a lot of time abroad. Amsterdam. Didn't drugs come from Amsterdam? Those youngsters dying at parties. Ecstasy. Didn't Ecstasy come from Amsterdam? And the States. What, four – five times a year to check on his supply of spare parts. Not only that but South America. James had looked into it, and he found that everything Terry did with Gallyon was routed through Colombia. Cocaine came from Colombia.

The fees *had* been good though, and all it cost them was a little bit of information. But it's funny how the mind is concentrated when a ghost from the past suddenly slaps the words *Drug Squad* across the desk at you.

James had agreed to break the arrangement with Terry, tell him about Vanner's visit and put an end to it now. There was money enough to be made and he could not afford to jeopardise anything with Jane.

And Vanner's resurgence brought that old buzzard home to roost. She missed it, the fire. Fire was her nature. Oh, she needed the money, the house, the cars and everything that went with it. Eating in the best restaurants. Accounts at Harrods and Selfridges. She needed it, was born to it. But it did not replace the fire in her that was only sated by someone dangerous like Vanner. He thought the children would change her, but she was what she was. There had been lovers. A husband could always tell. He didn't mind really. None of them could match him for his ability to keep her. And she needed keeping. She knew it and she knew he knew it too. That, more than anything else was what kept them together. But now, Vanner, back as if from the dead. What if he tried to see her?

Fifteen

Vanner sat in the incident room with Ryan. They looked at one another. Pierce's witness had been in but he could not positively identify either Ninja or The Wasp. Ryan sat forward. 'Maybe we should pull the Gypsy.'

Vanner looked at him. 'I want whoever's behind it. We pull him now – we won't get him.'

Ryan rubbed his jaw. 'Everything's very quiet isn't it. He obviously knows we've clocked them.'

Vanner bought coffee from the machine and stood in the corridor watching the rain pressing the window. John Phillips had got his son into a drug rehabilitation centre in Norwich. His father had organised it. He really ought to visit his father. Christmas loomed on the horizon and he knew he would be stuck for excuses. He wondered at himself then. What else would he do, sit and brood in London? At least in Norfolk there would be someone to drink with.

He thought about Lucas Street in Chelsea. After eleven years he had finally looked her up. The desire to go over there. To stand maybe on her street, and have a look at the life she had now with Riley.

Michael Terry came out of James Bentt's office and kicked the bottom of the door. He thought by going to see him he could sort this. He needed the edge Bentt gave him. But the other directors were there and he had lost before he went in. That tight bitch Lisa. God, he wished they had killed her. He still had not told Bobby.

He picked Mark up from college and they went to McDonald's together. Terry watched him sucking milkshake through a straw like a child. He leaned forward. 'Don't make such a racket, Mark. You're seventeen.' Mark wiped his mouth on his sleeve. 'Look, I'm sorry about this weekend,' Terry said. 'But something just came up and I have to go away.'

Mark moved his shoulders.

'Come and stay in the week. I can run you to college.' Terry sipped his coffee. 'What've you been doing with yourself anyway?'

'Just college. Working. You know.'

'Nothing changes then.' His father sat forward. 'You know you really ought to think about what I told you. I know you think college is important and it is. But it isn't everything, Mark. There's other ways of learning things. What you need in this life's an edge. No academic's going to teach you that.'

'Education's an edge isn't it.' His father looked at him then and Mark held his eye.

'Well, isn't it?'

'That's better. Bit of fire, Mark. An opinion.'

'I've got opinions.'

'You just keep them to yourself, eh?'

His father sat back then. 'Things on your mind, Mark. Things you want to say.'

Mark dropped his gaze to the empty burger carton in front of him.

'Don't stop now. You've only just got going.' His father poked him with a stuff finger.

'Spit it out. Come on. Have a pop if you want to.'

Mark looked at the carton.

'Come on, Mark. I know you blame me.' He looked about the room. 'Get it off your chest for God's sake. Say what you want to say.'

Mark stared at the floor, fingers entwined in his lap. His father sucked breath. 'I can't change the past, son. But I can help with the future.'

'I've got a future.'

'Doing what?'

'University.'

'And after?'

Mark lifted his shoulders.

'Exactly. No direction. You can't afford to wait till you get there. You need to know what you're going to be doing after you've finished. You need to plan, Mark. Strategise. Find yourself a market. Make an opening and exploit it. I can help you with that.'

'I don't need any help.'

'No? Do it all by yourself will you? It's a big bad world out there, Mark. Everyone's looking to bring you down. You've got to know the ropes. Know how to handle yourself. How can you learn that if you never do anything? You won't even learn to drive. Most kids your age would be champing at the bit. You're nearly eighteen. All you do is play your bloody computer games.'

Mark sat where he was and looked down at the floor.

His father sighed. 'I'll take you home. Like I said. You can stay in the week. Why don't you bring a friend. There must be someone. Did you ever hear from John?'

Mark pressed his glasses against his forehead. 'He's in a drug clinic in Norwich.'

His father looked at him closely. 'How do you know that?'

'His dad told me.'

He stood over the bench where Cready had worked his magic and looked at the sheets of paper with Denny's face printed on them. Simple but brilliant really. Colour copier onto the paper. The only bit he could not do was mix up the solution. Still, what did it cost to fly in someone like Cready. Three hundred thousand squares was a million and a half on the street. Stocks were low now though. Sooner or later he would have to work the magic himself or get back on the phone to Cready.

He opened the last of the envelopes and piled the cash into bundles of the correct denomination. Beside it, he lay the smaller pile of Western Union slips and the statements sent over from Cready. The money was still pouring in. What had they really got when you thought about it? They thought they had him with Ringo, but they never got a look at the box. Maguire was sound enough. He knew they had pulled him. It was bound to happen sooner or later. But Maguire was out of the game.

He was well ahead of them now. When a pawn falls you take it off the board. Maguire's box was cold. Not so much as a sniff of a pickup. He knew that was what they needed. That's what Vanner would be looking for, a dealer with a box so he could watch for the pickup. Sooner or later they might find one. But by then it would be too late.

Sitting down at his computer, he loaded the accounts programme and ran a check on the numbers. Again he felt the surge of it all in his veins. Best of all was looking at the results, the bottom line profit, dotted here and there in little pockets of cash for collection sometime later. He switched programmes to the operatives and scrolled through the list of names. As he scrolled so his palms began to moisten. He stopped at the letter P. P for Phillips, John. For a long time he sat there. The past. The beginning. The end. Leaving the warehouse, he walked to the phone box and dialled The Wasp.

Vanner parked his car in a side street near Gallyon's nightclub and waited for Lisa Morgan. She had left a message on his answerphone and asked him to meet her here. She had not said why. He sat in the car with the sidelights on and watched the rain on the window. Ten minutes later a cab drew up and he saw Lisa climb out of the back.

She got in the passenger seat and shook the rain from her clothes. His head was thick with her scent, hair long and loose and gathered about her jawline, all but hiding her cheek. She fumbled in her bag for a cigarette and he lit it for her.

'So what's going on, Lisa?'

She crossed her legs and her skirt rode up her thighs. 'I'm going into the club.'

He stared at her. 'Why?'

'Because Michael Terry's in.'

Vanner looked through the windscreen. 'Why don't you just testify against him?'

'Because I couldn't prove anything. Come on, Vanner. You're the copper. What evidence have I got?'

Vanner moved his tongue over his teeth. 'Gallyon'll cut you in pieces.'

'Not if you're there he won't.'

He looked at her then and he laughed. 'Oh, I get it. Payback time.'

'Something like that, Vanner. Chance for you to redeem yourself. Play the protector you like to think you are.'

'Lisa. I can't go in with you.'

'Why not? You've been there before.'

He shifted himself in his seat. 'You've heard of the Regional Crime Squad?'

'Of course I have.'

'Well, they've been watching the club for months, watching Bobby Gallyon. I can't go in there again, Lisa. It'll jeopardise everything.'

'You mean they'll string you up by the balls.'

'In a word, yes.'

'Good. Let's get going then.'

She opened the door and stepped out into the rain. Vanner sat where he was. He watched her walk up to the corner, then he got out of the car and followed her. She was already inside when he got to the door. The two bouncers squinted at him. He moved between them and went up the stairs.

The dance floor was half empty, just the odd couple drifting together. He looked for the Regional plant but could not see him. That was something at least. He saw Lisa having a drink at the downstairs bar. The barman looked awkward but he poured gin anyway. Vanner bought a Becks and sipped it, standing against the wall. He watched Lisa. She did not look at him. Upstairs Michael Terry sat with his arm around a black girl, in a short white dress. He had his hand resting on her thigh, a bottle of champagne between them. There was no sign of Bobby Gallyon.

Two of the bouncers stood talking together at the exit. One of them nodded towards Lisa, who slid off her stool and made her way to the stairs. The bouncer stepped into her path. Vanner moved to the bar.

'What're you doing, Lisa?' The bouncer looked down at her.

'Having a drink, Billy.'

'You shouldn't be here. How come they let you in?'

She looked down at his crotch. 'Used my charm, Billy.'

'You've got to go, Lisa. If Bobby finds out he'll kill you.'

'No he won't.' Lisa pointed to Vanner. 'He's Old Bill. Touch me and he'll have you.'

Billy stared at Vanner. Vanner stared at Billy.

Lisa climbed the stairs, Billy following after her. Vanner watched Michael Terry. He was laughing. He emptied the bottle of champagne and snapped his fingers at the barman. Lisa was at the top of the stairs. Still he had not seen her.

She walked over to his table. He looked up, saw her and his face darkened visibly.

'Found a new friend have you?'

The black girl stared at her.

'What do you want?' Terry twisted his lip.

Lisa looked at the black girl. 'Has he used his belt yet? Jerked off in your face?'

The black girl got up. Terry gripped her wrist, but she pulled herself free and stumbled towards the stairs. Billy moved to the table.

'Time to go, Lisa.'

She ignored him. Terry sat where he was. Lisa leaned over him. 'You want to see what they did to me?'

Terry inched backwards. She pushed her hair from her face, then forced her scarred cheek up close to him. 'Not very pretty now am I.' As she said it, she picked up the heavy crystal ashtray and smashed it into his face. Billy was on her then, lifting her off her feet. Terry slumped in the chair, hands over his face. Blood pushed between his fingers.

Billy marched Lisa down the stairs and across the dance floor. Vanner caught up with them at the bottom of the steps to the street. He moved between them, face close to Billy's; big man, heavy-jowled, hair cropped close to his scalp.

'Leave her,' Vanner said. Billy half-closed his eyes, then looked beyond him to Lisa.

'Bobby'll remember this.'

'No he won't.' Vanner stepped into his space. 'He'll forget.' He flapped his warrant card under Billy's nose. 'If anything happens to her – I'll be coming back.'

They walked round the corner and Vanner took hold of her arm. 'You satisfied now?'

She walked away from him and looked up at the sky, rain falling on her face. 'You should thank me, Vanner. You can look in the mirror again.' She stopped then and looked across the street. A pale-coloured Mercedes was parked in the spaces reserved for the club. Lisa crossed the road.

'Where are you going?'

She took off her high-heeled shoe.

'Lisa.'

She started at the nearside wing and scraped the heel of her shoe the length of the car. Then she turned and started again. Vanner caught hold of her arm.

'Enough. All right. Enough.'

She laughed in his face. 'I haven't even got started.'

She pulled away from him and put her shoe back on. A taxi came round the corner and she flagged it down. Vanner watched her go. Then he looked at the car. The paintwork was totally ruined. Something under the windscreen caught his eye. He moved closer. Something small and brightly painted perched on the dashboard. He rubbed the rain from the glass. A dwarf. He was looking at a model of a dwarf.

Saturday morning and he stood in Oxford Street with buses pushing the length of the road. Across from him, Mark Terry sat in the window of System X and painted model figures. Vanner dropped his cigarette in last night's puddle and crossed over.

He looked down at the table. Mark leaned forward, dark hair falling across his glasses, tongue stuck to his lip while he concentrated on the strokes of the brush. After a moment he looked up.

'Hello, Mark.'

Mark looked blankly at him.

'The copper at your mum's house.' Vanner bent down, hands on his knees and looked at the figure he was painting. 'You're very good you know.'

Mark shifted his shoulders.

Vanner sat down next to him, watching his brushstrokes, the steadiness of his hand. He wondered what it would be like to have a son.

'How long've you been doing this?'

'Since I was fifteen.'

'Collector are you?'

'I was. Too old for it now.'

'Pocket money?'

'What?'

Vanner gesticulated around them. 'The job. Pocket money.'

'Oh, yeah. Right.'

'Who taught you to paint?'

'Taught myself.'

'Can you draw?'

'Some.'

'Get it from your mum do you?'

'Dad.'

Vanner nodded. 'And how is your dad?'

Mark looked at him then. 'He's all right.'

'Not seeing him today?'

'No.'

'You tell him we were at your house?'

'Might've done.'

'Where is he today? I thought you stayed with him on Saturdays.'

'He's away this weekend. He goes away sometimes.'

'Where's he gone?'

'Amsterdam.'

Vanner called Ryan at home. 'Give Customs a bell, Sid. Terry's on the hoof. Took a flight to Schiphol this morning.'

'Already done. I'm way ahead of you, Guv'nor.'

'Nice to know you're on the ball.'

'One thing, Guv. Customs noticed.'

'What's that?'

'Got a bloody great plaster on his face, right under the eye. Looks like somebody hit him.'

Vanner grinned and switched off his phone. Almost immediately it rang again.

'Vanner,' he said.

'Mr Vanner.'

'Jabba. Where are you?'

'At my restaurant. Have you had your breakfast yet?'

Jabba had a restaurant on Holloway Road. He worked it with his wife and five sons. In his spare time he was a property developer, a hosiery manufacturer and the best fence of precious gems Vanner had ever arrested. They sat across from one another in the kitchen, eating samosas and drinking thick, black coffee. Jabba talked with his mouth full, trailing spiced crumbs down his chin. He looked at Vanner from over the rim of his glasses.

'So sorry about the other fellow, Mr Vanner. My sources got it wrong.'

Vanner, smiled at him. 'Don't worry about it.' The thing he liked about Jabba was that when he did something it was never by half measure. He had cousins and brothers and uncles all over London. Most of them were bent in one small way or another, and through his network, Jabba was the best snout he had ever had. He had arrested him when he was a PC, almost ten years ago. Last prisoner – next informant. That was how it had been.

Jabba's wife came over with a tray of biscuits. She came back again with the coffee pot, then Jabba ushered her away. Vanner watched her go, then looked across the table again. 'You have something for me?'

Jabba sucked the food that was stuck in his teeth. He snapped his fingers and called out something that Vanner did not understand. A boy of fifteen or so appeared through the door of the store room.

Jabba put his arm round his shoulders. 'This is Danny. My son,' he said. 'Danny is what we call him in English.' He smiled widely, hugging the boy to him, showing all of his teeth. Vanner lifted his fists to his chin. Jabba clapped his son on the back and sent him away again. 'He's a good boy, Mr Vanner. Eyes and ears in his head. He goes to school near here. He told me a little story.'

Vanner sat further forward in his seat as Jabba told him how his son had watched a young boy dealing acid squares at school. Some of his friends had bought them. Jabba was at pains to point out that his boy was a good boy and he would not dream of buying the squares. But he had seen them, little scraps of paper with a red and white face printed on them.

Vanner sat back, his heart high in his chest. He looked at Jabba. 'The boy, Jabba. The boy dealing. What did he look like?'

'White boy, Mr Vanner. Blond hair. One of those studs in his nose.'

Vanner stood with Ryan and the others in the incident room. 'We've got a kid dealing Denny acid at Hawkswood School. He's got blond hair and a gold stud in his nose. He's thirteen. Name is Mickey Tomlinson.'

'Second tier, Guv'nor?' Ryan said.

Vanner made a face. 'He's far too young for a box. So yes, he must be second tier.'

'But maybe he's supplied by a boxholder.'

'That's what I'm thinking.'

He sat down on the desk. 'He's the first we've heard of in a school. But he lives on the Kirstall Estate.' He broke off and looked at Anne. 'We know that there are no boxes with two cards in Kentish Town. Hawkswood's in Tufnell Park. Get onto the Post Office, Anne. Find out if there's a box with two cards.'

Anne got up and went over to her desk. The phone was ringing in Vanner's office. He looked at the others. 'I want this kid watched. I want it round the clock if we have to. What we need is his dealer.'

He stepped into his office and picked up the phone. John Phillips spoke in his ear.

'Hello, John.' Vanner sat down. 'How's it working out for your boy?'

'Fine. Well as far as the programme's concerned anyway.'

Vanner frowned. 'There's a problem?'

'Not with the place. Your father really did us proud.'

'But?'

He heard Phillips sigh. 'His solicitor was in yesterday. And it doesn't look good. John's very depressed.'

'What did he say – the brief?'

'Well, we were hoping that the programme he's working would stand him in good stead, what with his age and everything. But the solicitor says the CPS are going to push for the maximum. John's got a record. He'll do a couple of years at least.

Vanner was quiet for a moment. 'He's only a lad. With remission he'll serve less than half.'

'Still too long. I've never seen him so down. I don't think he can hack it inside, Sir. He'll be straight back on the stuff.'

'I don't know what more I can do. He stole cars. It's as simple as that.'

'I know, Sir. But he's looking for someone to help him.'

'A deal?'

'Something like that. He asked me to have a word with you.'

'What about? Yarmouth arrested him. I'm not sure I can make any deals.'

'Well listen at least anyway. You're Drug Squad right?'

'Yes.'

'Does the name *Denny* mean anything to you?'

* * *

213

The Wasp took the map from Ninja and turned it the other way up.

'You stupid one-eyed fuck.' He worked his finger over the page and then scratched his head. 'Help if we knew where we were.'

Ninja looked out of the window. 'Norwich.' He pointed to a sign post. 'We're there.'

'So you can read all of a sudden.'

'I can read that.' Ninja stuck his elbow out of the window. The Wasp tightened his jacket at the neck. 'I ought to drag you behind on a skateboard. Fuckin' windows down, all the way from London. Don't you ever get cold?'

Ninja did not say anything.

'Well, I tell you – I ain't sleeping with them down.'

Ninja felt in his jacket for his sword. 'Told us there was a big job didn't he. Told you he wasn't phasing us out. You and your fuckin' paranoia.'

'Oh, yeah. Where'd you learn that word?'

'I know words.' Ninja rubbed his belly. He peered out of the window. 'Lot of trees up here ain't there.'

'Course there is, you wanker. It's the fuckin' country.'

'Yeah, but look.' Ninja pointed. 'Fuckin' hundreds of them.'

The Wasp lit a cigarette. 'You never been out of London then?'

Ninja shook his head.

'Some Gypsy you are.'

He stood in front of the window, looking out over the river. Cars moved on the far embankment, the dome of St Paul's glowing against the sky. The shower ran in the bathroom. He had the phone in his hand, the ringing tone of The Wasp's mobile in his ear.

'Yeah?'

'Wasp.'

'Yeah.'

'Where are you?'

'Just got there. Ninja can't read a map.'

'Too late for tonight then?'
'We haven't found the place yet. We've only just found Norwich.'
'Wasp.'
'What?'
'Be discreet. Don't make too much mess.'
'Tell that to the Gypsy. He's the one with the blade.'

Sixteen

Vanner parked alongside the river and crossed the footbridge by the Unicorn. Memories flooded back now. Himself and Kirston and Riley, three schoolmates. Drinking and talking. Boxing and winning. The cheering in his ears. The Army. The past creeping out to haunt him all over again. He wondered why he tortured himself so much. Other people had lives. Like Sid Ryan, for all of his front: he had a home and a wife and everything that went with it. But Ryan was other people. The needle was stuck in his own life.

The clinic bordered the river. The multi-storey car park on the other side. A shopping trolley sat upturned in the water. Beyond the clinic itself, a patch of undeveloped wasteground where people fished in the daytime. Vanner paused on the bridge, tossed his cigarette into the water and went up to the door.

He was met by Colin Mason: a skinny man with black and tangled hair, matching the moustache that covered his lips. His handshake was firm and his voice gentle. He smelled of coffee and cigarettes. He took Vanner into the office. 'John's taken well to the programme, Inspector. Your father did the right thing by getting him here.'

Vanner nodded, glancing round the room at the files and the flat computer screen that lifted from one of the desks. 'Is his father here?'

'Any minute. He phoned us half an hour ago.'

'Where's he staying?'

'Guesthouse by the station.'

217

Vanner nodded. 'Where's John now?'

'Day room. We'll wait for his dad and then I'll bring him down to the Doctor's office. It's quieter in there.'

Phillips arrived and Vanner met him in the hall, face grey, bags like bruises under his eyes. 'He's very cagey, Sir,' he said. 'Been really withdrawn since the brief was here the other day.'

Vanner nodded. 'Mason says we can use the doctor's office. You want to be there?'

'I'd like to. If that's all right by you.'

John Phillips Junior sat in the stiff-backed chair against the wall. Vanner took out cigarettes and passed him one. He offered his lighter and John leaned to the flame.

'So,' Vanner said. 'You know I'm looking for Denny. How come you know that?'

John hugged himself, his features pinched and drawn, hair lank about his face. He motioned to his father. 'He told me you were Drug Squad.'

'You know the cartoon?'

John nodded.

'Acid and E's. Fresh face on the street.'

'Not that fresh.'

'You know?'

'Yeah.'

'How?'

'I just do.'

Vanner made a face. 'I need to know how you know, John.'

John looked at his father, pulled on his cigarette and sat forward. 'The face is new. But the deal's been going for a while.'

'How long?'

John sat back again. 'Can you do anything about my case? That's what I want to know.'

'I don't know.'

'Well if you can't – I'm not saying anything.'

'John.' His father looked sharply at him.

Vanner held up his hand. 'It's all right,' he said.

He looked at the boy again. 'You were arrested in Yarmouth, John. I can make no promises.'

'Then, I don't talk. But think about it. What's a couple of cars compared to a major source? I can give you his name. The face behind the face. But if I do I get off this deal. Then I get protection till you've picked him up. I also get immunity from anything else that shows up.'

'Such as?'

John pinched the end of his cigarette. 'I can take you back at least three years with Denny.'

Vanner watched his face. 'How it began you mean? Street gangs. Robbing people at cashpoints. Handbags that kind of thing.'

'I can give you it all.'

'You know about the watches then. The bail hostels.'

'Don't know nothing about hostels.'

'You were involved though?'

'In the beginning I was.'

'Others?'

'All you want is Denny. He's the source isn't he.'

Vanner looked at him with his head on one side. 'Maybe I don't need you, John. Maybe I have suspects of my own.'

'Then why're you here?'

'Curiosity.'

'I'll bet.'

Vanner offered him another cigarette. 'I'll say some names. You can nod or shake your head.'

'No way. I'm saying nothing till I know I've got a deal.'

'How do I know you know?'

'Trust me.'

Vanner lit the cigarettes. 'Three years you say?'

'Small-time then. The face came later.'

'Last summer.'

'I don't know when. But I already knew the name.'

'Kirstall Housing Estate.' Vanner said it quickly and John

219

looked at the floor. He stood up and flicked ash in the direction of the table. 'That's it,' he said. 'You know I know. Get me off and I'll talk to you. I'm not saying any more.' He walked to the door and went out.

Phillips sat forward and made an open handed gesture. 'Never knew he could handle himself like that.'

Vanner glanced at him. 'He's a heroin addict, John. Been hanging around dealers long enough to know the score.'

'Can you help him? He's telling you the truth, Sir. I know when he's lying.'

'I'll do what I can. But I can't make any promises. You just keep him here. Make sure that he stays inside.'

Phillips looked keenly at him then. 'You think he's in danger?'

'No. Not while he's here. But you need to know, John. Whoever's behind this Denny – has already killed one person.'

Vanner stood up and Phillips touched his arm. 'By the way,' he said. 'They dropped the charges against me. The CID at St Anne's.'

'Really?' Vanner raised his eyebrows. 'How come?'

Phillips looked at him then. 'I don't know. But the landlord withdrew his complaint. Maybe somebody had a word.'

Ninja and Wasp sat in McDonalds. They had found the clinic, parked the stolen Transit and gone in search of food. Ninja licked mayonnaise from his fingers. 'How're we going to get the bastard to come out?' he said. 'We can't just go in and cut him.'

The Wasp was watching one of the waitresses swabbing the floor. 'He's a smackhead ain't he. Bet he comes out at night, sits by the river there and has a little drink. Can't come off that stuff without something. And he can't stay inside all the time.'

'What, so we just sit and wait do we? Could take fuckin' forever.'

The Wasp shrugged. 'We got to do it, man. Bastard knows doesn't he.'

'That ain't our problem.'

'Ten thousand quid, you fuckin' wanker.' Wasp bit into a Big

Mac and talked as he chewed. 'Besides, if he's a problem to the man then he is to us ain't he. If the man gets pulled then sure as shit we will.'

'What about the pigs though? They saw us in Neasden.'

'We don't know they were pigs.'

'What was it then – a fuckin' picnic?'

'That's London, Ninja. Relax. We're in Norwich remember.'

Ninja ate his chips. 'Oh, what the fuck,' he said. 'Maybe we can dump him in the river.'

'Ten grand, Ninja. Paid fuckin' assassins.'

Ninja made a face, and picked at the meat in his teeth. 'Still don't know how we're going to do it. What if he don't come out. Ain't like Ringo is it. Any fucker can just wander in there. Nobody gives a shit.'

Mickey Blondhair dealt Denny E's at school. An Asian boy stood next to him and rolled one between his finger and thumb. 'Fifteen quid?'

'Yep.'

'Ain't got the fuckin' dove on it. How do I know it ain't shit?'

'You don't need the dove. This is the best.'

The boy curled his lip at him. 'You'd know would you?'

'You don't want it. Fuck off.'

The boy paid him and pocketed the tablet.

Mickey watched him walk away. So much better than thieving. Pushing up his sleeve, he glanced at the face of his watch. Ten more minutes until dinnertime was over. There would be more yet. There was a rave by the railway tonight.

He was right. Two sixth-form girls made their way over to him, one of them smoking a cigarette. She dropped it on the ground as she got to him and blew the smoke in his face.

Across the road in the car, Anne and China watched him. 'Little sod,' Anne said. China focused his lens. 'Come on, Sunshine. Look at me.'

Mickey did not see them. He did not know they were there. He was concentrating on his trade. He wished he could bring out the little scales. Look real good with the scales. The girls hovered in front of him. He could smell them. He loved dealing to sixth-formers: when they bent down he could see their tits. 'Fifteen quid, girls. You got it?' The blonde one, Rachel whatever her name was, pushed strands of hair behind her ear.

'Not bad is it – contaminated? I don't want to die.'

'Don't take it then.' Mickey withdrew his hand. 'Or better still don't drink too much water.'

'Go on then.'

'Respect.' Mickey felt in his pocket.

Vanner leaned on Morrison's desk. 'He knows who Denny is.'

Morrison looked up at him, tapping his lip with one finger. Frank Weir sat in the other chair. Vanner had driven down from Norfolk and had gone straight to see Morrison in Hendon. He had interrupted their meeting.

'You're sure?'

'Why call me up there?'

'How does he know?' Morrison indicated the vacant seat next to Weir. Vanner sat down, took out his cigarettes, caught Morrison's frown and put them away again.

'I think he was involved at the beginning. He confirmed what we know about the street gangs, the organisation. They were probably very small-time then, the bottom rung of somebody else's ladder. He told me that Denny was at least three years old as a market before the face came on the scene.'

'Always Ecstasy and acid?'

'I don't know.' Vanner glanced at Weir. 'But he was a friend of Terry's son. Maybe the gangs were going first and Terry saw the opportunity when he was on the Kirstall. I mean, let's face it – it's a scam. Like something from *Oliver Twist*.'

Morrison looked at Weir. 'What do you think?'

Weir scratched his head. He glanced at Vanner and switched the gum from one side of his mouth to the other. 'Sounds about right. How did the Phillips kid get into smack?'

Vanner lifted his shoulders. 'How does anyone get into smack?

One thing leads to another. It's eighty quid a gramme, so he took to nicking cars.'

Morrison sat back in the seat and placed his hands behind his head. 'What does he want?'

Vanner looked at the floor. 'To walk away from the charges he's on.'

'Which are?'

'Car theft in Great Yarmouth. Ten other offences to be taken into consideration.'

Weir sat forward. 'That won't be easy.'

Vanner looked at Morrison. 'Do you want to talk to them – or shall I?'

Morrison leaned his elbows on the desk. 'I'll do it, Vanner. Diplomacy was never your strong point.'

Vanner nodded and stood up.

'And talking of diplomacy. I had Burke on the phone yesterday afternoon. Apparently the Tom, Lisa Morgan, went back to Gallyon's nightclub and hit our target with an ashtray.'

Vanner lifted one eyebrow. Morrison squinted at him. 'She said she had a copper with her, some sort of protection.' He paused. 'You know anything about it?'

'Didn't the Regional plant spot the face?'

'No. He wasn't working.'

Vanner shrugged. 'Lisa's up for it, Sir. She was probably winding them up.'

'You haven't seen her then?'

'Not since the last time. No.'

He opened the door. Morrison stopped him again. 'One other thing. The new dealer. The schoolkid.'

'Second tier. We're watching him.'

'There's something else about him.'

'What's that?'

'His description fits the Alan Boyd assault.'

Vanner looked back at him. 'I know.'

Ryan was rolling a cigarette when he went in. Vanner squinted at him. 'Getting late in the month is it?'

Ryan passed him the roll-up and pinched tobacco between his fingers for another. 'We've got a box in Tufnell Park, Guv.'

'Who?'

'Someone called John Smith.'

'Who the hell's he?'

'That's what I wondered. He lives on the Estate. The address is Carlton Bishop's.'

Vanner smiled. 'The Wasp. We still watching him?'

'We were, Guv. But he seems to have gone walkabout. Him and the Gypsy both.'

Vanner narrowed his eyes.

The Wasp stood in the shadows of the car park. Ninja was further down the path, almost to the far bridge, the other side of the river from the clinic. The Wasp looked behind him to the rising grey of the flats. He frowned. A lot of lighted windows. He looked again at the clinic and swore softly to himself. 'Come on, you fuck. Not another night in this carrot crunching shit-hole.' Ninja was making his way back towards him. The Wasp skinned his eyes and tried to penetrate the gloom on the far side of the river.

They had seen him today, spent the afternoon watching. Last night he had come out for a smoke with one of the others, but he had stayed close to the wall and they had not been able to get near him. Ninja was going spare. If he did not come out tonight then he would flip and go in after him. But this afternoon they had followed him into town, where he had gone into an off-licence and come out with a bag. Wonderfully predictable, smackheads. He had come back to the clinic from this side, jumping the fence to the wasteland by the underground car park. They had watched him stuff his package into the bushes that lined the bank. It was only a matter of time.

'Any sign?' Wasp asked as Ninja walked up to him. Ninja shook his head. The Wasp looked at his watch. Eleven o'clock. 'We'll get down there,' he said. 'Wait in the underground car park.'

They climbed the fence, The Wasp watching the flats behind them. Ninja dropped first and skittered down the bank, almost falling into the water. The Wasp landed next to him, feet deep in the mud. He grabbed Ninja's collar and hauled him up. They made their way over to the car park and took cover behind a pillar. A few cars were still parked, like squat, metal sentinels against the black of the night. The Wasp shivered and pulled the zip high on his jacket. He took out his cigarettes and lit one. Ninja laid a hand on his arm.

John Phillips made his way round the edge of the building and slid down onto the mud of the wasteground. He looked back, shivered and hugged himself. Then he bent down and pulled his bottle from where he had hidden it. He had been doing well, only cigarettes and coffee until that lawyer showed up with his glum face and his words of misery. Until then he had believed his father, started to believe Colin, that maybe there was some end to this after all. But after the bloody lawyer and then the copper – deal-making. He spent his whole life making deals. And Denny. How could he shop Denny? He unscrewed the cap on the bottle.

They climbed out of the shadows towards him, dark against the dark. He stood with his back to them, lifted the bottle to his lips and swallowed.

The Wasp cupped a hand round his mouth. The bottle slipped and landed with a slap in the mud. Phillips gurgled. The Wasp grabbed him tighter: one hand on his mouth, the other on his arm. Phillips struggled, tried to call out, but The Wasp pinched his cheeks together. And then Ninja lifted the sword. The Wasp felt warm blood on his fingers. Phillips' body went stiff and Ninja ripped out the blade. The Wasp pushed him into the river.

Vanner dreamed of Lisa. Michael Terry with a knife on her throat then drifting against her cheek. But then it wasn't Terry – it was him. He woke with her blood in his eyes. He could hear rain against the window. His head thumped as if he had been drinking all night. He got up, showered and dressed.

* * *

He stood under the arch that backed onto Lucas Gardens and the church. Rain fell in ribbons across the parked cars in front of him. He leaned against the chilled brick of the wall. Diagonally across the road, he could see the front door of number 73. Royal blue paint, not a chip or blemish in sight. The house, like those on either side of it, looked like a two-storey terrace. But he could see that the attics had all been converted and he knew there would be basements. Four-storey house in Chelsea. She had got everything that she wanted.

He had been here for half an hour now, just sheltering from the rain and watching. People came and went along the street, but the weight of the rain kept their heads to the pavement and not one of them gave him so much as a second glance. The irony hit him: he was in Chelsea, standing across the road from his ex-wife's house, and if he walked for another five minutes he would come to Lisa's flat.

He tossed away his cigarette and immediately lit another. Eleven years of silence and half a million pounds worth of house. Was she in? Was she out? Which was her car? He cast his eye along the line of parked vehicles: a BMW with the hood up. A Golf. A Saab. Which of those was her car? Did she work or did Andrew Riley keep her?

The buildings on his right were two-storey mews cottages with garages built underneath. On his left were a kindergarten and nursery. The arch separated them. Turning his eyes from the road, he glanced through the damp vegetation towards the park with its wire bordered paths and its Kensington Council flower beds. A small white sign indicated that there was an antiques fair in the church. He wondered if that was all it was used for. And then he thought of his father. He had married them, him and Jane, at Sandhurst. It was the one and only time he had been glad he was a priest. He could see him now in his robes of white and green and gold. Tall, white-haired, proud of what he was and of who and what his son was. Never once had he judged him; not in Ulster or the Falklands, or last year when he had assaulted Gareth Daniels.

He threw away his cigarette and moving further along the archway, he glanced through the window of the kindergarten. He saw a wooden, gymnasium-style floor and he was reminded of the carpetless solitude of his house. A row of children's pegs stretched across the far wall with paint capes hanging on them. He perused the name tags above each peg and then he stopped and stared. *Jessica Riley. Thomas Riley.*

Somebody walked across the cobbles behind him, the clack of a woman's shoes. Vanner still stared in the window. From the corner of his eye he could see a huge, pottery urn, gripped by hands with crimson-painted nails. He could not see her face but she almost walked into him and he moved smartly aside.

'Sorry.' Rain-spattered Burberry and smoothly arcing calves. She walked past him and crossed into the rain. He could see the back of her head: jet black hair, scraped away from her face and tied in a plait over her collar. And eleven years unfurled and her touch on his arm and her voice in his head and *sorry*.

He leaned against the window, with the names of her children in his eyes and *her* crossing the road and walking away from him with straight back and fine limbs, clutching the urn that was all but as big as she was. She moved between the BMW and the Golf and stopped outside the door to number 73. She put down the urn, fumbled in her pocket for keys and then she was in and gone and he was alone with the rain and the past and the names of her children on clothes pegs.

He felt the twisted emptiness in his gut; as if he was back on that plane to Belfast with the Green Jackets all around him and the whine of the engine, dulling the voice in his head. Then he saw the keys still dangling from the lock. Crossing between the cars, he looked closer. He looked right and left, then stepped up to the door.

The house was still, save the sound of somebody humming from below the stairs at the end of the hall. Her coat still dripped where it was laid over the banister. Footsteps on the stairs. He stepped through the door on his left. A study. Riley's things. Riley's desk. He was filled with a desire to smash them. But he stood very still and cut his breathing to nothing as the front door was opened. He heard the rattle of keys and then it was closed again. She fussed about in the hallway. He could hear every move, the rustle of her skirt across stockings. He could smell her, the same scent she had always worn. It took his mind back to his days in Sandhurst, the only cadet who had witnessed life on the street, with a tour in the Province already under his belt.

In his mind's eye he could see her, white dress off one shoulder, clutching at full and youthful breasts. Hair drawn back from her face, the high arc of her neck, creamy and taut and smelling of that scent that plagued him now like memory. And the others: who postured and joked and laughed with her, while he stood at the bar in silence. Then her standing next to him and looking in his eyes and him stirring and the way she sipped gin with half a smile on her lips.

She moved along the hall and he could hear her feet on the stairs to the first floor. Her weight above his head as she moved into the room at the front of the house. Bedroom? Sitting room? He stepped out into the hall. Her feet above his head, moving back to the landing.

He stood in silence and looked back to the front door, wondering what he was doing here. Then he heard her cross the landing once more and he went down to the basement. He came out into a white-tiled kitchen that gleamed even in the frail light that dipped through the basement window. The urn stood at the bottom of the stairs. On the other side, a dining room; huge oval table, guarded by eight mahogany chairs.

He heard a bath running as he went back up to the hall. She was humming again, walking across the landing, presumably from the bathroom to her bedroom and back again. Her bedroom – where she slept and made love with Andrew Riley, the best man at their wedding. He placed one hand on the banister and touched the cloth of her coat. Upstairs, she crossed the landing a final time and then a door was closed and taps were turned off and he heard the sound of her sliding her naked body into water.

He stood outside the bathroom, listening to the sound of water moving over her flesh. The door across from him was closed, but the other, at the front of the house was ajar. He moved towards it, paused and then climbed the next flight of stairs. Another closed door. He opened it and children's beds and clothes and toys seemed to squash against his face. Eleven years of nothing and the stain of red on a sheet. He closed the door quietly, climbed the remainder of the stairs and came out in a spacious attic lounge. Two white couches with a glass-topped coffee table between them. A fireplace with no fire. He went back downstairs.

And now he stood outside her bedroom, listening to the sound of her bathing. Still she hummed. She sounded very happy. He went into her bedroom. Unmade bed full of pillows and soft, down-filled duvet all crumpled and ruffled as if she had only this minute left it. And on the floor at his feet, her skirt and her blouse and her black, silk underwear. He could not help himself. He did not want to do it, but he bent and lifted her blouse. He touched her bra, panties, her stockings; lifted them to his face, closed his eyes and breathed. Then he moved back to the landing. The bathroom door was open: she stood with a towel wrapped round her.

For a long moment they looked at one another. Vanner felt the knots in his flesh. She stared and stared, her eyes growing ever wider. Fear: in her face, in her eyes, the last time he had seen her. He shallowed his gaze and stepped past her. No word between them, only the height of her cheekbones, the unbroken sheen of her skin and the fear that lit up her eyes.

He was on the phone to The Wasp, standing in the dull light that breached the window through the rain. He could see the phone box from here, see The Wasp, only The Wasp did not know he was looking.

'Done?'

'He's floating in the river. Fuck-off hole in his back.'

He nodded, as if to himself, a tingling sensation crisscrossing the palms of his hands.

'Good. Now we lie low.'

'The money?'

'It'll be delivered to your box. Just wait a few days.'

'Make sure that it is.'

'What did you do with the van?'

'Dumped it.'

'And your clothes?'

'What about them?'

'Any blood on your clothes?'

'What d'you think we are – fuckin' amateurs?'

Jane sat on her bed, still wrapped in the towel, and looked down at her clothes. He had touched them. She knew he had touched them. Sudden heat in her bladder. She shook as she felt in the night-table drawer for a cigarette. Andrew hated her smoking. Andrew. She looked across the bed as she lit the cigarette and his smiling face lifted out of the photograph. Tears filled her eyes then. She drew smoke in too deeply and coughed it out again. She picked up the telephone and, with trembling fingers, she dialled.

Vanner walked, hands low in his pockets. Above his head, above a weary city, a tired and cloud-blown sky. Away from her house, across King's Road and all along Chelsea Manor Street. He took out a cigarette, cupped his hand to the match and tossed it away. He inhaled, exhaled without removing the cigarette from his mouth and stared at the weight of Lisa's building.

She waited for him in the hall, black skirt, black skintight top. 'Back so soon, Vanner?'

'I figured I was in credit.'

The dressing was gone from her face, but she kept her right cheek from him. At this angle her beauty remained intact and the fire was back in her eyes. He stood where he was, coat still buttoned, hands rooted in pockets. She watched him, stiff-eyed, as she had watched him when first he had interviewed her. She did not say anything, just kept her disfigured cheek from his gaze and looked him up and down. And he could do nothing but stand there, desire on his tongue and an overpowering need to bury himself in her flesh.

Then he was moving towards her, pulling away his coat. He took her, lifted her off her feet and pinned her against the wall. She wrapped her legs round his waist, arms about his neck. He forced his face into hers, jarring her head against the wall. The hint of wine on her breath. Fingers under her skirt, probing moist and naked flesh. He felt himself suddenly stiffen, harder and harder and harder. Scrabbling now with his jeans, pressing himself against her, forcing her into the wall. Breath ragged in his throat, seeking and missing, seeking again and still missing. Then her hand, guiding him, flesh entering flesh and pain like heat in his loins.

Seventeen

Vanner walked into the incident room and the silence lifted against him. He stared at the faces around him. 'What?' he said.

Ryan dragged fingers through his hair. 'Call came in from Norwich, Guv. The Phillips lad's been murdered.'

Five-thirty: Vanner stood by the river and looked at the area cordoned off by the Norwich SOCO team. Ryan was talking to one of the officers. Vanner stared at the patch of ground where a scuffle had obviously taken place. There were at least three clear footprints, one in particular close to the bridge, cutting deeply into the mud: what looked like the soles of tennis shoes or basketball boots. The rest were a mish-mash, all pushed into one another. A discarded bottle of cheap whisky lay in a bush. They had dragged John Phillips from the water.

Ryan came over to him. Vanner glanced beyond him to where Colin Mason was standing with John Phillips Senior, resting a hand on his shoulder. On the bridge to the right, traffic rolled onward as ever. A few pedestrians walked down from the city and glanced in their direction. 'Didn't spot him till this morning, Guv.' Ryan nodded to the flats across the road. 'Student went out for a run. She saw him in the water.' He pointed to the upturned shopping trolley. 'He was tangled up in that.'

Vanner followed his gaze. Drizzle mottled the flat of the river. He looked to the other bank and the path that carried as far as the second bridge. Then he scanned the height of the car park. His eyes settled on the exit and he cocked his head to one side.

'Take a look, Sid.'

Ryan glanced at him, then looked where he looked. 'What?'

'Security cameras.'

Ryan saw them now, a three headed camera fixed at the height of a pylon.

Vanner lit a cigarette and looked again towards Phillips. Briefly their eyes met and Philips looked away.

'Poor bastard.' Ryan shook his head.

Vanner looked beyond the blue and white tape once more. 'Prints look as though they might give us something.'

Ryan leaned on the fence. 'Spoke to the SOCO over there. Tuck. Reckons he'll get a cast from one at least.'

Vanner left him then and walked over to Phillips. Mason moved aside. Phillips crouched against the wall of the clinic and stared down at the ground.

'I'm sorry,' Vanner said.

Phillips let air escape from his mouth and slowly he shook his head. His face was beaten, puffy about the eyes, as if all the fight was gone from him.

'You all right?'

A muscle twitched in his jaw. 'I told him to stay inside. Why didn't he stay inside?'

Vanner squatted next to him. He offered his half-smoked cigarette and Phillips drew heavily on it, then looked sharply at him. 'You told me he wasn't in danger.'

'Up here?' Vanner motioned around them. 'I didn't think he was.' He looked once more to the metal cask of the trolley, protruding from the dark of the water.

Phillips looked suddenly helpless, eyes roving the river as if he half-expected to see his son rise from the depths. He shook his head, lifted his hands. Tears formed in his eyes and for a moment his mouth worked soundlessly. 'How could it happen? I mean, how the hell could it happen?'

Vanner looked at the mud at his feet. 'Who knew he was here?'

Phillips moved his shoulders. 'You. Me. Your father.'

'Nobody else?'

'The doctors. People here.'

'You didn't tell anyone else?'

Phillips looked up at him then. 'One of the lads from college. Mark Terry,' he said.

Andrew Riley sat with his wife: not next to her; not holding her, but across from her on the other couch in their attic lounge in Chelsea. He wanted to comfort her; but all of a sudden he could not remember how. She stared at the emptiness of the fire. 'I can't believe he came here,' she said. 'I mean – why? It's been eleven years.' She looked at her husband and immediately he looked away. 'Andrew?'

'He came to see me,' he sighed. 'Last month.'

'Came to see you. Why didn't you tell me?'

'There was no need to tell you. It was to do with business.' He paused then. 'He didn't say anything to you?'

'I told you. I just opened the bathroom door and he came out of our bedroom.'

'But I don't understand how he could've got in?' he squinted at her then. 'Are you sure you didn't invite him?'

'Oh, for God's sake. I left the keys in the door. It was only for a moment. I was carrying that urn I brought from the fair.' Then she remembered. 'I bumped into him. He was standing under the arch. He must have watched me. Followed me over the road and then let himself in.'

Riley stood up and rested a hand on the mantelpiece.

'You still haven't told me why he came to see you,' she said.

He shifted his weight.

'Andrew. What aren't you telling me?'

He sat down again. 'It's nothing I've done, Jane. It's nothing to do with me at all really. One of James' clients. He came to ask about him.'

'But you said he was in the Drug Squad.'

'Yes.'

'You've got a client dealing in drugs?'

Riley paled slightly. The look in her eyes; the fear all at once, distrust. 'If he is – *I* don't know anything about it.'

'What sort of a client is he?'

'He imports plant. Dump trucks, that kind of thing. Sells them on again.'

'So, what's that got to do with you?'

'Some of them are insurance write-offs. We deal with loss adjusters. You know that.'

'Do I? You've never really told me what you do.'

He looked at her then with his chin high. 'Well if I haven't – it's only because it wouldn't interest you.'

'How d'you know it wouldn't – if you've never bothered to ask me?'

'I have asked you.'

'Then why're we having this conversation?'

'Jane,' he said. 'We're having this conversation because you're upset. I'm upset. I didn't want to see him. I never wanted to see him again. I don't want him back in our lives.'

She looked at the floor. 'He isn't back in our lives.'

He left her then and went down to his study. He picked up the telephone and dialled Scotland Yard. A receptionist answered him and he took out the card that Vanner had left him. 'I want to speak to whoever's in charge of the North West Area Drug Squad,' he said.

Vanner and Ryan drove back to London in darkness. They were silent for a long time, the length of the A11 rolling out in front of them, the single carriageway between Thetford and Mildenhall clogging up with lorries. Ryan was driving, looking every now and then for an opportunity to overtake.

'What about the dealers from the Bull's Head?'

'Could be.' Vanner stared into trees. 'I don't think so though. Phillips told Mark Terry that his son was in a rehab clinic in Norwich.'

Ryan stared at him. 'Why would *he* want to know?'

'I don't know. But it's something I'd like to ask him.'

* * *

Late the following morning, Vanner went down to the incident room. He saw McCleod sitting with Anne. They looked away from him. He peered at them for a moment, and then he saw Morrison, sitting behind his desk. Frank Weir was with him.

Morrison got up, said something to Weir, who came out of the office. Morrison beckoned Vanner. He passed Weir, chewing gum, hands in the pockets of his suit.

'See you,' Weir said, and walked up the stairs. Vanner looked again at the others. Still they avoided his eye. He went into his office and closed the door. Morrison sat in his chair.

'Sit down.'

'You want to hear about Norwich?'

'Not from you. Slippery can fill me in.'

Vanner could feel the hairs on the back of his neck. Morrison held his gaze, green eyes, very pale, and full now of contempt. 'You're a fool, Vanner. Whenever I think otherwise you go out and prove me wrong.'

Vanner sat down and placed one fist on the desktop. Morrison looked at it. 'That's you all over isn't it. Saw that in you the first time we met. I might've been wrong about the Watchman. But I was never really wrong.'

Vanner did not say anything.

'You don't play by the rules,' Morrison went on. 'You never did. This is the Met, Vanner. Not some two-bit bunch of mercenaries who make it up as they go along. You have to go by the book. Stupid little things, like details, matter. Procedure matters. Disclosure matters, Vanner.'

Andrew Riley. Jane would have told him. Why did he think she would not?

'You should have told me about Riley,' Morrison went on. 'I let that go. I shouldn't have. Like a berk I cut you some slack. I tell you this now: I did it for the good of the inquiry.' His lips soured in his face. 'But you – you don't give a toss about the inquiry. You only came back because somebody hit you. That's no reason to be a copper, Vanner. That puts you exactly where they are.' He made a sweeping motion with his hand. 'Out there on the street, with the thugs and dealers and pimps.'

'I take it I'm off the case.'

'You brought it on yourself.' Morrison shook his head. 'I can't believe you went into their house.'

'She was my wife.'

'She's *his* wife now. And if he makes this official you're history.'

'You mean you didn't suggest it?'

Morrison was on his feet, fists suddenly clenched. 'Get out, Vanner. Take a holiday. A long one. Go away somewhere. Anywhere out of my sight.'

Ryan caught up with him in the car park. Vanner stopped, key in the lock of his car door. 'What's the story, Guv'nor?'

'No story, Sid. I just fucked up that's all.'

He stared into the bottom of his glass. Ryan looked across at him, holding a cigarette between his fingers. 'This going to be a wake, Guv'nor?'

'Probably.'

'Handle the hangover can you? You've got no one to wipe your mouth when you chunder.'

Vanner looked at him over the rim of his glass. 'I've had more hangovers than even you have, Sid. And that's saying something. They're like war medals. You win 'em and you wear 'em.'

Ryan sighed. 'So, now we've got Weir.'

Vanner shrugged. 'Results man. He's all right.'

'He's a fucking empire builder.'

Later, glasses piling between them, Ryan smoked Camels. Vanner stared at the wall behind his head, as sober as the moment he walked in. 'Ninja,' he said. 'One of the scroats who jumped me.'

Ryan looked at him, head to one side. 'You said they had hoods on.'

'I also said one was IC1. Eyes were fucked up. How many others look like Ninja?'

Ryan squinted at him. 'That doesn't make any sense.'

'No. It doesn't does it. If it was Ninja then it was also the other one. Why have a go at me?'

'You've never come across them before?'

'Never.'

'Maybe they just mugged you.'

'Maybe the world is flat.'

Frank Weir was in Vanner's seat at seven the following morning. Ryan came in at eight and Weir called him into the office. 'You all right?'

'Sparkling, Guv'nor.'

Weir half-closed one eye. 'Nobody likes it when the Guv'nor gets switched in the middle of an investigation, Sid. Especially his minder.'

Ryan looked at him. 'I'm a copper, Guv. Like you. It happens. You're in the hot seat now.'

'That's right.' Weir sat forward again. 'And I need you on my side. You're the best there is in the Drug Squad. Word is the big boys are taking a look at you.'

'Is that who it is?' Ryan lifted his eyebrows. 'Wondered who was plotted up in the house opposite mine.'

Weir grinned at him. 'Always the joker.'

'Just blabby, Guv.'

Weir picked up a 50/20 form from the desk. 'I hear Phillips' old man told a kid at college where his son was.'

Ryan nodded. 'Target 1's boy.'

Weir put down the paper. 'I think we should have a word with him. Don't you?'

They found Mark Terry in a politics lesson. They summoned him from the class and sat him down in the staff room. He looked very small in the chair.

'You all right?' Ryan asked him.

He nodded.

'You and John were mates, yeah?'

Mark was shaking. He looked down at the floor.

'It's all right, son. You got nothing to worry about,' Weir said it kindly. 'We know how it is to lose a mate. But we need to have a few words. You understand. We have to find out who did this.'

Mark looked up again and touched the sleeve of his shirt to his eyes.

'John's father told you he was in Norwich. Didn't he, Mark?' Ryan said.

Mark nodded.

'Did you ask him or did he just tell you?'

Mark looked at him then, eyes bunched and reddened at the edges. 'I was worried about him. You see, I saw these three guys having a go at Mr Phillips in the car park. Back at the end of the summer term. I asked him about John then. We used to be really good mates.'

'We know that, Mark.' Weir laid a hand on his shoulder. 'The thing is only a handful of people knew where he was. Did anybody ask you about him?'

'You mean like the blokes I saw in the car park?'

'Anybody.'

Mark looked out of the window. 'Only my dad,' he said.

Outside Ryan got in the car. 'You want to bring Terry in, Guv?'

Weir shook his head. 'The boy'll tell him we called. I want him to sweat. Sweating makes people nervous.'

Mickey Blondhair did his sums. He sat on the floor of his bedroom and worked out the numbers. Then he wrote them down on the paper The Wasp had given him, and slipped the notes into the brown padded envelope. Pasting it down, he wrote the box number and the postcode on the front. Then he went outside.

McCleod walked past the café, leafing through the pages of a newspaper. He watched as Mickey slid the package into the post box.

Ninja sat in his girlfriend's flat with the windows open. The TV flickered but he ignored it. Rain fell in sheets, splashing the inside of the sill. His sword lay on his lap: he smoothed his fingers over the blade and grimaced. The Wasp came in from the kitchen, two bottles of beer in his hands. 'What's the matter with you?'

'Chipped my fuckin' sword.'

'Where?'

Ninja held it up to the light and The Wasp saw three little nicks, two thirds of the way down the blade. 'Ach.' He handed Ninja a beer. 'Still works doesn't it.'

The Wasp sat down and stared at the TV. Ninja put the sword on the floor beside him then he picked it up and inspected it over again. The Wasp watched him from the corner of his eye. He shook his head. Ninja put the sword back in its scabbard and laid it on the floor. He tipped the neck of the bottle to his lips, wiped his mouth with his hand, and tipped the bottle again. He looked at The Wasp. 'When do we get the money?'

'Not till next Friday. He reckons it'll take him that long to get it together.'

'You believe him?'

'What choice have we got?'

Weir took the briefing, his first formal one since taking over from Vanner. He stood at the front with his hands in his trouser pockets. Morrison sat on the edge of the desk.

'Just so you all know – DI Vanner is back at Campbell Row,' he said. 'No mystery. Personal interest became apparent so he could no longer be involved here. As we've got a second murder, albeit in Norwich, DI Weir will assist me from now on. The rest remains the same.' He glanced at Weir. 'Frank.'

Weir stepped forward, flicked his gaze across their faces and cleared his throat. 'Word from Bethel Street, that's Norwich CID, is that Phillips died from a single stab wound. The blade was very long, perhaps some kind of sword. Good news is that the FME found two splinters in his rib cage. If we find the blade we should be able to match them.'

Ryan said: 'Any positive ID yet, Guv?'

'Not so far. But if our two boys were there – it had to be for a couple of days at least.

'They stand out a mile. Some bugger'll've seen them.' He looked at his notes on the desk.

'The videotape from the security camera is being checked. It's possible they watched from the car park.

'Now. This morning Sammy clocked the dealer from Hawks-wood School, posting a package. If our guess about the second tier is right then it could be to the box in Tufnell Park. We know there are two cards. If we're to take this up the line we need the pickup man. The previous supposition – that it'll be one and the same man for every box – is likely to be right. If I was running this operation, I'd only want one body collecting my cash. This box could give us the man. We don't want to alert anyone unnecessarily, so for that reason we're laying off Targets 2 and 3. If we get a positive ID from Norwich we'll think again.'

'We don't want the weapon going walkabout, Guv,' Anne said.

Weir shook his head. 'Not likely, Anne. The shape of the wound is the same as the Bream Park killing. If he used it twice – I reckon he's quite attached to it.'

'What about the prints in the mud?' China asked.

'Very expensive boots. Basketball type. Over a ton a pair.' Weir grinned. 'Not the kind of thing that's going to get thrown away lightly. The print is distinctive. The heel worn on the inside. The wearer walks with his feet slightly in, not knock-kneed exactly but getting there.'

Pierce folded his arms. 'What about Target 1, Guv?'

Weir looked at him. 'We know from Phillips Senior that he only told one other person about John and the rehab clinic. That was Mark Terry. Sid and I paid him a visit. He told us – he only told his father.'

McCleod scratched his head. 'What about the dealers from the Bull's Head? They had as much reason as anyone.'

'Picked them up already,' Ryan said. 'Alibis all of them. They've got at least a dozen witnesses who'll swear they were in the pub on Wednesday night.'

Weir continued: 'We've got a plot cleared with the Royal Mail. We can place a boy behind the box counter.' He grinned then, showing his teeth. 'So, who wants to play Pat for a day or two?'

Vanner went into System X on Oxford Street. Friday morning, quiet in the shop, only one lad in a green sweatshirt, painting models at the table. He was intent on his work and did not look up. Another lad came out of a doorway behind the counter. Vanner nodded to him and then began to peruse the hundreds of tiny figures that lined the racks below the computer screens. He studied all of the packages individually but nothing caught his eye. As he turned to the battle table in the middle of the floor, the lad from the counter came up to him.

'Can I help you at all?'

Vanner looked at him. 'Denny.'

'Pardon?'

'Have you got a character called Denny?' He took a photocopy of Denny's face from his wallet. 'Looks something like this.'

The lad looked at the picture, glanced briefly along the shelves and shook his head. 'No. Sorry. Have you seen it somewhere?'

'Did you ever have one?'

'Not that I know of. But I've only been here a year.'

'Who would know?'

'Head Office, I suppose.'

'Do you have the number?'

Vanner rang the head office in Manchester. He was put through to the products department, who told him that the company was ten years old and that they changed their stock lines of models as and when the computer games went out of fashion. He said that he had not known of a Denny, but he would check. Vanner said he would send him a copy of the picture and gave him his home telephone number.

He went back to Campbell Row and bumped into Ellis. They eyed one another on the stairs.

'What's going on?' Vanner asked him.

'Hash bust. Bit of smack.' Ellis looked at him. 'Denny was the main event though wasn't he.'

Vanner said nothing. He made his way up to his office. Inside, he shut the door and the confines of the room closed about him. To his credit, Ellis had been efficient in his absence, most of the stuff they were working on was up to date. As far as Vanner was concerned he could carry on being efficient. Sitting back in his chair, he watched the clouds roll like smoke above the city. On the pad there was a message for him to call McCague.

'So what happened?' McCague asked him when he got through.

Vanner pushed at his eyes with stiff fingers. 'Oh, the usual. Me and Morrison.'

'Told me you had a personal interest that went undeclared. Then you went into somebody's house. Bright of you, Vanner.'

'My wife, Guv.'

'Ex-wife.'

'Yes.'

'Bloody stupid thing to do. Even for you. Morrison said you had leave owing. He reckons the pressure must be getting to you.'

'Morrison's . . .' Vanner began but stopped himself.

'Maybe he's right,' McCague went on. 'Maybe you came back too early.'

'You think I need a holiday?'

'Don't you?'

'What the hell would I do with it?'

'Relax. Enjoy yourself. Go and find some sunshine. That's what other people do.'

'Right. Other people.'

'Vanner,' McCague said. 'Just so's you know. Morrison's more than right on this one.'

'I know.' Vanner put down the phone.

Eighteen

Michael Terry sat in the club and watched Gallyon come up the stairs. He signalled to the barman for more drinks. Gallyon came over and Terry smiled at him. Gallyon sat down. They did not shake hands.

The barman brought them their drinks. Gallyon took his glass and held it slack-handed, elbow resting on the arm of his chair. He stared at the cut under Terry's eye.

'I hear you had some trouble.'

Terry touched the stitching. 'Nothing I can't handle.'

Gallyon nodded slowly.

'Where's Isabel?'

'She's not in tonight.'

'No?' Terry could not keep the irritation from his face.

Gallyon shook his head. 'You won't be seeing her again.' As he said it, he sat forward and plucked the freshened glass from Terry's grasp. He put it down very carefully on the table. Then he looked at Terry, a deadness in his eyes like a shark before it bites. 'You're barred, Michael. I don't want to see you again.'

'What?'

Gallyon leaned very close to him then. 'You brought a Drug Squad copper to my club. That wasn't part of the deal.'

Terry was aware of an ache in his gut as if his bowels were suddenly loose.

'That's nothing, Bobby. I . . .'

'I did some digging, Michael. Thought it best to check.'

Gallyon wrinkled his lip. 'You lost me my best fixture in years. Isabel isn't a patch on her.'

'Look, Bobby. You can't . . .'

Gallyon jabbed him with an index finger, suddenly hard in the throat. 'Shut up, little man.'

'But, South America . . .'

'Don't promise what you can't deliver.'

Terry's eyes widened and Gallyon slowly nodded.

'Word gets about, Michael.'

Terry sat where he was, suddenly completely lost. Gallyon's face was closed. 'Now. Get out of my club.'

Terry half-rose.

'One more thing.'

Terry looked back at him.

'You're on your own. You finger me in this – I'll carve you up and feed you to my fish.'

The following morning Jimmy Crack sat with Weir and Ryan. 'Something went down, Guv.' Jimmy glanced at Ryan as he said it. This was the first he knew about Vanner's removal. Weir watched him. 'What?'

'Don't know exactly. Regional plant told me. Terry and Gallyon and then Terry with his marching orders. They escorted him out of the club.'

Ryan crushed the plastic coffee cup in his hand. 'Gallyon knows something then.'

The phone rang on Weir's desk. He picked it up and spoke for a few moments, then he put it down and lifted his fingers to his chin. 'That was McCleod,' he said.

'Envelope just came in. Five hundred quid in cash.'

Vanner was in the shower when he heard the phone ring. He bowed his head to the water and closed his eyes. The answerphone would kick in. McCague's last words were in his skull, rattling around like the water on his flesh, harsh and evident and correct. McCague was right. He had messed it up. Morrison would win. His kind always did. He and Weir would get their result and Morrison would be a player again.

He towelled himself dry and listened to the voice on the answerphone. It was the products man from System X. There never was a character called Denny. Vanner felt his heart sink. Then it lifted again. Not Denny as in D E N N Y. But four years ago there had been a Deni. Sol-Deni V to be exact. A warlord and strategist in the Renus Four Meridian, some intergalactic war zone of the imagination. Vanner rubbed at his hair with the towel. Sol-Deni V. Half devil, half human. The products man said he would try to dig out an old brochure. Vanner reset the machine.

Ryan followed him, black leather jacket and long hair hanging from under the lip of his crash helmet. He rode an old blue Honda. Ryan drove on his own. Up ahead was a bike. It would take over if he lost him in traffic. He watched while he waited for the lights to change in Marylebone. The second cardholder. This morning he had collected Mickey Blondhair's money.

Late that afternoon, he sat in the incident room with Weir and Jimmy Crack and some of the team from AMIP.

'He made three pickups from boxes and then delivered to the Strand.' Ryan rubbed his face. Weir looked at the paper in front of him. 'Sven-Lido?'

'The company he delivered to at the mailing address.'

Weir passed the paper to the girl standing next to him. 'Get it fed into Holmes, love.'

Ryan stretched. 'What about Norwich?' he said.

'Getting there.' Weir stood up and took off his jacket.

Morrison came down the stairs. 'We're making progress, Sir,' Weir told him.

'I heard.' Morrison glanced at Ryan. 'Mailing address?'

'Company called Sven-Lido.'

'Do we have his name, this biker?'

'Jackson. Damien Jackson.'

'What about the address? What happens to the stuff that's delivered?'

'Get's collected, Sir,' Ryan told him. 'Cyclist. Smog mask, helmet. Never takes it off.'

Morrison sat down. 'So now we watch and wait. Anything more from Norwich?'

'We've got two bodies on the video tape,' Weir said. 'Not very clear, the cameras are high and it was dark. About eleven – eleven-thirty the night before. The tape's being sent over. We'll get it down to the lab.'

Morrison smiled then. 'Results. Not before time.' He glanced at Weir. 'Change of face – change of fortunes.' He looked then at Ryan. 'Sometimes it happens that way. Eh, Sid?'

Ryan had a drink with Jimmy Crack. 'Fucking Morrison gets right up my nose.'

'Don't let him bug you. He needs the result like all of us.' They sat down at a table and Ryan flipped beer mats. 'You seen the Guv'nor, Jim?'

'Nope.'

The door opened and Vanner walked out of the rain. Ryan said: 'You better get him a pint.'

Vanner sat down and Jimmy placed a beer before him. Vanner ran his fingers over the glass and wiped them on his jeans. 'So,' he said. 'What's the story?'

Ryan looked at Jimmy, who grinned.

'Come on, boys,' Vanner went. 'This is how it was when I beat Weir for IO. Cosy chats with the lads. Now it's the other way round.'

Ryan told him what they had discovered about the mailing address and the tapes from Norwich. Jimmy told him about Terry's sudden and abrupt departure from Gallyon's nightclub. Vanner hissed air through his teeth. 'Got himself in a corner. Now he's lost his cleaner.' He lifted the glass to his lips. 'The artwork,' he said. 'It's not Denny.'

Ryan scratched his head.

'I mean not as in D E N N Y,' Vanner went on. 'It's D E N I.' He explained all that he had discovered from System X and when he had finished Ryan cocked one eyebrow.

'I thought you were on leave, Guv'nor.'

'I am.'

'Sort of busman's holiday is it?'

'I never did like the sun.'

Vanner drove home and parked his car. His house was dark. He wondered why he was surprised. It was always dark. There was one message on his answerphone. He pressed 'play' and listened to it. *'Aden. This is Jane. I think we need to talk.'*

Her voice. The first words save *sorry* in eleven lonely years. He closed his eyes, rewound the tape and played it back. Then he rewound it once more and listened all over again. He could not call her back. How could he call her back?

He sat in the darkness and waited for the phone to ring. He did not know how long he waited, but he waited. The phone did not ring. Still, he sat there and looked at it. After a while he wondered why he sat there at all. He got up and went down to the kitchen. It occurred to him then that his kitchen was in the basement just like Jane's, only hers was crisp and clean and white and his had a cooker, a sink and a draining board. He poked about in the fridge, found nothing, and went back upstairs again.

He bought a bar meal and ate it in a corner. When he was finished he sat back with his eyes closed and heard her voice again. He saw her in his head, wrapped in a towel – only it was not her face. It was Lisa Morgan's face and it was scarred.

He doodled. Sol-Deni V, a character from somebody's imagination. An unwritten name on the street. He shook his head, piecing it all together. But some of it did not fit. He bought another beer and carried it back to the table. He looked down at his scribble, Weir and Morrison thick as thieves in his head. He was losing. Maybe he had lost already. Maybe he should just up and go and take the time that was owing. But go where? Norfolk, alone in the cottage with only his memory for company.

He looked again at the name on the slip of paper, curling before him on the table. He took up his pen, lit a cigarette and doodled afresh. He shifted letters, moved them around, rolled them into one another and separated them out again. And as he did so, idly at first, the letters took on new meaning. He listed them in capitals at the top of the page and then shuffled them again. When he was finished he laid down the pen.

SOL-DENI V – SVEN-LIDO.

In his house the phone was ringing. He heard it as he unlocked the door. Seven rings and the answerphone would click in. He picked it up at the sixth.

'Vanner,' he said.

Silence, the sound of somebody breathing and then her voice in his ear.

'Aden. It's Jane.'

His knuckles whitened about the phone. 'Hello, Jane.'

Again a silence and this time it stretched.

'This is really difficult,' she said at last.

The breath broke from him and he leaned against the wall. 'Yes,' he said. 'It is.'

'Can I see you?'

'Why?'

'You came to see me. You frightened the life out of me, Aden.'

'You told Andrew.'

'Of course I did. He's my husband.'

He was silent again.

'Aden. Let's meet. I can't just leave it like this.'

Can't you? He thought. No last word. You leaving me. Not me leaving you.

'All right,' he said. 'If you want to.'

'Neutral ground. Restaurant. Pub maybe.'

'Where?'

'What about the West End?'

'Okay.'

'Any suggestions? I don't know many places.'

Vanner thought for a moment and then he smiled. 'What about Blake's bar on Long Acre?'

'Okay. Next Friday. About eight?'

'I'll be there.'

He put down the phone, went up to the bathroom and washed his face. He stared at himself in the mirror, the look in his eyes haunting him. Dark eyes, dead eyes, bereft of any feeling and yet burning up with it. Downstairs again, he picked up the phone and called Ryan at home.

Terry sat in darkness, the lights of the city tracing the horizon before him. St Paul's glowed in its floodlights. He chewed his nails, the silence of the room deafening him. No edge. No Gallyon. No Isabel. Just the silence that broke from inside him. He lifted the little coloured dwarf from the table and squeezed it hard in his hand.

Ryan went down to the incident room, the hum from the Holmes Suite in his ears. China was there with Anne and Jimmy Crack. Weir was in his office on the phone. Morrison was nowhere in sight.

'You going to the plot in the Strand, China?' Ryan asked him.

China nodded.

'Wait a minute. Will you.'

Ryan went into Weir's office and Weir put down the phone. 'Result, Slips. We've got a positive ID on Targets 2 and 3 in Norwich. Waitress from McDonalds. She saw them there on Tuesday.'

Ryan nodded. 'Got something else for you, Guv.'

Weir looked at him. 'What?'

'System X. The shop where Mark Terry works. One of those space model war games places. You know computers and that.'

'What about it?'

Ryan sat down and leaned his elbows on his knees. 'The

artwork, Guv. I did a bit of digging. There is no Denny. Not as in *DENNY* anyway. It's *DENI*.'

Weir moved to the edge of his seat.

'The face on the squares. The cartoon. Comes from a character called Sol-Deni V,' Ryan went on. 'Made obsolete four years ago.'

'What kind of character?'

'Warlord, General . . .' Ryan flapped out a hand. 'Strategist. Boss man. Whatever.'

'And Terry's kid works there?'

'Yeah. He paints the models. And guess who taught him to paint?'

'His old man.'

'Exactly.' Ryan folded his arms. 'There's something else,' he said. 'Sven-Lido. It's an anagram of Sol-Deni V.'

The following Wednesday, Weir stood with Morrison and Ryan in the offices of the Financial Investigation Unit at Campbell Row, David Starkey was leafing through the papers on his desk before them.

'Results of the Inquiry Order?' Weir said.

Starkey nodded. 'Sven-Lido's only a trading style. In itself it tells us nothing.'

'What d'you mean a trading style?' Weir asked him.

'It's not a company in its own right. It's so and so trading as Sven-Lido.'

'So who's it affiliated to?'

'We don't know. You don't have to register trading styles.'

Weir sat back and folded his arms. 'So it doesn't tell us anything then.'

'Not in itself.' Starkey licked his lips. 'But, we've checked Terry's history. Every company he's ever had a connection with.'

'And?'

'He's been about. His main business now is a sole proprietorship – MTI. *Michael Terry Imports*. We can get very little on that other than the bank details. There's no accounts listed because it's not a limited company. The bank don't hold any because he doesn't borrow.' He pointed to the paper in front of him. 'We checked with Companies House, and he's a director of seven other companies. Six we've discounted. They're effectively run by other people. He just draws a dividend.'

'What about the seventh?'

Starkey smiled. 'Now that is interesting.' He tapped the papers in front of him. 'Company called Calgary Holdings. It was dormant until two years ago and it was known as Catskill Ltd. But then it was reactivated. A name-change was registered, the registered office changed too. Bank accounts going again.'

'Bank accounts?' Morrison looked at him. 'I thought bank accounts were closed if a company was dormant.'

'Not necessarily.' Starkey lifted his shoulders. 'As long as a company hasn't been struck off the register they can hold a bank account. Anyway, two years ago this Catskill became Calgary Holdings. Calgary Holdings has a number of subsidiary companies. None of them seem to trade very heavily. But the balance sheets of Calgary Holdings are strong.' He paused. 'Well, I say balance sheets – there is only one.'

Morrison scratched his head. 'What d'you mean?'

'It's been reactivated for two years. There should be two sets of accounts. But they had an eighteen-month period for their first year.'

Ryan cocked an eyebrow. 'Eighteen months for a year. That makes a lot of sense.'

Starkey grinned at him. 'Puts off the tax-man, Slips. In this case just as well.'

Morrison sat forward. 'Why?'

'Because the assets on the balance sheet are properties. It's a property rental company.'

'So what's significant about that?'

'The properties don't exist.'

Morrison looked at Weir, who looked in turn at Starkey. 'So what're you telling us, Dave?'

'That the company's turning money over which is listed as investment income. Only there are no investment properties.'

Ryan picked up the set of accounts and leafed through them. 'How do you know?'

'Bank gave me a list. They asked for it when the account went into overdraft for a while. They didn't have a charge on any of them. They just wanted to know what they were.' He made an open-handed gesture. 'I checked them out. None of them exist. Terry's pushed money through his account. It's not cash. It's clean enough, and there's not much of it considering. But he's putting it through as rental income only there's no properties to get rent from.'

Morrison drew his brows together. 'What can the bank tell us about Terry?'

'Nothing. They've never met him.'

'What d'you mean *they've never met him*?'

'Everything's done by letter. They don't need to meet him. He's got no borrowing facility.'

'What about the overdraft you talked about?'

'Blip. One-off, Guv. The property list reassured them. Couple of weeks – the account was back in credit.'

Weir leaned on the desk. 'I don't see how any of this links up with Sven-Lido,' he said.

'The registered office of Calgary Holdings,' Starkey said. 'It's the mailing address in the Strand.'

McCleod opened the parcel that was placed in the box by the Tufnell Park staff. Five bundles of used notes. Quickly he counted. Ten thousand pounds. He picked up his mobile phone.

The Wasp sang as he sprayed his dreadlocks with hot water from the shower. It dribbled into his mouth, making him gurgle. The girl watched him from the doorway, her arms folded across her chest. 'What're you so happy about?'

The Wasp switched off the tap and picked up the towel from the chipped enamel of the radiator. 'I'm in a good mood today.' He winked at her. 'You ought to make the most of it.'

* * *

Ninja waited for him, sitting on the raised wall above the arch at the front of the building. The Irish hags, who frequented the café opposite, were cackling away together on the corner. Ninja looked up as The Wasp came down the steps. The Wasp nodded across the road. 'Don't fancy yours much?' he said.

Ninja did not smile. 'I'm coming with you.'

The Wasp squinted at him then. 'Don't be silly, man. We've been through that. You'll only scare the girl behind the counter.'

Ninja rolled his good eye at him, lifting it so most of the white was visible. 'You fuck me and I'll kill you.'

'When you gonna learn to relax?'

'When I've been paid.'

'Today's Friday. He'll pay.'

'Well, he better fuckin' had.'

The Wasp wagged his head at him. 'You know what your problem is? You don't trust anyone.'

'I don't trust you, Wasp. Maybe you should remember that.'

The Wasp shook his head. 'You ain't going to spoil my party, man. Wait here and I'll be back in half an hour.'

'Longer and I'll be looking for you.'

McCleod saw him come into the post office. The Wasp was smiling at everyone. He sauntered across the floor and leaned on the sill, the other side of the glass. He looked at McCleod, face losing its smile. Then he pushed his card under the glass.

'You got a package for me?'

'Wait a minute.' McCleod avoided his eye. He took the card and went into the other room. The Wasp leaned on the counter and looked about him. People queuing. Old ladies waiting for pensions.

McCleod came back with a large jiffy bag in his hands. He set it down on his side of the counter. The Wasp licked his lips. McCleod took the form and slid it across to him.

'Sign please,' he said.

The Wasp picked up a pen and scrawled. McCleod took the paper back from him and inspected it. Then carefully he checked the signature against that of the card. He caught sight of the pager watch on The Wasp's wrist. Opening the glass panel, he handed him the package.

'Thanks,' Wasp said. 'Have a nice day.'

McCleod nodded. He watched him wander back across the floor and then he lifted his radio.

Ryan climbed out of the car, Pierce and China with him. They saw The Wasp come out of the post office and they moved up behind him. China stepped round in front of him. The Wasp stopped, stared in his face for a second, and then made a dive for the road. Ryan floored him, grabbing him round the middle and bundling him onto the tarmac. The Wasp rolled, the package still in his grasp. Pierce ripped it out of his hands and Ryan sat on his chest. 'You're nicked,' he said.

From the doorway of the electrical goods shop on the corner, Ninja stood and watched them.

Vanner sat at the table and waited, a bottle of Becks before him. He looked at his watch. Eight-fifteen already. He looked out of the window. Perhaps she would not come. Perhaps this was just her way of winding him up still further. He toyed with the bottle of beer, opened but still untouched. Then he saw her, moving between the black metallic bollards. She stepped into the bar.

He could smell her; the scent under the arch; the scent on the clothes in her bedroom: the scent he remembered of old. He did not say anything, did not rise from his seat as she sat down opposite him. She took off her coat and laid it behind her and then she turned and looked at him.

'Hello, Aden,' she said.

'Hello, Jane.'

Stiffened silence. Eleven wasted years. He looked at her face, eyes, hair. He looked away, half-lifted his bottle and then he looked back at her. 'Would you like a drink?'

'I'll have a dry white wine please.'

Vanner signalled the bar.

Her wine came and she sipped it. He could see the imprint of her lips on the glass as she set it down. He took out his cigarettes, shook the packet and offered one to her.

'You still use these?'

'Sometimes.' She took one and he lit it for her. His hand was steady. She looked in his eyes then and blew a trail of smoke at the ceiling. She crossed her legs and he heard the rustle of silk. Her suit, two-piece in pale blue, was expensive and neat and everything that said everything about her now. He sat back, put the match to his own cigarette and trailed smoke from his nostrils.

'Why did you come to the house?'

Such a simple question. But one for which he had no answer. He moved in his seat, feeling his trousers sticking to him at the thigh. The air had died in the bar. The murmur of other people's conversation. The movement of bodies at the door. He could feel them, half-see them. 'I had to,' was all he could say.

'You had to?' She arched her eyebrows. 'After eleven years?'

He did not say anything. He had nothing to say. He held her gaze more evenly now and the thudding had stilled in his chest. The sureness of old was back in her face, full lips about the cigarette, dark-painted nails and slim fingers. A charm bracelet in gold graced her wrist, drifting over her palm where she held the stem of her glass. He could sense every inch of her. Her face sought his for an answer. Little lines in her skin: he had not noticed them before. 'I avoided you, Jane. I didn't want to see you. I wanted to move on. Forget.'

'So, why didn't you?' She uncrossed her legs and, as she did so, her foot touched his under the table.

'I did. Had.' He looked in her eyes, wondering if she could see the lie in his own. 'Then your husband's name was thrust under my nose so I went to see him.'

'And because you saw him you had to see me?'

He shrugged. 'Something like that.'

She sipped again at her wine. Vanner drained his beer bottle and ordered another.

'Why didn't you just knock on the door?' she said.

257

'Because you left the keys in it.'

She smiled then and he smiled too. He shook his head. 'I'm sorry. Must've scared the life out of you.'

She nodded.

'Made a habit of that didn't I.'

She toyed with her glass. 'Times change, Aden. People change. We were so young. What I really needed you couldn't give me any more.'

'You didn't always say that. In the early days *only* I could give you what you needed.'

She touched her teeth with her tongue, looked away from him, a hint of colour coursing her cheeks. 'As you say – in the early days.'

He sat back. 'So when did they change – the early days? When did they become later days?'

She shook her head. 'You were always away.'

'My job.'

'I know.'

'Your father's job.'

'I know that too.'

'You knew how it was when you married me.'

She looked at him again, a sigh deep in her throat. 'I *did* love you you know.'

Pain crushing his chest. He pursed his lips. 'Did you?'

'Oh, yes. Aden.'

He lit another cigarette, drew smoke, harsh and ragged into his lungs. He exhaled stiffly, looked beyond her, glass all at once in his eyes. He felt the warmth of her hand over his. He looked down. She squeezed the top of his fingers. 'I'm sorry, Aden. So sorry I hurt you.'

'Do you love him?' he shot the question at her. 'I asked you that once before and you told me he loved you.'

'Did I? You remember?'

'Every word.'

She finished her wine and looked at the empty glass. Again he signalled the barman.

'What did you do when I left?' she said.

'I went back to Belfast and killed people.'

For a long time they faced one another in silence, her touch gone from his hand. Vanner said: '*Do* you love him?'

'He gives me what I need.'

'What you need?'

She lifted her head, arching her neck. 'What *is* love anyway?'

'I haven't got a clue.'

She laughed then and he smiled, scraping the end of his cigarette round the lip of the ashtray. She cupped her face in her hands. 'You were in my bedroom.'

He nodded.

'Touching my things.'

He hesitated then nodded again.

'My underwear.'

He looked right in her eyes. 'Stockings. Bra. Knickers.'

Naked, he trawled her flesh like a lover. She lay on her back, the points of her breasts lifted to the ceiling, the black of her hair on the rug. Andrew Riley's house. Andrew Riley's rug. Andrew Riley's wife. He roamed her breasts, her belly, her thighs and buried himself inside her. Eyes closed, mouth half-open; the light shining on the crimson of her lips. He moved with her, lifted her, drew her back and lifted her over again. She cupped his head, fingers like claws in his hair. He held her, arms tensed, muscle pushing at the skin; the glow of the lamp dulling the sweat on his limbs.

'Where is he tonight – your husband?' He lay on his back, his body long and supple and empty. She curled next to him under the crook of his arm, the weight of her – warm against him.

'Rotary meeting.'

He laughed then and sat up. 'Rotary? Oh, Jesus, Jane.'

She stared at him. 'He goes every other Friday.'

'I'm sure he does, darling. I'm sure he does.'

He looked about the room then, perfect room, perfect things; the perfect world she had created for herself. Then he stood up and reached for his clothes. She watched him, lying naked still on the rug, as if in some kind of memory.

'You leaving?'

He nodded.

'That's it?'

He stopped buckling his trousers and looked at her. 'What else is there?'

She rolled onto her side, pain all at once in her eyes. He pulled his shirt over his head and stuffed it into his trousers. He gesticulated round the room. 'You have everything else you need.'

Nineteen

Weir sat opposite The Wasp. 'You're in a lot of trouble.'

The Wasp watched him from under his hair, eyes the colour of coal. The duty solicitor sat alongside him, briefcase by his side, glasses pushed high on his nose. Weir looked at the pair of basketball boots in a polythene bag on the table.

'Those put you in Norwich on the 12th. They put you at the scene of a murder.' He placed both elbows on the table. 'You want to start by telling me where your friend is?'

The Wasp looked at the floor. Ryan lit a cigarette. He snapped the match in two and dropped it in the tinfoil of the ashtray. He looked at the solicitor. 'You've reminded him how the courts will view his silence?'

'I have.'

'So maybe you should tell him to talk to us.'

Weir said: 'Are you the one with the sword or is that your mate?'

'Ninja.' Ryan blew smoke. 'The Gypsy. Haven't seen him since he was a kid.'

The Wasp looked at him now and Ryan nodded. 'Nasty little sod even then.'

'On September the 15th you were on the Bream Park Estate,' Weir said. 'You paid a visit to Ringo May's flat. When you left he was dead.'

The Wasp shook his head.

Weir sat back. 'You were there.'

'Not me.'

'You're not listening to me are you. We *know* you were there.'

The Wasp looked suddenly less sure of himself.

'Oh, you wore the gloves,' Weir said. 'That was bright enough. Only you dumped them after you left. Now that was very stupid.'

The Wasp watched him carefully.

'Ringo May's blood. You didn't wipe it off properly.'

'I don't know what you're talking about, man.'

Weir smiled then, only his eyes were cold. 'Yes, you do. You see we took your fingerprint from the inside of the gloves. You didn't know we could do that. Did you?' He looked at the solicitor. 'He really should talk to us you know.'

The solicitor leaned forward then. 'Would you like to give us a minute?'

Morrison was in the incident room when Weir and Ryan went down. Morrison looked at Weir. 'What's happening?'

'Brief's having a word with him. So far he's not said anything. We've just told him about the print from the glove though. So maybe now we'll get somewhere.'

'And Norwich?'

'Tape's crap. But we've got the boots and the waitress at McDonalds. It's enough.'

Morrison nodded. 'We need the other body.'

'We're looking for him.'

'I want the dealer picked up as well. The kid. Mickey Tomlinson.'

Fifteen minutes later, Pierce came down the stairs and called to Weir. 'The brief says he's ready to talk now, Guv.'

Weir and Ryan went back to the interview room. Ryan switched on the tape. 'Interview recommencing at 17:32.' He sat down next to Weir and looked at The Wasp. 'Feeling more like it now?'

The Wasp folded his arms, unfolded them again and sat back. 'So I was there. Doesn't mean I killed him. I didn't kill nobody.'

Weir clasped his hands together. 'We're listening.'

The Wasp looked at his solicitor, who nodded. 'Ninja killed

him. I was there. But it was Ninja what did it. He cut him up with a sword.'

'Samurai sword?' Weir said.

The Wasp nodded. 'Half-length.'

'Fond of it is he?'

'Pride and fuckin' joy.'

'Where does he live?'

The Wasp shrugged. 'He don't live anywhere much. He's a Gyppo. Roams about a bit.'

'Roams where exactly?'

The Wasp shrugged his shoulders. 'Could be anywhere.' He looked again at his solicitor. 'I didn't want to kill Ringo. I thought we'd just frighten him. Maybe rough him up a bit. That's all.'

Weir narrowed his eyes. 'Who told you to kill him?'

The Wasp was silent.

'Your own idea then?'

'No.'

'Who then?'

'I don't know who he is. Just a fella who calls. He talks to Ninja not me. Ninja's the main man. I just drive the car.'

Ryan scratched his chin. 'The mobile phone in your flat?'

'Ninja's.'

Weir glanced at the watch on his wrist. 'He contact you with that?'

'Who?'

'Whoever's behind the cartoon.'

'Don't know what you're on about.'

'Come on, Wasp.' Weir looked coldly at him. 'Do yourself a favour. You telling us it *was* your idea to kill him? Just now you said you were ordered.'

The Wasp spoke slowly. 'I said, Ninja was ordered. Not me. I didn't know till he did it.' He looked at Ryan. 'You saw Ninja when he was a kid right?'

Ryan nodded.

'Then you know he's a fuckin' space cadet don't you.'

'You telling us you just went along for the ride, Wasp?' Ryan cocked an eyebrow at him.

'And what about Norwich,' Weir said. 'The clinic by the river. Another warning gone wrong?'

'Ninja likes blood.' The Wasp shook his head. 'Man has a sword. What d'you want me to do – take the fucker off him?'

Ryan shook his head. 'Wrong, Wasp. Wrong. In Norwich one of you held him. Marks on his face, bruising on his collarbone and shoulder. The other one stabbed him. Had to be that way – the sword stuck in his ribs. We found chips from the blade in the bone.'

The Wasp looked again at his solicitor, then he looked at the floor.

'Mickey Blondhair,' Weir said. 'You supplied him from your box. Too young for one of his own?'

The Wasp said nothing.

'We've watched him dealing Ecstasy at school. You supplied him, Wasp.'

'No.'

'He posted cash to your box.'

Ryan stretched. 'Tell us about the hostels, Wasp. The more you talk the better it's going to be.'

The Wasp scratched his head. 'How much worse can it get?'

'Not much. But it could get a little bit better.'

'Time's time. Don't matter how much.'

'Tell yourself that when you've been watching the bars for ten years.'

The Wasp twisted in his seat and looked at Weir. 'I don't know nothing about hostels.'

'Come on. You can do better than that. We've got photographs of you in Neasden. What were the hostels – breeding ground for dealers? Street kids nicking for Denny acid and E's?'

The Wasp made a face. 'I told you. I just drive. Ninja does the rest.'

'But you helped. Like with John Phillips for instance?'

He shook his head. 'I already told you, I thought we were going

264

to mess them up a bit that's all. That's why I was holding him. Just trying to scare him a bit.'

'Wrong again, Wasp.' Ryan was shaking his head. 'You knew you were sent to kill him. He knew who Denny was didn't he. No other reason to be there.'

The Wasp shook his head. '*You* got it wrong, man. Ninja maybe. But not me. Ninja did all the talking.'

Ryan looked at the ceiling. 'Okay then. So how come you're collecting ten thousand pounds from your post office box?'

The Wasp opened his hands. 'It ain't my box. It's Ninja's. I just do the signing. Ninja, he can't read or write. So he gets me to do it.'

'The box is registered to your address.'

'Yeah. Because he don't live nowhere. I just told you.'

Weir stood up, paced to the wall and leaned one hand against it. 'Who's behind the cartoon?'

The Wasp shrugged.

'You never met him?'

The Wasp tapped his wrist.

'The watches?'

'Yep.'

'You've never seen him?'

'No.'

'Ninja?'

'I don't know. Maybe.'

Outside in the corridor, Ryan shook his head. 'Nobody's seen Denny, Guv. Without that we can't lay anything on him.'

'Dealing we can. We've got the delivery boy. We can prove a link between the boxes and the mailing address. On top of that we've got Calgary Holdings.'

'Not murder though. Even if we know somebody ordered them to do it we can't prove it was him.'

Vanner waited for Ryan in the pub on the corner of his road. He sat with his back to the booth and thought about Jane. The pain was gone. And yet – Lisa Morgan. Here he sat having finally closed down a section of his life after eleven useless years, and the price felt like someone else's.

Ryan came in, rain on the shoulders of his jacket. Vanner signalled to him and he came over. 'We nicked The Wasp,' he said.

'And the other one?'

'Not yet.'

Vanner pushed out his lips. 'Is he talking?'

'He is now. We can put him in Milo's flat. His prints match the one we lifted from the glove.'

'Norwich?'

'Boot print. Walks with his knees close together. Hundred quid's worth of trainers.' He made a face. 'Vanity. Always gets you in the end.'

'Good you don't have to worry then.'

'Ha ha.' Ryan looked at Vanner's pint. 'You going to get me one of those or is this info for free?'

Vanner placed a pint of lager in front of him. 'We've got a positive ID from McDonalds,' Ryan went on. 'It puts them up there together. The print puts The Wasp at the scene.'

'Tape any good?'

'No. He's admitted it though. Brief knows we've got him by the balls. He's trying to make out it was the other guy, the Gypsy. Reckons he thought it was just going to be a bit of a scrap.'

'Will that stand up?'

'Will it fuck. When we lifted him he was collecting ten g's from his post office box.'

Vanner looked across the bar. 'Doesn't give you Terry though.'

'Not yet. But we're getting there. Sven-Lido. Sol-Deni V. Dave Starkey's been doing his bit. Accounts, the bank and that. Terry's got a company called Calgary Holdings that gets rental income from property investments that don't exist. It's registered at the address in the Strand.'

Vanner sat forward then and furrowed his brow. 'That doesn't make any sense.'

'What doesn't?'

'Why use Sven-Lido. The same mailing address? Why doesn't he just paint pictures?'

Ryan lit a cigarette. 'Taking the piss, guv. He likes the wind up. I've told you: pop too much stuff and your brain gets fucked. It's a game isn't it.'

Vanner frowned at him. 'You reckon that's all it is?'

Ryan yawned. 'You've seen him, Guv. Seen how he plays it up. He really thinks it's funny. Anyway, I don't really care. Just as long as we nick him.'

Vanner sat back, resting his hands on his thighs. 'Weir must be delirious.'

Ryan squinted at him. 'You should leave the fanny alone.'

'The fanny, Sid, was my wife.'

He sat alone. Ryan had had the one beer and gone home. It was late. He was tired and he thought it was time he reminded his family who he was. Maybe he was right. Mentally, Vanner shrugged his shoulders and told himself it was no longer his problem. It was Morrison's problem and it would be Morrison's result.

But it *was* his problem. Ninja and The Wasp had attacked him with a bat and a sword, when he was drunk and weak and helpless. He still did not know why. It was the only reason he was sitting here at all. And more than that, all through this investigation, he had known that somewhere he had seen the Denny cartoon before. But he could not remember where.

Ninja squatted like a pygmy in the boiler room. He hugged his belly where the pain burned like acid. Steam lifted from unlagged pipes by his feet. He watched the door out of his good eye, sword unhoused by his feet. He had not eaten since yesterday. He was not hungry. He thought about cutting up The Wasp.

Morrison sat in the incident room with Starkey and his colleague from Financial Investigation. Starkey tapped the papers in front of him. 'No mortgage on the flat. That's three hundred thousand at least. The yard is the same. He sat back and ran hands through his hair. 'He's asset-rich, Sir. Gearing is next to nothing.'

Morrison pursed his lips. 'Then he's making a hell of a lot out of plant – or he's being a naughty boy.'

'Customs watching his yard?'

Morrison nodded. 'Two boxes of engine parts came in last Friday.'

'From the States?'

'Yes.'

'And Amsterdam?'

'Bought two Used Diggers two weeks ago. They're two hundred K each when they're new.'

Starkey yawned and stood up. 'Nothing from the mailing address?'

'Nothing's been collected.'

'Maybe you should've waited before nicking The Wasp.'

Morrison shook his head. 'Had to take him out, Dave. Ten thousand pounds in the box.'

McCleod looked at the gold stud in Mickey Blondhair's nose. 'That hurt?'

'No.'

'Not at all?'

'No.'

'How'd you pick your nose?'

'Like this.' Mickey stuck a finger in his nostril.

Anne leaned on the table. Mickey's mother and social worker sat behind him. His young mother looked old: pale skin; weak, mousy hair.

'Mickey,' Anne said quietly. 'We've got you for dealing Ecstasy and LSD in your school. We've also got you for slashing a man's knees at a cashpoint.' As she said it, his mother thinned her eyes. 'You're thirteen years old. It doesn't have to be like this. If you help us – then maybe we can help you.'

Mickey looked up at her. 'I ain't no grass.'

'Oh, for God's sake.' His mother slapped her hand on the table. 'Aren't you in enough trouble? Did I bring you up on my own just so you could do this to me?'

Mickey looked at the floor.

'Mickey,' Anne went on. 'There's been two murders. They're both connected with the drugs that you've been dealing. How d'you think that's going to look in court?'

'I didn't kill nobody.'

'We know you didn't. We know who did. All we want is for you to help us find him.'

Mickey hunched himself up in the seat. 'I don't know nothing about it.'

'Tell me about The Wasp. He supplied you. Right?'

Mickey chewed his lip.

'Come on, Mickey. He's in custody. He can't hurt you.'

He looked at her then, thought about it and nodded briefly once.

'Good.' Anne said. 'That's better.'

'Why's he called The Wasp?' McCleod asked him.

Mickey patted his hair. 'Used to have it short. When he was a kid. Dyed it in yellow stripes.'

Anne smiled. 'Tell us about Ninja.'

'I ain't talking about him.'

'He's still out there somewhere.'

Mickey shook his head. 'I ain't talking about him.'

Vanner sat in the café across the road from the Kirstall Estate. On holiday. He glanced at the picture of the desert island on the wall. The Indian woman brought him a cup of tea and he thanked her.

'Tell me,' he said. 'You live above the café?'

She nodded.

'You know many of the kids on the estate?'

'Some.'

'Like the two with dreadlocks?'

She looked at him then. 'I know who they are.'

'When did you last see the white one?'

She scraped at the floor with her shoe. 'I don't remember.'

'I'm a policeman,' he said.

She smiled. 'Always in some kind of trouble aren't they. Children today. He was sitting on the wall above the arch over there last Friday. I was putting out the rubbish and I saw him.'

Vanner looked where she pointed. A woman toiled up the ramp with a shopping trolley.

'Not since?'

She shook her head.

He thanked her and drank his tea.

He crossed the road and walked under the arch. The buildings lifted around him, not high and imposing like some of the estates, but strung out in a warren of five-storeyed front doors. Brown, withered stone, smeared in white and yellow and red. The children's playground, the swing seats missing, he moved between the red posts of the frame. The buildings ran straight down to the railway line from here and back to the road behind him. Cutting a path between the two main blocks, he came out on Leith Place. Above his head he could hear the whirring of sewing machines.

The sky leaked cloud, grey and white and in places black where rain threatened. He stood on the corner, with his hands in his pockets and looked to the far end of the road. It was blocked off by the rising red of a wall. Four separate businesses and then a filthy green door; daubed over with paint. The downstairs window was boarded where it had been smashed, only a small piece of glass was left. Stepping across the road, he cupped his hand but saw nothing.

'Can I help you?'

He turned and saw a squat-set man looking at him. He was wiping his hands on a rag, the tailgate of his van raised to eye level. Vanner squinted at him.

'You live round here?'

The man laughed. 'No,' he said. 'I don't.'

'Work?'

'I run the Art Workshop.' He pointed to the building that butted

270

against the west wall of the estate. Vanner looked it over, wire on the windows, wire on the door.

'Has to be like that.' The man nodded towards the flats.

Vanner showed him his warrant card. 'They've smashed my windows more times than I can remember,' the man said. 'At least the wire keeps them out.'

'You rent it all?'

'Yes.'

Vanner indicated the lofts. 'What about those?'

'All occupied. I don't know what they do. Design agency at the end, and the factory up there.' He pointed to the third floor of the middle block. 'Saris, I think.'

'What about that one?' Vanner pointed to the green door.

'Don't know.'

'Empty?'

'I've seen a light on.'

Vanner looked back at him. 'At night you mean?'

The man nodded. 'I work pretty late sometimes.'

'Have you ever seen anyone in there?'

'No.'

'But a light.'

'Yes.'

'Which floor?'

'Second, I think.'

Vanner looked back at the door.

Michael Terry stood at the window of the first-floor portakabin and watched the car parked at the far end of the road.

'Coffee?' his secretary asked him. Terry did not reply. She asked him again and he looked round. 'What?'

'Do you want any coffee.'

'No. I don't want any coffee.'

'Sorry,' she said. 'Only asking.'

Terry ignored her. He moved to his desk once more and sat down.

'Are you okay, Michael? You're not yourself today.'

He looked witheringly at her. 'Will you just leave me alone.'

She shook her head and turned once more to her typewriter.

Terry stared at the desktop. The nagging sensation squatted in his belly like an unwanted visitor. Every time he moved it irritated him. He got up again and went back to the window. The car was still there. Who was watching him -- Drug Squad? He had a good mind to go and ask if they had everything they needed. He shook his head as if to clear it. Gallyon gone. His edge gone. He looked again through the window and then sat down in his chair. He snapped at his secretary and she removed the dictaphone set from her ears.

'Yes?'

'The two Cats. They're arriving tomorrow. I want to know what time.'

Pierce took the call and stared hard at the wall. Morrison was pouring coffee. Pierce gesticulated to him. 'Right,' he said. 'Right. Thank you. Thank you very much.' He put down the phone.

'What is it?' Morrison asked him.

Pierce sat back, hands behind his head, eyes suddenly shining. 'That was Van Gelder, Sir. Drug Squad in Amsterdam. They've had a tip-off.'

'And?'

'Consignment of Ecstasy tablets – arriving in Tilbury tomorrow.'

'How?'

'Freighted in two used diggers.'

McCague was in the incident room. Ryan nodded to him as he came down from interviewing Damien Jackson, the second cardholder.

'Result?' McCague asked him.

'Yes, Sir.' Ryan lit a cigarette. 'We've got one body for the murders. Fingerprint at the flat and a bootprint at the Norwich scene. We've got a couple of dodgy pictures from the car park tape, but I don't think they'll stand up.'

'Positive ID from a waitress though.'

Ryan nodded.

'And you've got a thirteen-year-old dealer who likes to cut people at cashpoints.'

'Yeah.' Ryan grinned then. 'IC1, Guv. Bit of a blow for the Commissioner.'

McCague did not smile.

'Little bastard,' Ryan went on. 'In a couple of hours he'll be home with his mum. System's shot to fuck. We're trying to get the whereabouts of the Gypsy from him. But he's keeping his trap shut on that one.'

'What about the hostels?'

'Loads of bloody pager watches. Operation spreads right across North London.'

'Nasty.'

'Very. Not sure what Joe Public's going to think about street crime being set up from hostels.'

McCague sat down on the desk. 'So Vanner was right about that then.'

Ryan nodded.

'You seen him?'

'No. Said something about taking off.'

'He needs to. Came back too early.'

'Only came back at all because somebody spanked him.'

'I know. My mistake that. I should have let him be.'

Morrison addressed the briefing. McCague sat at the back of the room to listen.

'Okay,' Morrison lifted a hand and the conversation died. 'We're halfway there. For those of you who don't know we've got two bodies in custody. Target 2, The Wasp. He's spinning us a story about the Gypsy – but we're humouring him. He just might give us a location. We can place him at both murder scenes. The glove from Milo's flat and his footprint on the bank of the river in Norwich. He wears basketball boots which fit the cast exactly, right sole sitting slightly inwards. We've also got both him and the Gypsy in McDonalds the day before.' He paused and caught McCague's eye.

'We've now picked up the second cardholder, Damien Jackson. He makes the collections from the post office boxes and delivers to the mailing address in the Strand. We caught him delivering a package full of cash, with half a dozen cards in his pocket. So far he's not talking, but it's only a matter of time.' He paused again and sipped at a plastic cup. 'The girl at the mailing address can tell us nothing except the packages are collected by a messenger. Cyclist. No distinguishing mark, i.e. no badge or logo or anything. Wears a one-piece lycra suit and a helmet with a smog mask. So she never sees his face.'

McCleod shifted in his seat. 'What about Target 1, Sir?'

Morrison glanced at Weir. 'This morning we had a call from the Dutch Police. They've had word from an informant that a consignment of Ecstasy is crossing the water this evening. The word is the drugs are being carried in two used diggers. He paused again. 'The surveillance over there's paying off. If we're very lucky – we'll all be home for the weekend.' He looked over at Starkey. 'Dave's team have done the works on his business. Asset-rich. Very little borrowing. Both his flat in Blackfriars and the Dartford yard are unencumbered.

'We can link him to the mailing address and by definition the boxes. That's good enough. If we can take him with the drugs we'll be laughing.'

'But we can't tie him to the killings, Sir,' Anne said.

Morrison scratched his head. 'Circumstantially we can. Milo was a dealer and an informant. John Phillips Junior told DI Vanner that he knew who Denny was. Phillips told Mark Terry where he was. Mark Terry told his father.'

Ryan folded his arms. 'Brief'll pick away at the holes.'

'Maybe.' Morrison held up a finger. 'But, The Wasp has told us they were ordered to kill both Milo and Phillips Junior. Contacted by phone on the night of Milo's death, and two days before John Phillips'. We have the mobile phone they were called on.'

'Check Terry's records then,' Ryan said.

'Exactly.' Morrison made a gesture with his hand. 'We're looking for a mistake. Just maybe here he made one.'

'What about Gallyon?' It was McCague who asked the question, standing up at the back of the room. Morrison looked at him for a moment and then glanced at where Jimmy Crack was sitting on a desk.

'He got wise to the fact that we're into Terry,' Jimmy said. 'Looks like he ditched him. Unless Terry is very very desperate we're not going to get to Gallyon.'

Morrison continued: 'Tomorrow we set up a plot in Dartford. I want the whole team there. There's buildings we can use and a van. Customs'll be at Tilbury and we follow the diggers from there. They'll be transferred by crane to a low-loader and then driven to Terry's yard. When they get there we hit him.'

Michael Terry sat in the darkness, idly flicking through the Sky channels on the TV. The sound was turned down. He was not really watching. Traffic moved outside: he could hear it although only vaguely through the window. Gallyon's face in his mind. He touched his eye and thought about the bitch, Lisa Morgan. Switching off the television, he got his coat and went out.

Ninja walked the balconies, the chill of the night in his hair. By day the boiler room choked him. It was all he could do to sit there with the steam and the confines of the room and the door blocking his exit. At night he could breathe. He bought a kebab from the shop on the corner and ate it, squatting in the darkness with his sword hugging his side. He ought to go walkabout but did not have a clue where to go. He licked his fingers, the remnants of chilli sauce burning the skin.

The cloud of the day had gone and the sky lifted black and silver above the lights of the city. He sat with his back to cold concrete and let the breeze filter his hair. His stomach burned and he pressed one hand against it. Along the balcony something moved and instantly he felt for his sword. Voices, a girl and a boy.

He saw them come together against the yellow light at the head of the stairs and then they broke. Laughter in the breeze and then feet on the stone of the steps. Ninja let go of his sword, pushed himself to his feet and made his way back to the roof.

He stood by the light of the computer screen, rubber over his fingers as he trawled idly through the names as if he knew it was over. Damien taken. The Wasp taken. Ninja loose somewhere, like a wounded animal waiting to strike. Silence around him, nothing even from the street. Sitting down, he looked once more at the screen, thought briefly about erasing the hard disc and then switched it off. Downstairs, he stood by the doorway. When he was sure it was clear he pulled the door to and walked away. The padlock hung on its chain.

Twenty

Michael Terry woke early. He did not remember sleeping, just lying in the dark with the curtains spread wide and the clouds massing above him. With the dawn he rose, showered and dressed and drank a cup of coffee. Outside he got in his car. From the dashboard the dwarf seemed to haunt him.

He pulled up outside the gates to his yard. Seven o'clock and nobody had arrived yet. He glanced back down the road that led in past the diesel dump. No red car from yesterday. They were late or they had left him alone. Either way, the fact brightened him and he unfastened the chain on the gate. A few cars were parked outside the building opposite: a Mercedes, a Cavalier and a white, unmarked van. Terry ignored them, left his car by the portakabin and climbed the steps to his office. Inside he brewed coffee and watched as light grew over the city.

In the van across the road Ryan yawned. He shifted his position and glanced briefly at China. Anne sat in the front seat, flicking through a copy of the *Express*. Ryan looked over her shoulder. 'No tits,' he muttered.

China moved alongside him. At the back window McCleod was watching the yard through binoculars.

'What's he doing?' China asked.

'Drinking coffee.'

Ryan looked at the flask by his feet. 'Be all right if there was somewhere to pee.'

In the upstairs window of the office block, Weir sat with

Morrison. Pierce and two other AMIP officers stood at the window and peered through the blinds with binoculars. A mobile phone sounded. One of the officers answered it, then he looked over at Weir.

'Customs, Guv. Low-loader's arrived.'

Weir looked at his watch. 'Be a few hours yet.' He glanced back to the window. 'Better let them know in the van.'

Ninja shifted himself where he lay, the condensed heat of the boiler room catching his breath. The door stood half-open, but even like that his skin was alive with his sweat. A sound by the door. He threw off the blanket and scrabbled between pipes for his sword. On his haunches now, peering at the door. A boy's face appeared, half-hidden in the hood of the sweat top. Ninja grimaced at him. 'What do you want?'

The boy did not say anything.

'Get me some food.' Ninja got to his feet. 'Go on, you little bastard. Get me something to eat.'

He ate a sausage, cold and full of fat. The boy squatted before him, staring at the sword. Two others, a girl and her brother watched from the doorway. Ninja licked his fingers and looked at the kid in the sweat top. 'You seen The Wasp?'

The kid shook his head.

Ninja glanced at the others. 'Anyone got a spliff?'

The low-loader moved slowly into the yard. In the far corner, the operator climbed to the cab of the crane. Terry watched it all. The dirty yellow excavators, squatting on the reduced back of the truck. The cabs had been burnt out, an Eco' protest in Guinea. Let them protest away. Made his job a damn sight easier. He had fresh parts for the cabs: instrument panel, console, seat. But he no longer had a buyer.

The crane lifted them as easily as a mother a baby. Weir watched from the window. Morrison stood next to him, his coat buttoned.

No heat in the room. 'Let him get them down and we'll move.'

Terry was in the yard, the two excavators sat side by side and the crane was silent. His men stood around him, waiting. The foreman said: 'You want us to fill 'em up and shift 'em?'

'Not yet.' Terry was thinking about Gallyon. He took out a cigarette. The foreman signed the paper for the driver of the low-loader. Terry lit a match, held the flame for a moment and the wind took it from him. Wheels screeched on the road outside. He looked up as a white, unmarked van sped in through the gates. Driver's door open, the back doors open, and three men jumping from it. Terry stood where he was. His men stared. One of them reached for a crowbar. Then Ryan was in his face. 'Police, Sunshine.' He looked down at the crowbar. 'Not a good idea.'

A car pulled up behind the van and Weir got out with Pierce. Morrison climbed from the back seat. Weir walked up to Terry: he chewed gum, skull glinting in sunlight that broke through the clouds.

'Michael Terry,' he said. 'My Name's Weir. Area Major Incident Pool.'

Terry gaped at him, still holding the unlit cigarette. Weir spat the gum from his mouth.

'I'm arresting you on suspicion of dealing in Ecstasy and LSD. And of conspiracy to murder.'

Terry stared at him, face wasting under his eyes. He dropped the unlit cigarette.

Terry watched, lips compressed, as Ryan crawled on one digger. The foreman stood alongside him with his hands on his hips. His face was a blur, no expression at all. Ryan looked down at him. 'Where's the petrol tank?'

The foreman climbed up next to him and directed Ryan to the tank. 'It's diesel,' he said. 'It doesn't run on petrol.'

'Whatever.' Ryan worked on the cap, gloved hands to protect him against the freezing cold of the metal. 'Stiff as a stallion,' he moaned. The foreman watched him. 'Empty right?' Ryan said. 'Can't ship 'em with gas in?'

The foreman nodded.

Ryan freed the cap. A tube of rubber was fastened to the spring and extended down into the tank. It was flexible like gas hose. Ryan looked at the foreman, who was frowning. 'Not normal then.' Ryan wound in the hose. It was weighted at the end. Reaching down, he took hold of a cylinder of plastic, eighteen inches long. The cap was sealed in rubber and bound thickly with tape.

They found a second one in the other tank and took them to Terry's office. He stood there in silence as one of the Customs men took a knife to the tape and unscrewed the cap. The cannister was stuffed with plastic bags. The bags were full of tablets.

Vanner knocked on Mickey Blondhair's door. Rain fell in sheets. He got no answer and knocked on the door again. He was supposed to be at home. His mother was supposed to be at home. Vanner pressed the bell now. Still no answer. He shook his head and went back along the balcony. Outside the café, he waited in his car with the rain pressing against him. He sat in silence, coat buttoned, and stared at the wall of the building.

Ninja coughed blood. He stared at it, muddy against the palm of his hand. His gut burned. Nothing since that shitty sausage this morning. He leaned in the door of the boiler room. Outside the rain fell like ice, but it freshened the fire in his skin. From here he could see the railway and beyond that the High Street and the neon sign of McDonalds. What he wouldn't give for a burger. Fuck it. Maybe he should just stroll down there and buy one. Then he saw the lights of a police car cut the intersection beyond the station, and he moved back from the door.

Weir and Ryan faced Terry. He sat clutching himself on the other side of the table. The twin cannisters of Ecstasy lay before him, wrapped in plastic and tagged. Ryan flicked cigarette ash. 'Denny

E's,' he said. 'Or at least they would've been when you stamped them.'

Terry glanced at him. 'Is my solicitor here yet?'

'He's coming.'

'I'm not saying anything till he gets here.'

Ryan looked at Weir, then back at Terry again. All at once he thought of Milo lying in his flat, staring at his own dried blood with one arm twisted beneath him. 'We found them in your diggers.'

Terry shook his head. 'I don't know anything about them.'

Weir stretched and stood up. 'Tell us about Sven-Lido.'

'What?'

'Sven-Lido. You know where Damien drops off the cash.'

'I've never heard of Sven-Lido. And I've told you: I'm answering no more questions until I see my lawyer.'

Weir switched off the tape. 'We can wait,' he said.

The others were back in the incident room. Weir walked down with Ryan, and China handed them coffee. Spirits were high. Jokes flying. Morrison was on the phone. Starkey was making notes at a table. Ryan moved alongside. 'What you got, Dave?'

'Owns a boat down in Southampton. Not huge but big enough. Moors it on the Hamble. Member of the Yacht Club. Everything.'

'What else?' Ryan sat down and put his feet up on the table.

'Two cars. Merc and a TVR. You know the grunty kind. V8.'

'HP?'

'All bought and paid for.'

He showed Ryan the papers he was looking at. 'This is an FHR. MTI, his import company.'

'What's an FHR?'

'Financial History Report. Barclays Bank.' He pointed to the figures. 'There should be more than this.'

'What d'you mean?'

'The stuff he buys. The diggers, dump trucks and that. It's expensive. His costs are high. The sale price will be too.' He scratched his head. 'Not enough going through the account to pay for all he's got. Should be more than this.'

* * *

Weir stood with Morrison in Vanner's office. 'We're waiting for the brief,' he said.

China tapped on the door. 'Phone records are on their way, Guv. The yard. The flat and his mobile.'

Morrison glanced at China. 'What did you find at the flat?'

'Nothing.' He held up the painted dwarf. 'But we found this in his car.'

Terry's solicitor had grey hair and circular, gold-rimmed glasses. He sat next to Terry with his briefcase on the table. Weir showed Terry the acid square from the hostel.

'You supplied Ecstasy and LSD with this logo. It's Sol-Deni V, a character from System X. Where your son paints little models.'

'You left him,' Ryan said then. 'Your son. When he was twelve. Dumped him and his mother and ran off with a floozy. How come you started going to see him again after three years of nothing?'

Terry looked coldly at him. 'I'm his father.'

'You were his father when you legged it.'

Weir leaned on his elbows. 'You started seeing him again because of where he lived. You figured on a nice little supply of dealers. Bung them each a pager watch. Fifty quid for a post office box and you're dealing all over the city.'

'I don't know what you're talking about.'

Vanner watched the Kirstall Estate, darkness falling with the rain. He could smell the Gypsy through the gloom. He lit another cigarette, the inside of the car clogging with smoke. He stared at the kids messing about by the arch. Then it occurred to him – why did Terry need kids? Mickey Blondhair cutting up people at cashpoints. The robberies from the hostels. Stake money? Surely he had enough stake money.

'Calgary Holdings.' Weir faced Terry, who dragged fingers over his eyes. His shirt was loose, tie ragged about his neck. Ryan pressed one more butt to the ashtray.

'I've never heard of Calgary Holdings.'

'It's your company. This is a copy of the registration document. Once upon a time it was Catskill Ltd.'

Terry sat forward then, picked up the page and stared at it. His eyes slowly widened.

Ryan said: 'That's your signature.'

Terry looked at him. 'I didn't sign this.'

'It's your signature.'

'Yes. But I didn't sign it. Catskill's been dormant for years.'

Weir shook his head. 'It's alive and well and for the past two years it's been Calgary Holdings.'

Terry glanced at his solicitor. 'I've never seen this before. I did not sign this paper.'

The solicitor pushed his glasses up his nose. 'I'd like a moment with my client now please.'

'Not yet.' Weir pressed himself towards Terry. 'Tell me about Bobby Gallyon.'

For a moment Terry went white. 'I don't know him.'

Ryan laughed then. 'You've been seen with him. In his night-club. You know – where you used to pick up Lisa Morgan, the Tom you screwed on E's. The same Tom who won't work again because she fell over and cut her face.'

'What was it with Gallyon – he clean up the cash for you?' Weir jabbed out the question.

Terry closed his eyes, then he folded his arms and looked at his solicitor. 'I'm not answering any more questions.'

Vanner was dozing. A shout across the road jerked him upright. Very dark now. He sat up and wound the window down. Two kids were chasing each other through the estate. He pulled back his sleeve and looked at the illuminated face of his watch. He got out of his car, and saw Mark Terry walking up the ramp to the stairs. Vanner almost called out to him, but stopped himself. Mark walked with his head down, bag over one shoulder.

Mickey Blondhair's mother opened the door. Vanner showed her his card. 'Detective Inspector Vanner,' he said.

She looked weary, eyes blackened into hollows against the white of her face. 'What d'you want?'

'You were out today.'

'Shopping. I have to go shopping.'

'I want to speak to Mickey.'

'He's not here.'

Vanner looked along the balcony. 'Well, if he's not – when I come back tomorrow, I'll have him banged up so fast he won't have time to get dressed.'

'MICKEY.' She called over her shoulder.

Vanner stared at him, sitting on the edge of the worn-out chair with the TV silent but flickering still in the corner. Mickey avoided his eye, the stud in his nose reflecting the light from the lamp.

'Ninja,' Vanner said quietly.

Mickey looked up at him.

'Where is he?'

Mickey looked away.

'He's here isn't he, Mickey? Somewhere on the estate?'

'I don't know.'

Vanner glanced at the TV. 'Scared of him are you?'

'No.'

'I would be. Psycho like him, running around with a sword.'

'The one with the eye.' His mother shivered in the doorway. Vanner glanced at her, then looked once more at Mickey. 'You know where he is. Don't you.'

'No.'

'I think you do. Tell me, Mickey, where would the Gypsy hide out?'

Mickey looked at the TV. Vanner switched it off. 'Look at me.'

Mickey gaped at the floor.

'I said, *look at me*.'

He lifted his eyes. He had to: Vanner dragging his gaze from the carpet. 'It's over, Mickey. He can't hurt you. Now. Tell me. Where is he hiding?'

Mickey watched him. He wanted to look away but Vanner held him where he was. Outside, a train rumbled into the station.

'Come on, Mickey.'

'I don't know.'

'Okay. Where *might* he be then?'

Mickey glanced at his mother. All the swagger was gone from him. He looked back at the floor. Still he was silent, lips bunched together. Vanner stood over him. Mickey looked up, looked down again. Still Vanner stood over him.

'I'm going to stay here till you tell me, Mickey. You need to tell me. You're in so much trouble you really need to tell me. He's a killer, Mickey. Give up a killer and the court'll remember you did it.'

Mickey shook his head, then all at once he sighed. 'Boiler room,' he mumbled. 'He used to come to the boiler room.'

Ryan sat in the half-dark of the incident room with Weir and Morrison and Jimmy Crack. 'He blanched when I mentioned Gallyon,' Weir was saying. 'Hasn't said a dicky bird since.'

'Terrified.' Jimmy looked at the floor. 'Gallyon's warned him off.'

Ryan yawned. 'When do we get the phone records?'

Morrison looked at his watch. 'Sometime in the morning.'

Ryan nodded and stood up. 'I'm going home then,' he said.

Vanner moved his car into the side road and parked it outside the Art Workshop. He switched on his mobile and dialled Ryan's number. The phone rang as Ryan got to his car. He cursed and almost switched it off. 'Yeah?'

'Sid.'

'Guv'nor.' Ryan yawned.

'Keeping you up.'

'As a matter of fact you are.'

'What's happening?'

'We nicked Terry. Got him with a shitload of E's.'

Vanner looked at the roof of the Kirstall Estate. 'You ever

wonder why Terry would use kids to nick on the street?'

'Not now, Guv. I'm knackered.'

Vanner laughed softly. 'What're you doing?'

'Going home for some shut-eye.'

'Meet me at the Kirstall Estate.'

Ryan shook his head to clear it. 'What's going on?'

'I think I've found the Gypsy.'

Ryan met him in the side road. Vanner leaned against his car and dropped his burning cigarette. The rain had stopped falling, but it was replaced by ice on the wind that cut Ryan's flesh to the bone. He looked at Vanner then at his watch. 'What the fuck am I doing here?'

'Ninja,' Vanner said.

'Where?'

Vanner pointed to the roof, darker than the sky above them. 'Boiler room at the top.'

'How d'you know?'

'Mickey Blondhair told me.'

'That little gobshite. He kept his trap shut with Anne. How come he told you?'

'He knows it's over, Sid. Wants the best deal he can get.'

Ryan got his baseball bat from the boot of his car. 'You not tooled up, Guv?' Vanner shook his head.

'Good job I'm here then.'

'Pretty good in a fight are you?'

'Me – fight? I can't fight, Guv'nor.' He shifted the weight of his bat. 'But I spoil it for those who can.'

They climbed the stairs to the roof. A final corridor then the iron steps to the boiler room. At the end of the corridor Vanner stopped. 'Give me your bat,' he said.

Ryan looked at it, then shrugged and passed it over. Vanner closed his fingers over the shaft. 'I'm going to go in on my own. You wait here and stop him if he comes out.'

'Tell you what, Guv.' Ryan leaned on the balcony. 'If he comes out and he's still got his sword – I'll just wave him past.'

Vanner left him in the darkness and moved across the roof. The wind tugged at his face, the buildings falling away on all sides. He gripped the bat in one hand, flexed the fingers of the other and felt the hairs rise on his neck. As he got closer, he saw a dim light creeping from the boiler-room door. There was no handle, just a broken clasp of metal where the lock had been. He took hold of the edge of the door in his left hand. One long breath, then he wrenched it open.

He felt the heat, the stench of old sweat. The Gypsy squatted between two pipes. For a long moment they faced one another. Vanner showed him the bat. From inside his coat Ninja lifted his sword; one white eye, one dark eye fixed on his face. Slowly he rose to his feet, the sword in both of his hands. Vanner stared at him. 'I'm a policeman,' he said. 'You going to put that down?'

Ninja shook his head.

Vanner tested the weight of the bat. Ninja stretched to his full height, long matted hair hanging beyond his shoulders. He wore a combat jacket and jeans. For a second Vanner was in Ulster. He shifted the bat, sliding his hand all the way to the handle. Ninja stepped over the pipe.

And then he came at him, leaping almost, across the space between them. Vanner stepped to the side, the blade falling towards his head as it had done once before; only he was drunk then and there had been two of them. Now he was sober and the baseball bat was part of him. Ninja passed. Vanner parried and the blow jarred up his arm. Ninja fell back. Then he came again, and this time, a guttural cry in his throat. Vanner tingled: every sinew, every muscle. Ninja swung the sword and Vanner blocked, forcing him back. Ninja fell away, lost his grip on the sword, regained it, and crouched like an animal. Vanner stood his ground, the bat in both of his hands now.

'You can still put it down.'

Ninja shook his head.

Ninja came again, frontal this time, thrusting the blade like a rapier. Vanner moved aside, tripped on a pipe and fell. The bat clattered away from him. And then Ninja was on top of him. Vanner forced a fist into his face, the white of the dead eye in his.

Ninja rolled. Vanner rolled and crashed against the water tank.

He reached the bat, on one knee. And the Gypsy was at him again. He swung the sword, left and right and up and down like a warrior. Then he gripped it with both hands and came again. Vanner lifted the bat and the blade rattled against the tank. Ninja lost his grip, reached for it and Vanner tripped him. And as he did so, he brought the bat down very hard. Ninja cried out. From the corner of his eye, Vanner saw Ryan standing in the doorway.

Ninja rolled. Vanner was after him, kicking away the sword. He dropped the bat and then he was lifting him, two hands at his collar, hauling him to his feet. Ninja spat at him and Vanner tasted blood. He butted him in the face. Ninja cried out, both hands to his nose. Vanner hit him again, fists this time, left and right to the body. Ninja fell to the floor.

Then Ryan was on him, hauling his hands behind him and wrapping the handcuffs about them. Blood on Ninja's face. Blood in his mouth. He coughed and spat more blood on the floor.

'Not very well are you,' Ryan muttered.

Ninja lay slumped against the pipes, his arms twisted behind him. Ryan picked up the sword and opening his lighter, he ran the flame the length of the blade. 'Guv,' he said.

Vanner came over and Ryan pointed out the nicks in the blade. Vanner looked at him.

'Two minutes,' he said.

Ryan stepped outside.

Vanner squatted down next to Ninja and gripped a handful of hair. He twisted his face to the light. 'On March 4th you and The Wasp had a go at me.'

Ninja looked dully at him, the breath ragged in his throat.

'I want to know why.'

Still Ninja looked at him, blood on his lips, blood dripping from his nose. Vanner twisted his fingers deeper into his hair.

'I'll ask you again: why?'

Ninja squinted now, darkly, out of one good eye. The other a mass of dead flesh.

'Fuck you,' he said.

* * *

They locked him in Ryan's car and smoked against the chill of the night. Ryan looked at Vanner, face closed, eyes tight in his skull. 'Should've got the TSG.'

'Yeah.'

'Never mind.' Ryan looked at Ninja. 'You realise I'll have to go back with him.'

Vanner nodded and tossed away his cigarette. 'I'll come with you,' he said.

They booked him into the custody suite and the duty sergeant summoned a doctor. Ryan went home. Vanner finished up and found Weir outside in the corridor.

They looked at one another. 'I thought you were on leave,' Weir said.

Vanner took out a cigarette. 'I found the Gypsy for you.'

He met Morrison at the top of the stairs. 'Ryan tells me you picked up the Gypsy.'

Vanner nodded.

'Apparently he needs a doctor.'

'He didn't come very quietly.'

Morrison shook his head. 'You're supposed to be on leave.'

'I'll take him back again shall I?'

Morrison stepped back, eyes cold in his face. 'Did you get the sword?'

'Of course we got the sword.'

The call into the Communications Room at Scotland Yard. Male voice, low in the sergeant's ear. 'I'm phoning from the Kirstall Estate in Kentish Town. There's some trouble in Leith Place. I think someone's breaking into a building.'

'Right,' Sir,' the sergeant said. 'If I can just have your name.'

The phone clicked dead in his ear.

Two uniformed officers from Kentish Town drove along Leith Road by the estate. They turned right into Leith Place.

'Which unit?' the passenger asked.

'Didn't say. We better check them all.'

'Looks quiet enough.'

They drove to the dead end, swung the car round and parked. Then one by one they checked the entrances to the units. At the green door they stopped. The passenger looked forward. 'That padlock's loose,' he said. Standing back a few paces, they shone their torches the height of the building. Nothing. No movement or light or sound.

The stairs opened onto a huge loftlike space, with a door in the far wall. They bathed the floor with torchlight and then the driver found the light switch. A desk stood in one corner with a computer screen on top of it. The driver moved closer. He saw a pile of padded envelopes and alongside them an empty bottle of spring water. He bent and opened the top drawer. A pile of papers and two unopened watches. They looked at one another.

They moved more cautiously now, across the floor to the door in the end wall. One of them stood back. The other one twisted the handle. Inside, the atmosphere was thick, choked almost, like a weight in the air. They found a long, flat table. Half a dozen photographic development trays were stacked on top of each other. A metal rule alongside. At the far end was an old-fashioned washing mangle. They glanced at one another, then moved to the trays. A torn sheet of blue absorbent paper lay in the top one. Denny's face stared up at them.

The following evening Vanner sat in the pub across the road from his house. He had the Gypsy but still had no answers.

'On your own then?' McCague leaned on the bar beside him. 'Guinness,' he said to the barmaid, and eased himself onto the stool next to Vanner. The legs creaked under his weight.

'You got the Gypsy,' he said. 'His nose is broken. Glasgow kiss was it?'

'He came at me with a sword.'

'Reckon it was him who whacked you?'

'Him and the other one, yes.'

'The Wasp.' McCague shook his head. 'Ninja and The Wasp. Right pair of amateurs.'

'They managed to kill two people.'

'Got caught though didn't they.'

'Only after they did it.'

McCague watched the Guinness settle. 'The blade matches the splinters in John Phillips' rib cage.'

'Finished then.'

'We're waiting for DNA.'

'The shit he took on the floor.'

'We'll match it with blood from his nose.'

Vanner glanced at him then. 'And Terry?'

'Denying everything. Won't say a word about Gallyon.'

'I'm not surprised. Are you?'

'We've got him for it anyway.'

'For the drugs. Yes.'

'And the rest.'

Vanner frowned at him. 'That's all circumstantial.'

'He doesn't know it yet, but we got his phone records this afternoon. The night Milo was killed, The Wasp's mobile was phoned from Terry's flat. Two days before Phillips was stabbed it was phoned again. Silly mistake to make. He should've used a call box.'

Vanner sat back and lit a cigarette. 'Result then.'

'Sorted. Going to look very good. Major source off the street.'

Vanner smiled then, only not with his eyes. 'Morrison'll be laughing. Back in line for promotion.'

McCague frowned at him. 'He's a good copper, Vanner. He always was. Okay, he made a mistake. But we're all entitled to one.'

McCague bought whisky and they moved to a booth. Vanner tapped the table methodically with the edge of a beer mat.

'You came back too soon, Vanner. This all got too personal.'

'It is personal.'

'So you keep saying. But you don't know it was them.'

'Yes, I do.'

'How? You never saw them.'

'I saw Ninja's eyes.'

McCague cocked his head at him. 'It was dark, Vanner. You

said yourself they wore hoods. And when I left you – you were barely able to stand.'

'It was them.'

'Not Christian Tate? At one time you thought it was him.'

'Hard man shooting his mouth off. It happens. Remember Jo Hawkins?'

'How could I forget.'

'Lots of so called hard men like to crack on about hitting a copper. I killed Tate's brother. Tate is away and when he gets out I get hit. Can't lose can he.'

McCague looked long and hard at him. 'You know you ought to take that holiday.'

Weir stared into Terry's face. 'We have your phone records. Twice you made calls to The Wasp.'

'I've told you.' Terry kneaded his eyes. 'I've never heard of him.'

'Come on.' Weir arched his eyebrows. 'The Wasp. Black. Dreadlocks. Hangs out with a white boy called Ninja. He's got dreadlocks too. Come on, Michael. You know them.'

'I *don't* know them.'

'They live on the Kirstall Estate. We have them both in custody. The Wasp we can place at both scenes. The other one, the Gypsy . . .'

'I don't know who you mean.'

'The Gypsy,' Weir went on, 'he left us his calling card. Know what I mean? Took a crap in the middle of the floor.'

Terry stared at him.

'You didn't know he did that?' Weir sat back. 'Happens all the time. Takes a lot of adrenalin to kill someone.'

He took a stick of gum from his pocket, unwrapped it and put it in his mouth. 'You're in a lot of trouble, Michael. You're looking at twenty years.'

Terry stared at the ceiling.

'You can help yourself.' Weir moved very close to him. 'Give us Bobby Gallyon?'

Terry rested his forearms on the table and looked at Weir out of red and broken eyes. 'I can't give you Gallyon.'

'Why not?'

Terry took a breath, glanced at his solicitor and shook his head. 'Okay. Okay. Lisa Morgan. I gave her Ecstasy. I bought it from an Irishman in Covent Garden. I liked the woman on E's. It was fun. All right, I admit it. But that's all it was.'

Weir looked at the table top.

'One of your men must've picked her up,' Terry went on. 'And I guess she informed on me. They ended up in the club.'

'She had her face cut open.'

'I didn't do it.' Terry stared wide-eyed at him. 'You think I'd do something like that?'

'You told Gallyon though.'

'I didn't know he'd cut her.'

'What did you think he'd do – pat her on the head?'

Terry sat back again and raked his hair with stiff fingers. 'Look. I'm telling you the truth. You've got the wrong man. I didn't do any of this. Somebody's set me up.'

Weir raised one eyebrow. 'Like who exactly?'

Terry opened his hands.

'Gallyon laundered your cash. Why go down alone? Give me Gallyon and I can help you.'

Terry shook his head, face like parchment, lined and grey and suddenly very old.

'Come on, Michael. We've got a bogus company registered at a mailing address where drug money was delivered. We've got phone records which prove you called the killers prior to both murders. We've got a warehouse used as an acid factory. We found a bottle of water with your fingerprints all over it.'

Terry stared at him then and gooseflesh broke out on his arms.

'Give me Bobby Gallyon.'

'I can't.'

'Why not?'

'Because I can't.'

'Won't, you mean.'

'Look. All I did with Gallyon was sell dump trucks.'

'Why would you want to do that?'

'Because he had the right contacts.' Terry looked at him then. 'You say you have a bottle of water?'

Weir nodded.

'What kind of water?'

'I don't know. Spring water. What does it matter what kind? It's got *your* prints all over it.'

Terry reached for the plastic coffee cup. It was empty. 'I sold plant through Gallyon,' he said. 'We shipped it to South America. Diggers. Dump trucks. Big stuff. Two, three hundred K's worth a time.'

'Why South America?'

'Gallyon's got contacts there.'

'What kind of contacts?'

'I don't know. All I know is that you sell from South America.'

'Sell where?'

Terry tightened his lip.

'Sell where?'

'Iraq.'

Ryan drank with Vanner. 'Result, Guv, whichever way you look at it.'

'Charged is he?'

Ryan nodded. 'You know there was a computer in that warehouse with a list of all the dealers on it. Had a password but the eggheads cracked it.' He grinned then. 'We've even got him for selling trucks to Iraq.'

'Iraq?'

Ryan nodded. 'You can't sell to Iraq, Guv. DTI get shitty about it. Trucks could be used for shifting weapons. Anyway, that's what Terry reckons him and Gallyon were doing. We can't get Gallyon on the cash. But Regi are picking him up regardless. He'll only get a slap, but it's better than nothing. Their plot's knackered anyway.' He finished the last of his drink. 'Told you didn't I. The ones who do their own stuff – always the easiest to nick.'

Vanner looked at the table. 'Why the street kids though?'

'He's nicked, Guv'nor. Let it go.' Ryan shook his head. 'Why anything? Why Sven-Lido? Why kill Milo? Why do any of them do anything? Because they can. At least we've got the bastard.'

Vanner went home to his empty house and closed the door behind him. A brown envelope lay on the mat. He picked it up and carried it downstairs. When he opened it an old catalogue fell out. It was from System X. He sat at the worktop and flicked through it.

He came to the picture and stared. Sol-Deni V. Strategist. General. Commanding an army of wasted lives from the street. Corruption to fight a corrupt empire. He shook his head and smiled. Sol-Deni V. Not just a face now, but the rest; the cloak and the hood in three prongs, pointed and stiffened and sharp. And then he remembered where he had seen it before. Slowly a chill crept over him. He looked back at the text. An army of wasted youth. Sol-Deni *V*. Roman numeral. Five. The Fifth.

He took a pen from his jacket. SOL DENI V. He began to move the letters. Hairs rose on the back of his neck. He stared at what he had written.

SOL DENI V – DEVIL SON

Twenty-One

Vanner drove to Loughborough Street, the lights of a city in his eyes. He met Sergeant Jackson in the charge room.

'Guv'nor. Long time no see.'

'Hello, Jack. How goes it?'

'Quiet night. So far.'

Vanner nodded, glanced at the cells and remembered. A year ago, longer now. A lifetime seemed to have passed. He looked back at Jackson. 'You remember Gareth Daniels?'

Jackson made a face. 'How could I forget? Never lost a prisoner. Thought I might that night.' He grinned then. 'He's away now anyway. Took it on the chin in the end. All lost and young and very apologetic.'

Vanner looked beyond him. 'Certainly worked with the judge.'

Jackson squinted at him then. 'You're not here about him are you?'

'As it happens, I am.' Vanner leaned on the desk. 'His property records. You still have them?'

'It's all on the system.'

'Figured that one out have you?'

'Did the course, Guv'nor.' Jackson got up from his seat and led the way into his office. He sat down in front of the computer. 'What did you want to know?'

'I want a list of exactly what he had in his pockets.'

Michael Terry lay in darkness. Above him he could see the roof of the cell. A drunk muttered softly to himself through the wall by

297

his head. Every now and then he would cry out. Terry was still shellshocked. None of anything registered, except a bottle of water.

Vanner drove to the Technical College in Kentish Town. Parking his car, he made his way into the building and climbed the stairs to the Electronics Department. Mid-morning: a number of classes were changing and teenagers with book-laden arms filed past him. On the third landing he looked out over the concourse area and saw a familiar figure, locking his bicycle at the gate. Mark Terry shouldered his bag and made his way to the building. Vanner watched him, all the way to the door.

He found John Phillips putting his books away. The lab about him was empty. He looked old and drained and empty.

'John.'

Phillips looked up, his eyes tightened and then he looked down again.

'I called at your house,' Vanner said. 'Your wife said you were here. I didn't expect you to be back . . .'

Phillips rested a hand on the table. 'Work, Sir. Life goes on doesn't it.'

'How's the rest of the family?'

Phillips inclined his head, drawing breath into his chest. 'They're okay.' He snapped the fastener on his briefcase.

'We've got the ones who did it.'

'I heard.' Phillips looked to the window. 'Mark Terry's father.' He shook his head. 'I'd like to have a word with him.'

Vanner sat on the edge of a bench. Shouting echoed on the landing. Vaguely, Phillips glanced at the door.

Vanner said: 'When John was at school he and Mark were friends right?'

'I already told you that.'

'Was there anyone else?'

'What d'you mean?'

'I mean – who else was he mates with? Was there anyone specifically?'

Phillips looked at the desktop. 'John had a lot of friends.'

'I mean somebody in particular. Maybe someone who was mates with Mark as well.'

Phillips looked back at him. 'Nobody I can think of.'

Vanner scraped fingers over the wood of the bench. 'How is he – Mark, I mean?'

Phillips shrugged. 'Seems to be handling it. Just getting on with his work. Bright kid that. Go a long way he will.'

Vanner stood up and offered Phillips his hand. 'Take care of yourself, John. I'm sorry it ended this way.'

Lisa wore jeans and a T-shirt, hair pulled back from her head. She held a coffee cup and looked at him from the doorway of her kitchen.

'Just can't keep away. Can you, Vanner?'

'I haven't come for that.'

'No? What then?'

He stood there, suddenly impotent. In a way he ought to thank her. She had been instrumental in him facing down a past that had plagued his emotions for almost a third of his life. She sipped at the coffee, blue eyes on his.

'They've arrested Michael Terry,' he said.

'They?'

'I got taken off the case.'

'Indiscreet were you?'

'After a fashion.' They looked at one another. 'Terry's going away.'

'You want me to be grateful?'

He shook his head. 'I just wanted you to know.' He paused then. 'Gallyon's been nicked as well.'

She looked up sharply.

'Not for anything major I'm afraid. Or at least not major enough. Apparently, he and Terry were selling dump trucks to Iraq, routing them through South America.'

She looked blankly at him.

'It's illegal.'

'What will he get?'

'A fine, knowing his brief.'

She sat down on the settee. 'So Mike Terry was a drug dealer.'

'He'll lose everything,' Vanner said, as if in consolation. 'His flat, his yard, the lot. None of it has any real borrowing against it. He says he got his money because Iraqi plant is a cash business, but there's a pile of evidence against him. He can't prove he didn't get his assets from drugs,' he opened his hands, 'so he loses them.'

'And you win, Vanner.'

'No.'

'Course you do.'

'No longer my case, Lisa.' He took a breath and exhaled heavily. 'Look, I'm sorry. I mean about everything. If I'd stayed away you'd never . . .'

She quashed him with an upraised palm. 'I told you before: don't say you're sorry when you're not.'

He looked at the floor and then he turned to go. 'Anyway,' he said. 'I thought you'd want to know.'

She touched her cheek. 'So, this wasn't for nothing then?'

He half-lifted his shoulders.

'Pretty poor consolation. Considering I didn't want to be involved in the first place.'

'What will you do?'

'I'll survive. Don't pretend you care.'

For a long moment they looked at one another. 'Goodbye then, Lisa.'

'Bye, Vanner.'

He opened the door and left.

He stood at the barred window of the visitors' room at Wandsworth and tapped his upturned packet of cigarettes on the sill. Pigeons gathered in a cluster on the roof opposite. His back itched. This morning in the shower, the scar tissue raised against the heat of the water. Gareth Daniels, schoolmates with Mark Terry. John Phillips' words from the clinics. It fitted. Like the pieces of a puzzle in his mind. Sven-Lido was not a piss-take. Neither was Calgary Holdings. They were part of a little trail, sort of insurance policy. Ryan's words: *The easiest dealers to nick are those who do their own stuff.* Mark Terry did not do his own stuff, but his father gave it to prostitutes. The irony hit him then. Terry had bought Denny E's from Maguire. That was his statement to Weir. He knew now it was true.

Behind him the door was unlocked and Daniels walked in, followed by a prison warder. Vanner looked at him, slightly built, blond hair, one time shaved to his ears, but longer now and dripping before his eyes. The warder marched him to the table and he sat down. Vanner moved across to them. 'I want to talk to him on my own.'

The warder looked at him. 'I can't leave you alone with him.'

'Yes you can.'

The warder shook his head. 'He doesn't want to be on his own with you. Said so himself.' He looked apologetic. 'Sorry.'

Vanner looked at Daniels, sitting with his feet pushed out under the table and his arms folded. The innocence of childhood. The guilt-ridden lamb from the courtroom. When questioned about Vanner assaulting him, he had been specific in his view that it was no more than he deserved. Sympathy from the jury. Acceptance from the judge. Now he just sat there with the same truculent expression Vanner had witnessed through a cell door a year ago. He sat down opposite. 'Treating you well are they?'

Daniels avoided his eye.

Vanner watched him for a long moment and then he sat forward. 'Got what you wanted then?'

'What?'

'Clever. Very clever.'

'Don't know what you're on about.'

'Course you do.'

Daniels looked at him then as if he had a bad taste in his mouth. 'I don't have to talk to you.'

'Yes you do. You can't quite help yourself. Just one time. Set up something like that and then get to gloat about it in the flesh.

What kind of a buzz does that give you?'

Daniels looked away from him.

'Makes you a bit of a player doesn't it.' Vanner leaned his elbows on the table. 'I suppose you know your mate John is dead.'

'Never had a mate called John.'

'Yes you did. You were in the same class at school. You and him and Mark. Funny how things go. Mates one day, enemies the next.'

Daniels glanced at him again. 'I don't know what you're on about.'

'It could happen to you. Word to the right face in here. Find you one day, hanging from your pyjama cord. Poor lad killed himself.' He stared right in the eyes. 'But you learned to keep your trap shut didn't you. Saw the benefits. Few years and you're out. What're you going to do, the pair of you – start it up again?

'March the 4th,' he said. 'That'll be a date you don't forget.'

Daniels was looking at the wall. 'I don't know what you're talking about.'

'Somewhere there's money tucked away for you. That's why you keep your mouth shut. The firm looking after its own. Read a lot of books on the Mafia did he? Bright boy like that. Business and politics. Ended up with quite an army.'

He leaned more closely towards him. 'Stitched up his old man – big-time. Were you in on that part?' He sat back once more. 'I have to say you did well. Wonderful little scam. Pity about the kids dying at parties. But then what's another body? Tell me, Gary. Where does he put your money?'

Daniels looked over at the warder. 'I'd like to go now please.'

The warder took a step towards them and Vanner lifted his hand. He looked into Daniel's face. 'Sol-Deni V,' he said. 'You had a little model in your pocket. The night we arrested you. That what you used for the pattern?'

Daniels looked at the warder.

'Mark can draw can't he,' Vanner went on. 'He's got a really steady hand. I've watched him in the shop on Saturdays. How long did it take him to get the hang of the signature?'

Daniels lifted his eyes to the ceiling, then he pushed back his chair from the table. He signalled to the warder and stood up. Vanner sat where he was. Daniels looked at him and then offered him his hand. 'Nice to see you again, Mr Vanner. I'm glad you came. No hard feelings I hope.'

Vanner stood in the Governor's office. 'Behaving himself is he?'

The Governor looked over steepled fingers at him. 'Model prisoner so far.'

'I'll bet he is. How long will it take to get the phone records?'

'March you say?'

'Particularly the 4th. And the few weeks beforehand.'

'You can have them in a couple of days.'

On the street outside, he lit a cigarette and pulled so hard on it he felt dizzy. He coughed and flicked it away. He walked, alone, through the grey streets of South London. The impassive face of Daniels at eighteen was almost terrifying. At a pelican crossing, he spotted a café over the road and he waited for the traffic to slow. On a billboard hoarding opposite, the face of Leah Betts looked down at him. He could not prove this. He knew he would never be able to prove it. Morrison had his man. Weir had his man. Even Sid Ryan thought he had his man. An Ecstasy source removed. The PR would be wonderful.

Ryan was with him when the phone records came in from Wandsworth. March 4th. He knew he would find it and he did. A call from the Wandsworth Prison payphone to Mark Terry's house. He showed it to Ryan. 'I'm right.'

Ryan looked at it and scratched his head. 'So he called him. Doesn't prove anything. You said yourself – they were good mates from school.'

'I know.' Vanner took the sheet of paper from him and screwed it into a ball.

'The evidence against Terry's rock solid, Guv.'

Vanner looked up at him. 'You really think it's him?'

'Yeah. I do.'

'So you think all this is just me looking for a reason?'

Ryan opened his hands.

He sat there long after it got dark, hunched in his seat like the dwarf he had seen on Michael Terry's dashboard. The office outside was silent. Everyone else had gone home. He picked up the phone and dialled Hendon.

'Morrison.'

'Morrison, this is Vanner. There's things we need to talk about.'

Morrison looked at his watch. 'I hope this won't take long, Vanner. I'm due at a dinner party tonight.'

Vanner looked at him.

'I thought you were on leave anyway.'

'I am.'

'Other people go away, Vanner. They rest. You know – relax.'

Vanner sat down across from him. Morrison sat back in his chair, the red of his hair like a low fire on his scalp.

'You've got the wrong man.'

Morrison laughed at him. 'Take the holiday, Vanner. You're getting to be ridiculous.'

'Your evidence is circumstantial.'

Morrison sucked at his teeth. 'This is going to take a while isn't it.'

Vanner sat back once more. 'It's not Terry. It's his son.'

'His son?'

'Yes. They have the same initials. They're both M. A. Terry. You only need initials on company figures. The bank account was already open. No need for anyone to see anyone. Particularly with no borrowing. He only needed to forge the signature.'

'Vanner, I haven't got the time . . .'

'Listen to me.'

Morrison compressed his lips.

'Mark Terry works in System X,' Vanner said. 'Sol-Deni V was a character from five years back. He was a victim of the environment he was brought up in. Greed. Arrogance. Ruthless competition. He was dumped into it. Just like Mark Terry. To survive he had to adapt to his surroundings. Just like Mark Terry. He was good at it. Not at first, but in time. He was educated. He used what he found around him, an army of wasted kids. The long-time losers of the society he lived in.

'He looked around him, saw the game, and then he fought back from the street. Mark Terry used to collect the models. He knew all about Sol-Deni. He sat in that shop week after week and painted figures. He was good at painting, good at drawing. He learnt it from his dad. His dad had dumped him when he was twelve. He went from Hampstead to the Kirstall Estate. He didn't see him for three years. Long time to brood that. Long time to plan. Long time to think about getting even.'

Morrison looked sour. 'You're fantasising, Vanner.'

'No, I'm not. Mark Terry was friends with John Phillips. There was a third member of the team, but I'll come to him in a moment. Terry and Phillips started this. The third member knew The Wasp. The Wasp knew the kids on the estates. Some of them ended up in the hostels.'

He sat forward again. 'One of the things that doesn't add up here is the hostels. Why would Michael Terry bother with street kids? He'd only do that if he needed stake money. He was making cash from his sales to Iraq and wherever else he was selling. He and Bobby Gallyon had a great deal going. James Bentt's information. Access to the goods before they ever got to auction. What did he want with street thieves?'

Morrison was watching him more closely now. 'Think about it.' Vanner said. 'He didn't need a stake. He didn't need to bring in E's or acid or anything else for that matter. His son went abroad with him. To Amsterdam. E's are everywhere in Amsterdam. Anton Cready's set up acid lines in Amsterdam. He must have made the contact there. It wouldn't have been difficult. You can get the gear anywhere. Cready's an acid man from the sixties. He's known all over the world. But no one's been able to nick him.'

'The evidence, Vanner.'

Vanner nodded. 'A warehouse by the estate rented by *M. A. Terry*. Why would his father do that? Sven-Lido. A name-change on a dormant company. Mailing address. A bunch of dodgy accounts.'

'Fingerprints on a bottle, Vanner. The phone calls to The Wasp's mobile.'

'The Wasp.' Vanner sat straighter. 'Resident of the Kirstall Estate, where Mark Terry lives.' He thought for a moment. 'Those two calls came on a Saturday night. Right?'

'No. One did. The other was in the week.'

'You're right. I forgot. That weekend Terry was in Amsterdam. Mark must've stayed in the week. Did you ask Terry where his son was on the night of those calls?'

'Why should I do that?'

'Because he was there in the flat with him.'

Morrison sat forward. 'Vanner. This is all supposition. What evidence have you got?'

'I've got a catalogue from System X.'

'That's evidence?'

'Sven-Lido's an anagram of Sol-Deni V. You know what else it spells?'

'I'm sure you're going to tell me.'

'Break up the letters again – they spell *Devil Son*.'

Morrison looked at his watch. 'I'm late, Vanner.'

'There was a third body.'

'Who?'

'He's in Wandsworth Prison. I visited him. It was just like old times.'

'Who?'

'Gareth Daniels.'

Morrison shook his head.

'When we nicked him for killing Eileen Mitchell he had a model of Sol-Deni V in his pocket,' Vanner said. 'I knew I'd seen it before, but the face on the squares was just that – a face. Without the rest – I didn't recognise it.'

Morrison was quiet for a moment and then he smiled. 'You know something, Vanner. I wonder if you've thought about seeing the doctor. There's nothing more stressful than carrying a personal grudge.' He sat forward. 'Eats away at you. Believe me. I know.'

Vanner stared at him. 'I got hit by Ninja and Wasp.'

'You don't know that.'

'Don't I?' He leaned forward. 'Gareth Daniels was the third member of the team. He recruited The Wasp and in turn Ninja and so it went on. Trouble is, like John Phillips, Daniels liked to do the gear himself. With Phillips it was smack. Daniels E's and acid and whatever else he could lay his hands on. He was high as a kite when he hit Eileen Mitchell. That's why he got away with manslaughter.'

'You're not telling me anything, Vanner.'

'Daniels got put away. He kept his mouth shut, but for that he wanted a favour. He's also receiving money.'

Morrison looked at him. 'You can prove that?'

'No. But it's somewhere. Safety deposit box maybe. Cash piling up for when he gets out.'

Morrison started to get up. 'I don't have time for this.'

'Remember how he dropped his assault charge against me? Remember how meek and mild he was in the dock, all tears and apologies and innocence? The night I was hit on Eversholt Street, Daniels phoned Mark Terry from Wandsworth.'

Morrison stood up. 'None of this proves anything. So he made a phone call. You said just now they were friends.' He leaned his hands on the desk. 'Listen, Vanner. I lost my way once because of you. I'm not going to do it again. Nothing you've told me holds water. All you have is supposition based on your own desire to get even. They mugged you. That's what they did, Vanner. They mugged you.'

He lifted his coat from the peg. 'Michael Terry's been charged. We'll get a conviction. It's a result, Vanner. A good one.'

Vanner stood up then and looked at him. 'Of course,' he said. 'A result.'

Morrison pointed his finger, stiff, like a dagger at him. 'Don't make waves.'

Vanner moved to the door. 'I hope you enjoy your dinner.'

After Vanner had gone, Morrison sat down again, still holding his coat in one hand. For a long moment he stayed there. Soon he would be late for dinner. He had better phone Jean. Vanner's face assaulted him; grim, cold, dark eyes that penetrated until you bled. He would be glad of the move when it came. He looked at the neat, closed file on his desk and stood up. He paused and half-lifted the cardboard cover. Then he shook his head and let it drop again. Switching off the light, he went out to his car.

Vanner saw Mark Terry get off his bike by the steps to his mother's flat. He called out to him. Mark stopped, looked round and Vanner crossed the road. He leaned on the wall, lifted his hands and clapped.

'Very clever, Mark. Very, very clever. Your mother out all night and you with time on your hands. Tell me: what did you do with the money?'

Vanner opened his coat. 'It's all right, Mark. You can talk to me. I'm not wired or anything.' He let his coat drop again. 'Where'd you find out about Cready – on a little trip with your dad?'

'What're you talking about?'

'Hitting me would be Gary's idea wouldn't it. I mean – you're too clever for that.'

Mark looked away from him. 'I'm late,' he said.

Vanner paced around him. 'Why d'you leave all the names on the computer? Unnecessary that. Those boys were loyal to you.'

Mark looked at him then. 'There's no loyalty in business.'

'Ah. You do talk. *No loyalty in business*. Learn that at college did you?' He stopped pacing. 'Don't you care about your father? He must be a very bewildered man. What did you do – take a bottle of water from his flat – plant it over there?' He pointed towards the warehouse. 'He's going to be gone forever, your dad. You know – you only get one.'

'He shouldn't have done what he did.'

'You mean dump you and your mother?' Vanner moved closer

to him. 'Is that what it's about, Mark? Revenge? Or did you just look about you, see what the world was like and play the game yourself. Sol-Deni V. Isn't that what he did?'

He sat on the wall and folded his arms. 'Is that how it was – business rather than revenge? Was the revenge just a nice little sideline? Little bit of insurance, sort of underwriting your risk.'

Mark did not answer him. Vanner cocked his head to one side. 'You learned a lot from your dad didn't you, Mark. Business. Politics. Revenge. You looked at what he did and then you did it yourself. Only you did it better.'

Mark said nothing.

'But killing people, Mark. John Phillips. What's it like to kill your friends?'

Mark looked at him coldly. 'There are no friends in business, Vanner. And business kills people every day. Union Carbide: they killed people in Bhopal. Governments kill people. Our government kills people. They killed a whole bunch of them in the sixties: revoked the British passports of Ugandan Asians – retrospectively. That meant they couldn't come here. Idi Amin was pleased. He got to massacre them all.' He wheeled his bike a little closer. 'I learned that in politics.'

Vanner stared at him. 'You made the call to Holland didn't you. Set up the tip-off with the Dutch police. Tell me: what d'you do for an encore?'

Mark lifted his bike to his shoulder. 'I have to go now. My tea will be ready.'

Vanner stood on the ramp and watched him climb the steps. 'I'm going to watch you, Mark. You've been a naughty boy. Naughty boys get punished.'

At the landing Mark paused and looked back. 'No they don't. The clever ones walk away. He smiled and looked out across the estate. 'The game's over. Face it, Vanner. You lost.'

Also available from Headline

THE HOUR OF OUR DEATH

The second Sister Agnes mystery following her first
compelling investigation, SACRED HEARTS

Alison Joseph

The fragility of human existence is a familiar fact of life
for all who work in the London teaching hospital of St
Hugh's, as Sister Agnes Bourdillon, standing in as a
hospital visitor, well knows. But when an assistant in the
Pharmacology Department collapses at her desk it seems
to Agnes that her sudden death is being handled with
indecent haste. According to the Professor of Surgery
dealing with the matter, the woman was a member of
Agnes's church and so it is down to Agnes and her friend
and confessor, Father Julius, to organise her funeral.
That, he would have them believe, is the end of the story.

But Agnes cannot let the matter rest – for a start neither
she nor Julius have any recollection of the woman, and
something about the Professor's imperious insistence that
the hospital conduct the post-mortem both provokes and
worries her. When she discovers their post-mortem
results are entirely false she knows she owes it to the
shadowy victim to find out what lies behind her death.
Led from the bleak tragedy of a lonely woman to the
subtle, bitter politics of the medical fraternity, Agnes
finds herself at the heart of a hornet's nest of murderous
intrigue, torn by conflicting desires and loyalties
of her own . . .

FICTION / CRIME 0 7472 4894 X

The Mushroom Man

Stuart Pawson

There's nothing Detective Inspector Charlie Priest hates more than a case involving children. When Georgina, the eight-year-old daughter of local businessman Miles Dewhurst, goes missing, Charlie and his colleagues soon start to fear the worst. And Charlie's suspicions are focused on Dewhurst – is his performance as desolate parent a little too pat?

Meanwhile, these are dangerous times for clergymen. Three have died suddenly, and a picture of a Destroying Angel mushroom has been left beside the body of the most recent victim. It seems that something more than coincidence links the deaths – but why would a serial killer focus on men of the cloth?

As he races against time to find Georgina, and happens upon the first real clue in the hunt for the Mushroom Man, Charlie Priest has another preoccupation – his tentative pursuit of bishop's widow Annabelle. And Charlie's courtship is about to take a dramatic turn – for he is more deeply embroiled in one of the cases than he realises . . .

0 7472 4897 4

HEADLINE

A selection of bestsellers from Headline

OXFORD EXIT	Veronica Stallwood	£5.99	☐
THE BROTHERS OF GWYNEDD	Ellis Peters	£5.99	☐
DEATH AT THE TABLE	Janet Laurence	£5.99	☐
KINDRED GAMES	Janet Dawson	£5.99	☐
ALLEY KAT BLUES	Karen Kijewski	£5.99	☐
RAINBOW'S END	Martha Grimes	£5.99	☐
A TAPESTRY OF MURDERS	P C Doherty	£5.99	☐
BRAVO FOR THE BRIDE	Elizabeth Eyre	£5.99	☐
FLOWERS FOR HIS FUNERAL	Ann Granger	£5.99	☐
THE MUSHROOM MAN	Stuart Pawson	£5.99	☐
THE HOLY INNOCENTS	Kate Sedley	£5.99	☐
GOODBYE, NANNY GRAY	Staynes & Storey	£4.99	☐
SINS OF THE WOLF	Anne Perry	£5.99	☐
WRITTEN IN BLOOD	Caroline Graham	£5.99	☐

All Headline books are available at your local bookshop or newsagent, or can be ordered direct from the publisher. Just tick the titles you want and fill in the form below. Prices and availability subject to change without notice.

Headline Book Publishing, Cash Sales Department, Bookpoint, 39 Milton Park, Abingdon, OXON, OX14 4TD, UK. If you have a credit card you may order by telephone – 01235 400400.

Please enclose a cheque or postal order made payable to Bookpoint Ltd to the value of the cover price and allow the following for postage and packing:

UK & BFPO: £1.00 for the first book, 50p for the second book and 30p for each additional book ordered up to a maximum charge of £3.00.
OVERSEAS & EIRE: £2.00 for the first book, £1.00 for the second book and 50p for each additional book.

Name ....

Address ....

....

....

If you would prefer to pay by credit card, please complete:
Please debit my Visa/Access/Diner's Card/American Express (delete as applicable) card no:

Signature .... Expiry Date..............